CAPTURED
BY THE
VAMPIRE KNIGHT

CAPTURED BY THE VAMPIRE KNIGHT

A.N. PAYTON

This book is a work of fiction. Names, characters, places, and incidents either are products of the author's imagination or are used fictitiously. Any resemblance to actual events or locales or persons, living or dead, is entirely coincidental and not intended by the author.

CAPTURED BY THE VAMPIRE KNIGHT
Eternal Alliances, Book 1

CITY OWL PRESS
www.cityowlpress.com

Cover Design by MiblArt. All stock photos licensed appropriately.

Edited by Danielle DeVor.

For information on subsidiary rights, please contact the publisher at info@cityowlpress.com.

Paperback Edition ISBN: 978-1-64898-556-0

Digital Edition ISBN: 978-1-64898-558-4

To Jake.
For everything.

Fields of Death
Awriban
Dynasty

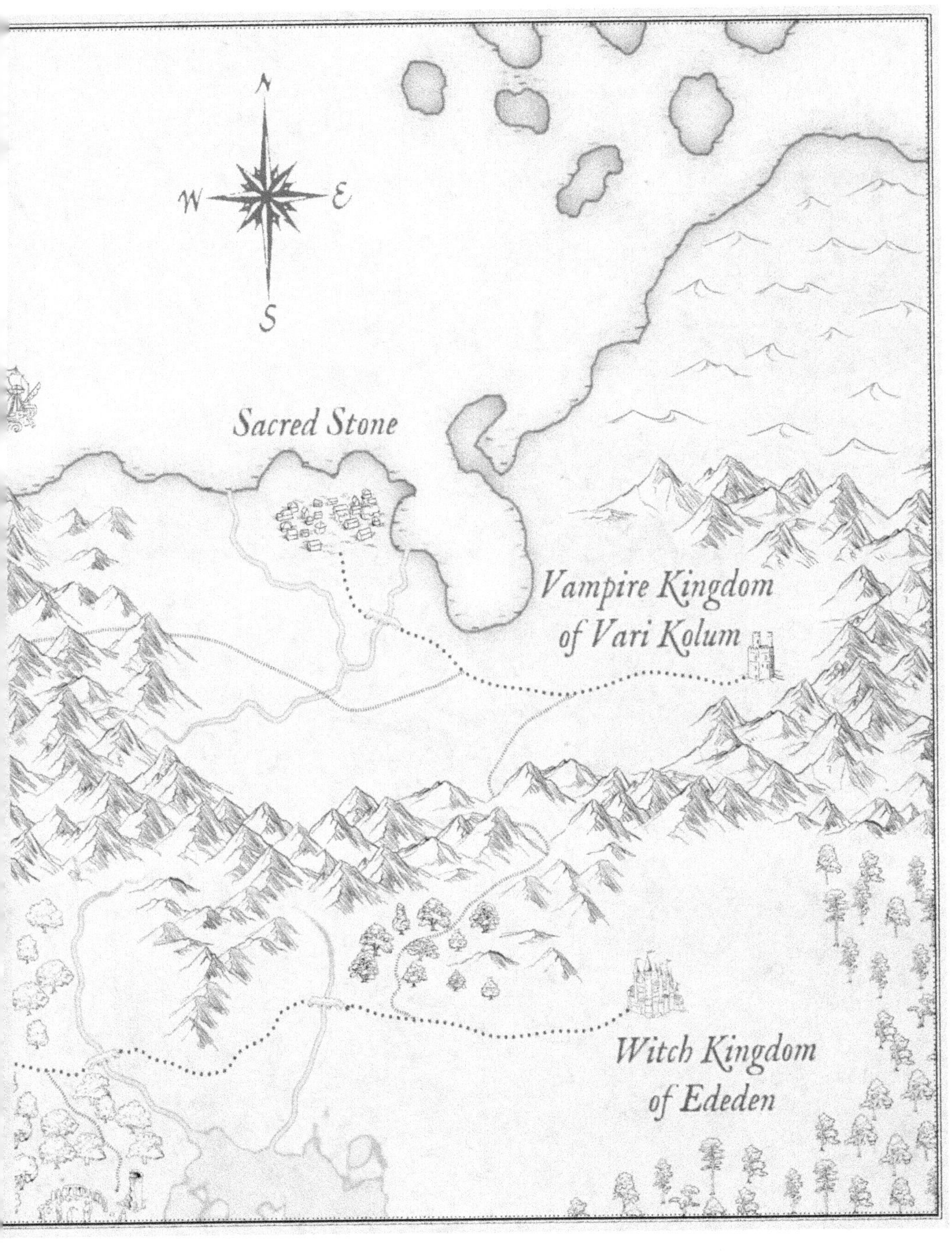
N
W
E
S
Sacred Stone
Vampire Kingdom
of Vari Kolum
Witch Kingdom
of Ededen

CHAPTER ONE

Movement flickered at the edge of the tree line. My hand froze, inches above a cluster of green herbs. My muscles locked, refusing to turn toward the twisting phantom in the shadows. The ghostly image faded, and I sighed.

"Are you seeing it again?" Penelope reached for a yellow flower, her fingers short and thick with youth. "You're supposed to tell us if you see it again."

"I didn't see anything."

"You have to tell us before something bad happens." She studied the bud, then let it fall. Not the right one.

"Something bad doesn't always happen."

Between the weeds, under the hot sun warming our hair and the gentle rustle of wind through the trees, I knew we were both thinking about the cat. Starving, pregnant, and sick, my ghostly stalker had poured magic into the animal and healed her in a heartbeat. Now, she and the six kittens meowed and rubbed our legs whenever we left our cottage.

"That's true." Penelope brushed a strand of golden hair from her face. Sweat streaked down the sides of her hairline and dampened her locks.

The heavy weight of regret sunk deep in my chest. An eight-year-old should be playing with friends in the river on such a hot day. "But it's usually bad."

Memories trudged from the depths I tried to drown them in.

A thief on the road.

The silver flash of a knife.

His heart stopping under my palm.

I pushed the thoughts away, but Penelope's face twisted as the memory ran through her mind.

"I promise to tell you if I see it again," I lied.

She bobbed her head in acceptance, and I bit my lip to hide the guilt.

Grass crept up a gently sloping hillside and disappeared into the edge of a thick forest. Yellow flowers popped up here and there, taunting us as we searched for the correct herb. The recipe for our father's medication required tansy flowers, but the blooms mirrored dandelions, wild sunflowers, and golden orbs of chamomile. My mother's spellbook displayed a single, hand-drawn image of a tansy flower, and Penelope and I took turns squinting at the page. No luck so far.

I reached for another bud, plucked it from the woody stem, and brought it close to my face. A sweet, floral smell escaped from the plant, a chemical warning to its neighbors that danger lingered nearby. The other plants quivered in the wind, unable to run.

I pulled the spellbook closer and smoothed a crinkled edge of the worn paper. The tiny flower in my hand matched the elegant sketches from my mother's pen. Finally. Only a few more and I'd be able to concoct another batch of my father's medication.

The pages shifted beneath my fingers. My brow creased. The wind could barely flutter a page at its current strength, much less move such a hearty spellbook. I lifted the book, and the ground shook under its wooden cover. The vibrations strengthened until a low rattle buzzed inside my chest. I pressed my palm to the damp grass, and the roughness scraped against me.

"Natalie?" Penelope said.

"Just a moment." The sensation intensified. The earth rocked beneath us in smooth, rhythmic motions. An earthquake?

"Natalie!"

"Penelope, I'm busy."

"Look!" Her shaking finger pointed to our little house nestled in the crook of a shallow valley.

A black and silver tide swelled through the cluster of houses composing our village. Men and women on horseback, dark clothes buckled into armor that flickered in the sunlight. Thundering horse hooves rattled the ground, enough of the creatures to shake the earth from nearly a furlong away. As the soldiers neared, war cries drifted to us, followed by a more distant sound of screaming.

The twist of fear turned in my gut.

"Vampires?" Penelope's face reddened.

"It's a raid."

"A raid?" Her throat bobbed as she swallowed. "The last time that happened..."

"I know." I didn't need to hear her say the words.

The soldiers flung open doors and rummaged through houses. They poured out, dragging goods and people in their wakes. The dark tide flowed closer to our perch on the hillside, and the smacks of horse hooves pounded a constant drum beating in my ears.

"Will they go to our house?"

I chewed my lip and tucked the spellbook under one arm. "I don't know," I answered honestly.

"We don't have anything expensive." Her voice sounded quiet but strong, and her little face hardened with courage much greater than her age. "And Papa's too sick to be a soldier."

"You're right," I said.

But I'm not too sick. Or too old.

Penelope wrapped her fingers around mine. I squeezed her hand as we watched the flood envelop our village.

The mass of soldiers paused at the edge of the community. Our house sat at the end of the valley, half-hidden by a swell of overgrown wheat that was once farmland but recently returned to wilderness. Two men peeled away from the rest and trotted toward it.

Penelope sucked in a breath and clutched my fingers until the tips turned white. I held hers just as hard.

More memories crept through my mind. Slick, warm blood on my fingertips. Pain in my throat as my useless chanting became screams. I shook my head. I couldn't drown in my past failures. Penelope's safety relied on my focus.

The men burst through our front door, and the frame buckled. My heartbeat filled my ears, blocking the shouts and horse cries. A red haze covered my vision until the only things left in the world were Penelope's grip on my hand and the reassuring weight of my mother's spellbook under my arm.

The pair retreated from the house almost as quickly as they'd entered. Nothing they wanted.

My breath released. The red haze slipped away.

"They're leaving," Penelope whispered.

"Looks like it."

One of the men swung onto his horse. A giant man, practically dwarfing his partner, with thick red hair as visible as a beacon from the slope we stood on. His monster steed reared, stomping the ground and snorting with its ears pushed back. The man jerked the reins, and the animal turned the other way.

My heartbeat slowed. They were leaving.

The redhead glanced over his shoulder. He scanned the terrain and paused, looking in our direction.

Penelope stilled at my side. "Do you think he sees us?"

One arm, buckled into silver armor, lifted and pointed at us. His partner, mounted on a smaller steed, turned our way and nodded. The two directed their mounts toward us and started up the hillside.

Butterflies beat against the confines of my stomach. Penelope's grip should have been painful, but panic numbed me. Bile clenched up my throat as my thoughts focused on the pair trekking closer.

"Can you do magic?" Penelope's voice shook more than her hand in mine.

Good question. I glanced into the distance for the hovering phantom. Nothing. Of course, when I needed it, the creature disappeared completely.

I drew a breath. Maybe I didn't need the phantom's touch to direct my power this time. Maybe it would be different.

I closed my eyes and reached for my magic. I could feel it, a fluttering entity that shared a part of my soul, but it remained wrapped in a tight spell that felt faintly like my mother.

Come on, work just this once.

I fought against the invisible cage that trapped my abilities. Mother may be dead, but the spell she cast to contain my magic remained as strong as ever. Every time I tried to purposefully wield the power, it failed to answer my call.

The spells slipped like sand through my fingers.

"No," I said.

"What do we do?"

The men galloped closer. Weapons weighed them down on one side, but their horses appeared unhindered by the massive weights on their backs. I couldn't see the vampires' eyes, but I imagined the depths filled with fury and hatred. Two hundred years of war had clouded all our gazes with the same expression.

"Run." The word fell from my lips as a combination of instinct and reality. Outrunning a vampire on or off a horse held little promise of success—but we had to try.

"What?" Penelope's eyes pinched and glistened with unshed tears.

"Run!"

I pulled her up the hill. After two or three steps, her body caught up and she sprinted beside me. We ran toward the tree line while the smacks of hooves on damp ground grew closer behind us.

The trees stretched higher as we neared. Their shade should have been a welcome respite from the heat, but it felt like an ominous shadow swallowing us up. Vampires could easily outrun us, but dodging the trees would slow them down. The wooden pillars would either be our salvation or the bars on our cage.

The wet grass turned to mud at the forest's edge. I conjured a mental map of the terrain. I'd grown up browsing these woods for ingredients for my mother's spells. I never expected that the same places where lifesaving plants grew would become a haven from vampire pursuers.

I pulled Penelope to the left, and our feet sunk into the chalky forest floor.

Someone swore. The mud would make their pursuit miserable, maybe deter them completely. Surely, two witch girls weren't worth following into the treacherous terrain.

"Did you see where they went?" asked the deep gruff of a man's voice, much closer than I expected.

"No. I'll go left. They can't be faster than us in this damn muck."

Heavy footsteps sloshed nearby. They had abandoned the horses.

I darted right, deeper into the trees. Penelope's grip on one hand and the spellbook in the other slowed my speed. Vines dripped from the overhead canopy and spilt like poison into the dirt. Animals scurried out of our way, brushing across branches and rocks, an eerie symphony for our escape.

There!

I ground my heels into the mud when I saw the downed tree. At some point, the giant had succumbed to disease or a storm and fallen to the forest floor. Years had carved away the inside of the trunk, leaving behind an empty space the perfect size for an eight-year-old.

Skidding to a halt, Penelope ran into my legs. I jerked her forward and stuffed her toward the opening of the log.

"Get in and be quiet."

She ducked into the hollow, then froze. She tried to pull herself out.

"What are you doing?" I pressed against her back, squishing her inside. "Get in there."

"There's not enough room!" she chirped. "You won't fit!"

"Of course not." The lies clung to my lips like expensive wine. "We have a better chance if we hide in different places."

Penelope hesitated, caught between fear, logic, and trust. Regret cut deep into my chest. Her brown eyes, set into her paled face, looked at me with naïveté. If I didn't stop lying to her, one day that trust would disappear.

"Okay." She wiggled into the hollowed space and settled in the darkness.

"Here, take this." I held out the spellbook, and it filled her arms, cradled against her quivering chest. "If you beat me home, put it under my bed with the others."

I stepped from the log and dragged my feet through the mud until the evidence of a second set of footprints faded away. Relief washed over me in a cold wave. Penelope was smart. She would be quiet when they came.

More curses filtered through the trees. One of the men walked beyond the clearing. It wouldn't be long until he caught me.

I bit my lip and did another scan of the area. I ached to find a place to hide, but the rocks and barren trunks offered little concealment. If I ran, the sound of my steps would give away my position.

Instead, I waited. Resolve became a noose around my neck, tightening with every moment of stillness. I fought against my flight or fight response as adrenaline coursed through my veins. My fingers shook. My breath came out ragged. Imaginary blood slipped down my fingertips. Would I meet the same fate as my mother?

The crashing grew louder, snaps of broken branches were almost on top of me. My mind filled with the sound of rushing water, a great icy river washing away logic, trapping me with only one thought: protect Penelope.

The redhead giant emerged from a thicket of clustered trees. Mud and grime marred his armor. Cuts he must have gotten from stubborn foliage healed as I watched. The skin knit together into an unbroken line, without even the hint of a scar. My mother would have been jealous.

Up close, the vampire was impressive. His massive form boasted ancestry from the gods of old. Those golden-red locks sat in neat rows, adorned with beads that glimmered in the wisps of peeking sunlight. They piled on his head like a crown, a radiant deity calling for my soul. A straight nose centered on his wide face, above full, rosy lips that broke into a smile when he raised his ocean-blue eyes and caught sight of me. Two pointed teeth shone sharper than the rest.

The frantic beat of my heart paused. My tongue turned to lead. The sweat on my skin became icy daggers, warning of the danger before me. Just like those plants I plucked from the soil, I had nowhere to run.

The intensity in his expression shifted. They flicked across my body, and my cheeks burned. I rolled my shoulders back and jerked my chin up. Laughter wrinkled the creases in the corners of his eyes. My defiance amused him.

"You're a civilian." His deep voice sounded like a stampede about to trample me.

I peeled my tongue from the roof of my mouth.

"Y-yes." I flinched at the smallness of my tone. If my power wasn't bound, I wouldn't have been so weak.

"There were two of you." He glanced around. "Where's the other one?"

"She went a different way. If you haven't found her by now, then she's already gone."

Please, Penelope, stay hidden.

He tilted his head, studying me. Something rolled across his face under the smooth mask he wore. Something dangerous.

"Come here." He beckoned with one hand while the other palmed the top of a great battle axe, almost affectionately.

I shook my head. *No way.*

"You can't be more than a hundred and twenty pounds soaking wet. What do you plan to do?"

He reached toward me, and I took a step back. His lips turned up in a grin, and a flash of silver rolled through his irises. I'd heard rumors of vampires showing emotion through their eyes. Seeing it in real life drew a shiver down my spine.

He clutched at me again, and I backed away, but he proved too fast. One hand caught a firm grip on my shoulder and the other grabbed the bottom of my chin. Though bands of muscle suggested his strength, he kept his hands soft. Tight enough that I couldn't escape, but not to leave a mark on my skin.

He lifted my face up to the hint of illumination filtering through the trees. The smell of evergreen and mint wafted over me, taking me to the vague remains of an almost memory. A layer of surprise escaped through the fear. I expected the sharper scents of sweat and blood.

He pushed my chin up and turned me to the side. The sunlight warmed my neck, and his gaze flicked to the place where thin skin shielded my thundering pulse. I stilled, suddenly aware that this man was a bloodthirsty vampire and I was witch, and we'd been enemies for over two hundred years.

His finger brushed across my throat. "What're you doing out here by yourself?"

The depth in his voice shallowed to a soft whisper between us. Air tried to escape my lungs.

"I-I was collecting herbs." I swallowed thickly. "My father is sick. I have to make him medicine."

"Your mother doesn't care for him?"

"She's dead."

The beads in his hair chimed as he bent his head. "I'm sorry for your loss. My father passed away last year."

"I'm sorry." What else could I say? We weren't friends or even acquaintances. He had an axe on his belt and wore silver armor with marks from my people's weapons.

"Me too," he said.

He towered over me, probably six and a half feet tall, and thick in a way that said he could lift very heavy things. He looked between the mere inches of space between our bodies, and his touch under my chin softened to a gentle caress. Heat slipped between us, warming parts of me that I hadn't noticed had become chilled in the damp forest. The hand on my shoulder slid down my arm as the man's brows creased.

"What's your name?" he asked.

I opened my mouth, but the word halted on my lips.

Behind the giant, the shimmer of a shadow moved in the tree line. Rolling waves of darkness spiraled together, and the shape of a sinister phantom formed. A ghost, a specter, or whatever it was staggered into a dark cloud of existence. It stepped toward us, one hand outstretched.

"No," I whispered.

The man's brows pinched again, and he tilted his head. "I promise I won't hurt you, girl. I'm just asking your name."

The phantom didn't alter its course. It stood five steps away, continuing its pace. Four. Memories of the thief it had killed undug themselves from the shallow grave in my mind. The blood leaking from his face. The frozen scream of agony. Worse, Penelope's wide eyes spilling with tears and the horror as she backed away, not from the dead man, but from me.

"Please, don't. Not right now."

Three steps. Two. Penelope would see it all again. She would watch me kill someone, and maybe this time the scars would be too deep to heal. The thought caused more pain than death at the hands of this vampire. How many lives could I take before even my family couldn't forgive me?

"Look, I promise not to hurt you." My mind barely registered the man speaking as the shadow crept closer. "We're not here for civilians. I just want to be sure you're safe out in the woods. There could be animals or who knows what."

The phantom lingered, barely one more step to go.

"Go away," I told it.

The vampire's face darkened. His eyes snapped back to my throat. "You're not really in a position to make demands right now."

Too late. It was here.

A shadow hand pressed against the vampire's back, and ghostly fingers slipped through his skin.

Magic screamed inside me, a terrible yell of anger and power. It beat against the bonds of the spell my mother had cast years ago. The cage she created was strong, but this phantom was stronger, and it controlled me. Slivers of magic reached between the bars as the being stole my power. Magic pulled from me and jumped to the vampire. His breath caught, and the hand on my chin moved to encircle my neck.

The magic rippled over the man, tasting the salt on his skin, and it purred a happy tune in my ear. It liked him.

Goosebumps broke out across his arms, and he shivered. "If you try to do anything with that magic, I will kill you right now."

I sought his gaze. I knew he could see the fear in my eyes. I didn't know what the phantom would do. These could be his last moments.

"I'm sorry," I whispered.

"Sorry?"

The magic forged a battering ram and pounded into the vampire. It filled his body and ran an iron fist through the depths of his mind. It dragged me along, trapping our minds together. Memories, thoughts, fears, and desires swirled into my head, none of them my own.

A woman in a deep green tunic handing me my first axe.

The pain during my first battle as a witch's sword cut into my flesh. The triumph as my axe met her head.

The memories zeroed in on a man I didn't know, but one this redhead vampire knew well. *He lifted me from the horse and wrapped my wound with layers of thick bandages. He ruffled my hair, and a beam of pride streaked across his face. The man's smile mirrored my own, a perfect replica. My father.*

No, not mine. His.

A body. Bloated and gray with days of decay. The fragments of a last conversation. Betrayal, suspicion.

"Your father was murdered." The unwanted words poured from me. "The coroner said natural causes, but you think someone betrayed him. Your greatest fear is that you'll die without avenging your father's death."

The magic slipped away, and the phantom disappeared. For now, at least.

I sagged in the stranger's arms, exhausted.

"What was that?" The vampire jostled me.

"I don't know," I said. That was honest. I never knew what the being would make me do.

"How did you get into my head? All those memories. Did you see them too?"

I nodded.

He looked at me again, as though for the first time. My brown curls pinned into a loose ponytail, and salt crystals clung to the back of my neck from sprinting. Mud crusted the front of my dress, but my face felt mostly clean. His gaze settled on my lips, and the grip at my throat loosened.

"You're coming with me."

Surprise trapped my tongue. *Excuse me?*

The man shifted his grip to my left wrist. He pulled me the way he had come, where the distant huffs of a horse waited. It took three of his great steps for my mind to catch up.

I buried my heels into the ground. The mud slowed me, and my scarce weight became enough to halt the vampire's tracks.

"I'm not going anywhere with you," I said.

The man paused. His shoulders tensed, and he turned to me. He grew close until my chest brushed his armor, but I refused to move back. Hot anger mixed into a fire of desperation and stubbornness. He had broken into my home, chased me and my sister into the forest, and had the audacity to demand that I leave with him.

No way.

"Oh?" He tilted his head to one side. "Maybe I can change your mind."

His gaze shifted over my shoulder to the hollow log of Penelope's sanctuary.

"No!"

His stride carried him to the felled log before I could get halfway there. He plunged his reach into the cavern and pulled my sister from the space. She gave a startled scream, and he muffled the sound with his hand over her mouth.

A blade appeared against Penelope's throat. She stilled.

"I don't want to hurt her." The man's blue eyes were soft, but darkness swirled inside.

"What do you want?" I asked, but it didn't matter. I would give him anything.

"Rayhan?" a new voice yelled into the forest. The second man. "Where the hell are you?"

"Listen," the redhead, Rayhan, said. His hand did not quiver at my sister's neck. "My friend is on his way here, and he doesn't care if witches leave our presence alive or not. You get to decide. You can come with me or stay here and you'll both die."

I twisted my fingers, but I didn't have a choice. Footsteps thumped closer, one rhythmic step after another. Where was my phantom when I needed it?

Tree branches cracked as the second man drew near.

"Yes, yes. I'll go with you."

Rayhan's lips split into a toothy grin. "Wonderful."

He pushed Penelope forward, and she caught herself in the mud. Her arms trembled as she lifted her dainty chin to look at me.

"Nat?" Her voice quivered.

"Back in the log."

"Nat—"

"Now!"

Her lips pressed, but she disappeared into the damp space. A knot in my chest loosened.

Rayhan strode to me, grabbed a handful of my hair, and pulled me to my feet. I swallowed a yelp. He didn't deserve any satisfaction from my fear. I staggered to match his pace, and my scalp ached, but I strained to keep the mossy log in sight. I needed one last glimpse of Penelope. I needed to memorize her face in case...in case I never saw her again.

She didn't peek out.

I barely felt the rough edge of tree bark bite into my skin as the vampire pushed me against a narrow evergreen. I didn't know how long Rayhan planned to keep me. My father's medication was low, and Penelope couldn't make the complicated recipe yet. I bit my lip. My father wouldn't survive long without his medicine.

"If I feel any magic, I won't ask questions this time." His hot breath crossed the back of my neck. He jerked my right hand behind me, and the cold touch of silver chewed through my skin.

"Is this necessary?" I asked. "I promise I can't fight you."

"These chains are silver. They'll make it harder for you to use magic, but not impossible. Remember, I don't have a problem killing two witches if one acts up."

Penelope.

The cold metal clicked as it tightened on my wrist. Each notch was another step away from my life, my sister, my father.

Click.

"You should have thought about the consequences when you bespelled me."

Click.

"Now you're mine."

Click.

More swearing, then the trees parted, and a shorter man stepped from the foliage. Black armor stretched over his chest, highlighting eyes so dark they almost swallowed the irises. They cut across me, and his hatred threatened to imprint a physical pain on my body. I resisted the urge to flinch. One of his lips curled into a sneer.

"About time you got here, Kadence. I thought I'd have to send a rescue party," Rayhan said.

"What did you find, Rayhan?"

Rayhan's heavy hand pinned my back against the tree while the other did a quick search, revealing that I didn't carry any weapons.

"Just the one," Rayhan said. "The other got away."

"A civilian." Kadence took in my dirty dress and lack of weapons. "Leave her here."

"She's coming with us. She used magic on me. It's personal now."

Kadence narrowed his eyes. "You usually avoid taking civilians."

"You don't know what she did to me."

"We could kill her."

"Like I said, it's personal."

The two faced off. My heart thumped in my throat. I craned my neck to see both men, but only Kadence was visible from my place against the trunk. His blank face hid the hint of suspicion that his tone carried.

Finally, he shrugged. "I don't care. We need to leave before their reinforcements arrive."

"Let's go, then."

Rayhan pulled me from the tree and dragged me into the trenches of the forest. I went willingly, looking back for as long as I could. Penelope's life was far more important than mine. As fear turned the thick bile in my stomach, relief ran through my nerves. Penelope and my mother's spellbook remained safe. Only that mattered.

Nothing moved from the hollow darkness of Penelope's hiding space, but I thought I heard the sharp inhale of a smothered sob before the terrain stole my view.

CHAPTER TWO

Moisture from the muddy ground soaked through my thin fabric shoes and pressed cold cotton socks against my feet. More water seeped inside with each step. Despite the hostile vampires, my mind fixated on the sloshing shoes.

Branches snapped against my arms and my breathing quickened as Rayhan pulled me unrelentingly through the forest, while Kadence's face twisted with displeasure beside him.

"The horses," Kadence said. "Finally."

The trees broke apart, revealing two horses perched on the edge of the grass, grazing merrily in the summertime sunshine as butterflies and dragonflies sprinted through richly colored flower buds. It could have been the canvas of an exquisite painting. Instead, it displayed the backdrop to my nightmare.

"I'm ready to get out of this godsforsaken forest." Rayhan glanced back over one shoulder. An undercurrent of unease tightened the corners of his eyes. He turned, but caught my gaze. He studied my face. Wrinkles creased his forehead, and his brows deepened. He opened his mouth, and I could almost see words on the tip of his tongue, but he closed his lips and looked away.

"Couldn't agree more." Kadence stopped at the nearest horse, a small brown steed that bristled under his hands. He reached below the animal and tightened a thick leather strap around its stomach.

The second mount flicked its red tail at our approach. Its white-socked feet stomped the ground while it grunted and groaned. Rayhan jerked me toward the animal and set a heavy hand on my shoulder.

"Stay here." He turned away.

I clenched my fists behind my back. Anger tightened my chest until it felt almost too hard to breathe. Insults lingered on the tip of my tongue. It would be smarter to keep my mouth shut, but the temptation proved too great.

"And what if I don't?" I asked.

Rayhan froze with one hand plunged into a saddlebag. His wide shoulders tensed under the line of leather armor. The side of his jaw sharpened from clenched teeth.

"What did you say?" He didn't turn to me.

Laughter spilled beside us. Kadence leaned his elbow on the brown horse's saddle and watched.

"This ought to be good," he said.

Rayhan turned, and his ocean-blue eyes came alive with flames.

The man stalked toward me and paused a handspan away. The wallowing scent of earth and mint combined with the heat of his body to warm even my cold, wet feet.

"What happens if I refuse to go with you?" I asked. "You don't have anything to threaten me with now."

"Don't I?" He stooped until his face leveled with mine, but I held my ground. "Maybe not at the moment, but there's nothing stopping me from coming back here."

The blood rushed from my head. "What do you mean?"

"I thought I was clear in the forest, *Nat.* If you don't come with me, then I'll have to pay a visit to your family in the future. The cottage in the valley is your home, isn't it? The man in bed looked your twin."

Rayhan had seen my father during their search of the house. Angering the vampire would bring him back, for both Penelope and Father. Images flashed through my mind. Blood spilled on the rough wooden floors. Penelope's body draped over the loft bed. A rattling hiss as my father drew his final breath, not from the autoimmune disease claiming his life, but from a sword in his chest. I knew I would be last. Rayhan would keep me alive until the very end.

Rayhan saw the decision on my face. A spatter of emotion dashed across his features, softening them. The blue waters in his eyes drowned the dancing flames and washed over me with a cooler look.

"I'm sorry," he whispered.

Surprise swelled in my chest. I wasn't sure I'd heard the man right. "What?"

"I said," Rayhan's voice grew loud. "Shut up and hold still so I can tie you to the horse."

I hadn't noticed the coiling rope stretched between his hands. The thoughts of my family's demise fresh in my imagination, I remained immobile as the vampire circled behind me.

"That's it?" Kadence straightened, his lips twisted down. "That was boring."

"Did you want me to kill her for asking a question?" Rayhan tied the rope around the metal shackles and pulled it between my arm and my waist.

"I've seen you kill for much less," Kadence said.

"She's a civilian."

Kadence mounted the horse instead of responding. The frown hardened on his face.

Rayhan pulled the rope and jerked me forward. Fresh water sloshed against my feet. He secured the other end to his saddle. The ginger stallion snorted and sidestepped the vampire, pulling me to the right. Rayhan lunged for the reins, but the animal stepped again, flicking his ears and lifting his lips in a sly grin.

"Foresti, you dumb creature, hold still." Rayhan snatched the leather straps, and the beast rubbed his velvet nose over the vampire's face.

"Gross, stop that." Rayhan flicked a glob of horse slime to the ground, but he couldn't hide the smile. He mounted the animal and affectionately ran a hand through Foresti's braided mane. Rayhan pressed his heels into the horse's side and set a brisk walking pace. He never glanced back at me.

Layers of emotions billowed in my gut, but resolve settled on the top. There would be a time for anger and revenge, but first, I had to survive. If I survived, I would find a way to unlock the binds my mother had tightened around my magic and kill all the vampires between me and my family, and I would do it before my father's medication ran out.

The thought of Rayhan's death warmed my wet feet.

We went down the back of the hillside, slipping through the uninhabited areas to avoid the edge of town. Distant yells and shouts floated over us, but the two pressed forward, unfazed, dragging me in their wakes. We crossed a tiny bridge over a rippling stream, and the clear scent of fresh water washed my mind. I would do whatever it took to survive and escape.

The wet socks rubbed against my skin and blisters formed, even though we'd only walked a short distance. My feet may not arrive at the final destination. Anxiety clawed up my already raw throat. I didn't know where the vampires were taking me, but the heavy saddlebags suggested they'd rode from far away. I wasn't prepared for a long journey.

We turned from the village toward a narrow valley pass. The horses strode side by side, and the cliff edges pressed golden stones against them. Scrub brush grew along the thin trail, unworn by passing footsteps. It wasn't a frequented path, but etchings in the rock proved people had walked it before. Perhaps it served as a secret spy passage, where the vampires watched our troops and reported intel back to their king. Or simply a game trail accidently discovered. Foresti's red and white behind blocked my view, but more and more voices filtered through the air. Men and women laughed and yelled in ominous, celebratory tones. The sounds of vampires commemorating their raiding victories.

The tight walkway opened suddenly into a shallow bowl. Dry sagebrush turned to dark green grass that paused at the cliffsides. The sun-cooked soil proved too hard for the tendrils to climb, but the bowl retained water to feed the foliage. Not even this desert valley offered my feet a dry respite.

Two rows of witches sat in the grass, hands bound and tied together with coils of thick rope. Probably twenty or so altogether, a mix of men and women, able-bodied with military haircuts. The prisoners of war rounded up from the village. Several vampire guards stood around the captives while even more soldiers congregated at the opposite end of the clearing. They all rested one hand on their weapons.

Rayhan picked up the pace, forcing me to half sprint behind him. He jerked to a stop at the rows of witches, and my hands lurched in the bindings. I bit my tongue to smother a groan.

A dark-skinned witch sat crisscross on the ground. He grimaced at the vampire, then turned to me. His eyes widened, and his face flushed red.

"A civilian?" Anger boiled in the witch's words. "What's the point of taking a civilian? Just to prove you really are monsters?"

"Shut up." Rayhan slipped from the saddle and circled behind me. He unwound the rope from the chains. As he worked, I caught flashes of white-edged scars across his fingers. I dropped my stare. These hands had seen many battles, had killed many of my people.

"Only a bloodsucker would kidnap an innocent woman from her family," the witch hissed.

A blur of darkness streamed past as Kadence spilt from his horse and appeared beside me. The cold edge of his sword touched my throat. I lifted my chin, caught between Rayhan's hard body and the cutting side of a blade.

Recognition filled the witch's face.

"That's what I thought," Kadence said. "Civilian or soldier, her life means as little to me as yours. Consider your words before speaking again."

The man's lips pressed tight.

"I told you I wasn't going to kill her." Rayhan pushed the flat side of Kadence's sword down. A tremor stirred his hand, but I was the only one close enough to see it.

Kadence shrugged. "He needed an example, and I provided one. I don't see a problem."

Rayhan shook his head and moved past the vampire, dragging me along.

"Sit here." Rayhan sat me at the end of the row of witches. Chains clinked, and my hands found freedom until the vampire pulled them in front of me and resecured the shackles. One rope connected all my people, and Rayhan wrapped the loose end around my silver binds. He tugged the restraints, and they held fast.

"You'll march with the others." Rayhan stood and turned to his horse. "We leave in an hour."

Rayhan and Foresti disappeared into the throng of vampire soldiers.

Kadence watched Rayhan's back as the man rode away. He flicked his black eyes over me, burning a trail of hatred across my skin. I knew he imagined my death in a thousand different ways.

I looked down. That much pain and rage felt too intimate for a stranger to see. When I glanced up, Kadence and his horse had trotted back toward the others.

"What did you do to piss off the king?" the man beside me asked.

"The king?"

He nodded. "That was King Kadence and his best friend, Rayhan. They usually don't go on prisoner raids. Kadence prefers his opponents to be dead."

"Then why are we alive?" I leaned around the stranger to look at the other witches huddled along the rope.

"No idea." He took in my ragged dress and the line of red where the silver shackles had started to irritate my wrists. "What's your name? How old are you?"

I couldn't blame him for his question. The round face I inherited from my mother, combined with my father's wide eyes and slim nose, made me look young. He probably wouldn't be surprised if the bloodsuckers had kidnapped a child.

"Twenty-five." I had no reason to lie about my age. "And my name is Natalie."

"Reef." He held one hand awkwardly in front of me, wrapped around the rope. A smile tilted my lips as I returned the handshake.

"Nice to meet you," I said.

"Did they hurt you?" Concern sparkled in Reef's dark eyes. His gaze rolled over my body with a medic's precision.

"No." Although my feet throbbed, and my waterlogged socks worsened the pain. "But these shackles are irritating my wrists."

"They're silver," he said. "It hinders our magic, but it tends to bother the skin. Here, let me look."

I froze my tongue before it could refuse the offer. A familiar determination filled his face, one that used to appear on my mother's when she saw a new patient. I held my hands toward him, and he peered under the metal.

Reef grimaced, pulling tight the edges of laugh lines. No laughter sprang from his lips today. I tried to imagine his slim form tucked into silver armor with a sword in hand, but the image refused to appear. Perhaps he had served another function in the war than fighting.

"The skin is already turning red," he said. "You must be more sensitive to the silver than normal. It'll probably blister before we reach Vari Kolum."

The name of the vampire kingdom drew a sense of dread across my shoulders. Blistered feet, blistered wrists. Wonderful. I pulled my hands back and rested them in my lap.

"Is that where we're going? How far is it?"

Reef shrugged. "Where else would we go? Unless they've dedicated a camp to prisoners, I imagine we're headed straight for the dungeons. And nobody knows how long it'll be. We've never been able to find their kingdom."

They'd found Ededen rather easily. It wasn't fair that they could do raids and round up innocent people and off-duty soldiers.

The vampires broke from their groups, and a new murmur ran through the ranks. Some mounted horses, others packed supplies into pale canvas bags. They wore similar dark uniforms, but their armor varied. Most had standard silver plates, but smatterings of black and gray also appeared. One man's helmet had a bright red feather protruding from the back. They all carried weapons, mostly hammers or swords, but a few held axes and bows. Suspicious gazes scanned us, monitoring for unruly behavior.

A tall, spindly bloodsucker stopped in front of us.

"Everyone up!" he yelled. "Prepare to march out."

The man grabbed the rope and pulled. His strength outmatched ours, but we didn't dare fight anyway. The silver shackles slowed our magic to a trickle, and the vampires would have plenty of time to kill us. One outlier could be the end of everyone.

The rope jerked my hands up, and my body followed a heartbeat later. My feet groaned in protest, but I shoved the complaints away. The men and women tied next to me were in the same situation. We wondered if we would ever see our families again, if we would survive imprisonment in a vampire dungeon, how long we would travel before they gave us food and water.

Wondering what the price of freedom would be.

Reef put one foot in front of the other, and I followed him. We walked at the tail end of the progression. The ropes pulled taut, and I quickened my pace. Already sore and exhausted, I hoped a break would come soon.

"Are you okay?" Reef asked, half-turning to speak in my direction.

"Yes," I said, another lie from my mouth. Physically, my feet and wrists hurt, but the ache felt shallow and bearable. The turmoil rolling through my head was the truth of my perseverance. If Penelope halved my father's medication dose, he would have enough for two weeks. I had to be home before he took the last one, and nothing would stand between me and my family. I would do anything to get back to them, even if it left these witches —my own people—as bodies in my wake.

Anything.

CHAPTER THREE

The second day proved worse.

The vampires had marched most of the night to put miles between them and possible witch reinforcements. They established a rough camp last night, cozied around dots of fire, and bickered about who needed to watch the prisoners. One lone guard stalked up and down our rows and offered an occasional bitter word or blatant threat. We had slept on the ground, huddled for warmth, but not too close because we were sore and tired. They brought water once, but my throat still felt dry as a bone.

Up and walking again before the sun rose in the morning.

The moisture harbored in my socks had dried, but new liquid drenched the fabric as blisters popped. Each step shot hot agony into my feet that spread up my nerves. If the ragged limbs weren't bleeding yet, they would be soon.

The setting sun illuminated sage green plants along our path, although that was a generous term for the game trail half-hidden in overgrown bushes. The vampires didn't seem to notice as they perched on their horses and fondled their weapon hilts.

A low branch snaked across the route, and my toe caught the harsh wood. I staggered and smothered a gasp as sharp pain stabbed through my raw feet. The fumble pulled the silver shackles taut on my wrists, and the metal burnt. The rope connecting me to the rest of the witches tightened, and Reef looked over his shoulder.

"Are you okay?"

"Yes." I bit my lower lip, but tears poked the corners of my eyes. More pus and mystery fluid oozed from my injured foot. The stick must have broken a fragile blister.

"Tell them you need a break," Reef urged me for the dozenth time since we'd begun the punishing pace that morning. "They can't expect a civilian to be as physically capable as a soldier."

"I'm okay, Reef." I tried to convince a smile to stay on my face, but the constant aches forced my lips to twist. "Just a little stumble."

"They need to give you some water, at least. We all need water."

My mouth turned to paper. The thought of water consumed me. A ravaged animal yearning for the mere basics of survival tore through my thoughts. Primal instincts threatened to overrule logic.

"No." I fought the beast. Asking for anything from the vampires risked heating their anger and making our lives worse.

"You're going to hurt yourself," Reef said.

I couldn't hurt more than I already did.

"I'm okay." I strengthened my voice, but I could hear the falsity.

Our footsteps blended into a monotonous tone. The crunch of sore feet across rocky soil ate away hour after hour. Shrubs transitioned into tall prairie grasses before the lingering rays of sunlight faded and the terrain turned dark. A few vampires lit torches to illuminate our steps, but I wasn't the only one tripping over the uneven ground.

I licked my lips, but no moisture remained on my tongue. Its sandpaper edge rubbed the cracks on my skin. With every other step, the world swayed and rocked. Reef's figure stayed the only solid point that kept me on my feet.

I watched Reef's back as random thoughts and twisted memories trailed through my mind. My father had enough medicine to last two weeks, if Penelope limited his doses. He wouldn't feel well, but he would survive. Thinking about Penelope sent a new pain through my heart. The fear in her eyes as the shadow figure killed the vampire in the clearing.

No, wait, that wasn't right. It didn't kill him. The phantom read his mind, his memories. The dehydration and chronic throbbing of my feet were playing games with me.

Homesickness bubbled up and stuck in my throat. Each step put me farther from my family, who needed me, relied on me. Penelope deserved better than the life I could give her. It was my fault she didn't have her mother anymore. I let our mom die, and I could never change that.

The wetness of hot liquid trailed down my fingertips. The metallic scent of blood tickled my nose. I jerked my hands to my face. Speckles of dirt and grime covered my palms, but there was no blood. I rubbed my fingers together and still felt the slickness of the memory.

I needed water. Insanity brushed against my mind.

Somewhere amid the prairie reeds and crunch of thin shoes on gravel, I noticed a new pattern of footsteps. Solid and strong, they stomped a familiar rhythm among the waist-high weeds.

I recognized them.

My pulse beat in my throat.

"Mom?"

"Natalie?" Reef's voice sounded distant and muffled, as though he was screaming at me underwater. "Who are you talking to?"

I scanned the foliage, arching over my shoulder to search the dark landscape. It had been years since my mother's death, but I couldn't forget the sound of her pace. I'd spent hours walking through the woods, collecting herbs and healing supplies, with my mother's hand tucked in mine.

Eagerness replaced the pain in my feet and parchment in my mouth. Maybe my mother had defied biology and had returned from the dead. Dehydration and exhaustion reassured me that this was possible. She could be here, in this very place, right now.

I sought her figure with a hunger reserved for the starving.

There. There she was.

My mother appeared beside me, matching her steps with mine. Her brown hair was wrapped into a tight bun, and she wore a simple tunic and breeches. Leather shoes pulled up to her knees and tied with a single strap. Her body glowed as though a flickering torch illuminated her from the inside out.

"Mother!" My arms ached to hold her, to feel her warm skin, but something held them bound. The impossibility of the situation—that we had cremated my mother and scattered her ashes into the wind—didn't matter. Logic and years of studying told me this was a hallucination, probably from stress and physical ailments. But truth had no place in my fractured mentality, and I knew my mother was real and walked before me.

"Mother!" My throat was too dry for more than a hoarse scream. "Come here! Mother!"

"Natalie! There's nobody there."

I tuned out Reef's calls.

"Help me. I want to see you, but I need help."

She turned her copper eyes into my soul and wrinkled her nose as though she didn't like what she saw. Her high cheekbones tightened, and her lips pulled back into a toothy sneer. Along the surface of her glowing skin, black streaks began to twist.

"Help you?" Her voice sounded deeper than I remembered. It sent a chill down my spine. "I would never help you."

The dark lines spread over her body. They swirled around her neck and disappeared under her clothes. Some of them thickened and froze, revealing a dark crack through my mother's skin and only shadow on the inside. My eyes grew wide, and my throat tightened.

"You are the reason I'm dead." The cracks deepened. "If you had been a better witch, a better daughter, I would still be here. Penelope would have a mother. Jardel would still have a wife."

"I tried." It came out a whisper. "I tried to save you."

"Did you?" She lifted one hand toward me. Around the fractures, skin slipped off her limbs and floated to the ground as gray, decaying snow. "Just like you tried to save the thief on the road after you'd already killed him?" She shook her head and clumps of her hair fell. A curling darkness danced beneath her skin, so similar to the familiar depths of my stalker phantom.

"No," I begged.

"You don't even have magic," she sneered. "Killing you would do this world a favor."

My mother's skin floated in the summertime air and disappeared into the weeds. She looked down at me and took slow steps forward, her hand outreached. Each step ate away more of her body until the only thing left was the black phantom, the ghostly creature that haunted me. It kept coming, one hand out, and I knew that when it touched me, I would die.

My foot caught on the ground, and I dropped to my knees. Weight on my wrists dragged down with me, and a murmur of complaints filtered through the night. Only half-aware of the line of witches that my stumble had halted, I watched that shadow hand draw near.

"Please." Tears tried to form, but my body didn't have enough water. I didn't know if I begged for the creature to leave or to end it all now.

The phantom stopped a breath away, and its reach clawed through my heart. I couldn't feel it and there was no pain, but a scream ripped from the depths of my chest and escaped through my mouth.

I didn't die. I had wanted to die.

"Shut up, the lot of you. You magic asses are going to get us all killed. What's going on? Who stopped back here?" a new voice boomed, one of the vampire guards that had been on duty last night.

"Natalie, get up." Reef twisted as much as the binds allowed and grabbed one of my wrists. Cold and numb, I couldn't feel his grip. He tugged at me, but I sagged in the chains. Exhaustion turned my legs soft.

"Here's the problem." The vampire sounded close. Agony exploded through my ribs and stole the little breath I had. The hard ground caught me, and my wrists pulled sharply against the silver cuffs, half-holding my arms above me. The vampire launched another sharp kick into my side. The hot pain combined with the rest of my aches into a whirlpool of numbness. I didn't have enough energy to feel anymore. "Get up."

I couldn't move.

"Or, you can die."

Yes, yes. Death would be the sweet release of this pain. The memory of my mother's disappointment would fade forever.

Rough hands grabbed the back collar of my dress and forced me to my knees. The cold blade of a knife touched my throat.

"Get up or die where you lay." The scent of raw meat oozed from the vampire's mouth.

I closed my eyes. I didn't want to see my death.

Vibrations beat against the ground, and a moment later thundering horse hooves grew near. An animal huffed above me, and a trail of warm air blew across the side of my face.

"What's going on here?" Rayhan asked.

A calm nothingness claimed me.

"She's making a racket," the guard said. "She has to shut up, or her screams are going to attract the Suo."

The word felt familiar, but my broken memories couldn't place it.

"We can't handle a Suo?" Rayhan asked.

"Sir, it's birthing season."

Silence.

"I'll take care of this."

"Yes, sir."

The man dropped me, and I fell forward, trapped upright by the bonds on my wrist. Through the blur of darkness that crept on the edges of my vision, Rayhan dismounted and drew closer. He pulled a knife from his belt and cut the rope tying me to Reef. Arms tingly, I fell, but Rayhan caught me. His warmth soaked into my dress, finally heating my icy skin.

He picked me up, and my head rolled onto his shoulder.

"What's wrong with her?" Rayhan asked.

"She's sick," Reef snapped. "She's not trained for this level of physical endurance, and we've only had water once. Last night."

Rayhan's eyes creased. He looked to the second vampire. "Is this true?"

"I'm not sure, sir."

Rayhan turned his back to the stranger, but anger rumbled through his chest. "Get them water, immediately."

"Yes, sir." Hurried footsteps shuffled off.

"Here."

Cradling me in one arm, Rayhan pressed a cool glass to my lips. Sweet water, more intoxicating than the finest wine, spilled between them. I guzzled it, savoring the trails that ran over my parched face. Too soon, the liquid disappeared.

"You'll throw up if you drink too much."

I moaned, the most that my mouth could form. I craved more, but the words wouldn't come through my lips.

"Ten-minute break for water, then we march again." Rayhan turned, keeping me in his arms.

"What are you doing?" Reef asked, and a murmur of agreement spilled from the witches. "Where are you taking her?"

Something cold and smooth rubbed over my legs, and a rough jostle forced my eyes open. The familiar brush of unconsciousness beckoned me. My mother's books would diagnose me with syncope, but the symptoms listed in her dainty handwriting didn't describe the dizziness and nausea quite right. Both enveloped me, making the darkness more tempting.

I sat atop the red and white stallion, perched carefully across the wide leather saddle. Rayhan held me steady with one hand and leapt up. He wrapped both arms around me to settle his hands on the reins.

"She's riding with me," Rayhan said.

"The hell she is," Reef protested, but Rayhan jerked the reins and Foresti lunged forward. He snorted, flicked his ears, and tried to angle his head for a better look at the new rider on his back.

"Come on, you stupid horse." Rayhan manhandled the straps against the animal, but his voice sounded gentle despite the commands. "Ride straight for once."

My strength was drained. My mother's words weighed too heavy for my broken mind. Rayhan's chest felt warm, and his breathing turned to soft white noise in my ears. Dehydration and the constant aches in my feet beckoned me to sleep, and I happily followed.

CHAPTER FOUR

Consciousness dragged me kicking and screaming back to reality. I didn't want to wake up. My throat would be dry and sore, and my feet were likely ragged stumps. Immobility stiffened my body. The grogginess in my head suggested I had slept for a long time, but not well.

Darkness lingered behind my closed lids. The distant memory of a horse perched in the archives of my mind, but I wasn't moving now. Scattered sounds echoed through the space. The slithering of fabric on rough stone. A gentle drip of water nearby. It smelled musty, a kind of humidity that clung to my nose with a tinge of bitterness. A low murmur of whispered voices slipped around me, and one that sounded particularly familiar.

"Have you heard anything from her?" a woman's voice asked. She seemed far away and muffled.

"Not yet, Jolie. Hopefully soon," Reef echoed, much closer, but not beside me. The rope that connected us must have been severed.

"He's going to be back with more water."

"Good," Reef said. "It's their own fault for taking a civilian as a prisoner. They should take care of her."

Lower murmurs of agreement floated around me.

I peeled my heavy eyelids open. Faint torchlight illuminated a small, square cell. Ten by ten paces and lined with a rich orange stone. A crisscrossing iron door secured the room. A tiny window, two feet across and blocked by three thick bars, displayed a vibrant sky filled with twinkling stars and an almost full moon.

I laid on a stone bed, really more of a narrow bench, that stretched the back length of the cell under the window. The rest of the space remained empty except a metal bucket that sat unobtrusively to one side. I wrinkled my nose when I realized its purpose.

Surprisingly, I felt good. My muscles ached a bit, and I wished sleep would call me again, but I had expected worse. The silver shackles remained around each wrist, but the chain between them was gone, allowing me to move my hands freely. The metal rubbed against my skin and ached more than the slight throbbing from my injured feet.

We had survived the journey to Vari Kolum's dungeons, although it may have been a close call. A flash of triumph wound through me. I had fulfilled my first goal. Next, I would figure out how to escape this prison—which had never been done before—and travel home, even though I didn't know the way. No problem.

I smothered a sigh.

"Reef?" My voice cracked halfway through the word, and I cleared my throat.

"Natalie!" Relief etched in his tone. "You're awake! How do you feel?"

A solid rock wall towered between us and distorted his words. I couldn't see him, but I could hear him well enough.

"She's awake?" the same woman, Jolie, asked. She must have been in a different cell.

I sat up slowly, and the walls stayed in place. The nausea and dizziness had faded. My tattered shoes perched on the stone bed beside me, and bandages covered my feet. An herby smell emitted from them, and I rubbed my toes together. They felt slick and wet, slathered in some kind of oil or balm.

"Yes, she just woke up. Natalie, are you okay?"

I ran a finger along the edge of the bandage to collect the salve. I gave it a little sniff. Beeswax, calendula, and chamomile. A simple but effective healing lotion.

"I'm alright," I said. "How about you?"

"We didn't pass out halfway through the journey, Natalie," Reef said. "We're fine."

"How long has it been?"

"You slept almost a whole day." That explained the stars through the window. It was the next night. "Rayhan comes by every two hours or so and forces you to drink more water. You've been pretty unresponsive until the last couple times. That's why I thought you'd wake up soon."

I scooted to the edge of the stone bed and placed my feet on the ground. Stabbing aches poked into my soles but settled quickly. I stood, and they bore the weight with only slight discomfort. Maybe the balm held something I hadn't identified, an ingredient with pain-killing properties.

I crossed the cell and studied the iron gate. Thick bolts held the metal door in place. I wrapped my fingers around the cold bars and jerked them, feeling for give. Nothing.

I peeked through the rails. Rows of torches lined the walls, one parked in front of every cell. Only three stretched to my left, and a dark hallway continued unseen. On the right side, they stretched endlessly until the angle of the gate blocked my view. Beside me, Reef's outstretched hand hung between his cell's bars, and I barely made out the edge of his pointed nose and high brow.

He smiled at me. "You look better."

"That's what every girl wants to hear."

He laughed, but the sound was small. "You were knocking on death's door last night. I'm glad to see you up and walking."

"Me too." And that was the truth. As much as sleep had been restorative, I needed to be awake to escape this place.

Somewhere overhead, a door creaked open. An exchange of voices filtered to us, and heavy footsteps clambered down an unseen flight of stairs. They grew louder, closer.

"That's him." Reef drew his hand back into the cell. "It's Rayhan."

I pressed against the unmoving bars to angle for a better look. Rayhan was four cells away before I saw him. Even bigger than I remembered. He swallowed the space between the rock wall and the iron gates. He had shed the armor, revealing a muscular chest and thick arms beneath a thin tunic. His oval face boasted a square, bearded jaw and a nose that flared at the tip. He was a plain sort of handsome, until you saw his eyes. The ocean had bled its heart's blood into the irises and stained them a promising and wild royal blue.

Watching the ground as he walked, Rayhan's brow pressed tight and his lips puckered as though his teeth clenched. Furrowed anger lined his expression. But when he looked up and saw me, his features smoothed and a smile settled for a heartbeat before fading to a flat, blank look.

He stopped in front of the bars. He studied my body–drawing warmth to my cheeks–and fingers curled around the metal between us.

"You're awake," he said.

"I am."

"I brought you these." He held up a pair of black, fur-lined shoes. I squinted at them. The fur would probably come alive and eat my feet.

He frowned at my silence. "Move away from the door so I can come in."

"And if I don't want you to?"

The ocean of his eyes turned to a hurricane.

"I'd hate to have to visit a specific witch kingdom again, so soon after such a debilitating raid." His words came out flat, but they felt like solid hits to my chest.

I stepped back from the bars until my knees hit the stone bed and I perched on the edge. Rayhan made quick work of the lock, and the cell door swung inward. He strode inside and shut the gate with a final click.

The fury left his eyes, and he hunched his shoulders.

"I'll leave these here." He set the black shoes on the floor. I didn't move toward them, although my fingers itched to feel the soft pelt. Three days of travel had worn my dress to sandpaper ribbons, and the bandages on my feet weren't the same as luxury rabbit fur.

"You want to go home," he said.

I wrinkled my forehead. That may have been the stupidest statement I'd ever heard.

"Yes," I said.

"I want to help you."

I took an exaggerated look around the stone prison, then raised my brows at the man.

"I want to help you, *if* you help me," he clarified.

I was locked in an enemy camp as a prisoner of war. I possessed only a cream-colored, threadbare dress, a pair of holey shoes, and new black slippers on my cell floor. I had nothing to give him.

The air in my lungs turned to lead, and my throat tightened at a sudden thought. Rayhan was a very large, inhumanly strong man, and I was an untrained civilian under his mercy. He could ask anything from me.

He must have seen the thoughts play across my face.

"If you'd open those ears for thirty seconds, girl, you would have heard my promise not to hurt you back in the woods." He reached a hand toward me, but I flinched out of the way and pulled my knees onto the bed. "Gods, woman. You're more skittish than my dumb horse. Here, look."

Rayhan snatched the iron bucket with one finger under the handle and gave it a quick scan. Seemingly content that it remained unused, he flipped it upside down and perched on the pan. The metal bowed under him, but it held. There was something comical about the redheaded giant sitting on the edge of a tiny bucket, but I couldn't find the air to laugh.

"Does that make you feel better?"

"Sure," I said.

"Sure? Suddenly you have a sense of humor, huh? Look, I want to get you home, but there's something you can help me with. Remember the magic you did to me in the forest?"

I nodded. I remembered the brush of foreign memories invading my mind.

"Can you do it again?"

I tapped my tongue on the roof of my mouth. Only the shadow creature could control my crazed and unpredictable magic. Telling Rayhan the truth would trap me in the cell forever, and my father would die when his medicine ran out. Some vampires could identify lies. Something about hearing the changing heartbeat or smelling sweat on the skin. I couldn't risk angering this man.

A half-lie then.

"Yes," I said. I could technically do it again, I just didn't know how or when.

Rayhan raised an eyebrow. A moment passed, and he raised the other.

I tilted my head.

"Go on then." He flicked his fingers at me. "Do it."

My mouth dropped. "You want me to... right now?"

"Yes."

"Magic... here? Now?"

He leaned forward. "Are you hard of hearing, woman? I don't want to involve too many people, but we have a man upstairs who knows sign language. I can bring him down."

"No, no, I can hear you." I just couldn't believe him. "But...that's not how magic works."

He narrowed his eyes. "You did it in the forest."

"Th-that was different," I stammered. "I was on edge. There was less control."

"You need to be on edge then?" He rose from the bucket like a king from a throne and stepped to me. He put one hand on either side of my legs and bent down until our faces hovered a hand's width apart. Woodland green and peppermint sprang through the air, with another deeper and muskier scent underneath. "Tell me, does this do it?"

He was too close. I couldn't breathe.

"I need..." What? A book? A sacrifice? "A circle."

A circle, Nat? Stupid. I should have told him some exotic herb and made him trek days through the wilderness to find it. Maybe a terrible beast would eat him and one of my problems would be solved. But a circle? A piece of chalk would solve that.

He leaned back, and I gasped for cool air. He looked over the cell and squinted at the flat stone floors.

"Here." Rayhan pulled a folded knife from his belt. Small and less than three inches long. He pushed the thin blade out with a click. "Carve a circle into the floor."

Oh gods. Only the vampire and I stood in the space, leaving plenty of exposed ground. Curse the shadow creature for never showing up when I *wanted* to kill something.

There remained little choice. I had to make a circle and hope some magic would happen.

The knife sank coldness into my palm. Rayhan retreated to his bucket, and I settled my feet onto the floor. Walking around the room, I pulled at my power. It rushed forward, hungry and eager, but caught on the bars of my mother's spell. I tried to gather the tendrils reaching for escape, but they slipped away.

I didn't feel anything. No draw toward a position of power or that tiny space where natural energy clusters. The magic sat flat and timid. This would end badly.

I chose a random place and knelt on the hard rock. The knife tip complained against the solid floor, and I forced my weight onto the blade. It cut into the stubborn stone. My shaking hand began the edge of a wobbly circle.

Sweat broke out on my forehead, from either the stress or the effort to push the blade into the stone. After a few minutes of drawing as slowly as possible to buy time, the edges connected and the circle was complete. I wiped my brow and waited for the snap of power to emit from the, admittedly, misshapen circle.

Nothing.

"Is something wrong?" Rayhan asked.

"No," I said and smiled. The man pressed his lips together.

Witch Lesson 101: If a circle fails, try chanting. I folded myself into the space. My arms and legs rubbed the line. Why had I drawn it so small? I closed my eyes and took a breath. Mother taught me to ground myself in the senses before calling on the magic. I felt the chill of cold rocks soak through my clothes. The sound of Rayhan's rough breathing. The scent of herbs on my healing feet.

My lips found a simple chant, a general spell to guide the power into action. I repeated the phrase under my breath, pushing it between the tight chains that trapped my magic, and tried to drag my power into the circle. The rhythmic words couldn't overlap the beating of my heart.

A screeching drew my eyes open as Rayhan pushed from the bucket hard enough to tip the metal pan over. It clanked on the floor, drawing yells from Reef and neighboring cells, which faded into the background behind Rayhan's approaching figure.

"Nothing's happening." The man ground his teeth until his jaw reddened. He sent an angry look my way but turned and threw a solid punch into the stone wall. The structure shook, and mortar dust speckled onto my head.

He spun back to me.

"Why is nothing happening?" One pointed finger danced in front of my face.

Anger heated my bones. I stood up from the floor, and my power, still chained and unusable, flurried around me in response. It painted me in a black cloak, pretty to look at, but not functional.

"I don't know why nothing's happening." I grabbed his finger and forced his hand down. "Maybe it's because I almost died last night, and my kidnapper continues to threaten me. Maybe it's because I haven't eaten in three days. Maybe it's because I'm trapped in a cell instead of at home taking care of my family!"

Rayhan snapped back from me. His mouth went slack, and he ran one hand over his jaw.

"Okay." He tapped a finger on his cheek. "Maybe that's the problem."

I sagged, still standing in the center of the haphazard circle. "That I'm too exhausted and afraid to do the spell?"

"No. Maybe it's not personal enough down here in this cell. Come on."

The man opened the metal door and held it. He gestured at me with his other hand. "Come on, woman, I said let's go."

I shook my head. The best way to be murdered is to go to a second location. If he wanted to kill me, he could do it here.

"Okay, look. You said you're hungry, right?"

My stomach twisted in knots. I bit my lip.

"I know you're hungry. I can see it on your face. Food sounds good, right?"

My mouth watered.

"What do you want?" he asked. "Want some honey ham?"

Yes, please.

"Hot bread rolls with fresh butter?"

Oh my.

"A glass of water *and* milk, to top it off?"

He had me and he knew it. The satisfaction settled in the square of his shoulders.

"If you go with me, then I'll bring you a plate of all that. No prison porridge, I promise."

I looked down the rows of torch-lined cells. Rayhan followed my gaze.

"Yes, yes, them too. I'll have a whole damn banquet for all of you. Just come with me. I promise I won't hurt you."

I took his outstretched hand, and his fingers enveloped mine. He tugged me through the gate, and I trailed down the hall. Discreetly, while the giant focused on the path forward, I retracted the tiny knife he'd given me and hid the weapon in my fist.

"Natalie?" Reef craned his neck to watch as we walked past. "Don't become a martyr for us."

"Don't worry, Reef." I tried to make my voice light. "I know what I'm doing."

"Natalie, I'm serious. Don't hurt yourself because you think it will help us."

"Shut up," Rayhan said. "She's going to be fine."

Following in the giant's footsteps, I prayed he was right. Between one step and the next, I slipped the knife into my shirt, between my breasts, where it thunked like a cold heartbeat beside my own.

CHAPTER FIVE

"Shouldn't you be concerned that you're showing me the exit?" Rayhan's grip on my hand remained constant but careful. I didn't know how many hands he had held, but he was aware of his strength.

"You won't see an exit out of this castle."

The orange-tinted stones wrapped around a spiral staircase that stopped at a landing before a wooden door. One guard sat in a chair with a book on his lap. His brows shot into his hairline at our approach, and he stood to a quick attention. He looked at our clasped hands and opened his mouth.

"Not a word, soldier." Rayhan pushed the door open, spilling us into a hallway lined with plush black carpet and more torches. Sculptures and paintings hugged the walls. One side of the hall dipped into a small alcove with a cluster of gold-painted chairs. "We were never here."

It slammed on the guard's gaping mouth.

"Look." I half ran as the giant pulled me along to another stairwell. "He doesn't think I should see the exits either."

"You have a lot to say for someone wearing shackles on her wrists. Maybe adding the chains again will shut you up."

I bit my lip. The silver bands alone bothered my skin. I didn't want to add the constant tugging of a heavy chain.

We climbed one more set of stairs, and darkness spilled from the next landing. Shadows pressed along the hallway, sparse of torches, and shrunk the space. Movement flashed in my peripheral vision, but it was only the flicker of our silhouettes on a blank wall. No artwork or decorations adorned the walls, unlike the lavish lower level. The floors were flat, naked stone.

I moved closer to Rayhan and hoped he wouldn't notice.

"Kadence's room is on this floor." Rayhan muted his voice to an almost whisper. "So be quiet for a minute."

My lips sealed. After feeling his sword against my neck, I didn't want to ever see the vampire king again.

Rayhan led the way down the dark hall. We passed identical doors composed of solid wood boards with three decorative iron bands looped around them. Whispers slipped from one or two rooms, but the rest remained quiet. An eerie mood drifted through the space, slow and melancholy, like these people mourned for something.

Rayhan stopped at the fourth door from the end and pushed it open. He moved slowly, with not a hint of sound escaping the old hinges. He peeked inside and, evidently satisfied, pulled me through the entryway. The door shut, trapping us in a dim room.

"Let me light these candles."

The vampire wouldn't have a problem seeing in the darkness, but I could only make out looming shapes and creeping shadows. A match scratched against paper, and a bright spark erupted. Rayhan lit a cluster of candles on a low table beside the door. He cradled the flame with one hand as he crossed the space and ignited more candles perched on an ornately carved bedside stand. The largest bed I'd ever seen sat between the nightstands. The headboard climbed halfway up the twelve-foot-high wall, dancing flames etched into its wooden slab.

"This was my father's room." Rayhan looked around, and the edges of his lips curled. A twisting shadow moved through the ripples of his blue eyes. He must not have fond memories here.

"You said he died?" I phrased it as a question, but I knew the answer.

Rayhan nodded. "He did. They said it was something genetic, something our blood couldn't heal."

"But you don't believe that."

"No."

Silence pulsed between us. Living without a parent was hard, and despite centuries of war, there was comradery in that.

"Try your magic here." Rayhan's voice broke the spell.

I looked around and frowned.

"This was his home," Rayhan said. "You said you needed to be in his home."

"I said *I* needed to be home. *My* home."

His brows creased. "Well, that's not an option."

"Only because you say it isn't."

"Are you going to do a spell or not?"

I held up a silver, shackled bracelet.

"We both know those slow the magic, they don't stop it," Rayhan said. "Do something or I'm taking you back to your cell."

The knife sat against my chest, but I didn't dare pull it out. The small blade would be a paper cut to a man of Rayhan's size, and I didn't know how to wield it anyway.

I sighed. This was a waste of time. Hopefully, he wouldn't kill me when I failed.

I reached for my power, but the chains around it remained tight and secure. Magic was supposed to fade when the spellcaster died. My mother had been gone for seven years. I wished her spell would figure that out.

I didn't pretend to need a circle this time. When my attempt proved futile, my lies would be caught and I'd be trapped in the dungeon forever. I ground my feet into the smooth stone and tried to center my mind. A salty flavor lined my lips from the dried sweat still coating my skin. A light chill through the room brushed against my bare arms. I ran through the senses again, hoping for something new to spark my magic and help it rip free.

Nope.

"I'm sorry." I shook my head.

Rayhan's shoulders sagged. He put one hand over his face, and I pretended not to notice the tear in his eye. I turned away to avoid looking at my enemy's grief.

A dark figure loomed in front of me. The phantom.

I gasped and stepped back, but it reached for me. My heart drummed in my ears as fear wrapped a tight coil around my chest. It grabbed me with a clawed hand, and its fleshless skin dissolved into me in a cold rush. The being pulled my magic from the depths of my soul, higher and higher, until it piled into a powder keg and the phantom lit the match.

I exploded.

Magic pulsed through the room, and new shapes formed over the dark space. It grew brighter as rich sunlight stretched through the window. The temperature rose ten degrees, and all the candles were illuminated, not just the few Rayhan had started.

A man perched on the edge of the bed, pulling his shoes off. Tall and wide, a little shorter than Rayhan, and bald. Despite the lack of hair on his head, he had a brilliant red beard, well maintained and trimmed, that tumbled down to cover his collarbones. An odd color tainted his skin tone. He wasn't quite solid, but I could see him clearly. I stepped near and reached out. My hand slipped through the mirage, and the image flickered, then settled. He continued to pull his socks off, unhindered.

A knock sounded at the door. The man smiled and pushed from the bed. He opened it and caught the edge of a silver platter. He pulled the tray inside and ushered in a woman behind.

"I told you not to carry everything yourself. There are plenty of young men who would help with the load."

She looked about my age and lugged two canvas bags filled with food. Beautiful honey-brown locks dropped down her back and ran along the edge of her waist. Her arms tightened, and finite muscles protruded beneath her dark silk dress. The man settled the tray on the table beside the door. It held a simple teapot and a pair of white cups.

"I can carry a couple bags up a flight of stairs, Manveer." The woman twisted her hair into a tight bun. "Anyway, I've got to go. I'm late for sparring."

"Just a moment, Hayleigh." Manveer caught the girl in a hug. She tensed, then hugged him back with a big smile.

"I missed you too." She laughed. "I'm glad you're home."

"Me too." Manveer turned to the teapot and grabbed the handle. He froze. "Won't you stay and have a cup of tea with me?"

Hayleigh's eyes widened, and she flicked her gaze to the door. One hand clenched into a fist, then went slack. She smiled and half-shrugged.

"Sure, I can be a few minutes late to spar."

Manveer flipped over the cups and tipped the teapot. Wisps of a new scent twirled around me. The golden tea turned to black ooze, but Manveer poured as though he didn't notice the thick sludge. Maybe he didn't. Maybe my magic affected the imprint.

Hayleigh lounged across the bed accepted the cup Manveer offered. She raised it to her lips and grimaced.

"No sugar?"

"Of course not." Manveer sat at the edge of the mattress. "You need to learn to drink tea like a man."

Hayleigh rolled her eyes and took another unhappy sip.

"Listen," Manveer said in a tone that sounded too familiar. "I wanted to ask how your mother's doing. Wilson's been demanding with his projects, and she was in the library a lot before I left. Has she been acting strange?"

Hayleigh rose and crossed back to the silver platter. She set her cup on the far edge and ran her finger along the rim.

"Mom is Mom." She shrugged, but her face tightened. "They were both disappointed when Nadeem rejected Wilson again."

"He must have a good reason for it," Manveer said.

Hayleigh turned, abandoning the cup of black ooze on the tray.

"Maybe you could talk to him?" she asked, and eagerness lit her eyes. "Maybe if Nadeem let Wilson in the lab for a few days, it would change his mind."

Manveer pressed his lips. "Nadeem knows what he's doing," he said softly. "I trust the old vampire's decisions."

"Fine." Hayleigh crossed her arms. "Was there anything else you wanted? I'm really late now."

Manveer shook his head and opened his mouth, but Hayleigh jerked the door open and let it slam shut before his words escaped. Heavy silence filled the space, and Manveer sighed. He wrapped two hands around his small cup and settled against the headboard with his tea.

I stepped closer. The inky liquid bounced but never spilled a single drop. Manveer lifted the cup to his lips.

Unlike the haunting image of my mother on the road, I knew this wasn't real. My magic floated over me and twisted into this projection of the past. But knowing that Manveer was already dead—and that magic composed this vision—couldn't convince me to leave it alone. Though my actions could not save his life, my arms raised with a will of their own.

I snatched the tea from his hands, and hot liquid burned my skin. I threw the cup, and it shattered on the ground.

Manveer's gaze snapped to me, his mouth gaping. His blue eyes resembled Rayhan's so clearly, it was like looking at a twin.

"Who are you?" He stood and plucked a knife from somewhere behind the pillow. He lunged at me, but the blade sunk through my chest without leaving a wound. I staggered back, and the horror on my face matched his. I clutched at the strike, but my threadbare dress stayed unmarred.

Manveer's eyes widened.

"What are you?" His lips kept moving, but the words were distorted.

The image flickered like a dying torch. Manveer raised one arm toward me, freezing and jerking, until the scene paused, then faded away.

I remained in Manveer's room, except it was dark again and I was crying. Rayhan hadn't moved from his back corner, but he watched me with a guarded expression.

"What was that?" he asked.

I wish I knew.

"You father was poisoned." I wiped the tears from my eyes for a man I'd never met. Manveer had felt so real. He had looked directly at me. It was impossible. Magic couldn't alter the past.

"It was in his tea," Rayhan said. "It can't be right. Vampires are immune to poison."

I snapped at him. "How did you know it was the tea?"

He gestured to the floor. Between me and the vampire sat a thousand shards of white porcelain, covered in a thick black sludge.

My hands shook. I backed away from the cup. It didn't exist. It couldn't.

Rayhan crossed the room and grabbed my shoulders. He kneeled in front of me, blocking my view of the shattered cup.

"I need you to help me." His voice was muffled with the edge of desperation and depression. He looked at me the way a blind man would look at the sun. With perfect abandon.

I needed help too. Help to get out of here, to go home and take care of my family. This broken vampire was the obstacle between me and them.

"If you help me, I'll let you go," he said.

One knot in my gut loosened.

"What?" I whispered.

"If you help me find my father's murderer, I'll let you go home. I'll put you on a horse and ride you there myself, and I'll promise to never go back. You could live in peace, without fear."

The words painted both hope and despair into my future. He didn't know I couldn't control my power. The phantom was as likely to kill him as it was to help. But I had to get home to protect Penelope and take care of my father. I'd do anything to escape, even drive a knife through Rayhan's chest if I ever had the opportunity. Helping solve this murder should be a lot easier.

"Okay," I said. "I'll help you find your father's killer if you agree to let me go."

"Done."

Rayhan held out one hand. I closed my fingers around his palm, and we shook on it.

"There was someone else in here with your father," I told him. "A girl with long honey-colored hair."

"Hayleigh? She poisoned my dad?"

I shook my head. "No, she drank the tea too. Is she dead?"

"No, she's fine. I saw her yesterday." He paused and tilted his ears toward the door. "Someone's coming."

"Maybe they're going to another room."

He listened for a moment longer. "No, they're coming this way." Dainty footsteps clicked on the stone floor, loud enough for my inferior ears to hear. "You have to hide. If anyone sees you outside of the dungeons and tells Kadence, he'll have you killed. Quick, under the bed."

Under the bed? Surely, we could do better than that. Rayhan pushed me down as the steps grew closer. I dropped to my knees and pressed one hand to my chest to hold the hidden knife in place. I rolled beneath the bedframe a heartbeat before the door cracked open.

"Rayhan!" a woman said. "What are you doing here?"

"Ella." I could hear the smile in Rayhan's voice. "I didn't expect to see you."

"It's been a while, hasn't it?" She crept closer, and the hem of her long black dress appeared. Some kind of emerald green sash draped down the garment and hovered inches above the floor. "Come here, give me a hug."

Silence for a moment.

"Let's sit on the bed. Manveer wouldn't mind. His room was always an open door." Ella said, and the mattress above me sank.

"Why are you here, Ella?" Rayhan asked.

"I visit from time to time. It's been lonely since he's left." The words came out soft, as though she held back tears.

"I know what you mean," Rayhan said. "Sometimes, it's the only place where I feel close to him."

"It looks like you're making yourself comfortable. What's all over the floor?"

A bubble stuck in my throat. The shattered cup.

Rayhan let out a low chuckle.

"I brought up a cup of tea," he said. "The way Dad used to always have tea in here. Then I..." He let his sorrow peek through his words, and I didn't know if it was the truth or an act. "I felt so empty inside. The cup slipped before I knew what happened."

The man deserved a theater award.

"Come here. You need another hug."

Clothes shuffled and someone laughed.

"Now that's out of the way, do you want to tell me who's hiding under the bed?"

My tongue stuck to the roof of my mouth. My opportunity for freedom might evaporate before it even began.

"What do you mean, Ella?" Rayhan asked.

"Don't play dumb, boy. Your father didn't marry me just for my looks, you know."

A heavier silence settled between them.

"Alright, Natalie," Rayhan said. "You can come out."

Oh, I didn't think so. My muscles locked.

"I said, get out of there." One massive hand sprawled under the wooden frame. I scurried away, but his reach stretched too far. Strong fingers wrapped around my forearm and pulled me across the woven rug.

Two faces peered from atop the bed. The woman, Ella, had large, round eyes and a slim nose. Her rosy lips pursed into a puckered smile. She wore a black dress with long, draping sleeves, and the green sash I noticed earlier pinched her waist.

"A girl." She smiled and exposed a hint of sharp fangs. She looked me over and settled on the cuffs around my wrists. "And a witch. I didn't expect you to pose a jailbreak, Rayhan." She crinkled that dainty nose.

"That's not it, Ella. Natalie thought she could help me connect to Dad."

"With magic?" The disdain was plain in her voice.

Rayhan itched the back of his neck. "Well, yeah, with magic."

"Did it work?" Ella asked.

I bit my lip and wondered what Rayhan would say.

"No." He shook his head. "It didn't work."

He lied better than me. I needed to take notes.

"Your name is Natalie?"

It took a moment to realize Ella was talking to me.

"Y-yes," I stammered. I backpedaled from under the bedframe and stood on shaking legs.

"Natalie, this is Ella." Rayhan gestured to her. "She's my stepmother."

What was I supposed to do with my hands? She didn't offer a handshake or even a wave. She tilted her head a bit to one side and watched with a flat expression.

"They don't look as scary as the war stories the soldiers bring home," Ella said.

My mouth turned up in an involuntary smile. It had been days since I'd really smiled, and my lips felt stiff and unused.

"I'm actually very scary, ma'am," I said. Ella's laugh echoed low and rich, and I could see the appeal of having her by one's side as a partner.

"I like this one, Rayhan. You should keep her around."

"I have to take her back to the dungeons before someone tells Kadence she's out."

Ella's face darkened. "Kadence wouldn't be happy about a prisoner running through the castle. He may be gone by now though."

"He's leaving?" Rayhan's voice hitched in surprise, and his eyebrows tightened. "Where?"

"He didn't tell you? He never goes anywhere without you. I assumed you'd decided not to go. He's heading to Sacred Stone in the north to negotiate more supplies."

"Why doesn't he send a team out? The king shouldn't be bothered with supply negotiations."

"I'll let you inform him of that," Ella said. "Maybe that's why he didn't tell you he was going."

"Maybe," Rayhan agreed, but a dark shadow etched across his face.

Ella rose from the bed, and the dress billowed around her like a sorcerer's cape. She held out one hand, palm down, and I caught it in my fingers. Her hand was soft and warm, and her skin radiated a floral scent.

"It was a pleasure to meet you." She smiled, squeezed my fingers, and left the room.

Relief fluttered in my gut, and my racing heart settled. Ella seemed to have a problem with the king, and I doubted she would run to him and blab about my temporary prison escape.

Rayhan touched the side of my arm. "I have to take you back."

I nodded, but dread lingered at the bottom of my chest. There were several unpleasant places I'd rather go than the dim cell of Vari Kolum's dungeon.

The trek back proved uneventful. A new guard perched on the prison landing, but he didn't blink as Rayhan led me down the winding staircase. The vampire unlocked my gate with an iron key and held it for me.

My breath hitched as I stepped inside and the lock clicked shut. Something squeezed in my chest and stole the fledging freedom I had almost tasted tonight.

"I'll have food brought soon," Rayhan said.

I looked out the tiny window where the faint rays of sunlight beat against the dredge of night and nodded. After a moment the giant left, and his steps faded up the stairs and disappeared.

"Natalie?" Reef asked once the last door thunked shut. "Are you hurt?"

"No, Reef." I made my voice strong and loud and sprinkled an edge of laughter into the tone. "Nothing happened to me at all. I'm fine."

I dug the tiny knife from my shirt and clenched it in my fist. I could feel the pulse in my fingers beating against the dull metal edge, and I wondered if I was lying to Reef or to myself.

CHAPTER SIX

Rayhan kept his promise of good food, and the cell block cheered when guards carried carts of steaming plates down the stairs and rolled them from door to door. The young woman who delivered my plate also pressed a note into my hand.

Don't expect this every day. R.

I crumpled the page and tossed it into the metal bucket that I'd returned to its rightful corner. Fresh rolls, honey-glazed ham, and some type of wild mushroom soup melted in my mouth and stretched my empty stomach. I ate until my gut cramped and I wanted to throw up, then I ate some more. Full and almost sick, I crawled onto the stone bench and fell into the first proper sleep I'd had in days.

I woke up with the knife clenched in my fist. With the blade folded tight, the silver weapon looked small and innocent. It wouldn't do much in a hand-to-hand fight, but it was a sliver of power I refused to relinquish.

The cell bore signs of old age. Watermarks marred the stones where moisture had lingered for a long time. Divots and scratches painted a grim picture of previous occupants' fates. A crack as wide as two fingers ran along the place where the ground met the raised platform of the bed, and the mortar fell away in some places.

I settled my knees on the cool rock and dug my finger into a weak spot in the sealant. My nail broke from the rough edge, but I wedged it in deeper. Biting my tongue as the rock scratched my skin, I hooked my knuckle around the lip and pulled up the mortar. It groaned in protest but lifted away from the stone. Repositioning for a better angle, I squeezed two fingers underneath and urged the chunk out.

The knife fit perfectly in the hollow space. I tucked it into the hole with the fragility of a baby bird. The piece of mortar crumbled in my hand, and I pushed the pieces over the deep break to cover any hint of the shiny weapon.

I sat back to examine my handiwork. The crack looked as dull and drab as before. Perfect.

"A lot of ruckus over there," Reef said in a weary tone.

"Sorry, did I interrupt your beauty sleep?"

He laughed. "No, but you should still be getting yours. How are your feet today?"

I squinted at them, smothered in the bandages from yesterday. They didn't hurt anymore, thanks mostly to the plush slippers Rayhan gave me, but I hadn't peeled away the wrappings.

"I'm scared to look," I said.

"You better do it anyway. You don't want an infection to sneak up on you in here."

I sighed. Reef was right. The wrappings uncoiled into a sticky mess of beeswax and oils. A distinct floral smell, a little rosy with an undercurrent of chamomile, spread through the air. My skin appeared raw. Red tokens of blisters splattered here and there. The pain was gone, though, and there was no ooze or pus or other signs of infection.

"They look good," I said.

I wished the same could be said for my wrists. My flesh split under the silver bands, and they itched constantly. I wanted to put some of the healing ointment beneath the shackles, but it was used and dirty. I wouldn't ask Rayhan for more. I refused to be in the vampire's debt.

"I'm glad," Reef said, and a heavy pause followed. "Look, Natalie, we don't want to sound unappreciative, but whatever you did to get the food last night, we're not going to ask you to do it again."

"What do you mean?" I crinkled my nose. It was part of my deal with Rayhan. Working with him benefited all of us.

"We don't want you to...use yourself as a bargaining chip. For us." The words carried an awkward weight.

Oh. The other witches thought I slept with Rayhan for the food. It wasn't an unfair assessment. I was young and Rayhan was, well, a man. Discomfort scratched at me as I considered what to say next.

It might be safer to let them make assumptions. The vampires had been our mortal enemies for centuries. Helping them made me a traitor of the crown. I wasn't sure if sleeping with one looked any better.

My throat tightened. I hadn't thought about that. I may return home to a trial for treason.

"I promise not to do anything I don't want to." The words sounded neutral enough to settle Reef's mind, for the moment at least.

"I hope you know what you're doing, Natalie."

I had no idea.

"I do, thanks, Reef. Your concern means a lot."

"Well, we're all stuck in here together. We have to be on the same team."

I scratched at the floor with my broken nail. Steam rose from the damp stones as sunlight warmed the cell. Maybe it would be dry before nighttime. Probably not.

"I thought dungeons were underground," I said.

"I guess dungeons can be wherever they want. I've never been in one before. The window is a nice touch."

"Could be a bit bigger!" Jolie yelled from two cells down, and a clamor of laughter followed. My own lips formed a hesitant smile. Jail cell humor. The only thing better was death row humor.

I walked to the window and wrapped my hands around the bars. The rough iron had turned red with age. I tugged on the outer bars, and they held fast. It might be pointless, but I had to try.

The middle one slipped when I grabbed it. My heart jumped into my throat. Maybe my escape hid here all along.

I circled both hands over the metal and pulled. My arms screamed and burned as my muscles locked. I ground my teeth until my jaws ached. The bar spun in its grooves but held fast. I plastered one foot against the wall to gain leverage, but the iron refused to budge.

I dropped my head. The thick bubble of a scream built in the center of my chest. Tears stung my eyes and blurred the monotonous confines of my cell.

Wait. I glanced around the room. It wasn't the swell of frustrated tears obscuring my sight. Something seeped through the iron gate behind me.

Gray mist enveloped the space. Transparent but turning opaque by the second, it swirled and twisted like hungry grapevines. The mist oozed thicker than fog and carried a faint, bitter smell. It rubbed along the inside of my nose and burned my exposed eyes.

"Hey, does anyone else have fog in their cell?" Reef asked, followed by the rattle of bars as he pressed against his door.

"It's a little foggy over here," Jolie said. A chorus of no's echoed from the others.

The mist looked magical, but vampires couldn't do magic. It pulsed with an unnatural movement as it ebbed and flowed. I retreated into the back corner of the space, but the gray fog proved persistent in its search. It wrapped around me and thickened until I couldn't see the looming iron gate or even the metal bucket across the way.

Between the foggy sheets, dark, reaching arms danced toward me.

My heartbeat filled my ears as two long coils flashed through the mist. Twin ropes snapped in front of my face, and a sharp scream escaped my lips. The cords turned, searching for me, and a sound like a cracking stick erupted. The tendrils flicked around one of my wrists, a dark bracelet to match my silver shackle.

I pulled my arm, and the black rope followed. Resistance met on the other end, as though someone invisible in the mist held that side. I ran a finger from my other hand over the material, but its coiled length betrayed no secrets.

A blue-gold spark danced through the rope. Lightning over an ocean backdrop, beautiful but deadly. Power poured through the coil and burned my skin. A sharp, hot pain pressed into my arm and lit a fire through my nerves.

I screamed. My fist involuntarily curled tight, and the limb refused to move. The current paled, then that blue-gold sparked again and molten lava surged into my blood. I didn't have air to scream.

The coils tightened and jerked me forward. I stumbled on the uneven ground and smacked my free hand to catch my fall. The coil zapped me again, painting a fresh layer of pain over the old. Someone jerked on the rope and dragged me across the rocky floor. I reached for my magic, but it remained locked. I gasped for air, and sour fog filled my mouth.

The ropes pulled me toward the door.

"Hey!" Reef screamed through his gate. "We need help down here!"

I took another ragged breath. I ached to scream, to add my pleas to Reef's yells, but my lungs lacked the space.

The iron door sharpened. A dark figure poised behind the crisscrossed bars, with wide shoulders and slim hips, oddly feminine despite wearing all black.

I fought against the ropes. Blinding blue flashes pulsed through me, catching my cries and tensing my muscles into knots. Relentless, the stranger dragged me closer. My struggles didn't slow them. The waves of pain merged into a constant pulse that slowly strangled my willpower.

My body gave up. My mind urged it to fight, to keep struggling, but the embers sliced my nerves and the agony became overwhelming. Limp and exhausted as the rolling mist suffocated me, the coils heaved me to the iron door.

The figure kneeled. Two warm fingers pressed against my neck, and a woman's groan filtered through a black hood. She sounded surprised I was still alive. I was too.

She pulled a long, silver blade from behind her back.

Reef continued to yell, and new shouts stacked on top of his, but I tuned them out. The pain faded away as my mind lost its ability to cope.

I closed my eyes. I didn't want to see my death, although I'd seen many other people die. Usually, I was trying to heal them. But not always. Maybe I deserved to die. Maybe I should watch the punishment for my crimes.

I squeezed my eyes tighter and waited for the sharp cut of the knife. It would be a relief to escape the fiery pain of the rope weapons.

"The hell is this?"

Rayhan's voice.

The figure froze with her blade a handspan from my throat. She swore under her breath and pulled the weapon back. She turned on her heels and disappeared down the deep hallway, dragging the twin ropes in her wake. Something creaked on old hinges, then only silence.

Rayhan ran after my attacker, a blur of red and gold and silver armor. His steps crashed down the hall and faded.

"Natalie!" Reef said. "Are you alive?"

I sucked in as much air as my lungs could hold. My stomach protested, and adrenaline sharpened the edges of my vision. I rolled to my hands and knees and took careful breaths until the nausea eased.

"I'm...okay." My throat felt dry and hoarse. My arms ached, and red marks shined where the ropes had wrapped around my skin. Blisters had formed.

"What was that?" Reef asked. "It looked like..."

Magic. The mist looked like magic.

"I don't know," I said. The fear peeled away, and anger bubbled in its place.

Whoever had killed Rayhan's father must be keeping a close eye on the son. They knew I was involved. Well, not anymore. I would find another way to escape this prison, and not in a body bag.

By the time Rayhan appeared in front of my cell door, empty-handed and with creased brows, anger flushed my skin and sweat beaded on my back. I was here because of him. I needed to be home, taking care of my father and Penelope. Instead, the vampire jerked me around like a puppet on a string and was going to get me killed. No thank you.

The door swung open, and Rayhan stepped inside without an invitation. It took the entirety of my self-control to avoid plucking the tiny knife from its sanctuary and stabbing the man just to prove I could.

"The attacker got away," Rayhan said. "I don't know where they went. This hall is a dead end."

"I'll show you a dead end." I stalked to him. Blinded by rage, he didn't look as big in the moment. I pointed a finger at his sprawling chest, then back at me. "This. This agreement we had. It's over. I didn't sign up to die for you."

The ocean in his eyes swirled.

"What do you mean, girl?" His voice turned deadly quiet.

"I. Mean." I bit off the words. "This. Is. Over." I lowered my tone. "Whoever slipped that poison into your father's cup knows we're working together. You promised to get me out of here. I assumed I would be alive when that happened."

Rayhan moved close to me. His towering figure reminded me he was a giant, and I was a barely-average-height, untrained-in-physical-combat woman. I stepped back to avoid touching the hard line of his body.

He slouched until our gazes locked. "This is over when I say it is."

He took another step, and I backed away. "We had an agreement."

Step.

"I brought you, and your friends, food."

Step.

"I promised to take you home."

My knees staggered against the edge of the raised bed. Nowhere else to go.

"You don't get to take back your word."

That earthy wisp of evergreen and eucalyptus brushed over me. He took the extra half-step, turning the space between us into mere breaths.

More sweat spilled down my spine, and my heart thundered. This close to a vampire, it might as well be the dinner bell. But he wasn't looking at my neck. His blue eyes danced around my face, then our bodies, as though he just noticed the lack of distance.

My lips turned dry, and I ran my tongue across them. Rayhan caught the motion and followed the trail with his gaze. His stare burned, but unlike the sizzling welts on my arm, this heat simmered low in my body, alive and needy.

Oh no. I did not need the hots for a vampire.

Denial added fuel to the flames.

"Did you have something to say to me?" The ocean flared into a full hurricane, twisting and twirling and threatening to pull me in. I couldn't let him trap me in the depths of his eyes. The beautiful lure would drown me.

I pointed my finger in front of his face.

"I don't belong to you," I snapped. Anger. Rage. A hint of something else, something I didn't dare name.

Rayhan grabbed my wrist, sending hot tingles trailing through my arm. He pulled my hand to his chest, and I set my palm against the silver armor plate. The cold metal beat away that senseless heat and refreshed my mind.

"Let's see. You're in my dungeon, wearing my shackles and—" He looked down to our feet. "—my shoes. Yet you say that you don't belong to me?"

"I'd rather be naked in the woods, if given a choice," I hissed.

A shadow flickered across his face. "That can be arranged."

I blushed and bit my tongue.

His fingers stroked my cheek, and I jumped.

"Shh." He tucked a strand of hair behind my ear. "I've promised not to hurt you. Here, feel this."

Rayhan unfastened the leather straps at the shoulders of his chest plate. The metal slipped away, and he settled it on the ground. He found my hand again and pressed it to the thin black shirt, the bare threads that lingered between us.

"Do you feel that?"

His chest was solid and warm.

"Your heartbeat?" I asked.

"Exactly. I bet you thought I didn't have one of those."

I'd never considered a vampire's heartbeat before. His drummed steadily.

"I know you miss your family, and I'm sorry you got hurt tonight." He ran his other hand over the blisters on my arm. His touch was butterfly kisses. "My dad is dead. I'll never see him again. You can go home and be with your father and sister, and I promise to make that happen, but I'll still be here alone. The only thing I'll have left of him is closure, knowing his killer found justice."

The edge of his voice turned hard, and I recognized the sharpness. He was lying. I used the same voice with Penelope a thousand times, even days ago in the forest. Maybe the words were true—he would deliver revenge with the swift swing of his axe—but the tone and the touches weren't. He was playing me.

I jerked my hand from his chest, and he smirked. We both knew he let me go. The man deserved a punch in the face, but it wouldn't be my fist that delivered the blow. As much as I hated to admit it, he remained my best chance out of here. I would try to find the killer, but the next attack would put Rayhan's body between me and those shocking ropes.

"Fine," I said. "I'll help you, but you have to secure this cell block."

He squinted.

"I can't do that," he said. "I have duties to perform."

"Kadence is gone, and I'm sure none of your superiors would dare question the king's best friend. After all, wouldn't you do anything to catch the killer and preserve the last piece you have of your father?" Malice lingered in my every word.

The hurricane made landfall, trying to rip through me.

"Fine," he said. "I'll make sure you're well guarded."

He pushed away from me and sulked to the cell door. Looking back over his shoulder, he spit out, "But you won't like it."

He slammed the iron gate shut, trapping me inside. I didn't know which hurt worse: my wrists as the shackles burned through them, the blistering welts wrapped around my forearms, or the soft ache in my heart I refused to acknowledge.

CHAPTER SEVEN

"Isn't this the morgue?" I asked.

The orange tone of the stone walls dimmed as we descended staircase after staircase. My flimsy dress, torn and dirty since being tossed in my cell, barely warded away the underground chill. After the second set, there were no more landings, and the way became a twisting spiral descent into the bowels of the castle.

"The morgue is down here." Rayhan's words were aimed at my back. He followed, despite my slower pace, presumably in case I turned around to run. I wasn't sure what he imagined would happen if I ran. I had yet to see a way outside.

Part of me wondered if Rayhan had given up after I yelled at him that morning and thought the morgue was a nicer, cleaner place to kill me.

The staircase ended. I expected a haunted hallway, complete with a moaning specter rattling chains in the corner, but it opened into a spacious lounging area. Black leather couches formed a semicircle around a low table where a board game rested as though the players would return at any moment. A walkway branched off the back of the room, and an arched doorway peeked into a wide space lined with rows of tables.

My heart started pounding. Maybe he really was taking me to the morgue.

"Come on." Rayhan snatched my hand and pulled me toward the archway. I sunk my weight into my heels.

"What?" He looked between me and the gaping door. He rolled his eyes. "It's not the morgue, girl. Come here and I'll show you."

He tugged at me again, and I reluctantly followed.

The doorway opened into some type of laboratory. Three metal tables spanned the length of the room, and fire burners spread every four feet in the center. Rows of glass cabinets lined the walls, and beakers, metal instruments, and fragile scales peered through. Everything had a clean label pressed to the front, written in blocky penmanship.

One man in a wheeled chair worked at the farthest table, next to a lit burner. A beaker perched over the flame and bubbled while he stirred with a glass rod. A puff of smoke escaped the narrow spout, and the stranger hurriedly wrote in a bound book at his side. He looked about fifty, with dark skin, curly hair, and thick glasses that made him appear a bit bug-eyed. I pressed my lips to hide my surprise. I'd never heard of a vampire needing a wheeled chair.

"Nadeem." Rayhan greeted the man warmly.

Startled, Nadeem jerked up from his beaker and repositioned his frames on his nose. He looked Rayhan up and down and spared me a quick glance. The man smiled.

"Rayhan." He pushed the wheel of his chair with one hand and angled it toward us. "It's been too long, my boy. What brings you here?"

"Not that long, I don't think." Rayhan bent to give him a gentle hug.

"I haven't seen you since the funeral. If I didn't know better, I'd say you were avoiding me."

"Never, Nadeem. That's not my way." Rayhan's face crinkled. "Has it really been so long? The funeral was..."

"A year ago." Nadeem nodded. He waved one hand in the air. "But no worries now, lad. It's tough to lose a parent and tougher to see the faces that remind you of them. I knew you would come when you were ready."

His gaze shifted to me, and I noticed the hint of stubble across his face. "And you've brought a friend."

Rayhan pushed me forward. I plastered on a fake smile.

"This is Natalie," Rayhan said.

"And a witch too." A new expression widened Nadeem's eyes, and he leaned toward me for a closer look. "I thought they weren't allowed to leave the cells."

"Kadence isn't in the castle right now. He's traveling."

"Then I guess a short field trip would be relatively safe." The man reached for me. I stepped away but was caught by the iron block of Rayhan's body at my back. Nadeem smiled and lowered his hand without touching me.

"My apologies, miss. Sometimes curiosity has its way with me. My brain usually catches up quickly. I'm quite curious about you. Your power is overwhelming. I've never seen anything like it."

As far as I knew, vampires couldn't sense a witch's magic unless they were using it.

"How do you know that?" I asked.

"It's my life's work to determine the weaknesses of our enemies and how to exploit them." Nadeem stared over my left shoulder, and I thought he didn't see me at all. "To learn a weakness, you must first identify the strengths. Your magic is written across your face and your skin, if one learns how to read them."

He looked at the silver shackles. "These chains would not bind an inch of your power if you knew how to use it."

Silence wrapped around us. Goosebumps broke over my arms, and I rubbed them for warmth or comfort.

Rayhan watched me with a frown. Suspicion wrinkled the corner of his eyes.

"I don't know what you're talking about," I lied. Maintaining Rayhan's trust remained my priority. If he knew the extent of my power, even trapped under my mother's spell, he wouldn't let me waltz around so blatantly.

"No," Nadeem said slowly. "I imagine you don't."

He blinked, his eyelids magnified to three times their size.

"Rayhan." The warmth sunk back into his voice, and the weight of forbearance slipped away. "What can I help you with?"

"I wanted to talk about my father's death," Rayhan said.

"Such a shame." Nadeem headed toward his lit burner, and we followed. "A vampire should not die so young, barely in his prime. Only sixty-five years old, less than one fifth of my age. One should not lose a friend so soon."

"Did you see the coroner's report?"

"The report?" Nadeem shook his head. "I saw the body, lad. After the official autopsy, of course. They wouldn't let me perform it myself, too close to the deceased, they said. Psh. The coroner was very good, I'll admit. He was seasoned."

"What did you see?" A knot tensed Rayhan's voice, tight and hard, that he tried to hide but didn't quite succeed.

Nadeem pressed his lips. "Nothing, lad. I agree with the original report. Manveer had a chronic disease, perhaps something he was born with. The evidence was sprawled through his body. Desecrated blood cells, nerve damage, organ failure. He'd probably been hiding his illness for weeks, maybe years. He went in his sleep. Perhaps not the way a battle-hardened warrior would want, but a good way to go."

"You don't think it could have been poison?"

"Poison?" A shadow fell over Nadeem's face. "Listen to yourself. The only poison that can kill a vampire is Lexliv, and the witches lost that recipe generations ago."

I'd never heard of Lexliv before, but I wasn't brave enough to ask more.

"I know." Rayhan turned away from us. I ignored the glint of sorrow on his features. "His death doesn't sit well with me, that's all."

Nadeem patted Rayhan's hand. The bubbling brew beside him made a cracking noise, and sparks erupted through the spout.

"Eek!" Nadeem spun the dial to dim the gas and wrinkled his nose. "There goes that lot."

I peeked to see the steaming sludge solidifying in the beaker.

"What are you making?" I asked.

Nadeem's face lit up. "Well, I shouldn't tell trade secrets to the witches, but I suppose it would be fine just this once." He looked around the lab as though scanning for lurkers that may tattle. "It'll be better if I show you."

He rolled to the back cabinet and plucked a key from his pocket. The door opened and revealed lines of tiny glass balls filled with brown slime.

"This is a bubble of sodium nitrate and sucrose. I heated the mixture and divided it into individual uses. If you look through here..." He tilted the orb so I could see inside. "...there's a matchstick on one side. Simply pull the lighting paper from the stick, which ignites the match and activates the chemical reaction. Roll the ball wherever you want and BAM!" Nadeem shouted the word, and I jumped. "You get smoke."

A wide grin cut his face in half, and a rosy joy spread across his cheeks. "I call it a smoke explosion."

"It's like a little bomb." I tapped on the glass with one nail, but the thick components didn't even jiggle. "A smoke bomb."

Nadeem's brow creased. "Well, that does have a catchier ring to it. Maybe I'll pitch that phrase to the king next time he ventures down here. He isn't very invested at the moment. Who needs smoke, he says, when we can just cut their heads off? He's not very innovative, that man."

"You were going to show me?" I said.

"Yes, yes, of course."

His nimble fingers plucked the paper from the opening at the top, and a spark erupted when the match lit. Nadeem rolled the ball on the floor toward the doorway and it sat there, alone and unobtrusive.

We watched it.

Nothing happened.

"Well, sometimes the mixture doesn't catch." Nadeem shrugged. "It's still a prototype."

The tiny orb flashed again, and smoke poured through the top, more aggressively than the fragile bulb looked capable of producing. A thick, odorous scent wrapped around us, and Rayhan started coughing as the haze covered our vision.

Mist gathered over my face, reminding me of this morning. My hands curled to fists and my throat closed, not because of the chemicals in the air, but from the fear of another attack. I twisted through the smoke, searching for a threat and anticipating the coiling snap of a lightning rope, but there was nothing.

"Nadeem, how do you turn it off?" Rayhan's faint outline attempted to fan the fog away.

"I can't turn it off, but go kick the bulb through the door, lad. I'll drop the failsafe covers, and we can wait it out in here."

Rayhan's footsteps thunked. "I kicked it," he sputtered. "Close the cover."

A whining noise sounded behind me, but I didn't move to investigate. I was as likely to run into the cabinet full of smoke bombs as I was to locate the sound.

"Let me open the vent too," Nadeem said, and a sharp clatter of metal on metal followed his words. "There. Just give it a moment."

The mist thinned as a current of fresh air pulled it upward. Nadeem sat in the back of the room, holding the pull string of a metal grate in the ceiling.

"It'll smoke out the rooms upstairs, but that's not my problem." The vampire gave a toothy smile. "That was fun. Say, should we do it again?"

"No!" Rayhan and I yelled. My hands shook from the memories of the attack, and I wiped them on my dress to hide the quiver. The sweat from my palms blended into the dark stains on the dirty fabric.

"They've got to be sick of you doing that, Nadeem. Plus, having to carry you down the stairs every day. When are they going to build you a lab upstairs?"

"Psh," Nadeem said. "They've already offered, and I told them to shove it. This lab was made for me, just for me, and it's where I've worked for over two hundred years. If they build a new lab, they can get a new scientist."

"Maybe you're stuck in your ways, old man."

"Or maybe the youth are ruining this kingdom." Nadeem waved one fist in the air. "They sent a contractor down here last week. Do you know why?"

Rayhan shook his head.

"They want to demolish the catacombs. The castle was built on those catacombs. If they're removed, the whole place might crumble down with them."

"Then why remove them?"

"Eh, something about the water table rising." Nadeem opened and closed his hand like a puppet's mouth. "It's a flood risk, they say. I'd say they'd be ruining a perfectly good supply of witch intelligence we should be studying more." His dark eyes flashed over me and caught my surprised expression. "But I shouldn't say any more about that."

"No," Rayhan said sharply. "You shouldn't."

This conversation was proving to be more interesting than discovering the origin of the smoke that had filled my room and covered the appearance of the attacker. I wanted to ask more, but the hard look on Rayhan's face made me pause. What resided in the catacombs that pertained to witches, and why didn't Rayhan want me to know?

I shoveled the curiosity away. Escape came first, but if I found myself back in this lab, I had a few choice questions for Nadeem.

"Look, lad," Nadeem said. "Since we're stuck in here until the smoke explosion stops, you should know I never emptied your father's cabinet. It's probably full of junk, but it's your junk now. You go take a look and I'll...I'll give you some space for it."

"Thank you, Nadeem." Rayhan nodded and grabbed my hand.

Black wooden cabinets lined a small nook at the back of the room. There were several tall, narrow cupboards, but most gaped open to display empty shelves. A golden nameplate screwed at the top of one cabinet read *Nadeem Patel* and the other said *Manveer* in sloppy white paint.

Rayhan ran his finger over his father's name.

"Has your magic said anything?" Rayhan asked.

"What?"

"About Nadeem? Could he be my father's murderer? Have you had any visions?"

I dropped my gaze to the floor to hide my shocked expression. I should have known Rayhan dragged me down here to investigate Manveer's murder.

"If the person who killed your father also attacked me last night, it couldn't be Nadeem," I said. "The assailant didn't use a wheeled chair."

"Nadeem may be physically fragile, but don't underestimate him. Other than Kadence, he's probably the most dangerous creature in this kingdom. He has legions of assistants who would bend backward to do his bidding, no matter how dire."

I looked over my shoulder at the man swearing at the beaker in the sink as he manhandled a scrub brush through the narrow opening.

"Okay," I said slowly. "I'm not getting anything from my magic about him." That wasn't how magic worked either, but I wasn't going to bring that up.

"How did your dad know Nadeem?" I asked.

Rayhan pulled open the cabinet bearing his father's name and grabbed a stack of paperwork from the top shelf. He thrust it into my hands, and I pushed the papers into a neat pile.

"They were best friends," he said. "Nadeem is older than Dad, but Dad did an apprenticeship under him before taking a spot in the army. Dad thought he'd be a scientist for a while."

"He changed his mind?"

Rayhan shrugged. "He wanted the war to end. He figured killing all the witches would be the fastest way."

"Why would Nadeem want to kill his best friend?"

"I don't know." Rayhan's tone was sharp. A tremor tightened the muscles of his arms. He tugged hard on a black sweater, and the fabric tore under his hands. The two pieces hung limp as a body on the scaffold, and Rayhan gingerly gathered them. He pushed the halves together as though his will might repair the garment.

He took a deep breath and spoke with a faux calm. "I don't know why anyone would want to murder my dad. But if someone could make a poison to kill a vampire, it would be Nadeem."

I clamped my mouth shut. Speaking about Manveer would only trap Rayhan in a deeper hole of anger and frustration. I needed him to function. The sooner we found the killer, the sooner I could go home.

"Why is Nadeem in a wheelchair?" I changed the subject.

"I don't know." Rayhan handed me another set of papers. "He doesn't talk about it, and I don't ask."

As Rayhan shoveled more and more things from the cabinet, I flipped through the pages in my arms. Scientific equations scrawled across the top few and some observations of experiments I didn't understand. I flicked the pages I'd read to the bottom of the stack, careful not to drop the whole set.

The next revealed a hand-drawn map.

I turned the pile sideways and studied the squares and rectangles that composed the image. Sketched to perfect scale, tiny aerial snapshots of rooms and hallways filled the sheet, with initials in each corner.

Wait a minute. I recognized this place.

"Hey." I nudged Rayhan's shoulder. "I think I found something strange."

"Hmm?"

Rayhan paused the systematic unloading of his father's locker and peered at the page. "It's a map."

I closed my eyes to prevent a dramatic eye roll. "Good job, Captain Obvious," I whispered. "It's a map of the hallway with your dad's room."

Rayhan grabbed the sheet, and I flinched as his giant fingers wrinkled the pristine parchment. My mother would have been furious at such disrespect to the paper.

"It's the fifth floor. Look, here are his initials at the bottom of his room." Rayhan pointed to a tiny *MW* at the edge.

"It has the king's too."

The square of Kadence's room held a small *KH*, circled in red ink. Red Xs peppered the walls.

"These Xs are windows and the balcony door," Rayhan said. "Why would Dad have those marked?"

I could think of a few reasons, none of which I dared say out loud to a giant, angry vampire. Instead, I went through the next pages. Jotted at the bottom of the last page was a note in sloppy, quick handwriting.

KH - IS KILLING ONLY OPTION? RECONSIDER? WINDOWS SECURE.

Rayhan remained absorbed in the map, and I slipped the second sheet from the pile and folded it. I pushed the paper square into the waistband of my dress, hoping the fabric stayed intact enough to hold it there. I didn't want Rayhan to see the page and jump to the same conclusions as I did. Rayhan wouldn't be able to handle the implications on this paper, and he was my ticket out of the vampire castle, these shackles, and this prison. If he fell apart on me, I would be trapped here forever. And the note would certainly unravel this giant man who exuded strength but quivered at the thought of his dad's death.

I was certain that Rayhan's dad had been planning to kill Kadence, Rayhan's best friend. And if Kadence had discovered Manveer's plans, that would give him plenty of motive for murder.

CHAPTER EIGHT

I was looking forward to my stone bed and whatever food they would bring tonight. Even something called "prison porridge" made my mouth water. The folded paper in my waistband weighed more than it should. Maybe telling Rayhan that I thought Kadence murdered his father would fulfill our agreement and he'd take me home. Or maybe it'd send the man into a spiral and he'd end up in a cell beside me for killing his king. Better to wait until I found more evidence.

The leather shoes Rayhan gave me cushioned my healing feet, but my wrists continued to worsen. The silver bands ate away at my skin, and tender blisters formed beneath the metal. A constant ache radiated up both arms, and I ground my teeth to hide the pain. The welts on my skin from the attacker's blue whip paled in comparison.

We were halfway to the dungeons when a petite vampire with long, black hair passed us in the hall. She reached out and snatched Rayhan's arm.

"Where do you think you're going, young man?" She stood shorter than me, but laugh lines pinched her face. She looked about forty, but I'd learned enough about vampires to be skeptical of her appearance.

"Madeline." Rayhan tipped his head in greeting.

"I'd heard a rumor you were traipsing around with a witch prisoner," Madeline said. "I'd hoped it was just that—a rumor."

"She's wearing the silver shackles, Madeline. Plus, she's a civilian. She wouldn't be able to overpower me to escape."

"Hmm." Madeline pressed her lips, but something flashed across her face. Humor. "Kadence wouldn't like it."

"Kadence, His Royal Ass, isn't here, is he?"

"Tsk." Madeline pointed a finger at Rayhan. "You'd be careful with those words in public. This isn't a council meeting." She leaned back to study the man's expression. "He was agitated with you before he left. Is something going on?"

"Nothing, Madeline." Rayhan waved one hand. "I don't know. You know how he gets."

Madeline nodded, and dark hair curtained her curvy figure. "And your name?"

Oh, she was talking to me. I peeled my tongue from the roof of my mouth. "Nat-Natalie," I sputtered.

"Natalie," she said warmly. "Why is Rayhan dragging you all over the castle?"

"I, um..."

"She had a vision," Rayhan interrupted.

I forced a smile, but unease sank my chest.

"A vision?"

"About my father."

"You're brave to use magic in Kadence's castle," Madeline said.

"He'll recover," Rayhan said. "My father won't."

The words fell between us. Madeline touched Rayhan's shoulder.

"Manveer is very missed," she said. "I hope you know what you're doing, Rayhan."

Madeline dropped her hand and continued down the hall until she disappeared through another corridor. I thought I saw her turn back at the last moment, but Rayhan had already dragged me away.

Reef perked up when we passed his cell, which looked like a mirror image of my own. He wore new clothes—a thin, light brown muslin shirt and matching breeches. His face appeared clean and freshly shaved.

Rayhan pulled open my door. I had never been more relieved to see my prison cell. Fresh clothes had been stacked on the raised platform beside a pail of water with a folded washcloth draped over the edge.

The gate rattled shut.

I wanted to wash my face, but a dark hand of terror clutched at my chest. I stumbled back to the bars to look at Rayhan's retreat.

"Hey!"

He paused.

"You promised to protect me! Aren't you going to put a guard down here?"

"Don't worry, Nat." He didn't turn around. "I'll make sure you're well protected."

His footsteps thundered through the hall and up the stairs, and the wooden door banged shut.

"He's the worst," Reef said, and I chuckled.

"He sure is."

"What did you do with him?" he asked.

"He took me to the basement."

"The morgue? That's ominous."

"No, it was their laboratory. I think that's where the smoke from the attack came from. They have a cabinet full of chemicals that make smoke."

"It wasn't magic?"

"I don't think so."

"Was the attacker in the laboratory?"

"No, the scientist was in a wheelchair," I said as Rayhan's warning about Nadeem's assistants tumbled in my mind.

"That's all you did?"

"Yes, Reef, that's all we did."

"You swear?"

I didn't have the energy to maintain the facade of being Rayhan's secret lover tonight. "I swear."

The bucket of water beckoned me, and I submitted. I dipped the washcloth into the cool liquid, and soapy bubbles tried to sputter to life. I was much too late. The liquid had probably been warm and bubbly hours ago. I washed my wrists, biting my tongue as the sensation stung like acid. I rinsed the rag and pressed the fabric to my face. The dirt and grime from the last few days wiped away. The water had turned deep brown by the time I carried the bucket to the cell door and heaved it between the bars.

I pulled Manveer's letter from my waistband. I wasn't sure what to do with it, but I couldn't show it to Rayhan yet. The cold stones met my knees as I crouched beside the crevice hiding my little knife. The paper didn't fit as well as the weapon, but it hid well enough.

The shackles grated unbearably against my injured wrists. Ooze and blood peeked around the edges of the silver, and the skin next to the wound held an angry red hue. If I wasn't careful, infection would set in soon.

I ran a hand over my dress. Its original cream color had become an ugly gray-brown, and the hem was tattered. I gathered the bottom of the garment in both hands and pulled at one of the worn edges. The fabric gave way and split up the middle, stopping at the waist seam. I tugged at the stubborn edge, and it ripped, leaving me with a long strip of material. I wrapped the makeshift bandage under the silver band until it formed a barrier between the metal and my skin.

Relief came immediately. I sat back on my heels and sucked in my first deep breath in days.

I turned to the new set of clothes as thunderous footsteps cascaded down the stairs. I recognized them by now.

Rayhan.

I paused and listened as the steps drew near. The man's shadow covered the torch in the hall. I pinched the edges of my ripped dress closed and staggered to my feet.

The vampire carried a rolled mat, blankets, and an extra-long pillow. He dropped everything in a heap and unrolled the mat beneath the torch.

"What do you think you're doing?" I approached the gate as he smoothed a black, quilted blanket across the thick pad.

"You wanted protection." He gestured at himself. "Here it is."

"This is not what I asked for."

Rayhan waved one finger in the air, mocking me from our previous argument. "You demanded that I personally guard this cell block."

"I meant by assigning more guards to the row, not camping in front of my door."

He stepped closer, leaving the half-inch of the metal gate as the only barrier between us. His lips turned up in a smile, and his smugness rolled over me in waves.

"I told you that you wouldn't like it."

Stubbornness and pride locked my legs. "Are you planning to sleep outside my room indefinitely?"

"We have a bargain, girl. I need you to be alive or that bargain disappears. If I have to sleep in this cold, musty hall every night until you figure out who killed my father, then so be it."

I smothered an eye roll. So nice of him to selflessly care about my safety. "Fine. But first, turn around."

"Why?" His tone twisted, curiosity leaking through.

"I have to change clothes." I held up the clean outfit.

The frustration on his face faded into something that burned through my thin dress and warmed my skin from the inside.

"I'm not stopping you." A slight growl marred his words.

"I'm not a painting for you to gasp at," I snapped.

Rayhan pushed from the gate and folded himself across the rectangular pad. He set both arms behind his head and crossed his feet in front of him.

"Looks like you have two choices. You can wear clean clothes or dirty clothes. Neither choice involves me."

I turned my back to the man and narrowed my eyes at the innocent pile of tan fabric. Anger tightened my throat. I wouldn't have ripped this dress if I'd known I would be stuck wearing it. I released the ragged edges, and it gaped open to the top of my stomach. Definitely not appropriate to wear around the castle.

Rayhan's gaze danced across my back, but I refused to acknowledge him.

The clothes felt soft as I scooped them from the bench. I tugged the breeches beneath my skirt and stepped into the legs. The waistband sat a little loose, but the cotton was rich and breathable.

I pulled the dress over my head. My hair tumbled down in waves and tickled my bare back. I imagined the vampire eyeing my exposed skin and waited for the anger to flare again. Instead, something else burned hot in my core, something awfully close to desire.

No. I flung the feeling away. I only needed to use Rayhan to escape. Anything else would muddy my fastest route out of here.

The tunic clung to my curves without settling too tight. It fit well, better than I expected for an inmate's outfit.

I clenched my fists and turned around. My mouth opened, and a stabbing insult perched on my tongue.

The words faded.

Expecting the vampire's burning gaze, surprise caught me instead. The man stretched across the cot, covered by the black blanket, with his back toward to me.

A little unbalanced, I sat on the stone ledge. Silver moonlight peeked through the window to blend with the dancing torches. Rayhan's chest rose in even movements, and I remembered the steady thumping of his heart under my palm. I laid on the stones and used my arm as a makeshift pillow.

I buried the thought as soon as it erupted, but with the giant sprawled in front of my door, I finally felt safe.

CHAPTER NINE

Rayhan left before I woke up. Sunlight flickered through the cell, illuminating his empty bed pad and the missing black blanket. The blanket wasn't really missing though. Sometime in the night, the vampire had slipped inside my gate and draped the fabric over me. I wanted to be irritated, and perhaps it was a little creepy to imagine Rayhan sneaking beside me while I slept, but the quilt was warm and held a distant scent of sea salt.

The light also revealed an unexpected visitor. A woman perched on a wooden chair next to Rayhan's abandoned bedding. She hunched over to rest her elbows on her knees, but the position couldn't hide her excessive height, probably close to six feet standing. Her wide shoulders looked like they missed the sagging weight of armor, and a battle hammer rested in a leather loop on her waist. Her hair was pale blonde and cropped short.

I sat up, and the blanket cascaded to the ground. She remained still, but I knew her sharp eyes caught every motion.

Annoyance ground in my gut. I was tired of strangers appearing by my cell when I didn't expect them. The last one had tried to kill me and nearly succeeded.

"Who are you?" I asked. "Where's Rayhan?"

The woman tilted her head, but her lips remained closed.

I refused to squirm from her intense gaze. Her eyes cut through me and buried into my soul, shifting through the layers inside. I was sure she knew the horrors in my heart, the ones I had never spoken.

As the silence stretched, a burning pain sliced across my skin. The fabric I'd stuffed beneath the shackles last night had slipped away. Brown blood and hazy white fluid trailed down my arm.

I squatted next to the bench and fished my old dress from the floor. It remained my only option for bandages.

"You're hurt?" the woman said, and I jumped. Her voice sounded solid, a deep gong that vibrated through my chest.

"I'm okay." I shredded the fabric and wrapped it around the silver band until the pain eased.

Her nostrils flared as she scented the air. Great. Another vampire.

"It doesn't smell okay." She leaned back in the chair and crossed her arms. She wore a thin, pink cotton tunic and tan breeches, different from the black and gray the other vampires donned. "It smells like old blood and rot."

Gee, thanks, lady.

"I said I was okay. I didn't say I was great."

The woman smiled.

I used my teeth to tie the ends of the fabric, and the pain dulled. It would be a temporary respite. The wound needed proper treatment soon. Hopefully, I would be home before then.

"I supposed being trapped in this cell isn't great anyway." Her wide eyes took in the iron gate, the latches hammered into the solid stone, and the excuse of a window emitting hints of fresh air.

"I wouldn't vacation here." I picked up the black blanket and draped it over my shoulders. The breeze held a chill today.

"It's probably worse when it rains," the woman said.

Hmm, I hadn't thought about that.

"Can I help you?" I asked. I had nothing better to do than shoot the breeze with a tall, strange vampire carrying a hammer and inhaling the scent of my blood, but something about the interaction dredged up caution in my gut.

"I've heard rumors you've been spending time with Rayhan," she said.

I dropped my head into my hands. Everyone wanted to know what Rayhan was doing with his toy captive.

I considered lying, but it felt wrong. "Yeah. He's been showing up a lot."

"Do you want to get rid of him?" Her voice held an edge.

I shrugged. "It's nice to leave the cell once in a while, but..." The sentence trailed off.

"But?" she prompted.

But indeed. But I couldn't give him what he wanted, what I promised. I had no way of helping Rayhan solve his father's murder, and it was only a matter of time before he discovered the truth. A jolt struck me. If Rayhan learned I had lied to him, I may suffer a fate worse than imprisonment.

The woman waited for an answer.

"But nothing," I said, though the words were hollow.

"Has he hurt you?" She leaned forward again, her attention rapt on my face.

I scrunched my nose. "No. Annoyed me, frustrated me, sure. He's a little scary sometimes, but he's never hurt me. I just can't seem to get rid of him."

The woman's rich laughter caught me off guard. "Good." She stood from the chair in a fluid display of grace and confidence. "If that ever changes, you let me know and I'll take care of Rayhan."

The woman turned and walked away with long strides.

"Wait!" I shed the blanket and ran to the cell door, straining my neck to keep her in sight. "Who are you?"

She didn't look back before disappearing from my view.

"You sure get a lot of visitors, Natalie," Reef said, and I could see the side of his face pressed against his own bars. "And I don't think that's a good thing."

"How long was she sitting outside my door?"

"I don't know," he said. "I didn't see her walk over."

That proved to be the second time someone entered the cells without being seen. It meant another entry hid somewhere deeper in the dungeons, and it was going to be the death of me.

"They brought food though," Reef said. "I did see that."

A plate piled high with food sat on the ground outside the cell. Flaky oatmeal, a mound of scrambled eggs nestled around strips of pork and topped with a fat sweetbread. It would likely be cold, but my stomach rumbled anyway.

"Wow, did everyone get the same platter?" I slipped my fingers through the cracks and persuaded the plate into my room. Saliva drenched my tongue, imagining the sweet bite of the bread.

"I don't know. What did you get? I got some mystery porridge with a glass of lukewarm milk."

I froze with the pastry halfway to my mouth. "You didn't get sweetbread?"

"Sweetbread? No!" The bars rattled as Reef angled for a better look.

"Oatmeal?"

"No!"

"Pork? Eggs?"

"I think the porridge had some raisins, but that's about it," Reef said. "You have all that on your plate?" His voice turned dark. "What are you doing to get food like that?"

I wasn't doing anything, but Reef would make his own conclusions. Guilt lessened my appetite. I wouldn't be able to eat any of it.

"Here." I pushed the platter through the gate and scooted it as far as I could with my fingertips. Reef's hand slipped through his bars and pulled the edge of the dish until he slid it into his room.

"Oh no." He shoved it back. "This is yours."

My mouth had turned dry, and despite the knots in my stomach, I knew I wouldn't eat a single bite. Besides, if my escape came down to a physical altercation, these soldiers needed to be in better shape than me. Feeding them would help my cause.

"I kept some," I lied. "I don't need all of it."

Reef's fingers paused. "You have some?"

"Yep." I pretended to take a loud bite and faked exaggerated chewing noises. "Yum, it's delicious."

"It doesn't feel right," Reef said, but he poked the plate into his cell.

"Eat some and pass the rest down," I said. "We can share a little with everyone."

"Good idea." Reef's voice came out muffled with a full mouth. "Jolie, Jolie."

"Hmm?"

"Reach through the bars. I have more food for you."

"Oh!" Excitement colored her words. "This is incredible."

"Take something and pass it down. It'll be close, but there might be enough for the whole row."

Happy murmurs followed the scratching of the plate as it slid across the ground. The atmosphere of the dungeon changed as it trekked down the row. People, my people, laughed and whooped with contagious joy, and a smile tilted my lips.

"You did good, Natalie," Reef said, soft enough that only I could hear him.

"Thanks," I said, but my throat tightened. I didn't deserve his appreciation. I would abandon them all at the first opportunity.

The door upstairs opened and shut, and silence spread as we all strained to listen.

"Ma'am!" A sharp screech of a chair scratching against rough stone. "You...um...you don't have clearance to come in here."

The footsteps paused.

"Don't I?" A woman's shrill voice stabbed at the guard, and I recognized the tilt of an accent. Rayhan's stepmother, Ella.

"Ma'am, I'm sorry, but your status has been revoked to civilian since..." He trailed off.

"Since my husband died?"

"Y-yes, ma'am."

"And you think my status was only derived by the man who stood next to me?"

"It's the rules."

"Listen here, dear." Ella's voice dropped to a deadly tone. "I never needed my husband's permission to go about this castle, and I don't need yours now. I'm going to collect a prisoner and walk out of here, and if you open your mouth about it, it will be the last time you're able to open it. Do you understand?"

I could picture Ella's round face and squinted eyes. She probably waggled a finger at him, the way every mother knew how to do.

The guard didn't respond.

"That's what I thought, dear."

The footsteps resumed, and I guessed where she was headed before she appeared at my door. She looked around the meager room.

"Tsk," she said. "This is no place for a woman to live."

"It's no place for anybody to live," I said, thinking about Reef sleeping on the same stone ledge, in the same musty air as me.

Ella waved her hand. "Of course, dear, but women especially need some finer touches."

I suddenly felt self-conscious of the thin cotton garb that had been akin to royal robes last night. The bucket of soapy water had peeled grime from my skin, but my hair remained a ratty mess and fresh bloodstains wrapped around my wrists. Ella's eyes discovered every granule of dirt, and a bit more I hadn't noticed.

Ella pulled a silver-plated key from the pocket of her dark gray dress, tied with a lilac ribbon this time, and unlocked the iron gate. It swung open, knocking into the waste bucket, and Ella wrinkled her nose.

"I can't keep you out of this cell, unfortunately, but I can provide you a few hours to wash up and eat."

Ella held out her hand, palm up.

A feeling gnawed at my chest. My fingers curled at the thought of taking her hand, although her words and offer suggested no malice. It would be nice to leave the dungeon for a while, and pleasant tingles trickled down my spine when I imagined washing up. Still, something kept me back. A distance stretched between us, a crevice I wasn't sure I wanted to cross.

But Ella knew Manveer better than anyone. If he was plotting to kill

Kadence, Ella might have heard. It would be stupid to pass by this opportunity to search for more information, solve Manveer's murder as soon as possible, and head home.

I forced myself to smile. Her palm felt cool and sticky.

"Wonderful." Ella tugged me down the hallway and tucked my palm into her elbow. We trekked up the stairs and reached the guard on the landing. He hastily rose from his chair, mouth open and one hand outstretched. She didn't glance at him, but I turned back as we walked out the door. The man lowered his hand slowly, defeat sprawled across his face. The wooden door shut and latched, cutting him off from view.

Ella pulled me through the halls. Most were lined with plush carpets that cushioned each step, reminding me how stiff my ankles were from the stone floors of the cell. Statues and sculptures watched our journey with blind eyes. Vivid, intricate artwork adorned the walls. One memorable tapestry stretched across an entire wall in a rainbow of colors and shapes with silhouettes of people working a field in front of a setting sun. I wanted to linger and take in the talented weave, but Ella's hand was steady on my arm.

"Here we are!"

Ella pulled open a black door, and I stepped into her room. An archway connected two spacious suites. We walked into a living area with a pair of black velvet fainting couches around a low marble table blocking most of the lit fireplace at the opposite end of the space. More paintings hung on the walls, rich landscapes full of light and color and people. A queen-sized bed peeked through the wide arch, dressed in white sheets and adorned with far too many pillows.

"This way." Ella dragged me behind the couches, and a generous copper tub appeared, parked in front of the fireplace, filled with steaming water. Desire blossomed at the sight.

Ella looked between me and the tub. "It's for you, dear. Go ahead."

"Oh no, I couldn't." Hot water was a luxury I didn't even have at home. We bathed in the shallow creek behind our house, which was blessingly cool in summertime and icy cold the rest of the year. Taking a heated bath now would be a slight against my brethren in the dungeon.

"I have to insist, dear. I want to talk to you, but the smell has become quite distracting." Ella patted my hand, but my cheeks burned. I tried to take a breath, but only the soft fragrance of lavender oil in the water wafted around me. "Go ahead and get in the tub, and I'll send my girls in to help you."

"I don't need any help." My brows creased. I hadn't needed assistance bathing since I was a child.

"Don't worry, Natalie, they're very wonderful. You'll have such a lovely time. I've laid a clean outfit on the bed when you're finished. Maybe we can burn these." Ella scowled at the tan outfit, and I resisted the urge to cover myself with my arms. She patted my hand again and left the room.

I knew it was weakness, but I peeled my clothes off. The steaming, perfumed water was impossible to deny. I stepped into the tub and bit my lip to suppress a sigh. The warmth soaked into my cold bones and loosened the tight muscles. I dunked all the way under and massaged the knots in my hair, persuading them apart with my fingers.

A few minutes later, the door slipped open and two women came inside, carrying armfuls of supplies.

"Hello." One dainty woman smiled, and strawberry curls danced around her head. "My name is Ruby, and this is Kenzie. We're here to help you get ready."

Unease surrounded me, but Ruby's gentle smile settled my nerves.

"Sure, I guess." I leaned against the back of the tub.

The girls washed and brushed my hair, then sprinkled conditioner and scented oils into the wet strands. They scrubbed my fingernails with long-haired brushes until they shined. Ruby's lips pinched at the sight of the mangled skin beneath the silver shackles, but she silently rubbed some thick ointment on the wounds.

The dress Ella chose for me held a deep lavender hue, dark enough to blend into the vampire style without turning invisible. A chiffon fabric composed the outside of the garment, with silk lining the inside. The neckline plunged low, and a tight sash pinched my waist. It turned my soft curves into a womanly shape that made me bite my lip when I caught my reflection in the mirror.

“You look lovely.” Ruby brushed my hair near the fire, and the warmth combined with her careful strokes persuaded my eyes to close in contentment.

“Thanks,” I murmured.

The door opened, and Ella walked in. A male staff member pushed a cart filled with food behind her.

“Just leave the cart here by the couch. I’ll put it outside when we’re through.”

The man nodded. Ruby and Kenzie followed him out with murmurs of well wishes to me, and the three disappeared.

“Come sit next to me and let’s eat.” Ella piled thin slices of meat onto a seed-peppered roll and ran a small swatch of spiced mustard across its face. “I skipped breakfast this morning and I’m simply starved.”

“You can eat food?” The words tumbled out before I could think twice.

“Of course, dear. It helps us last a little longer between blood meals. We do make our own blood, although it’s not enough to survive long. Eating food helps build our supply.”

I suppressed more questions, sank into the plush velvet seat, and piled food onto my plate. My guilt had drained with the used bathwater, and I devoured the warm meal before my mind could find a reason not to.

Ella poured two cups of tea, took one, and leaned against the couch.

“Rayhan said you were helping him connect to Manveer in the afterlife,” she said.

I choked on my bite and reached for the second cup. The liquid cleared my throat, but it burned when I swallowed again.

“Yeah,” I said slowly. “I was trying to help him.”

“Did it work? Were you able to reach his spirit?”

Magic couldn’t speak to the dead. Once someone crossed over, they were gone from this world, magic or not. But some powers could glimpse the past or the future, and that was sometimes as good as reaching the afterlife.

I bit my lip. Rayhan had lied to Ella that day in Manveer’s room. I didn’t know his reasons, but I trusted him more than I did her.

“No,” I said. “My magic hasn’t told me anything about Manveer.”

"Well, that's a shame." She set the tea on a porcelain coaster. "It would do Rayhan some good to hear Manveer say it wasn't murder. The man has gone crazy since his father passed. He's a completely different person now."

I resisted the urge to rub my arms. If my father died, I hoped I would become a different person too. I knew I had after my mom's death.

"The coroner's report said it was a genetic disorder," I said.

"I suppose that must be right. I didn't see the body, of course. It didn't feel appropriate. But the report was very thorough. It said Manveer's insides were a mess, full of disease. That doesn't happen overnight." Ella shook her head. "My poor husband. He should have had many more years."

"Why would Rayhan think his father was murdered?" I took another sip of the tea. I couldn't identify all the herbs. A hint of jasmine and something with an earthy tone. "Did Manveer have any enemies?"

"Of course he did. Manveer was very high-ranking in the army, only two generals were above him, and the king, of course. You don't get that high up without knocking a few people down."

"Who did he knock down?" The rich, warm tea settled the twirling nerves low in my stomach.

"Well, there was one person he did particularly dirty." Ella's eyes danced with old laughter, and I could almost hear the remnants of Manveer's voice telling the story along with her. "General D'ar Zhao. Manveer and Zhao went to the same promotion board, but Manveer got the spot and Zhao was forced to lead recruit training. He was very bitter, threatening to end Manveer's career."

Killing someone would certainly end their career. A high-ranking general might also have access to a secret toxin that could kill vampires.

"Although Rayhan's biological mother had enough reasons to kill the man as well," Ella said.

"His mother?" I raised my brows. Rayhan had never mentioned her. I assumed she was also dead.

"Oh yes. Maverick Stott. Rayhan is her only child, and she never married Manveer despite years of proposals. She was more interested in the battlefield than child-rearing. Manveer basically raised Rayhan himself."

"Why would she want to kill Manveer then? If he was raising her child?"

Ella shrugged. "That woman has a vicious streak. She acts before she thinks. Maybe she thought Manveer would stand in her way like he was in Zhao's way. Maverick is not someone to mess with, and I avoid her as much as possible. Thankfully, she lives on the battlefield and is almost never here."

I couldn't picture Rayhan's mother as anything other than a sweet, round woman with fresh cookies and arms ready for a hug.

"Plus, Maverick had relations with several men. That's her choice, of course, and she wasn't married to Manveer. But he was angry about it, anyway."

Passion was a great motive for murder.

"Enough about our drama. I want to learn more about you." Ella's eyes narrowed onto me, and my cheeks flushed.

"M-me?" I stammered.

"Yes, dear. Rayhan has been spending a lot of time with you these past two days. I'm curious what's so intriguing about the little witch prisoner."

I set the tea down and scratched the back of my hands. "I think he just wants to connect with his father one more time. I don't think he's interested in me."

"Nonsense." Ella smiled. "He looks at you like a game of chess and he's guessing your next move. Men only want one thing when they look at women that way."

I swallowed, and my throat tightened. Was Rayhan genuinely attracted to me?

"Tell me about your mother."

A weight sunk in my chest, but I kept my face flat. "She's dead."

Ella nodded. "I'm so sorry to hear that. How did she pass?"

The question wasn't appropriate. We both knew that, but something compelled me to answer, something warm and sweet bubbling in my gut.

"She was attacked during a raid almost seven years ago. I tried to heal her but…" But my worthless magic was locked away and she died. Tears pushed to the corners of my eyes, but I refused to let them fall. My cursed power had taken too many tears from me.

"Tsk, I'm so sorry, dear. It's unfair to lose something important to you." She sipped more tea. "How does your magic work, if I can ask that? Do you have a lot of it?"

Enough to drown you, bring you back to life, and drown you again—I just don't know how. I didn't tell her that. That knowledge would make the vampires lock me in the dungeon and toss the key. They wouldn't wait around to see if I could actually use the power or not.

A phantom itch spread along my skin the longer I kept Ella waiting.

"I'm powerful, but I don't have an affinity for anything." The persistent need to fill the silence faded.

"An affinity?"

The itching demand to answer her returned. I ground my teeth, but words slipped off my tongue.

"Some witches have specific powers that others don't have. It's called an affinity. Mind reading, teleportation, stuff like that."

"But you don't have that?"

"No." *I have nothing special.* "My mother had an affinity for healing. I didn't inherit it. All the healing I do is from recipes and studying."

"Shame," Ella said. "That would have been useful."

I bit my lip, but the homesickness had already sprouted. Nausea tilted my stomach, and the sweet roll I was halfway through looked as appealing as raw wood.

"Tell me," Ella said, and I shifted to the edge of my seat in anticipation of her next question. I wasn't sure why, but I wanted to tell her anything. "Has Rayhan found a motive for Manveer's murder?"

I tapped my tongue against my teeth. Rayhan hadn't seen the note I'd tucked away with the folding knife. He didn't share my suspicions that the king may have ordered Manveer's death.

"No," I said.

"That's good, dear." Ella patted my hand. "That man needs to accept the truth."

I thought of the map and the clear *KH* initials in the corner. Kadence Hendrick.

"What about King Kadence?" I asked.

Ella's nose wrinkled. "What about him?"

"Does he have any enemies?"

She rolled her eyes. "Kadence's people love him. They think he's the answer to all their problems, their salvation in disguise. He's not, of course. I watched him grow up as a scared little boy to a man in king's clothes. He's as broken as the rest of us."

"Would someone try to kill him?"

A current flashed over her mild expression. "They'd either be very stupid or very brave to try."

Someone knocked on the door. Ella's face bunched, then smoothed again. She looked at me, and for a pointed moment, I didn't recognize her behind a dark mask. Then she smiled and my discomfort settled.

"Come in!"

A young woman in a pastel dress entered the room. Her hair was folded into pigtail braids, and her full skirt cast an aura around her. I recognized those honey locks and her voice immediately and forced my face into a flat expression. Hayleigh, the woman who brought Manveer his poisoned tea.

"Mother," she said, her gaze darting between me and Ella. "Wilson is looking for you."

"What does he need?"

"I don't know, something about pyrotechnics."

"We're just about finished here. Tell your brother I'll be a moment. He's in the library, I assume?"

Hayleigh nodded.

"Thank you, love."

The door closed behind her.

Ella stood and reached out her hand. I circled my fingers around her palm. She pulled opened the door for me, then turned back and locked it.

"Thank you for chatting with me. It's been lonely since Manveer passed. Hayleigh and Wilson are from my first marriage, so they don't mourn the loss as much as I do. It's nice to have Rayhan to share the load of grief, even if his pursuits blind him to the truth."

Heavy footsteps ground against the stone floor, punishing the rock slabs into submission.

"Speak of the devil," Ella said as Rayhan rounded the corner. His blue gaze locked on his stepmother, and he stalked to us.

"The guard said you took Natalie from her cell this morning."

"Yes, I did."

The man towered over Ella, but she held her ground and met his glare with a calm, focused determination. Even slipping a hint of a smile.

"Where is she?" Rayhan clenched his teeth.

"She's right here, dear." Ella pulled me in front of her, positioning me as a blockade between her and the rigid line of Rayhan's chest.

He glanced at me, opened his mouth in rebuke, then did a double take. His ocean eyes widened and skirted across my body like a sea wind, a warm and gentle caress.

"Natalie?" he asked.

I crossed my arms. "Maybe if you gave your prisoners a bath, they'd all look a little nicer."

The enchantment fell from Rayhan's face, and that hurricane force filled his expression. That was better. That was the Rayhan I was used to.

"I'm off to help Wilson with another one of his projects. You two have fun," Ella said. Rayhan didn't turn to look at her.

"He's almost thirty years old. He can do his own projects." Rayhan grabbed my arm and pulled me to his side. I bit the inside of my cheek but didn't protest. His hand was more comforting than Ella's smaller grip.

"Yes, but he is a man." Ella winked at me as she walked past. "They always need a woman's help."

CHAPTER TEN

Rayhan watched Ella until she turned down a hallway and disappeared. He sighed and looked at me with fresh eyes.

"You weren't in your cell when I came to get you." Rayhan shifted his grip on my upper arm to trail his fingers to my hand. "I was...worried." His lips had formed a different word first, but he settled on the other.

"Ella offered me a bath and food. The best you've offered is dragging me to the morgue and thinly veiled threats against my family."

Rayhan turned, but my palm remained wrapped in his. "Well, I have something else for you."

"This is still about finding your father's killer, right?"

"What else would it be, girl?"

Ella's words about men wanting one thing from a woman swirled in my head.

"Nothing," I said and followed the giant down another staircase.

I wished my feet would turn to lead. When we got to our destination, Rayhan would expect me to use my magic and I would face his wrath when nothing happened, again. I chewed the inside of my lip. My freedom depended on him trusting I could solve Manveer's murder.

I'd have to devise a way to trick him into believing I controlled my power.

Rayhan paused before an arched entryway.

"This is awkward," he said.

"What?" I peeked around the corner.

"Bria lives on the castle grounds."

"So?"

Rayhan rolled his eyes. "I can't show you the exit."

"I mean, you could. I'd appreciate that."

Rayhan shook his head, sending those reddened locks into a cascade. He scanned the room, and his gaze landed on a navy-blue throw pillow.

"Here." Rayhan ripped apart the seams until a wide square remained. He folded the fabric into three sections, creating a long, slim satin band.

"What is that?" I asked.

"It's a blindfold. See?" He wrapped the cloth around his head, but the back edges barely met. "It'll fit you better."

I squinted at the material. On the one hand, I'd rather return to my cell than be willingly blinded and led by my mortal enemy into who knows where. On the other, the quicker I found Manveer's murder, the sooner I would be home and able to take care of my father.

"Fine." I turned around. "But if I open my eyes to the morgue, I will find a way to kill you."

The fabric carried a chill as Rayhan settled it over my face. His warm fingers batted the cold away and sent out trails of heat as they fluttered across my hair. His hands moved carefully, precisely, and he knotted the edges without trapping a single strand. Rayhan hesitated when the band was secure, as though he didn't want to pull away. The scent of evergreen and an herbal spice washed over me, stronger and more intoxicating than the lavender in the bath.

Rayhan grabbed my fingers and pulled me forward. "This way, girl." Something husky roughened his voice.

Rayhan had slept only steps apart from me last night, had crept into my room to drape a blanket over me, but his hand in mine as he guided me through the castle instilled more intimacy. There was a promise between us, a guarded covenant, but neither one of us knew what it said. We lingered somewhere between a prisoner and a jailer, two people in the throes of loss, and a man and a woman.

"Watch your step here. There's a bit of a staircase." Rayhan pulled me down each step, and my hands perspired, but not from the rich rays of sunshine that suddenly warmed my skin.

"How much farther?" I asked, but I didn't know if I hoped for a longer or shorter timeframe.

"We're almost there," he said.

The sun faded, and the lingering edges of brightness dimmed. Rayhan released my hand and set both palms on my shoulders, grounding me with his weight.

He rolled the blindfold down, and his touch quivered. His face spanned a breath's width from mine, his body even nearer. He studied me, examining every movement for a flinch away from him. There was none. Desire bubbled from my core, spilled through me, and supercharged my nerves.

Rayhan stepped closer, and I moved away, but my back caught against the edge of a stone wall. He shifted his hand on my shoulders to brush his thumb across my throat. My pulse pounded harder for him, stealing his attention to my neck.

I put my palms on his chest, and he froze. Any hesitation, the slightest push, and I knew he would leave. I fisted his tunic fabric between my fingers and pulled him closer. He obliged, and a rumbling growl sprouted from his core and sank into mine.

I expected him to kiss me, but the vampire tilted his head at the last minute and his lips brushed over my jawline. Tingles webbed through my skin, spiraling down my chest, digging into the center of my body. I moaned and leaned my head back to give him more room. The rough stubble peppered across his jaw tickled as he trailed over my neck, heightening every tender brush.

Suddenly, Rayhan's touch disappeared.

Without his support, I toppled forward and caught myself on a stack of firewood. Rayhan stood several steps away, his back to me and both hands on his head. His breathing echoed like he'd just run a hard race.

"Why'd you do that to me, girl?" he asked, still turned away.

I rubbed my fingers across the places he'd kissed. The doubts that began in Ella's room unfolded in my chest. I was too plain and boring to excite him. He grew up in a castle as the king's best friend, and I grew up bathing in an icy river. He expected things from a woman, and I had nothing to offer. Resolve hardened me. I didn't want him either.

"What do you mean?" I sharpened my words. "You kissed me."

He spun on his heels. "You practically begged me. You pulled me closer." He ran one hand over his stubbled chin. "It's been too long since I've fed. You're lucky I didn't take a bite just now."

That explained the missed kiss. He only saw me as food. Curiosity outweighed the cut of rejection for a moment. I had never imagined a vampire's bite. Would it hurt? It must not be that bad. The vampires had hundreds of humans volunteering to feed them.

"Why didn't you?" The words were bolder than I felt.

"Why didn't I...bite you?" Rayhan's face pinched. "Did you want me to?"

I shrugged. I wasn't sure I wanted him to, but it hurt that he thought I was so disgusting to even merit the chance.

"Never mind," I said. "Let's talk to whoever you dragged me to see and get this over with."

I stalked toward the cabin door, but Rayhan blocked me.

"Well, there's another thing," he said.

I crossed my arms. "What?"

"She's not actually here."

"Then why are we here?"

"I was hoping you'd be okay with some recreational breaking and entering."

"Recreational...what?"

"Recreational breaking and entering." Rayhan gestured as he spoke. "I'll break the door, we enter, you do magic, and we leave." He smiled.

Unbelievable.

"What's the penalty for breaking and entering in Vari Kolum?"

"I don't know. Maybe a fine?"

"What's the penalty for an escaped prisoner breaking and entering a vampire residence in the midst of wartime?"

Rayhan rolled his eyes. "You're not an escaped prisoner."

"But the rest is true."

"Look, girl, it's easy. I'll break the door..."

Rayhan's foot launched faster than I could track. He connected with the door, and the wooden latch splintered into a thousand pieces. It smacked against the wall and ricocheted back toward us. Rayhan pushed it open and bowed in a grand gesture.

"... and now we enter," he said.

I balled my hands into fists. Several responses rested on the tip of my tongue, but I refused to give him the satisfaction of a reaction. I shouldered past Rayhan into the cottage. It would be best to get in, snoop with whatever kind of magic Rayhan expected, and get out before the vampire came home.

The interior of the cabin stretched small, but comfortable. The rounded stones resembled river rocks, the sharp edges smoothed away. A wide fireplace sprawled against most of the back wall, and bright paintings and tapestries decorated the rest of the room. Unlike the stone floors in the castle, this one was composed of slabs of polished wood. A couch perched at the foot of a full bed, and several bookshelves rose on the opposite side. An obviously handmade table, barely long enough for two plates, sat by the door at the edge of a petite kitchen. I ran a hand across its face, and the wood was soft and worn.

"Who lives here?" I needed a name to fit into the house. The colors were rich and warm, but underneath it all, something unsettled twisted. The table, the bed, the meager couch. It all felt lonely.

"Her name is Bria Ofperalta. She was my father's mentor for a long time."

I pulled out the wooden chair and sat on it. Not even a wobble.

"The decor is rather masculine."

"Bria used to be married." Rayhan looked around the room, but he lingered in the doorway. I had a feeling he didn't want to do the entering part of recreational breaking and entering. "I don't think she redecorated after her husband died."

"Why not?"

"There's always been some questions about how Sion died," Rayhan said. "Maybe she thought redecorating would draw more suspicion."

I pulled my hand from the wood like it was hot. "Questions?"

Rayhan shrugged. "Bria was never indicted of a crime, but a perfectly healthy vampire doesn't kneel over and die without an explanation."

"Your father did," I pointed out.

Rayhan shook his head. "The autopsy showed a lot of problems with Dad's body. Sion's looked normal. The cause of death was undetermined, and Bria lived a quiet life after that. She used to be Head Advisor to King and Queen Hendrick, before..."

"Before what?"

"Nothing. They've been dead a long time now."

"Do you think Bria's husband was poisoned too?"

"You're the one with the magic. You're supposed to answer these questions, girl."

Oh right.

Rayhan narrowed his eyes. "Are you actually going to do any magic, or are you planning to sit around all day and wait for lunch to be served?"

A spark of anger coursed through me, but it doused quickly. I had promised to do magic and by golly, I needed to do magic.

"Fine." I scooted from the table, scratching the legs unnecessarily loud on the wooden floor. Maybe I could stall long enough for Bria to come home, report us for breaking and entering, and be hanged. Can't do magic if I'm dead.

I found the center of the room and tried to persuade tendrils of my power from its locked cage. My mother's spell ground around my magic and trapped it inside me. I pulled harder, expecting more resistance.

Instead, a wisp grabbed at me. One faint sliver of power escaped my mother's binds and circled through the space. It was thin and weak, but I clutched at it like the last rays of light before an endless winter.

The magic ran through the cabin and lingered at the right edge of the room, near the bed and a square window. I followed it, attempting to build its power. Once I reached the place it had settled, the fleeting wisps disappeared.

I kneeled on the ground and pressed my fingers into the floor. I pulled at my magic, but nothing else happened. There must have been some reason it called me here. I studied the space, but the floor appeared unremarkable, as were the bed and the walls.

"What?" Rayhan's voice raised an octave. "Did you feel something?"

"Yeah," I said, but I didn't know what it was.

"Is it something from my father?"

No, it felt like something else—warmer, happier. But the sensation faded.

"Can you be quiet? You're ruining my concentration." Apparently, I needed a lot of concentration to pretend to do magic. Even though the power had fled, I had to convince Rayhan that I could solve Manveer's murder. Rayhan's jaw snapped shut, but those broody eyes tracked my every move.

I sank to the floor between the humble bedframe and the rock wall and crossed my legs. I rested my palms on my knees and grounded myself in the space, the way my mother taught me. An earthy scent of stone and wood filled my nose. Coolness from the rock beneath me seeped into my skin. With each inhale, I pulled more of the surroundings into myself and tried to expel my magic with every exhale.

The power didn't move. The phantom wasn't here.

Time to fake it.

I began a slow chant, feeling the shape of each word as my tongue clicked against the back of my teeth. The rhythm I picked wasn't musical, it vibrated deep and tonal and chunky, but it fit the rustic warmth of the house. As the chanting grew louder, I increased the speed, letting my voice flow through the home and the gaping hole a stranger's death had left behind. An invisible wind swirled over me as the cabin responded to my voice.

My magic couldn't fill the space, but nature held its own raw power.

The wooden floor and rich stone walls sang a song of grief and loss. My voice became the catalyst, the permission to ease the sorrow that Bria had wrapped around her for so long. I chanted until the current of natural magic faded away and only the sound of my own voice echoed in my ears.

I threw my head back and let the silence settle. The home felt happier, content, a cocoon for Bria to rest in instead of a shrine for her mourning.

"Did it work?"

Rayhan's words broke my focus. For a moment, I had forgotten he was here, had forgotten why I was here.

"Um..." I had to give him some sliver of hope to keep working with me. I had to get home. "Yes. It worked."

"What did you see?" The vampire couldn't hide the eagerness in his tone.

Yeah, Nat, what did you see?

"There's a heaviness lingering here." That was true, at least. "The house feels empty, alone. Loss has settled in this place."

Silence.

I opened my eyes, and Rayhan stared at me.

"What?" I asked.

"That's it? There's a heaviness here?"

"What did you expect?" I crossed my arms.

"Last time, you saw my dad. A cup shattered on the floor. Now, you say the house feels heavy? Of course it does, it's a stone house."

I pressed my lips, and anger and frustration rolled through me. He was right, my words were weak, but it annoyed me anyway.

"I've told you a dozen times that magic doesn't work the way you want it to." Especially mine, which didn't work at all. "If you don't like it, you can cut the deal and take me home right now."

"I'd rather lock you in the dungeon and throw away the key."

That option grew more tempting by the day.

I pushed up, and my wrists groaned as the silver shackles brushed over them. The salve Ruby applied had soothed the sting, but the fabric refused to stay around the metal. It wouldn't be long until my flesh became broken and bleeding again. I clenched my teeth and ignored the pain.

"Well?" Rayhan crossed his arms too, and his muscles bulged far more menacing than mine. "Is there anything else you can do?"

I opened my mouth, armed with a harsh reply, but a breeze slipped around Rayhan and a cluster of green-gold leaves furrowed through the doorway. The debris drifted into the cabin and ground to a stop on Bria's furniture.

"I suppose you did that?" Rayhan watched the leaves fall.

"You don't know what I'm capable of," I snapped.

"You don't seem to be capable of anything." The vampire stepped inside and snatched a leaf. When he opened his hand, green powder lined his palm. "Let's clean these up and get out of here before Bria comes home."

I bit my tongue and grabbed a wide leaf from the bedside table. The only personal item on the nightstand was a leatherbound book with a title imprinted in gold lettering. When I reached for another leaf, the corner of a folded note nestled inside the pages of the book brushed my hand.

I let the foliage scatter to the ground and pulled the paper free. Letters scrawled across the page in the same handwriting as the one from Manveer's cupboard that I'd hid in the secret crevice with my knife.

MW - 8:30 PM - BB

"What is it?"

I couldn't hide the paper this time. "It's a note."

"What's it say?" Rayhan stood behind me. I pretended not to notice the parts of his body that almost touched me.

I handed him the note, and his face pinched.

"What's it mean?" he asked.

"I don't know."

"BB? Could that be initials for a poison?"

"I don't know."

"Why does Bria have a note with my dad's initials?"

"Rayhan, I don't know!"

The vampire curled his fingers into a fist, crushing the page.

"Dad's been dead for over a year, why would she keep it this long?" The words barely hissed through his stiff lips. A roaring sea twisted around me. Rayhan became the eye of the storm, and I got caught in the violent current. "She did it. She killed him the way she killed her husband."

"Rayhan, we don't know that."

"You said there was a heaviness in the house. What's heavier than plotting to kill your mentee? Someone who looked up to you?"

I ran through a list in my head. *Grief, sadness, depression.* Emotions carried weight based on the person feeling them, not the feeling itself. I didn't say it out loud. These weren't the words Rayhan wanted.

The vampire spun around and thundered to the door, dragging the fury of a tropical storm in his wake. He had death in his eyes, and he wouldn't stop until he found Bria, wherever she was.

I couldn't let him go. Maybe Bria was involved in Manveer's murder, the note seemed suspicious, but I wouldn't allow Rayhan to administer justice based on my lies. The only thing my power did was help heal the hole Bria's sorrow had cast. I refused to be the judge and jury in her execution.

I grabbed Rayhan's elbow and dug my heels into the floor. The man pulled me along, not even noticing my weight. We slipped through the busted door and over the two steps of the front walkway. The grass didn't help my quest. My feet glided along the damp strands.

"Rayhan, wait!"

His face turned an unhealthy shade of red, and sweat scattered on the back of his neck. This wasn't working. He would just drag me all the way.

I dropped his arm and sprinted to the cabin. Hopefully, fury would cloud his judgment and he wouldn't start running. I'd never be able to outrun a vampire. I skirted through the kitchen drawers, tossing spoons and forks to the floor. *Come on, every kitchen has knives.*

There. A butcher's block on the counter held a selection of knives, ground into the wood with precision-carved slits. I pulled out a flat-edged blade and ran after Rayhan.

He was halfway to the castle, his back to me, hard lines of determination squaring his shoulders.

"Hey!" I screamed, but his steps faltered for only a moment.

Alright then. My grip shook as I lifted the knife to my forearm. I took a steadying breath. I didn't need to cut my whole hand off.

The sharp edge sliced into my flesh, and blood welled from the wound. The ruby drops pooled together, lingered for a moment, then cascaded down my skin into a macabre waterfall. It hurt, but the spinning red ribbons appeared so stark against my pale flesh. The pain faded away as the rose trails drew twisting lace down my arm. I tilted my hand, letting the liquid flow to my fingertips, a river of life fluid sacrificed to the ground.

I hadn't heard his return, but Rayhan's wide shadow settled over the dripping blood. His eyes trailed the liquid across my hand.

"What have you done?" His flat voice sounded almost like a whisper.

"You wouldn't listen to me." I matched his tone. "I didn't know what else to do."

Rayhan circled his fingers around my wrist and drew my arm close to him. He dipped his finger into the trail of blood, and it smudged on my skin.

"Not this," he whispered. "Never this."

He held me, his attention entrapped in the fluid leaking down my fingertips. Our body heat fused together, blending a spicy mix of mint and breeze between us. His gaze trailed over the wound and up to my eyes, thrusting me into a sea brimming with desire. For my blood or my body, I was afraid to ask.

He dropped my hand and pulled his shirt over his head. "We have to cover this or the whole castle will smell the blood. This was stupid, girl. There're other ways you could have gotten my attention."

"I called your name."

"Something can be effective *and* stupid." Rayhan's nostrils flared as he wrapped the black fabric around my forearm. "Come on, let's get you cleaned up. I don't need you to get an infection."

"Then I wouldn't be able to keep helping you." I rolled my eyes.

"Exactly."

Rayhan dragged me up the castle steps, hesitated for a moment at the doorway, then fixed the makeshift blindfold over my eyes. He led me through a twisting hallway and pulled the cover off. I followed him, pressing his shirt over the gash in my flesh, and tried to ignore the bare skin on his back. It was a very nice back, admittedly, but all men had backs. This one shouldn't be able to light a smoldering fire in my gut and make me wonder if he would feel as soft as he looked.

"Here." Rayhan stopped in front of a nondescript door and pulled me inside.

The room resembled a small cave. The orange-toned walls had been painted matte gray, and a lush carpet spanned the floor. A mahogany headboard towered catty-corner to the door behind a wall of windows. The space begged for a fireplace, but there wasn't one. Double doors hinted at a balcony, but thick curtains covered the glass panes and blocked my view outside. Two additional doorframes nestled into the walls, one to the right and the left.

"Sit on the chair." Rayhan gestured to a leather armchair near the foot of the bed. A twin sat next to it. He went the other way, digging through a wooden cupboard and swearing beneath his breath.

The material felt cool under the chiffon dress, and the chair swallowed me with comfort. I pulled Rayhan's shirt away from the gash. The bleeding had already stopped, leaving a red haze smeared across my arm.

"Alright, this one will be cold." Rayhan slapped a wet rag over my forearm before I could protest. The chill seeped through the wound and into the muscle underneath. He kneeled in front of me and rested my wrist on his knee. He wiped the cloth around the cut in gentle circles, careful not to split the skin.

He leaned very close to me. His sprawling chest hovered inches from my fingertips and beckoned me like a moth to a flame. Hard lines of muscles creased his abs, not thick, but lean and flexible from years on a battlefield. He had an expanse of freckles across his shoulders, caused by a combination of his fair skin and sun exposure, but they faded before his pecs. I clenched my fingers into a fist, avoiding any temptation to test how those muscles would feel.

I remembered when he pulled away from me at Bria's cabin. I forced my gaze somewhere else. He wasn't interested in me. I was weak, magicless, and couldn't bring him one step closer to avenge his father. I hadn't been able to save my mother years ago, and I was running out of time to save my dad now.

Escape had to be my priority, my only desire.

"And this one will sting." He smacked a second rag down and sharp tendrils stabbed into my cut. I tried to pull my hand back, but Rayhan held it tight. "I told you." A hint of a smile touched his face.

He pulled the cloth away and set down a gauze bandage. He wrapped medical tape around it, secure enough to keep the edges closed, but not to interfere with circulation to my arm.

Unspoken words sat between us.

"Thank you," I said. They weren't the right words, but they were the only ones I had.

"Yeah." Rayhan released my wrist and remained kneeling by the chair. "I need you to be healthy."

I pulled my hand to my chest and nodded. He needed me to solve Manveer's murder.

Rayhan tilted his head and his face pinched. Like an ocean current, a riptide pulling me out to sea, something lingered in his gaze. He opened his mouth, then paused and glanced toward the door.

"Someone's coming."

Why did someone always arrive in the moments I very much wanted to be alone?

"Crap. I know who it is." Rayhan looked between me and the doorway. "She can't see you. Quick, in here."

He pulled me from the chair and peeled open the door on the left. I expected a washroom or closet, but surprise caught me when it opened into an art gallery. Rayhan pushed me inside, and I stumbled as the lock clicked shut. A moment later, voices tumbled through, Rayhan's and a woman's.

Curiosity tore me. I wanted to know what mystery woman barged into Rayhan's room, but the paintings captured my attention. I ventured deeper into the gallery.

Two easels each held a half-finished piece on their wooden frames.

More canvases were stacked around the room, some covered with a thick sheet while others remained bare. The space was a cascade of rich color. Most of the paintings depicted landscapes, but humanoid figures and silhouettes peppered some of the fabrics. They had similar short brushstrokes, soft but vivid colors, and an impression of a picturesque setting. Too bright and brilliant and colorful to be reality, but detailed enough to second-guess that thought.

I studied the nearest easel. The displayed canvas held a mellow lakeside location and a rainbow sunset dropped behind the crystalline water. Unfinished beginnings of a yellow blanket spread over marbled grass. The sun wasn't visible, but thick streaks warmed the painting, and I could almost feel the rays across my skin. A woman's shape was sketched atop the blanket, but paint hadn't yet filled in the pencil lines.

Looking around the expansive space, surrounded by stone and vibrant artwork, I yearned for the grassy field this mystery silhouette perched in. I wanted to touch the icy water lapping against my feet as the sunshine warmed my hair. I reached for the canvas, half against my will, but paused. My natural oils would muddy the paint, and this art didn't deserve that fate.

Another painting caught my eye. A simple meadow, hues of green and yellow and gold, but the strong black strokes of the artist's signature drew me in.

Rayhan Whylde.

CHAPTER ELEVEN

By the time the door creaked open and Rayhan stepped into the room, I was halfway through the stacked canvases. I peeled them away one by one, trying to memorize the mesmerizing brushstrokes before moving to the next. The paintings themselves were beautiful, modern and timeless, but Rayhan captured more than color and landscapes in his work. Each harbored a trail of emotions that twisted a churn in my chest.

"What are you doing?" Rayhan slipped around the stacks of artwork and stood beside me. His fingers fidgeted at his side, like he wanted to snatch the canvas from my hand. He wore a new black shirt, and I smothered a hint of disappointment.

"Did you paint all these?" I asked.

"Yeah." He scratched the back of his neck and studied his feet.

"This must be years of work stacked in here."

"A few years, yeah."

"Why don't you display any of it?"

"Most are displayed. Some of the work, though, I want it to be private."

"Do you have a favorite?"

"What?" He turned to me, an unease I'd never felt from him before leaking through the question.

"Do you have a favorite painting you've created?"

Rayhan looked around the room, and that flat mask he wore cracked. He wrapped one arm over his chest, gripping the opposite bicep, and the stance shrunk his frame, making him look almost normal-sized.

His eyes settled on a stack in the far corner. I followed his gaze, but the paintings hid beneath a white sheet.

"Never mind it, girl." His hand locked on mine, and when I turned, the composed, careful expression covered his features again. "It's time for you to go back. I have stuff to do this evening."

"Like finishing this painting?" I gestured at the half-complete canvas as he pulled me past it.

"What?" He scowled at the art. "No, not that one."

"A different one then?"

"I said it doesn't matter. Leave it alone."

Rayhan slammed the door and flinched when something crashed from the other side. I couldn't suppress a smug smile. He deserved a little havoc when he flashed an attitude like that.

We ventured through the castle and down the stairs that dropped into the dungeon. The guard didn't look twice at us, and Rayhan opened my cell gate.

"I'll be back in a while," he said, but his attention was down the hall. "Your theatrical stabbing gave me an idea. I might know what BB stands for."

I wrapped my hands around the bars.

"You're not going to kill Bria, right? We don't have any evidence it was her."

"Bria will survive tonight at least," Rayhan said over his shoulder. "Depending on what I find out, she may not live beyond tomorrow."

"Let me know if you're going to kill her, please."

"I will." He disappeared up the stairs, and a short, dark-skinned female guard came the other way. She dragged a wooden stool in her path and set it up beside Rayhan's pad. She flicked open a newspaper without glancing at me.

Exhaustion weighed me down. The emotional toil of Rayhan's hot and cold act and the unexpected sensations from his paintings combined with physical fatigue. I lugged myself to the makeshift bed, snagged Rayhan's black blanket from the floor, and nestled inside its luxurious material. The rock bench had never been so comfortable.

"Natalie?" Reef asked.

"Yeah, what's up?" I called through the beginning tendrils of unconsciousness.

"Just making sure you're okay."

I was clean, fed, and bandaged. The sun barely sank through the shallow window, but I couldn't keep my eyes open any longer.

"I'm good," I replied and let sleep carry me away. Just before the darkness claimed me, I thought I saw the quick dart of a flickering phantom, but when I looked again, the cell was empty.

"I DON'T UNDERSTAND why you wanted to return here." Rayhan flopped on Manveer's mattress and laid across the bed so that his thick legs hung over the side. I tried not to look at him and pulled open the nondescript doors at the end of the room.

Because I think your father was plotting to murder your best friend wasn't a viable answer, so I kept my mouth closed.

Rayhan had been sleeping by the cell door when I woke that morning. I still wore the chiffon dress from Ella, although the hem quickly gathered dirt and debris. My wrists were red and oozing again, but they weren't bleeding yet. Rayhan hadn't mentioned murdering anyone, so I was half confident that Bria still lived. She probably wondered who had broken into her cottage and stolen a single piece of paper.

The doors opened into a narrow closet. Boxes stacked neatly to the top of the space, so adding another would prove impossible.

"What are these?" I pushed to my tiptoes and scooted the highest box down.

The bed squeaked as Rayhan sat up and strode to me.

"I don't know." He snatched the container from me, and I surrendered it. There were plenty more.

"Why wasn't the room cleaned out after Manveer died?" The second one felt lighter, and I set it on the edge of the mattress.

"I don't know," Rayhan said.

"It might be a shorter list if you tell me everything you do know."

He shot me a glare. "Kadence never asked for the room back." Rayhan shrugged. "I didn't think about doing anything with it."

I flicked the lid open. Junk was scattered on the bottom. A broken arrow tip. The worn string from a bow. A crude drawing of a child and a woman. A musty smell seeped from the box, and I discovered a pile of aged bones to be the culprit.

"Gross." I plugged my nose. "Why would he keep this?"

"Let me see." Rayhan abandoned his container, which was filled to the brim with paperwork, and leaned over me. "This is the first arrow I ever carved. And these bones were from my first hunt. I shot at three rabbits that day, but this was the only one I got." He gathered the tiny pieces in his giant hands and cradled them. "I didn't know he kept these." Softness lowered his voice, the disappointment of what could have been.

I let Rayhan sift through the keepsake box, and I dumped the paperwork onto the bed. Logs of soldiers' training records, names redacted with thick black ink, and recorded hours and outcomes of spars. The data would be invaluable to Ededen. Weaknesses and strategies were listed in plain text, but there were too many pages for me to steal. I ran a finger across the paper with a longing resolve.

Nothing here raised my "plotting to assassinate a king" hackles.

"Help me bring down the rest of the boxes," I said.

Rayhan gingerly placed the bone shards back into the container and shut the lid.

"Why do you want to look at them all?"

Great question.

"Maybe my magic will call out to something," I lied with a smile.

Rayhan's lips twisted, but he gave a stern nod.

We pulled them all down and sprawled them across the stone floor. The morning sun sank lower as we browsed through stacks of paperwork, small knick-knacks, and other unhelpful junk. My hopes fell with each box we declared useless. It appeared Manveer was just a sentimental guy with hoarding tendencies.

"This is strange." Rayhan held up a page. It wasn't clean, white parchment like the others. It had yellowed with age, and stains peppered the fragile surface. I scooted closer to the vampire and stared over his shoulder. Thick, black symbols marred the paper.

"Are these spellcraft symbols?" Rayhan relinquished it to me. I had stacks of my mother's spellbooks at home, but these didn't look familiar.

"Maybe," I said, but remembering the twisting smoke that filled my cell during the attack, I doubted this was witchcraft. The precise arrows and notated signs read like a science equation.

I folded the page into quarters and stuffed it in my waistband.

"You're keeping it?" Rayhan's face pinched. "Did your magic say something?"

"No, but if it is important, I don't want to lose it in this stack of paperwork." I leaned around Rayhan's arm and dug into the box. "What else is in here?"

"This too." Rayhan's voice turned hard. One fist crunched another piece of paper. He uncurled his fingers, and I plucked the page from his palm. Pressing it flat, Manveer's handwriting peered up.

BH, 8:30, BB.

"This matches the note from Bria's cabin." I returned the slip to Rayhan. "Did you find anything out about that?"

Rayhan's face paled. "I went there, but she didn't say anything useful."

"Went where?"

"BB," he said. "I went there."

"Well, where is it?"

"The blood bank." His lips pressed. "Bria works there."

I stood up. "Let's go then."

"No!"

Rayhan jumped and blocked my path to the door. I backpedaled, too late, and collided into his chest. He grabbed me before I could fall and pulled me against him.

I held my breath. I didn't want his intoxicating scent warping my decision-making. I needed to see what was at the blood bank, and Rayhan was an obstacle in my path.

"Why not?" I crossed my arms.

"You don't send a witch into the blood bank. That's where hungry vampires go."

I rolled my eyes. "Nobody's taken a bite of me yet. I'm sure it'll be fine."

"It might scare you."

"I've tended to the wounded on the battlefield." Memories of screams and blood bubbled through my mind. Instead of pushing them away, I leaned into them. Healing was dark and depressing and hard, and worth every minute. "I think I can handle a blood bank."

Rayhan opened his mouth for a rebuke, but closed it again. He shook his head, and the red locks flew around his face.

"Fine." He pulled open the door. "But I don't like it."

The blood bank sat on the second floor, near the entrance to my dungeon. A young, blonde secretary perched at a simple wooden desk piled with papers. She smiled at our approach, but her gaze flicked between us.

"Mr. Whylde," she said. "I didn't expect you back so soon. Would you like me to arrange your usual?" She turned her dainty, round face to me, and the simmer in her expression died a bit. "Are you applying as a new donor? We don't take anyone with recent injuries, but you're welcome to try again in a few weeks."

She must have noticed the bandage on my forearm, or maybe the blisters peeking beneath the silver shackles.

Rayhan stiffened. His wide eyes looked everywhere except at me, and his Adam's apple bobbed. He gulped with fish lips, but nothing came out.

"We're here to see Bria." I took a stab in the dark.

The blonde tilted her head for a moment. "I'll let her know you're here." She disappeared behind a flowing white curtain.

I dug my elbow into Rayhan's side. "What the heck is wrong with you?" I hissed. "Am I the only one trying to solve this murder?"

Rayhan swallowed and coughed into his elbow. "S-sorry," he stammered, his face turning red.

The secretary returned. "Bria is on the way."

"Thank you."

The curtain parted a moment later, and a tall, thin woman stepped beside the desk. Her dark hair pressed stick straight. Red rouge lined her lips, which emphasized her deep blue eyes. She looked older, although vampire appearances were deceptive, but age didn't touch the expanse of her beauty. The words I'd planned to say slipped from my mind.

"Hi." I smiled.

Bria, who had been looking at Rayhan, shifted to study me. She smirked and held out her hand.

"You must be Natalie." Her hands felt very soft.

"You know my name?"

"I saw Rayhan last night." She cast a sideways glance at the man. "He told me all about you."

The tops of my cheeks warmed, but I wasn't sure why. I couldn't picture her in the rustic cottage we'd broken into, but I could feel the barrier of grief that hung as a sash around her. I hoped the faint magic I'd welded would help heal that over time.

"Let's go back to my office." She parted the fabric with one hand. "I don't want anyone trying to taste the witch."

Me neither.

Rayhan called it a blood bank, but the word felt wrong. Brothel was more fitting, but the vampires probably didn't appreciate the negative connotation. A hallway stretched behind the curtain, composed of stone painted a warm white. Crimson-red carpet lined the floor, a little too close to the color of fresh blood. Most doors remained closed, but some flung wide open, affording me a look as we passed. The large rooms held roaring fires and luxury velvet furniture. Men and women lounged inside, some reading, knitting, or napping. Just waiting for the next customer.

"You don't store the blood?" I shifted my gaze as one woman made eye contact through her cracked door.

Bria pulled open the last door in the hall and ushered us in. Her office was also wide and spacious, but it had a neat wooden table instead of lounge furniture.

She sank into a plush chair and gestured at us to sit.

"We do, actually. We have cold storage pits underground that we refill with ice daily to maintain the temperature. But most of our customers prefer...a fresh meal." She gave an apologetic grimace.

I caught sight of the tips of her pointed teeth, and my curiosity burned.

"Does it hurt?" I leaned forward in my chair.

Rayhan choked. He wrapped one hand around my arm and tried to say something, but he couldn't get any words out.

Bria's expression flattened as she looked at Rayhan's grip on me.

"It can," she said slowly. "We can decide how the bite feels. Usually, it's very pleasurable. Would you like to try it?"

Rayhan's breath froze, and his face turned blue. I had a feeling Bria was trying to provoke the man somehow, but it didn't make me less interested. I bit my lip, thinking.

"I've never had witch blood before," Bria continued. "I promise you would feel no pain."

I half-nodded before I'd made a complete decision.

"No!" Rayhan's voice thundered through the room. He pulled my arm hard, although I hadn't moved from the chair. "Nobody is drinking anyone's blood here."

A shadow flickered over Bria's face and caught the edge of a smug smile. She shrugged those confident shoulders and sent me a look. I suppressed a laugh.

"What can I help you with now, Rayhan?" Bria settled into her seat. "I answered all your questions last night."

"Do you recognize these symbols?" I handed her the note we'd found in Manveer's box, and Rayhan kept a firm grip on me.

Her sharp eyes studied the page for a moment.

"No." She returned it. "It looks mathematical. Have you asked Nadeem in the laboratory? He would be the expert on this kind of thing."

"No, we haven't." Although that was a good idea.

"Why did you meet Manveer here in the blood bank?" I asked. "There are no dates on the paper, so we don't know how long it's been."

"Rayhan asked me that last night, after pretending he didn't break into my cabin." Bria shot him a sharp glare. "As I told him, I don't know what Manveer wanted to talk about. He never showed up. A week later, he was dead."

Interesting.

"Do you know anything about poisons that can kill vampires?"

"Shouldn't I be asking you that?" Bria said. "Is that what happened to Manveer? He was poisoned?"

"We don't know," Rayhan jumped in. "Natalie's magic gave her a vision. But it's been..." He shot me a look. "Temperamental since then."

I suppressed a grimace. Maybe my acting wasn't as strong as I thought.

"Actually, there is a story." Bria crossed her legs, and new creases folded in her breeches. Apparently, she didn't cross them often. "But it's a child's fable. I'm sure it has nothing to do with Manveer's death."

"Could you tell me anyway?"

Bria tapped her ruby nails on the arm of the chair, then stood up. She meandered to a towering black bookcase and tugged one volume from the shelf. I expected a leatherbound novel, but it was a thin children's book.

She handed it to me, and the paper cover felt smooth. The title, *Deathbringer*, scrawled in vivid gold letters. A strange name for a children's book.

"It's about a king," she said. "Who falls in love with a queen. She loses her mind and betrays him, but first she uses his blood to make a poison. At the end, she kills everyone in the kingdom."

"You read this to your children?"

Bria shrugged. "Growing up in war makes our children hard-hearted."

Or maybe reading terrifying stories did that.

"You can keep the book," she said. "I have a copy at home. Or at least I used to, assuming nobody stole it." She pegged Rayhan with a glare, and he shifted.

"Thank you," I said honestly.

Bria wiped her hands on her breeches. She held out her palm, and I shook it.

"I have to get back to work. You're welcome to stay and look around, but I wouldn't recommend it. The vampires that come here expect to be fed and have little patience." She flashed Rayhan a glance. "And I don't think your escort would like what may happen."

"Bye, Bria." Rayhan pulled me out and shut the door on Bria's laughing face. The redness on his cheeks spread down his neck and disappeared under his hair.

"That was a waste of time," he huffed.

I disagreed. The children's book was small, a bit bigger than my palm. Thick paper composed the cover and strips of twine bound the pages, instead of wood and glue—like hardback novels. I flipped through the carefully drawn images, skimming over the words.

"Have you read this?" I asked Rayhan.

"Of course. Everyone has."

Rayhan pulled the curtain back, and I jumped. My dark phantom twisted and turned inches away from me, its featureless face a gaping black hole. I tensed until my muscles hurt, but it didn't reach for me. My heartbeat settled. It wasn't ready to wreck my life, at least not yet. I swallowed and let out a rush of air.

"You okay, girl?" Rayhan looked back as he dragged me along. "Don't let that silly story scare you. It's all myth."

"I won't," I said, although the story hadn't bothered me at all. The phantom was gone when I turned again.

Rayhan stammered to a stop. He raised his face to study the ceiling. I paused and followed his gaze. White specks floated from above, peppering me in a faux snow. Cupping my palm, I caught a few flakes and ran them between my fingers. They felt hard, but brittle, and broke into a fine powder.

"What is this?" Pale dust stuck in Rayhan's hair, aging him with gray in a moment.

"It's mortar," I said. "From the ceiling."

The stones overhead vibrated in a gentle rhythm. White mortar slipped between the rocks and rained over us in small chunks. A deep rumbling echoed from above, screeching through the floors and wrapping around my head.

I pressed my palms against my ears, but the growl grew deeper and deeper. Rayhan ground his teeth at the unpleasant noise.

An explosion boomed from above. The castle shook for a heart-wrenching moment. I tensed, expecting a tumble of stones to smash me. The building groaned, then the shaking ceiling settled. The raining mortar stopped.

Something replaced the tension in my gut. Something twisting and dark and heavy—dread.

A wild current ripped through Rayhan's eyes. He grabbed my hand, and sweat coated his palm. I knew mine felt the same.

We raced up the stairs, dodging concerned vampires and staff members trying to evacuate the castle. We were salmon moving upstream, and I shouted apologies as Rayhan barreled through the crowd.

Finally, we reached the third floor, and Rayhan pushed past a single guard attempting to halt our stride.

A gaping hole replaced where Manveer's room used to be, filled with brittle rays of sunshine.

I looked away when Rayhan's tears began to fall.

CHAPTER TWELVE

The guard shut the gate and settled into the chair in the hallway. Rayhan hadn't said anything when I left him at his father's door, but I knew he wouldn't be down here tonight. Nothing remained of Manveer's room. The place where his father had lived and died and stashed away cherished childhood memories became nothing more than a gaping hole in the side of a castle.

I wrapped the blanket over my shoulders and hunched in the corner on the bench bed. A new stream of water dripped onto the floor, possibly caused by the vibrations of the explosion. It trickled between the stones in a cascading escape through the cracked stones.

There must have been evidence in Manveer's room. That was the only reason someone would blow it up. We had been close to discovering something, and instead it slipped away. My hands clenched, and the shackles rubbed against the sensitive skin at my wrist. A dark ribbon of warm blood trailed down my arm. I couldn't feel the pain anymore. The constant ache had become a part of me.

"Natalie, are you okay?" Reef asked.

It was a good question. Physically, my wrists were the only thing wrong with me. The gash on my forearm looked healthy, and I had taken the bandage off to let the wound dry. I hadn't had a bowl of prison porridge yet, since the staff members kept bringing me fresh food. The dress Ella gave me had seen better days, but I had nothing else to wear. Hopefully, laundry would be delivered soon.

Emotionally and mentally, I was wrecked. I wasn't any closer to discovering Manveer's killer and getting home. My father's medication would be dwindling. Once it completely ran out, he would grow weaker and weaker and eventually...

I drew my mind from the thought. I would be back before that happened. I'd make sure of it.

"I'm okay," I called to Reef. "I'm just tired."

"I feel that." Scrapes echoed through the hall as he slid down the stones of his cell.

I turned the paperback book in my hands. I'd read the text a hundred times, trying to glean a hint of relevance to Manveer's murder, but I couldn't find any. The words were simple, written for children.

Once there lived a beautiful, young King and Queen. Their people adored them and were happy. Riches and prosperity filled the land.

Until one day, when the King was attacked. He fought the attacker with his sword and cut off their head! Although the King survived, the Queen became fearful of his life.

The Queen couldn't imagine living without her husband. She refused to let the King be alone. If she couldn't be nearby to protect him, she ordered many guards to keep him safe. But the King resented her actions. He believed he could protect himself. He grew angry at the Queen and avoided her.

The Queen realized she wouldn't be able to keep her husband safe. One night, alone together in their room, the Queen killed the King. She knew death would be the safest place for him.

The Queen knew that without a King, the people were no longer safe. She brewed a poison from the King's blood and hosted a feast for the whole kingdom. Everyone ate and danced and made merry. At the end of the night, the Queen served poisoned wine and all the people died.

The Queen drank the last glass, knowing everyone she loved was safe and she could finally rest.

Chills crept up my arms. I couldn't imagine reading this to a child. Our children, witches and vampires alike, were being raised to expect their own death on the battlefield. It provided comfort when one expected death to be a safe retreat.

But it didn't help with Manveer's murder. I pressed the fragile pages flat and set the book aside.

Looking up, the black wisps of my ghost loomed a breath away.

"Oh no," I whispered. I glanced around for a spot to hide, but I already huddled in the far back corner of the cell. There was nowhere else to retreat.

"What's wrong?" Reef asked.

"Uh, nothing!" I scrambled up the bench, arching back from the smoking hand that stretched toward me. Maybe if it couldn't touch me, it couldn't make me do anything.

"What's all that noise then?" I heard him scamper to the cage door, and the metal rattled on the hinges.

"Just, um, stretching." My nails tore against the stones, but they held fast. There was no escape. Bile crept up my stomach as the clawed fingers drew closer.

"It's awfully loud," Reef said.

"Sorry," I said, a squeak through my tight throat.

The phantom hand pressed against my forearm, an invisible stab of ice through my skin. My magic, wrapped in layers of my mother's spell, leaked between their bindings and the phantom soaked it up. I could feel the power twisting and turning inside the creature, then it spit the power back at me.

My vision went black. My hearing faded.

And then...they returned.

I remained in the corner of the same cell. Except now, moonlight streamed through the window that had been sunny moments ago. The vision appeared a bit distorted, the edges blurred if I turned my head too fast.

I crawled to the window and wrapped my hands around the bars. A chill from outside, which hadn't been there earlier, brushed against my fingers, carrying a scent of orange blossoms and wild musk. The moon sat full in the sky, a glowing beacon shining down.

Footsteps crashed from the stairs, and yells and shouts from the other witches escalated as the steps drew near. Voices melted together into a thick mob.

"Hey! What happened?"

"What did you do to her?"

"You're scum, the lot of you!"

I ran to the gate.

"Natalie, what happened?" Reef asked. I opened my mouth to reassure him I was fine, but my voice locked in my throat. Not a breath of air escaped my lips, and I realized I wasn't breathing at all.

I should have felt afraid, but sudden shock stole that emotion. Coming down the hall with Rayhan trailing behind... was me.

I blinked. It couldn't be *me*, of course. I was right here. I ran my hands over my body, and they met solid flesh. I was here. I existed.

But she did too. And that Natalie had a swollen split lip and a black eye.

"I'll kill you. If I ever get out of here, you'd better run." Malice leaked through Reef's words, and Rayhan flinched but didn't respond. The vampire's face twisted, and I wondered if he thought he'd deserve the fate.

Rayhan opened the gate, and I moved out of the way. Neither recognized my presence, and they brushed past me without a glance.

I hovered near myself. It looked different than seeing a reflection, not flipped around or backwards. My dark hair flowed almost to my waist, brittle and broken on the edges from infrequent washing. My eyes didn't line up quite right, and they angled down like an aging branch to where the corners bunched. I had changed from the gown into a simple prisoner outfit. I recognized the stiffness in my jaw as I clenched my teeth. I had a lie on the tip of my tongue.

"Natalie." Rayhan's words faded at the end of my name, and he drew a breath. "I'm so sorry."

The other Natalie's eyes flicked from the giant to the secret place I knew harbored a silver knife and the remains of a stolen note from Manveer's locker. Her lips tilted into a smile, and she settled one hand on

Rayhan's arm. The vampire looked at the point their bodies touched with hope brimming on his face.

"It's okay." My voice filtered through the space. "I've iced it, and the nurses put some ointment on it. I'll feel better after I've slept."

"I'll stay here all night," Rayhan said. "I'll watch over you."

Her expression flashed, then flattened out. "No, please don't." She flinched a bit, but the tension in her shoulders told me it was an act.

Rayhan took the bait, hook, line, and sinker. He nodded and reached one hand toward her. The other Natalie froze, genuine fear in her eyes, and he dropped his palm.

"I'll send a guard down to watch over you." He turned to the gate. "I'll be back in the morning."

The door banged shut, and the man's steps retreated from the stairs. The other Natalie's expression changed. Her brows pinched in concentration, and her fingers fluttered against the tops of her thighs. A moment later, she sprinted to the secret knife and plucked the mortar from its covering.

"Natalie, I promise you, I will kill that man." Anger and pain seethed through Reef's voice. Natalie's hands froze for a heartbeat, then continued freeing the tiny weapon. "Are you going to be okay?"

"Yeah, Reef." She pulled the knife free and flicked the blade from its folded sheath. Moonlight reflected an eerie glow across her skin. "I'm going to be fine."

Reef kept sputtering threats, but the second Natalie dashed to the window. She pressed the blade beneath the center bar and dug the silver tip into the mortar. I held my breath I didn't need. Could it be that easy?

The bar twisted and popped from its place. A slight thunk announced its arrival on the grass underneath. It wasn't a long fall, less than ten feet.

Natalie stuck her head through the new opening. It took some wrestling, but a moment later, her shoulders squeezed through. She turned around, gripping the tops of the other two bars, and looked back into the darkness. I swore her deep eyes locked on me, and a jolt of shock shattered in my chest, carving me from the inside out. Then her gaze fell away, she slipped her feet over the edge, and let go.

I ran to the window and tried to peer out, but the outside bled into a sea of black, unknown to the vision. Natalie—I—was gone, and I didn't know where.

Reef continued his rant. After a moment, he realized there was no response.

"Natalie?"

Silence.

"Natalie?"

Nothing.

The questions became screams and frantic shouting. The guard descended the stairs and yelled at Reef, then peeked into my empty cell. Her face turned purple, and she ran a hand through her hair before spinning on her heels and sprinting away.

I wanted to feel guilty about the other Natalie's departure. She had abandoned Reef and the rest of her people without even quenching their fears that she was alive. But a single thought swirled through my mind as the screams intensified, and eventually, Rayhan reappeared at the gate.

It couldn't be that easy.

Could it?

The edges of the vision turned black. The dark cell flickered as the magic spun back through me. Returning to my body, or my time, or from wherever the phantom had thrown me, felt like a breath of air after submerging from thousands of feet. I collapsed to my knees, gasping, and there wasn't enough oxygen in the room to fill my empty lungs. I gagged, and that made me more nauseous. I threw up bile onto the wet rocks until I finally caught my breath.

My head spun as air settled into my bloodstream and goosebumps sprouted across my skin. I shook as if with fever, but renewed hope pushed all of it away.

The phantom had shown me a way out.

I dragged myself up the cold stones and hunched on the bench. My arms felt weak as I pulled the black blanket over my body, but I didn't have the strength to sit up.

I itched to dig up the tiny knife and escape right now. I knew it would work. My magic had done terrible, deadly things, but it never lied to me. I could dislodge the bar, and it would set me free.

But the phantom had not only shown me *how* to get out, it also showed me *when* to get out.

The Natalie in my vision had been injured. I didn't want to do whatever would cause those wounds, but I would. Magic was temperamental. If I tried to escape at the wrong time, something bad would happen. Impatience fought against the logic in my mind, but I refused to break the vision I had just seen. I wouldn't touch the knife or the window until the full moon stared down at me and my face resembled tender hamburger meat.

The white orb shone through the bars, casting three grizzly, vertical shadows onto the opposite wall. Judging by the almost complete fill of the moon, my vision would be fulfilled soon.

I let images of freedom cover me in warm thoughts as my exhausted body drifted into unconsciousness. Underneath the layers of excitement to escape, something unhappy lingered, and I pressed it into a tiny ball in my mind until it didn't resemble longing for Rayhan anymore.

CHAPTER THIRTEEN

"Why are we going to the library?" Rayhan led, and I followed, trying to ignore how the rhythm of his hips lit a spark in my chest. His dark cotton breeches and black tunic weren't suggestive, but they hugged his body the way I tried to convince myself I didn't want to.

"What?" Admiring the view had distracted me.

"I said, why are we going to the library, girl? You're supposed to use magic to figure this out, and I don't want to spend the entire day locked in a room full of dusty books."

A well-kept library wouldn't have dusty books, but I bit my tongue. Rayhan's suspicion about my magic hung thick between us, and silence remained my only possible response.

"Besides," he continued, "it'd make more sense to talk to D'ar Zhao. He hated Dad. I always imagined he'd run a blade through my dad's chest, but poison wouldn't be beneath the man."

And that was another reason we headed to the library. Ella had painted a dark picture of Zhao, and I wasn't eager to meet him. I didn't want to see someone who Rayhan expected to stab his father. Something about it rubbed me the wrong way.

Speaking of rubbing, underneath the silver shackles, my wrists had turned bright crimson and streaks of red spread beneath my skin. The chills sending goosebumps down my arms suggested infection had finally festered in the wound and I had sprouted a fever. The symptoms weren't bad, but without treatment, they'd get worse.

"The library might help us decode these symbols." I smoothed out the crumpled page that remained the last surviving item from Manveer's room. Rayhan glanced at the paper, and his lip curled in doubt, but his steps didn't waver.

More people moved through the halls today. The pristine, warm stones almost shimmered in the sun's subtle glow through the open windows. Staff members in black uniforms hurried by, arms loaded with cleaning supplies or blankets or curtains to be washed and dried. A charged emotion shifted underneath their rushed steps. A hushed and excited whisper.

"Kadence must be on his way back." Rayhan watched one petite woman drag a packed basket.

A sludge of dread ran through me. "How do you know?" I wanted Manveer's murder to be solved and to return home before the king arrived.

"The staff always make it a big deal," Rayhan said. "Kadence has his issues, but his people love him."

I pressed my lips to prevent unwise words from spilling through them.

"Here." Rayhan jerked his hand out, almost smacking me across the face, and gestured to the left.

The library spread before us.

A simple, stone-lined archway seeped into a circular room. Plush black rugs, or perhaps furs, covered the floors, and a spattering of tables and chairs lingered in the middle. Lines of dark wooden bookshelves lined every hint of the sandstone walls, filled with hardbound books. An unlit fireplace sat between two shelves, and it looked out of place, as though it stole the space where more books could live. The scent of paper and old glue lured me like a wild beast to a pit trap.

A staircase spiraled along the side of the room to the next level. I scanned the twisting walkway and rubbed my eyes when I caught sight of the second floor. Crystalline glass composed the floor of the overhead story. The bottom of more bookshelves peered down, accompanied by the soles of library patrons' shoes. The third and fourth floors were also transparent, building to the stone peak of the top of the spire.

It appeared impossible. The sheer weight of the bookshelves alone would shatter a sheet of glass, but the people above us stepped with confidence.

"How?" Words died in my throat.

"Huh?" Rayhan was halfway through the round room and turned at my question. His brows arched, and he followed my pointing finger to the ceiling.

"Oh." He shrugged. "We don't know."

The muscles in my jaw surrendered, and my mouth gaped. "You don't know how the floor is made from glass?"

"Nobody knows," Rayhan said. "Mythology claims that before the war, witches and vampires lived together in the castle. The glass holds either because of physics or magic, and we're not willing to test which one."

Less impressed with the glass floors, Rayhan turned to the left. I trailed blindly, enthralled by the dancing steps of the people above us, seemingly unhindered by the transparent foundation.

"Rayhan." A warm voice stole my attention. Nadeem pushed his wheelchair from the edge of a table and wrapped his fingers around Rayhan's outstretched palm. He lifted one hand to wave at me, and I returned the gesture. "What are you doing here, lad? I'm certain I've never seen you in the library."

"Yeah, well." Rayhan shifted on his feet and pointed his thumb at me. "It's all her. I'd rather beat answers out of people, but she wants to do research first."

Nadeem's lips split into a smile. His teeth sat a little crooked, but the expression shaved years from his face.

"You've found yourself a smart one." Nadeem pushed his glasses higher and set a bookmark on his page. "What are you researching? Nothing more about poisons, I hope. I'm afraid you're going to talk yourself into nonsense at this point."

"Nothing about poison." I jumped in before Rayhan's red face and open mouth said something regrettable. "At least, I don't think so. We're looking up these symbols."

I set the paper on the desk in front of Nadeem, and he held it between his fingertips. There was a tremor in his grip, the only hint betraying his age.

His face darkened. "It's happening again," he whispered.

"What is?" I asked.

His gaze fixed on the parchment, but I knew memories had returned him to a different time and place.

"Lexliv." He ran his finger across the black ink.

"Lexliv?" I repeated. "That's the name of the witches' poison, isn't it?"

"What?" Nadeem snapped his gaze up. "I'm fairly confident I never said the word 'poison.' Did I say poison, lad?"

"No." Rayhan shook his head, and I shot him a glare.

"But do you know what it is?" I leaned down to peer at the paper over his shoulder.

"These are very old symbols. It's a detailed mixture of science and magic, it appears." He bent above the page, blocking it from view. "Some of these are symbols from the ancient language. I don't speak it anymore, I'm afraid. Time damages us all."

He turned it over, but the backside was blank. "Where did you get this?"

"It was in Dad's room," Rayhan said. "In a box."

"Hmm." Nadeem sat back in his chair. "I've been working on perfecting the smoke explosions. The detonator isn't particularly reliable, but this is curious. If it's okay with you, I'd like to look over this equation a bit more?"

"Yes," Rayhan said before I had the chance to protest. A bubble of annoyance squinted my eyes.

The redhead caught a glance of my face. "What?" He put both hands in the air in a universal surrender sign. "You wanted to know what it says. There's no better translator than Nadeem."

Nadeem nodded. "He's quite right, miss. I've studied ancient languages for three times your lifespan." He squinted, and his thick glasses made his eyes look massive. "Perhaps many more than three times."

"Fine," I bit. My hands were tied, but I didn't like it. Leaving the paper felt wrong.

Nadeem folded the page along the same creases and stored it in his pocket. A flash of motion turned his head as a muscular, pale-skinned man sauntered to the table.

"Are you ready to leave yet?" The man crouched down.

Frustration peered through Nadeem's eyes, and hot anger trailed behind.

"If I have to tell you again, Samuel—" Nadeem's voice held an edge of threat. "—not to interrupt me during my work, I will take your tongue so you can never ask me again."

Samuel snapped up from the table and sauntered into the corner. He crossed his arms, biceps bulging under a sleeveless tunic.

"I swear." Nadeem shook his head. "They keep sending me the most useless apprentices. Trying to get me to retire, I think. Well, the council has quite a surprise coming if they think I'll ever retire."

Nadeem laughed, but the menace in his tone had been real. I remembered Rayhan's warning that Nadeem had people willing to do his bidding. The pale man looked more like an assassin than a laboratory assistant. I imagined him slipping poison into someone's tea, but the image didn't fit quite right. He appeared more the type to run a knife across their throat.

"Since Nadeem is going to research the note, we have plenty of time to talk to Zhao." Rayhan sounded too eager, but I'd used my excuses. He snatched my hand in his massive palm and dragged me toward the arched exit.

A moment later, Rayhan paused. His blue eyes drifted to the transparent ceiling, and a frown caught on his lips.

I imagined what my lips would feel pressed against that frown, and the slow, sweet delight as they turned into a smile.

Stop it, Natalie. It's just the fever talking.

"Uh oh." Rayhan made a slight turn toward the stairs. "I'm pretty sure that's Ella."

Emotions twisted as we trekked up to greet Rayhan's stepmother. On the one hand, she was a lovely woman, and so kind to have offered me food and new clothes. But on the other, she had a casual way of insulting me, and the ache in my wrists already ate at my slight patience. I followed Rayhan anyway, and we stopped in front of her table.

Looking down at the glass floor, I peered into the room we'd just left. Nadeem's dark hair bobbed in his seat. My feet appeared to float on the clear glass, and the view blurred. My stomach turned sour as a wave of nausea swelled. My mind remained unconvinced that I wasn't falling, or about to fall, to my death. Lightheadedness twisted my vision, and my heart pounded hard in my ears.

"Don't look down, dear." Ella snapped her fingers under my nose, and I latched onto the movement. "First time in the library? It happens to everyone, of course. Who would ever think glass floors are a good idea?" She rolled her eyes.

"Breathe, girl." Rayhan slammed a hand into my back, and I pulled in a gush of air. The nausea faded. "Better?"

I nodded, although the spinning room suggested it may be a lie.

"Good."

Rayhan turned to his stepmother. She wore a navy blue dress, a silver sash pinched her waist, and a matching headband bound her thick, dark hair. Her feet crossed daintily at the ankles, and she peered around a pile of books.

"What are you doing here, Ella?" Rayhan looked over the woman, then searched for something else.

"I'm helping Wilson with some research, of course."

"Of course," Rayhan bit.

Ella frowned. "I don't know why it upsets you so much. Wilson's projects are only intended to help the castle."

"Nadeem rejected him as an assistant multiple times. There's a reason for that. If Wilson wants to help in the war, there are plenty of other things to do besides science."

Ella waved one hand. "He doesn't want to fight or clean up the bodies after battle. He wants to make a lasting impact. I think it's admirable."

"Dad thought it was stupid."

Darkness etched over Ella's face. "He's not here, is he?" she whispered, then her bubbly personality returned, and she gave a sharp grin. "Pardon my rudeness, you know how I get about my children. Look, he's coming down the stairs now. You're welcome to ask what he's working on."

I craned my neck around Rayhan and saw a young man about my age sagging beneath the weight of several books. He peered beyond them to watch his feet and still fumbled the last step. He staggered but regained his balance and didn't drop a single book.

Wilson had curly brown hair, almost the same color as his mother's. He was tall and skinny, not a runner or an athlete, but a scrawny guy. His eyes held a rich hazel hue, with a narrow-pointed nose centered under them. He crashed the books onto the table, and my heart pounded again, expecting the glass to give at any moment.

He sighed as the pile teetered, then looked at us. A scent of wildflowers and fresh earth drifted over me. Those hazel eyes turned from ordinary to striking, and the scrawny features aligned to create something much different from who had been hiding behind the tower of hardbacks. Wilson was very handsome.

His gaze trailed over my body, and his brows pinched at the sight of my dirty dress. My cheeks filled with warmth, and a pleasant feeling rumbled in my gut.

"Hello." Wilson extended his hand and caught my fingers. "I didn't catch your name."

My mouth opened, but only a hiss of air escaped.

"She didn't say it," Rayhan growled. His narrow gaze skirted between mine and Wilson's connected hands.

"Natalie," I said, breaking the word awkwardly into too many syllables.

"Natalie." My name sounded as sweet as red wine. "That's a lovely name."

Wilson turned his palm, nestling my fingers in his and lifting them to his lips. They were soft and warm.

Oh my. Butterflies flapped in my chest.

A hand wrapped around my bicep and yanked me away from Wilson. His palm slipped from mine, and part of me mourned for the departure. Rayhan's grip tightened on my arm for a moment, and his face pinched.

"Are you a witch?" Wilson's voice had a slight accent, an uptick at the end of every word.

"I am," I said.

"I've never met a witch before." He dragged his chair out and sat down, perching both elbows on the table next to his mother. "Well, not an alive one."

"Oh, um..."

"We were just leaving." Rayhan pulled on my arm, but I shifted my weight to drag my heels. It was as though Wilson was a magnet and I had turned to metal, unable to resist his call. The tilt of his head, the crooked smile on his lips, they beckoned to me.

"Don't leave on my account," Wilson said.

The world narrowed into his dreamy eyes and smooth, flawless skin.

"Okay." I pulled from Rayhan's grip, aching to feel Wilson's touch one more time.

"Natalie." Rayhan ground his teeth. "We have to go."

"What are you researching?" I dodged Rayhan's reaching grasp.

Wilson's face lit up. "We were studying pyrotechnics, but I think we've hit a wall there at the moment." He looked at his mother, and Ella nodded in agreement. "We've been dabbling in pheromones recently. Do you know what pheromones are?"

I shook my head. I had a distant memory of the word from one of my mother's lessons, but I didn't bother searching for the meaning. I wanted to hear more of Wilson's voice.

"They're chemicals that our bodies use to communicate. Every living creature secretes pheromones. It's part of what makes people attracted to each other."

"There are other uses besides sexual appeal, of course," Ella butted in. "Imagine halting an entire battlefield because the enemy thinks they're suddenly in love, or afraid. It could change the tides of the war."

Rayhan rolled his eyes and grabbed me again. "If it could impact the war, Nadeem would have figured it out by now," he said. "We need to go—"

Shouts erupted from downstairs. Rayhan's tug on my arm paused, and we peered at the floor underneath. Chaos played beneath us.

Three glass orbs with thick, brown ooze piled on the bottom and one orb that appeared empty settled on the plush, black carpet. Smoke trailed from the four balls, and one snapped with a spark as the concoction ignited.

"Hey!" Nadeem's voice muffled from below. He rolled his chair toward the empty-looking orb and studied it. "This is one of my smoke explosions."

The ball at his feet flashed, and thick mist coiled through the air. The other smoke explosions sparked, and soon the entire first story was engulfed in thick fog.

"Did you see the orb that was empty?" I asked.

"It wasn't empty," Rayhan said. "There's a clear liquid at the bottom."

I swallowed thickly. Rayhan's vampire eyes were more trustworthy than my own.

"What do you think is happening down there?" Wilson stepped beside me, and the scent of wild orchids overwhelmed me. I greedily sucked another breath, trying to memorize the smell.

Screams scattered up from the ground floor, and wisps of smoke climbed the staircase to our level. Distantly, wrapped in layers of swirling mist, streaks of blue light flashed.

My mind froze. The sight thrust me back into my cell, and the lightning pulses twisted through my skin. I inhaled sharply, but there wasn't enough air in the room.

"I don't know." Rayhan pulled a long, flat blade from under his shirt. "But I'm going to find out."

"Don't!" I grabbed Rayhan's arm, and my throat locked. He couldn't leave me. Not now.

The sea in his eyes settled to calm water. "Hey." He tucked a finger under my chin and studied my face. "The smoke's coming up here already. I need to go secure the stairs. I'll keep you safe."

Logic and emotion warred through me. I gave one stiff nod.

Rayhan ran, moving downstairs faster than his large frame should allow.

"He's going to get himself killed," Wilson mumbled behind me.

"Hush, dear," Ella said. "Don't worry the girl."

The words lit a fire of concern in my chest. The cold glass pressed against my knees as I dropped to the floor and tried to make out shapes in the swirling mist.

More screams and shouts and another flash of icy blue cut through the monotonous tones. The fog crept up the stairs until it swirled between my feet and rubbed my legs, thick and icy and alive. It covered my view downstairs.

My heart thundered in my ears. The memory of the blue-gold current on my arms stole my breath and sent the world into a spiral.

"I think she's going to be sick." Wilson's voice was distant, far away.

No, I would not be sick, but I also wasn't going to stand here and wait for the attacker to slip up the stairs.

I jumped to my feet and headed to the steps.

"Stop!"

"Wait!"

I pushed Wilson's and Ella's words from my mind and trekked into the rolling gray mist.

The air felt as thick as last time, maybe worse. It wrapped around my face, digging into my nose and mouth, coating them with oily slime. I took a ragged breath and held it, searching for a glimpse of movement through the smoke.

There. A flash of blue-gold lightning. My instincts screamed to go the other way, but I headed toward it.

Rays of light spilled through the mist. The archway leading to the hall filtered some of the fog, inviting fresh air inside. I let out my breath and drew a new one, holding it again. The vile smoke burned my lungs.

The thinner air revealed Rayhan fighting an attacker, dressed in all black and wielding twin ropes charged with blue current. Burn marks had already wrapped around Rayhan's exposed skin, but it didn't slow him down. He twisted the knife with sharp, accurate motions. The attacker's clothes bore several gashes, and Rayhan's blade tinged red with blood.

I recognized the shape, that dark outline with an edge of femininity. It was the same attacker from my cell, and her blue whips aimed for Rayhan this time.

She lunged and Rayhan sidestepped, dodging the tendrils by mere inches. She stepped again, forcing Rayhan back. Her whip swung, forcing Rayhan to retreat one slow step after another.

She snapped the rope, but Rayhan's blade streaked faster. His knife caught the tip of her charged coil, and it fell to the ground in a hiss of sparks. The entire weapon dulled, the charge broken. The assailant dropped the handle and switched the second rope to her dominant hand.

The two circled, tracking each other. I froze when the attacker's gaze locked on mine over Rayhan's shoulder. Only her eyes, dark and dancing, peeked through the tight mask, with a smug look of recognition.

"You," the voice growled. The tilting sides of the mask suggested she smiled underneath.

Rayhan lunged, but the attacker held her ground until the last moment, then spilled sideways out of his blade's reach. He staggered, but his weight and momentum were too much. She stuck her foot out, and Rayhan tripped over it. She pushed the center of his back and helped him crash to the floor at her feet.

My pounding heart skipped a beat. The woman straightened and flicked her lightning whip in a blurred motion. The end bound tight around Rayhan's neck. The vampire staggered to one knee and clutched at the coils, but she sent whatever magic or power through the weapon, and a blue-gold pulse shot into Rayhan's skin.

A loose sputter escaped his lips, and he convulsed. His face turned deep red, then purple, then edged with a hint of blue.

He wasn't breathing.

"Stop!" My held breath rushed out, and I dragged more smoke into my lungs. It simmered in my chest, a sludge of gray mucus, but I barely noticed under my mounting concern for the vampire.

The attacker looked at me over her shoulder. She flicked her eyes up and down my form and turned away.

"Don't worry," she hissed. "You're next."

She didn't see me as a threat, which was fair. Each rugged gasp of the twisting smoke sent ripples of fog into my head. My lungs burned for clean air. The phantom was nowhere to be found, and my magic remained trapped under my mother's spell. My hands were empty, so utterly useless.

Just like me.

The room spun, and the rims of my vision turned black. Rayhan's quaking form blurred, and my knees wobbled, then collapsed. Hard stones cracked under the carpet, barely cushioning my fall.

This felt different from the smoke that had consumed my cell. I remembered the single orb Rayhan said contained a different color sludge. Some kind of aerosol chemical.

Or poison.

The blue whips distorted into streaks the shade of river water, wrapping around Rayhan's ashen face. He slumped to the side, and his eyes locked on mine. He tried to drag a gasp of air through pressed lips, but the jolt froze his muscles.

He was going to die, and I was next.

Acceptance settled over me, heavy and warm and comforting. I hoped the poisoned smoke took me before the attacker could wrap her blue coils around my neck and shock me to death.

Rayhan's eyes closed.

That looked nice. Despite the unhealthy tint of his skin, he could have been resting, about to fall asleep. I longed for rest too. Each breath pulled me closer to unconsciousness.

Rayhan's knife sat abandoned on the floor, dripping blood on the carpet. The attacker didn't have any visible wounds, but slashes marred her clothes. She wasn't invincible. She was mortal, or at the very least, woundable.

I stretched for the blade, and my fingertips grazed the hilt. My body weighed a thousand pounds, but I pushed through the struggle. I'd dragged injured soldiers upstairs to my healing loft hundreds of times.

I forced myself to reach farther as my vision turned black and my head pounded. The cold metal chilled my fingers, but my grip was strong.

The attacker towered over Rayhan's still form. I just needed to move one more time. I needed to push from the ground and run the knife into her body.

I took a breath and held it.

Three. Two. One.

I lunged from my knees, half blind, and thrust the weapon at the shadowy figure. The sharp metal slipped through tender skin and skidded to a stop at a hard edge. I'd hit bone. Calling on the last of my strength, I twisted the blade and blood ran down my hand, hot and sticky. A distant voice screamed, the blue glow faded, and the sound of footsteps retreated down the hall.

Beside me, Rayhan drew a ragged breath.

He was alive. I put my head on the soft carpet, my energy gone. The air began to clear up, but not quickly enough. I would die before fresh air could clean my lungs.

"Poisoned aerosol," a female voice said above me. It was Ella. "Grab him and pull him out. I'll get her."

Strong arms looped under me, and I skidded across the floor, bumping against every rough edge. The gray mist turned to clear, bright light, and warm sunshine spread over my skin.

I gasped for fresh air and tried to cough. My weak lungs protested, and only a wheeze escaped. It was enough. For now, it was glorious.

Wilson dropped Rayhan beside me. He rolled onto his hands and knees, and a healthy pink glow returned to his face. He vomited bile, then wiped his mouth with the back of his hand.

"If I had my axe, their head would be rolling right now," Rayhan growled, every other word a gasp for more breath. Harsh burns wrapped around his neck, but they healed as I watched. The bitter scent of burned hair and charred flesh spilled from us. "That's it. I'm never going anywhere without my axe again."

"Her," I said, my throat feeling like I'd swallowed a hot poker.

"Huh?" The three vampires turned to me.

"The attacker was a woman," I said.

"I don't care who it was. Next time, she'll be dead," Rayhan said.

My gut twisted. He sounded confident there would be a next time.

"Who else was in there?" Ella peered through the archway, where wisps of mist escaped.

Rayhan's throat bobbed. "Nadeem," he said. "And one of his assistants."

Silence.

"I'll go check," Ella said.

"No." Rayhan pushed to his feet with a slight wobble. "I'll go." He disappeared into the darkness.

I remembered the thick press of the poisoned air inside me. Surely, if I could last that long, a vampire could do better. But I had been beside the vented doorway, where the mist was thinnest. Nadeem had been at the epicenter of the smoke bombs, where the poison that erupted would have been the most potent.

I bit my lip and twisted my fingers in my lap. Ella rubbed Wilson's shoulders as he sat silently at her feet. Whatever starstruck admiration I'd felt earlier had faded, and Wilson looked fragile and afraid.

Rayhan stepped from the mist, with Nadeem's limp and lifeless body draped across his arms. I didn't need to ask. The gray tone of the scientist's dark skin told me he was dead.

I turned away, guilt and pain and anger mixing at the sight. A dead enemy shouldn't shatter me so completely, but my heart tore at the limpness of his fingers. They'd been so alive moments ago.

Rayhan set Nadeem gingerly in the hall as shouts spread and staff members sprinted toward the library, carrying gurneys and shrugging into protective gear.

"The smoke is toxic." Ella met the first responders. "There's no hurry. Anyone left inside is long dead by now. Go straight to open the windows and get the paddle fans to clear the air."

I sat on my heels next to Nadeem. His glossy gaze stared up, and I ran my fingers over his stiff lids to draw them closed. A black tablecloth draped over the table beside me and I plucked it off and laid it over the body.

Tears pressed in my eyes, and I let them fall. It could have been me or Rayhan, but it was Nadeem, and it hurt.

"Natalie." Rayhan's voice sounded soft, as though his throat was tight too. "The paper's gone. The attacker stole the page from Nadeem's pocket."

Grief split open a black hole in my chest and swallowed me from the inside out.

CHAPTER FOURTEEN

Rayhan hadn't come for me in two days.

They'd finally brought us fresh clothes, and the dress Ella gave me was left in a purple heap near the barred door. The prisoner outfits may have been boring and drab, but they were soft and comfortable.

A shadow passed the door, and metal clanked against the stone ground as a guard dropped a tray of food. The scent of fresh bread greeted me at the gate. Thick yogurt piled high with assorted fruit and a stacked plate of eggs should have made my mouth water. Instead, nausea twisted my stomach, and I pressed the back of my wrist to my lips to avoid puking on the decadent meal.

The infection from the shackles had only grown worse. Pounding rhythms of pain ran up and down my arms while the fever came and went. I'd wrapped layers of cloth from Ella's dress around the metal bands, yet they were drenched in pus and other fluids. It didn't seem to matter how many coils of fabric I forced between the silver and my skin—it cut through me like a hot knife.

"Here, Reef." I pushed the plate toward the man's outstretched fingers.

"Are you sure you're finished eating already?" He swiped the bowl of yogurt and passed the tray down to Jolie's cell.

"Yeah, I ate plenty." I plastered on a fake smile, hoping it made my voice sound convincing. I hadn't eaten anything in two days.

Exhausted and weak, I staggered back to the bench and wrapped my tired fingers around a cup of cold water. If I took small sips and deep breaths, I could keep some fluid down.

My father's medication would be more than halfway depleted by now. If Penelope lowered the dose, it would buy him some time. He would grow weaker, possibly falling into unconsciousness, but he would survive until I got home. Penelope knew a little about tonic brewing. She might try to make a new batch, but she was so young and I hadn't finished teaching her the process. It took me two years to learn it, and that was with my mother's experienced guidance.

My vision hadn't come true yet. Impatience rattled my chest while I watched the spattering of blue sky through the small window. If the vision wasn't fulfilled tonight, I would leave anyway. The knife could slip the bar from the frame, I knew it could. The phantom was absent, and my face wasn't bruised, but I was done waiting. I needed to get home before I became too weak to complete the journey.

A bead of sweat trailed down my spine as the fever broke again. The distinct scent of salt layered through my clothes and combined with the wet musk of dripping water.

Drip. Drip. Drip.

Thud. Thud. Thud.

I raised my head. Had the illness stolen my sanity?

Thud. Thud.

No, only one person thundered down a staircase with such ferocity. Rayhan had finally returned.

I raced to the water dribbling down my cell wall and cupped my hands together. The cold fluid trickled into my palms, clean and clear, and I splashed the icy fluid onto my face. I ran it over my arms and hoped it would be enough to hide the pus and blood and sickly sweet smell.

A figure blocked the torch across the hall, and Rayhan towered in front of the door, slouching a bit to peer into the cell. His large fingers rattled at the lock, and the gate swung open. He wore all black, and a giant axe loomed over one shoulder like a second head sprouting from his right side.

We stared at each other for a moment, the steady drip of water from my arms the only sound between us.

"I'm sorry it's been so long," he broke the silence. "We had Nadeem's funeral."

I nodded, but a fist squeezed my stomach. I would have liked to attend the old vampire's funeral. He had been strange and erratic but also kind, and he had cared about Rayhan.

I raised my hand to touch the vampire, but a flash of hard emotion crossed his face and I let it fall to my side. He turned away from me, studying the ground.

Maybe he blamed me for Nadeem's death. I chewed on my lip. If I had been able to use magic the way I promised, Nadeem might still be alive. My heart thudded in my ears. Maybe Rayhan was here to cancel our agreement. Maybe he would lock me in here forever and my vision would never be fulfilled, and the attacker would return and strangle me with her lightning ropes.

The thoughts spun endless circles in my mind, wrapping around me like a noose I couldn't reach to loosen.

"I have a meeting with D'ar Zhao," Rayhan said. "Do you want to come with me?"

My pulse beat almost too loud to hear him. "You want me to come with you?" Disbelief bubbled in my tone.

"Yeah." Rayhan squinted at me. "How am I going to catch the bastard who murdered my father and his best friend without your magic to help?"

I swallowed, and the movement caught in my throat. He wasn't mad at me.

"Yes, yes." I scrambled toward the vampire, careful to hide the tilt in my steps from the dizziness. "I want to come with you."

"Here." Rayhan held out the silken blindfold. We must have been going outside.

I wrapped the fabric around my head and tightened it in the back.

Rayhan took my elbow, and his grip was firm and solid. I expected the faintness to grow worse with blindness, but some part of my inner mind settled into a comfortable rhythm as I followed the burly man.

"How was the funeral?" I asked.

Rayhan paused for a moment. "It was nice," he said, his words drawn and slow. "We built a great pyre and scattered his ashes to the wind."

I pressed my lips. I didn't have anything to say.

"What do I need to know about Zhao?" I asked, changing the subject.

"Zhao is an ass." Rayhan's voice harbored a hint of anger. "His and Dad's careers took off together. They ended up along the same path. At the promotion board, only one of them could be promoted, and the panel selected Dad. He didn't have a choice, but Zhao was really pissed. He threatened Dad multiple times, but it had been a few years since the last time."

"What did he threaten to do?"

"Stab Dad through the heart, cut off his head, the usual stuff." I felt the motion of Rayhan's shrug. "I wouldn't peg Zhao for poison, though, or to hire an assassin. He's the kind that likes to get his hands dirty."

"Then why are we talking to him if you don't think he did it?" The painting of D'ar Zhao in my mind was less than flattering.

"He's the only suspect that's actually threatened Dad," Rayhan said. "We should at least check it out. Maybe your stubborn magic will decide to make an appearance."

Maybe, but probably not.

The solid stones under my feet turned to the soft crunch of crisp grass. Dry heat pressed over me. The cells were hot from the open windows, but the constant water kept them moist and humid. Here, the sunshine was unhindered to spread across my skin and chase away the approaching fever.

"I'll get that for you." Rayhan plucked the blindfold off and stowed the sash in his pocket. I blinked at the assault of bright light and cupped my hand over my eyes. We had come from a different door than the one that led to Bria's cabin. A sloped walkway spilled straight to the grass, and fresh wildflowers swayed in the slight summer breeze. Trees surrounded us, but not the thick, foliage-full forests we had at home. There was no undergrowth or damp swampy ground, just segregated, lonely trees.

The gentle wind wasn't strong enough to soothe the heat, and sweat budded on my forehead, not a product of my illness this time. The rolling scent of new grass and evergreen floated through the air.

In the center of the field, less than one hundred yards from the castle, was a grand colosseum. Wide sheets of shining metal composed the massive circular structure. Screams and shouts trickled from the building, and beneath the fresh air was a faint scent of blood. Rayhan angled us straight for the building.

"This is the Lists," Rayhan said. He grabbed the handle of a half-hidden door and nearly tugged it from its bolts. "This is where our soldiers train."

The Lists opened into a wide arena. Black rows of benches followed the edges, nestled under an overhang to protect the audience from rain or snow. The center stretched open, exposed to the elements, and a cluster of soldiers sparred in the middle. A makeshift medical station sat to the right, and bloodied and bruised vampires occupied several seats. One woman screamed as a medic fixed a tight bandage around a stump where her hand should have been.

"Don't worry," I overheard the medic say as we strolled past. "It'll grow back in three or four months. We just have to keep it clean."

My tongue plastered to the roof of my mouth, and I forced my wide eyes away. My already queasy stomach turned in protest. I had helped heal the wounded after a battle, but the missing limbs were too much for my gentle potions and ointments. Those cases went to witches with a healing affinity. And our limbs didn't grow back.

Two men circled each other in the arena. One had dark skin and the other looked fairly pale. The pale one was tall, but stout and muscular. His shoulders spanned wider than his hips, like he'd been pressed between two walls, and his face matched. His eyes were dark, and his nose was short and squished. He wore armor over a black uniform, and the shoulder plates came to a sharp point at the tips. The letter Z had been etched into the metal. This must have been Zhao.

Zhao spun his sword at his opponent, but the edge didn't have the dull finish of a practice blade. He swung a real blade at his own soldier. The man jumped back a moment too late, and his skin split. Fresh blood poured onto the ground. It wasn't the first the dirt had consumed, and it stretched in matted, red clumps at their feet.

Zhao's twisted laugh slithered around me and settled an eerie chill into my bones.

"You're too slow." He spat at the soldier. "You couldn't kill a child with that speed."

His words set a sludge over my skin. I resisted the urge to rub my arms.

The smaller man spun his weapon, a thick battle hammer that was blocky and sturdy. His inhuman speed blurred the metal, and he launched toward Zhao with a loud grunt. His blade struck empty air.

Zhao twisted his sword across the back of the man's knees, and he collapsed.

"Medic." Zhao smiled beneath the words. "Come clean up another mess." There was a hiss at the ends of his sentences, soft and serpentine.

Zhao turned, and his eyes widened when he saw Rayhan. I had a feeling he knew we were here the whole time. A deep grin split his face in half, and an emotion slithered in his gaze that wasn't joy or surprise or fear. It was something darker, something hungry.

"Rayhan." Zhao reached for a handshake, but then pulled Rayhan close for a partial embrace. "It has been a long time since you've stepped into the Lists. Are you here to show them how it's done?"

Zhao gestured to the line of new recruits waiting for their turn in the arena, who all wore masks of fear yet tried to hide them.

"Not today, Zhao," Rayhan said.

"I heard about Nadeem Patel's funeral." Zhao dipped his head respectfully, but the gesture looked wrong on his broad shoulders. "He was close to your father. I didn't have time to attend, unfortunately. War waits for no man's death."

His black eyes slipped to me, and cold edged through me.

"That's the reality of it, I suppose." Rayhan stepped back and clasped a strong hand on my shoulder. "This is Natalie. She's been taking a second look at Dad's death for me."

Zhao's split smile crept impossibly high.

"A witch is helping you? Her mortal enemy?" He leaned close, and the scent of sweat and saliva rolled off his skin. "Curious." Zhao straightened. "I thought your father died from natural causes. An infection or something."

"A genetic disorder." Rayhan clenched his teeth. His dislike of Zhao seeped through his body language, and he stuck his chest out. "I'm checking all the options."

"Of course," Zhao said. His gaze rummaged over me, and I resisted the urge to step behind Rayhan. I jutted my chin into the air, and the defiance lit a spark in Zhao's eyes. His savage grin turned to something...else, and regret tumbled through me.

Zhao pivoted and sauntered to a nearby weapons rack. The rusty stand was peppered with swords, axes, bows and arrows, and other blades I didn't recognize. Zhao plucked a simple sword from its place and balanced the side of the hilt on one finger.

"Tell me," he said, studying the blade, "does she do magic to help you figure out the truth about your father's death? The silver shackles are supposed to prevent that."

"You know the silver just slows down magic. It can't stop it." Rayhan dragged his foot in the bloody dirt impatiently.

"No magic then? Does she have a truth-identifying affinity?"

"We're not asking that many questions, Zhao." Rayhan ground his teeth.

"Sounds like a no as well." Zhao flipped the sword and caught it by the blade without a single mark marring his creamy skin. "She must fight then."

He stepped close and held the hilt of the weapon out to me.

I shook my head and curled my fingers into fists.

"Come on." He pushed the sword my way, and the leather hilt touched my hand. The tip of his tongue skirted across his lips.

"I don't know what you're playing, Zhao, but knock it off." Rayhan reached for the sword, but Zhao was already several steps away.

"Here's what I'm playing, Rayhan." Zhao's words sounded rehearsed.

He had expected this meeting and prepared plans for us. "The little witch is going to show all our soldiers what her people are made from or—" He wagged a finger near Rayhan's face. "—the king will hear about your extracurricular activities, and she'll spend forever rotting in her cell."

"Are you threatening me?" Rayhan's voice turned more growl than speech.

"Threaten General Manveer Whylde's only son and King Kadence Hendrick's best friend? Never. I'm threatening the useless enemy witch we've been at war with for hundreds of years. Her feet don't deserve to touch our soil." Zhao spit on the ground in my direction. "Her kind has killed thousands of our people. Your friends and family have died on the field. Your mother fights them because she hasn't forgotten the pain and loss the witches have dealt to us. Tell me, Rayhan, do you forget? Do you forget your sister's last breath when the witches pulled her guts from the inside out? Do you forget the cries of her children when we lit the funeral pyre? Because I don't. And I never will."

Zhao paused and Rayhan averted his gaze, silent.

Zhao turned back to me and offered the sword again. "Take the blade, witch," he bit. "Or fight without it."

He dropped the hilt, and the weapon fell into the dirt. "So be it."

Zhao was fast. I never saw the hit coming. One moment, hatred and pain stretched into a fire of turmoil in his eyes, and the next, I was on the ground and blood pooled in my mouth. The pain followed, hot and blinding, and spread like acid clawing through my face. My lip throbbed with every beat of my heart. All my teeth remained in place, but they ached, and more pain radiated through my jaw.

I groaned and rolled onto my hands and knees. Blood dripped down my chin and scattered across my shirt.

"Hey!" Rayhan yelled, but he sounded far away. "I swear, Zhao, I'll kill you for that."

"Soldiers, hold him," Zhao said. "You have no authority here, Rayhan. This witch will be long dead before you can defeat all of my warriors."

Zhao's foot smashed into my side. The air rushed from my lungs. I tumbled into the dirt and drew a ragged breath. Pain circled my tender ribs and spread out, a fireball explosion through my nerves.

A shadow covered the sun. Zhao, holding the sword hilt again.

"What do you think this time?" he asked, his smile stretching too big and his eyes turning too dark.

I staggered to my feet. It hurt to stand upright, but I grabbed the weapon from his hands. He snickered while I stumbled to put distance between us.

My fingertips glided over the rough edge of my split lip, and I flinched. Blood flowed freely, and Zhao wasn't the only person watching now. Behind him, several soldiers raised their heads and sniffed the air, tinged with my scent.

This is what the phantom had shown me. It was the fulfillment of my vision, but the victory wasn't as sweet as I expected. My head spun and throbbed, my lip was on fire, and bruises would soon blossom across my ribs. It seemed I would pay a steep price for escape. I thought of my dad, of Penelope's warmth wrapping around me, and resolve hardened me. I would pay, whatever the price.

The sword felt unexpectedly heavy. Zhao handled the weapon as though it were weightless, but the metal pulled my aching arms down. Zhao circled me and I avoided him, dragging the blade tip in the dirt.

"Will you not come for me, little witch? I have killed many of your kind in battle. Do you not thirst for revenge?" Zhao was unarmed, but his tone betrayed no worry.

I'd never held a sword before. We hunted with bows and arrows at home, and Penelope's aim was great with her slingshot. I wrapped both hands around the weapon and heaved it into a sloppy swing at the man. The blade made a shallow arch overhead. Zhao lingered, then stepped lazily out of the way. I missed by several feet and the weapon jerked my arms when it pounded into the ground.

"You have to be faster than that," he said. "Shall I show you?"

His body turned to a dark blur as he launched at me. I swung around, heaving the sword, but he hammered a hard punch into my side. Burning pain raked through me. Bile climbed up my throat and I swallowed it down. The sword lugged behind Zhao's form, much too slow and much too late.

The weapon smacked to a halt. I leaned on the hilt, the only support keeping me standing.

"Don't you see, little girl, there's no hope for you here." Zhao gestured one hand toward Rayhan, whose giant axe swung at a dozen soldiers, each stabbing with their own swords. "These new recruits are no match for a seasoned warrior, but your blood will paint my arena before he finishes them. If you've ever considered any last words, now would be the time to say them."

I drew a deep breath into my aching lungs. My magic beat against its bonds, and I knew if it was free, this man would be dust in the wind. I adjusted my grip on the hilt and willed my arms to turn to hard iron.

"Last words?" My lip was numb, and the words escaped with a bit of a lisp. "Go to hell."

I stabbed at him. Pure ambition to see my blade through Zhao's heart drove my strike. A twisted smile locked on his smug face, and he turned to sidestep the lunge. He underestimated my speed, my determination. My sword tip ran through his clothes and brushed against his chest, running a thin cut over his skin.

Blood leaked down the blade, but the wound healed before a single drip fell.

Zhao cast his dark eyes to me, and a fire burned in their depths.

I didn't see his next strike, or the one after that, but they hammered into my gut hard and swift. I doubled over. The sword slipped from my hand. Zhao moved behind me, and a sharp jab into my lower back sent a spiral of stars through my mind. Blackness edged my vision. My knees buckled, and Zhao launched another kick at my face. Bright light tinged with the explosive force of his foot into my eye. I propelled backward. Dizziness and red streaks colored the world. The pain enveloped me. Even a slight breath stretched my gut enough to strain a whimper from my swollen lips.

A hand wrapped in my hair and jerked me from the ground. Zhao lifted my limp body until my face was inches from his. He looked blurry through my injured eye.

"Don't you see?" he whispered, and he pulled my head back until I could only see the rows of empty black seats. "Your kind deserves to die at my feet."

Numbness swirled through me. The distant edge of unconsciousness felt too far away. I needed it to come closer, to deliver me from the hurt.

Zhao's breath hovered over my neck, and a hot drip of saliva fell on my throat. His fangs cut through my skin.

I screamed.

Shattered glass and molten lava poured from his mouth into my body, stealing any hint of logic from my mind. Distantly, I recognized it as some kind of innate power, not true pain but imagined pain Zhao forced over me, but there was no reason left in the blend of terror. Oxygen fled my lungs, and I willed it to never return. Mere unconsciousness wouldn't fix this. Only the sweet nothingness of death could stop this torment.

Behind me, someone else screamed, a much deeper tone. Footsteps drew near, and something hissed through the air.

Zhao's head exploded over me. A shower of brain matter and white bone shards fell across my face. For a moment, his body fought gravity, but then went limp and lifeless as my back slammed into the ground.

I drew a breath. The pain from Zhao's bite faded immediately with his death, but my mind wasn't convinced. Surely, it was too much to ever stop.

Above me, Rayhan's axe held half of Zhao's face, squished into an impossible span of three inches. I wanted to throw up, but I didn't have enough energy to stagger to my knees. I could only close my eyes.

"Come here." Rayhan scooped me into his arms. My head fell back, too weak to remain upright. I glimpsed buckled and battered bodies trying to stand on broken limbs. Rayhan had beaten down his own people to get to me.

"Natalie?" His palm pressed against the side of my face. He must have felt the fever from the shackles, or maybe the possible fracture from Zhao's kick, but he frowned. "I'll take you to the infirmary. You need a doctor."

I needed a witch healer. Vampire medicine would heal me human-slow and leave scars, but I didn't have a choice.

The gentle rhythm of Rayhan's body rocked against me as we fled the Lists. I passed out between the expansive field back to the castle and woke up in a small cot with three women hovering over me.

"She's awake."

"Do we want her to be?" a tall woman with dark skin and curly hair asked. She wore the standard staff uniform, with the addition of a white apron around her waist.

"Give her something for the pain." Another woman uncorked a bottle and pressed it to my lips. I considered refusing the treatment, but I opened my mouth and swallowed it in one gulp. If they wanted to kill me, so be it.

"There." The first woman set a cold rag against my forehead. "We'll get some ointment for her wrists too. Most of the pain is likely from the bite wound. The physical injuries aren't so bad."

My throbbing face and burning ribs longed to argue with her. The medication seeped through my body, turning my limbs light as air.

"That's better, huh?" The woman settled a cold cloth on my injured eye, and blackness ringed my vision. "You can rest, dear."

My eyelids closed against my will.

I HAD NEVER BEEN MORE eager to return to my cell. The three nurses let me sleep for a few hours and iced my injuries. The swelling would get a lot worse before it got better, but the ice and lingering pain medication turned the sharp ache into a tolerable throb. I kept my back straight and stiff, shoulders locked, and hid the pain under sheer stubbornness. They had also slathered ointment on my wrists, but I knew it was too late. I would need strong medication or magical healing, and I wasn't about to ask the vampires for either.

I was leaving.

Every step hurt, and the fever turned my body slick with sweat, but joy tumbled in my chest as we neared the cell.

I had fulfilled my vision. The bruises on my face matched the exact ones the phantom showed me. Sure, my ribs and stomach were a mess of black and blue under my shirt, and there was a massive bite mark hidden beneath my loose hair, but it was time.

I was leaving.

The guard at the top of the stairs stood at Rayhan's entrance. He saw me, and his mouth opened and closed like a little fish, but no words came through.

I took the lead, trying to avoid skipping to my cell. I couldn't physically skip, and my head spun from either the fever or traumatic injuries. But the thought was there.

Moonlight tumbled through the windows in our row, illuminating the captive witches. As we passed, several caught sight of me and their expressions turned angry. Some staggered to the door for a closer look. Soon, shouts and yells trailed through the hall.

Reef was waiting, pressed against his iron gate, before we came into view. His face reddened when he saw me, and his eyes tightened with the promise of death.

"Natalie, what happened?" He twisted to keep me in sight as Rayhan poked at the lock. "I'll kill you. If I ever get out of here, you better run."

The door swung open, and I stepped inside. I studied the rivets of water trailing over the rock wall to avoid looking Rayhan in the eyes. He might see my eagerness in the depths.

"Natalie," Rayhan said. "I'm so sorry."

There's no need. I would accept a thousand beatings for the chance to escape and return to Penelope and take care of my father. Rayhan wouldn't believe me if I stayed quiet. I hunched my shoulders, trying to look weak, and it wasn't difficult. My body hurt.

"It's okay," I said. "I've iced it, and I have the healing balm from the nurses. I'll feel better after I've slept."

After I escape this place forever.

"I'll stay here all night," Rayhan said. "I'll watch over you."

No! Fear jolted me, but I pushed it down. He had to leave. I had to make him leave.

"No, please don't."

Rayhan's face fell. He nodded and reached for me. Those hands I'd longed to feel against my skin suddenly turned to bloody hands reaching for my throat. I jerked away before memories could remind me that Zhao was dead.

Rayhan lowered his hand. "I'll send a guard down to watch over you. I'll return in the morning."

The door banged closed. Disbelief spread through me. He was leaving. Everything was playing out the way the phantom showed me.

I jumped to get the hidden knife and pulled the mortar away. The folded note I'd stolen from Manveer's locker tumbled out, and I jammed the page back in. I didn't care if Manveer was trying to kill Kadence or if he had been murdered, or anything about the man at all. My opportunity for escape was narrowing.

"Natalie, I promise you, I will kill that man." I barely heard Reef's voice. "Are you going to be okay?"

"Yeah, Reef." I pulled the blade from its tiny sheath, and the moonlight danced across the silver, a special ballet just for me. My hope and treasure were so small, pressed into a slim knife. "I'm going to be fine."

A chill from the metal bars seeped into my palms, but everything felt cold against my feverish skin. I ground the blade beneath the center bar, the way I'd seen in the vision, and it popped from its place like an overripe grape on a dying vine. The bar slipped from my shaking fingers and tumbled down the steep drop to land softly on the grass.

I twisted my sore and stiff body through the narrow gap. My shoulders struggled, convinced they were too big, but freedom proved a great motivator. I found the right angle and pushed myself through. Each hand gripped one bar, my feet perched on the ledge, and I settled for a moment to wait for the dizziness to subside.

I hadn't seen this far in my vision. I didn't know what came next.

Guilt tore a rugged gash in my heart. I was abandoning Reef, Jolie, and the rest of my people in this treacherous prison. The witches had never found Vari Kolum. Their jailbreak would never come. This would be the last time I would see them, and instead of helping, I was running like a thief in the night.

I looked back into the dark cell. My shadow cast an eerie shape onto the wall, a creature perched on the window, more animal than human.

Somewhere, somehow, another me watched this moment. Faced with the same choice as the Natalie in my vision, could I make a different decision? Could I choose my people, our cause and our war, over my personal freedom and my father's life?

No.

I studied the cell, searching for an invisible observer. I tried to mentally give her every excuse for my cowardice, for my frantic fleeing in the middle of the night, for abandoning my people. Nothing moved inside, not even a sliver of unsettled air.

I couldn't stay. I had to go home.

I slipped my feet over the edge and let go.

CHAPTER FIFTEEN

The moon arched past its crest in the sky, and I veered away from it as I trekked through the dry forest, weaving around trees and avoiding puddles large enough to drown in. I wasn't very successful at the second task. My feet and socks were already wet, reminiscent of my march toward the dungeon.

It should have been easy to find the right way. I just needed to walk away from the giant celestial object in the sky. Except it kept moving. One moment, it would be at my back casting a deep shadow over my steps, and the next, it danced in front of me, close enough to touch.

Thoughts jumbled my mind and distracted me. I stumbled through a thicket of trees into an open clearing. Thick branches caught my legs and I fell forward, catching the ground with a knee and my palms. The world spun. Maybe the moon wasn't moving at all. Maybe I was the one having problems. I closed my eyes. Just a little rest and I would be back on my feet again.

Animals flicked through the forest. At first, they'd been wary, nothing more than a snapped branch and a quick flash as they darted away. The longer and deeper I ventured through the woods, the bolder they'd grown. A dark rabbit jumped near me, its pink nose twitching as it caught my scent. Birds chuckled when I walked under their nests, chastising my midnight interruption. I thought I snatched a glimpse of an old buck, weighed under heavy antlers, peeking between two narrow trunks. It may have been the fever or my injuries, though, because the animal disappeared at the next glance.

These woods made me long for home. The ground was too dry, the foliage too short. I craved the musty scent of my backyard trees, where mushrooms sheltered beneath rotting logs. The sun could barely cut through the forest at home, and animals wouldn't dare venture close. These weren't hunted often, or they'd be more hesitant to approach.

I dragged myself to my feet and tried not to sway. My eye was swollen shut, and red streaks, turned pink in the silver light, wrapped around my arms. For the first couple hours, I'd ripped the hem of my shirt and dampened it to combat the fever, but I'd since given up. Sweat streamed over my skin, and the summer air chilled me to the core.

A deep breath sent pain through my bruised ribs. I forced my feet forward. Each step drew me closer to my father, to Penelope, to our tiny cabin that we called home. At least, I thought it did. I looked up, searching for that dang moon again.

"Natalie." A man's voice, steady and strong, billowed through the night.

My heart pounded. I squinted at shadows moving through the forest.

"Natalie." It came from behind me, warm and familiar, and the darkness twisted together into a new shape. Tall and lean, my father stepped from the tree line, standing straight and healthy. He opened his arms wide.

Joy overwhelmed me, silencing the voice in my mind saying it was impossible. Even at the peak of his health, with plenty of medicine, my father would be too weak for this journey. Maybe someone had carried him, or he'd sold the house to buy a horse to come find me. I didn't care. I ran as tears stretched across my cheeks in the wind, aching for his warmth to wrap around me.

He loomed closer, arms open, the dimples in his narrow face prominent even in the dim light. I lunged for him and fell through the image. Chalky dirt spattered my face while sticks and rocks cut my skin. The pain blended with the pulsing throb already there.

It wasn't real. A hallucination, probably from the fever, or pure desire to see my father—but it wasn't real.

Tears flowed more, not for joy or excitement, but deep sobs that rattled my chest and tried to tear me in half.

"Natalie," Father called again.

I dragged myself from the dirt, more carefully this time. There was no reason to rush for a hallucination. I turned to face him. Father wore a plain tunic tucked into wool breeches and leather boots, the kind he'd wear for the little garden work he could occasionally do. His dirty blond hair was neatly combed. He looked good, healthier.

"Natalie." His tone changed, and his brown eyes flattened. "You abandoned us."

His words struck my already fragile heart.

"No." I tried to explain. He wasn't real, at least I didn't think so, but I still wanted him to know. "I was forced to leave. I had to protect Penelope."

"Penelope?" His teeth clashed together in a rugged white grimace. "You didn't protect her. You got her killed."

"What! No, she's safe, she was safe when I left. I made sure of it!"

My father shook his head and pointed behind me, deeper into the forest. I squinted as a humanoid figure limped from the shadows.

"This is your fault," Father said.

The moon illuminated the creature. Penelope's shape and size, the thing scuttled forward on one leg. The other was damaged and decayed, maggots peppering gaping holes in the flesh and falling behind like a trail of awful breadcrumbs. Her skin held a pale and gray hue, the color of milk after it's outside much too long. Rotten gaps thrust through her body, and blood and fluid and thick organs strained to creep out but were secured by tendrils of stubborn sinew. Her jaw had detached on one side and hung loose and broken. A deep red tongue, almost black, wiggled from the lower portion as she tried to speak. Words couldn't form, and her mouth emitted a constant screech.

"No!" I hurried back, as far from the creature as I could get without taking my eyes from its face. Penelope's hair, clumps missing from the skull, cast around the shape with each step, a golden cape to adorn its approach. "She was alive. I kept her alive."

"We buried her." The anger in my father's voice scalded me. "You should have left her buried. Look at what you've done."

The creature heaved her broken body toward me. My feet caught on the uneven ground, and I fell in the rough grass. Her decayed leg broke away, and she stumbled. A moment of relief washed over me. She wouldn't be able to move with one leg. She couldn't reach me. Her half-rotten head popped over the windblown reeds, and she dragged herself closer with disfigured fingertips.

"We would have rather buried you, Natalie." My father stepped around so I could see him and the corpse crawling toward me. "It should have been you who died."

My sobs grew louder as sadness and fear swirled inside me. The winds shifted, sending the scent of putrid flesh into my face. My stomach protested. I gasped for air, and the thick smell of death filled my mouth, sour and hot.

"It should have been you," Father said again.

"Yes, yes," I cried, afraid to cover my eyes and block the view of the vile creature. "It should have been me. I wish it was me." My sobs drowned out my father's words, but his mouth continued to move.

It should have been me. I deserved to die. If Penelope didn't live on this earth anymore, it held no place for me either.

I searched my bodice and found the knife I'd used to slip from my prison cell. My hands shook as I ran my finger over the blade. A sliver of blood rose to the surface. The blade was small but sharp.

My tongue stuck in my mouth as I set the edge against the blue vein on my wrist, barely visible under the red streaks of infection. After abandoning my family and my people, after Zhao's bite made me long for death, after seeing Penelope's corpse, death would be a sweet relief.

I dug the blade into my skin. There was no pain as the wound split open. Red liquid swelled and poured over my arms. The cooler air doused my fevered blood.

I switched hands and cut the other wrist.

"See?" I held up my bleeding limbs to show my father. "I did it. I'll join Penelope soon. She won't be alone."

He stared at me with disdain and loathing in his eyes. "No, she won't. She's never leaving you again." He pointed to the creature that had crawled several feet and now groaned near my legs.

"Please," I begged. I tried to kick it away, but my limbs wouldn't move. The corpse of Penelope screeched again, glass shards in my ears. "Go away. Go away."

Her rotting hand touched my bare skin, and the cold flesh stole the last of my sanity.

I screamed. She screeched. We wailed together until my voice turned hoarse and the air refused to fill my lungs again, and I screamed even though only silence left my body.

Behind Penelope and my father, something thudded the ground hard. A ripple of vibration cascaded through my chest, rattling my tender bones. Trees snapped and crashed to the forest floor. A deep, bellowing roar thundered from the woods, and it was very close.

My father's pale face sneered at me, then a massive beast sprinted through him. The apparition disappeared. A moment later, Penelope's dead hand faded from my leg. I was alone in the field except for the predator that breathed rancid breath around me.

The creature towered over ten feet tall. It held the general form of a feline, but with longer legs and a small, pinched waist. Spines ran from its shaggy tail to the low point between its shoulder blades. Claws the length of my hand protruded from its expansive paws and punctured deep into the rocky soil. Atop its back, five pairs of beady eyes studied me impassively. Babies, clinging with ragged claws and limbs with too many joints to the back of their mother.

I recognized the creature, but the beast scenting my blood in the air looked far different from the hand-drawn image in my mother's old books. It was a Suo, a territorial being with a passive temperament, except during the birthing season when it searched for fresh meat for its offspring.

The Suo roared, and the sound loosened something primal in my mind.

Instincts consumed me, screaming for me to find my feet and get out of there.

I scrambled up, even though I knew there was no way to outrun this creature. Adrenaline pumped through my body, pins and needles poking my fingers and toes, and I obeyed it. But the blood streaming down my fingertips and the dizziness from the fever told me that my life span would be measured in moments.

I ran. Trees sprouted at the edge of the clearing, and I ran into them, hoping the towering beams would slow the Suo down. I didn't halt to peek behind me, but her paws beat the ground at my feet. She didn't bother avoiding the thin trunks of several trees, but barreled over the tops of them, sending a deadly green cascade over my head. My mind blanked, and I let the drive to survive propel me forward. Death sounded sweeter a moment ago than it did with this creature at my heels.

My lungs burned. Each breath stretched the bruised skin from Zhao's beating, and my wrists throbbed as I pumped my arms at my side. My steps faltered at flat ground that my mind convinced me was sloped or pitted, and I lost any precious time I had gained.

Behind me, the beast roared, and her exhale brushed the side of my neck. The sickly sweet scent of rotten meat reminded me of my inevitable fate. Several small coos echoed from her back as her five little babies mimicked their mother's great roar.

I tripped. A traitorous branch peeked between a rocky, pine-covered section of ground and caught my ankle. Bark bit into my palms as I grabbed the nearest tree to recover my balance. The world spun, and I lost the fight against my dizziness. I sagged and fell to my knees.

The Suo's bounding steps halted. Her gentle breath against my neck was the only indication she was still there.

Slowly, I slipped to the ground and turned to my back. The beast covered the moon. Her nostrils flared at my scent, and her head tipped sideways as though wondering what had ceased my retreat. Her slanted red eyes caught mine, and her lips peeled away from those great jaws, displaying teeth half my height, dripping with saliva.

Zhao's demand for my last words filtered from the depths of my memory. What would my last words be? The failed promise to kill myself to join Penelope's corpse? That obviously hadn't worked, since I was alive despite the buckets of blood I'd probably shed in the forest. My begging plea for my sister not to touch me? Surely, words spoken to a fever-induced hallucination didn't count.

I leaned my head against the sharp needles and sought out the stars. The dizziness and blurriness from my injured eye combined, and the sky became inky blackness.

"I'm sorry." I let myself go limp. My sore muscles finally relaxed. A nearby river sang a joyful trickle, and somewhere deeper in the woods, an owl hooted. "I'm sorry, Penelope, Father, Mother." There wasn't enough water in my body to push tears through my stubborn ducts, but the depths of my chest heaved with the pain.

The Suo's shadow covered me as she crouched for the killing strike.

I closed my eyes and waited for the sharp press of her fangs into my skin.

"Hey!" a woman's voice jutted from the woods. It was deep and familiar. I snapped my eyes open and craned my neck, searching for the sound.

A tall, feminine shape sprinted from the trees toward the Suo. She lifted a hammer and swung the heavy weapon at the creature. The Suo sidestepped, a bit too late, and the weapon clipped the side of her jaw. She roared, spit flying, and shook her head from side to side.

The woman stood between me and the Suo. Two hands gripped the long hilt of the hammer, which was pulled back and prepared for another swing. Her clothes looked black in the shadows, but I had a feeling they were some bright color. Her hair was cut soldier-short into loose waves.

It was the stranger who had visited my cell after the first night Rayhan spent in the hallway. I hadn't gotten her name, but she told me to talk to her if Rayhan ever bothered me.

The Suo leaped at the woman, and the sudden jump tore a scream from my throat. Dry and cracked, it was more of a screech. She dodged the Suo's teeth, but one massive paw caught her legs. She somersaulted and popped back on her feet.

The two circled each other, sharpened claws and vampire fangs on display. The subtle moonlight illuminated the woman's eyes, and they resembled silver coins, eager and ready for bloodshed.

"Come on, little creature." Her voice sounded almost too deep, not masculine but inhuman. Closer to an instrument than something from a humanoid throat. She swung the hammer in a tight circle, warming her wrist. "Or are you afraid?"

The Suo looked at me over the woman's shape. A soft whine escaped, and the babies meowed from her back. Her lips curled from her teeth, but she turned and bounded away into the dark.

"That's what I thought!" the woman called after the fading Suo. She rubbed the hem of her tunic over the new bloodstains on her hammer, then dropped it in a sheath on her back.

She looked at me, and her expression twisted. I didn't bother trying to stand. I settled on the cool ground and let the trickle of relief run through me.

The stranger kneeled at my side and pressed her palm to my forehead.

"You've got a fever," she said.

I nodded.

"Too late for antibiotics," she continued. "We'd never make it to the castle in time, much less the human infirmary in town. They're the only place with medications."

I blinked. She was right. Medication took time to work, and I didn't have any left.

The woman ran her hands over her clothes and tugged a small, clear vial from her pocket. It was capped with a waxed cork, still sealed. She pressed her finger into the thick wax, then paused.

"Well." She tapped one finger along the edge of the glass. "Let's see what he says. He shouldn't be too far behind. Embarrassing that it's taken him this long."

I opened my mouth to ask who she was talking about, when another set of steps pounded the ground.

Rayhan, of course.

Rayhan's massive shape plunged between two trees to my right, and his gaze landed on the woman kneeling beside me. He squinted, and annoyance flashed across his face.

"I told you to wait for me, Mom." He jabbed his finger in the direction the Suo had run away. "What if it attacked you?"

Did he say *Mom*?

The stranger waved her hand dismissively. "If the worst thing I fight in a day is a Suo, it's been a good day. Besides, I found your witch, and she's dying."

Rayhan's protests locked in his throat. His eyes caressed my wounded and weakened body, and something dark pressed his lips tighter—fear.

He dropped to his knees, the two vampires forming a half-circle around me. He put the back of his hand against my cheek. I turned my head into his touch, craving more, and only partially because his touch felt cool on my hot skin.

"Look." Rayhan's mother—what did Ella say her name was? Maverick? —flipped over one of my arms. The long gashes had stopped bleeding, but bands of sickness crawled under my flesh. "Good thing these cuts are shallow and sloppy, or she'd be dead from blood loss by now. But the red streaks are signs of deep infection. We can't heal something like this."

"She-she's going to die?" Rayhan said.

"Yes." Maverick nodded. Rayhan's face froze in a twist of horror. "Or we can give her this." She held up the tiny vial.

"I thought you said medicine wouldn't heal her?"

"Not our medicine. This is witch medicine. It's magic."

Rayhan narrowed his eyes. "Where did you get that, Mom?"

"Does it matter?"

"Did you steal it from a witch soldier you killed?"

"I don't need to answer that."

"Mom!"

Maverick threw her hands in the air. "Look, either way, there's a dead witch. Would you rather it be a stranger or her? If you'd prefer she dies, that's fine too. I'm not particularly attached yet."

Rayhan snatched the bottle from his mother's grip with a sharp glare. She didn't try to hide her smug grin.

Rayhan popped the wax seal and pulled the cork from the top. He pushed his hand under my head and set the glass to my lips.

I swallowed the entire thing. I should have protested taking the potion stolen from a dead witch, but my body hurt and something in the back of my mind screamed that it didn't want to die. I guzzled the contents and Rayhan lowered my head, but he kept his palm between me and the ground.

They both stared at me.

"Nothing's happening." Rayhan lifted the container to his nose and sniffed. "Are you sure this is healing medicine?"

Maverick shrugged. "Either that or poison."

"Mom!"

"What? Without medicine, she's going to die anyway. If it's poison, it'll just hurry the job along."

Rayhan opened his mouth, then closed it with a snap. He looked away from me, but not before I saw a flash of silver in his eyes. He was angry.

Warmth sprouted in my stomach and meandered through my core, sending pleasant tingles across my nerves. If this was poison, it was a much better death than the ways I'd recently almost died. The heat became bubbly in my gut, and a smile spread on my face. The fever broke and sweat doused my skin, sinking into the thin prisoner clothes and covering me with a comfortable chill.

"There, see?" Maverick gestured at me. "She's coming around."

It was true. The tonic ate away my aches and pains. The throbbing near my eye and wrists faded. Dizziness slipped away, and the world finally held still. Maverick's form sharpened, and I could see the resemblance between her and Rayhan. They had the same shape head, the same long nose. Rayhan studied me cautiously, as though I were a piece of glass that might shatter beneath a sharp glance.

His rugged face looked different under the stars, which now shined bright and clear. His hair fell around him like a red-gold drape, accenting his defined jaw and deep blue eyes. His forehead creased with worry, betraying years of laugh lines, the signs of a good and happy life.

I reached for him and ran my finger over the tip of his full lips where the two points met. His eyes crinkled, but he held still, and I could see longing on his face.

A bubble of laughter escaped my mouth, and the vampires jerked in surprise. Their twin stares made me laugh harder.

"What's wrong with her?" Rayhan asked.

Wrong? Nothing! I hadn't felt this great in months.

"Sometimes the potion makes them a little...loopy," Maverick said.

"Loopy?" Rayhan's suspicious look drew more giggles, and I wrapped my arms around my sides. "You mean drunk?"

"Maybe that's a better description, yeah."

Rayhan curled his fist, then forced them to relax as he flattened his face.

"What?" Maverick asked.

Rayhan shook his head. "Nothing. Let's get her to the castle."

Rayhan scooped me up, eliciting another stream of laughter. My head tilted in a new way, not full of sickness and fever, but light as air. Time moved differently as I floated over the ground, up a set of stone steps, and into the dark, familiar halls of the castle.

We reached the turnoff to the dungeons, and Rayhan went left instead of right. I knew it was wrong, but the magic flowing through me, mending my aches and stealing my pain, didn't let me feel alarmed.

"Where are you taking her?" Maverick fell in step beside us.

"To my guestroom," Rayhan said, his voice sounding rough. "She'll be safer there."

"And it's harder to escape from the fourth floor."

"That too."

The darkness gave way to a hall lit with torches. Flames danced over our pale bodies, illuminating us for better or worse.

Dried blood covered my arms and clothes. I thought the slits on my wrists had been deep, but they barely broke through the skin. The magic accelerated my healing, and the red streaks were already gone.

Rayhan wore the same outfit as when he'd departed before my escape. Black on black, with the addition of the silver axe, minus Zhao's smashed face.

Maverick's light pink tunic settled over blood-covered blue breeches. She walked with her shoulders back and a confident stride that expected people to move out of her way, despite the halls being empty.

Maverick pushed open a door, and I recognized Rayhan's room. Curtains peeled from the balcony doors, giving me a glance of the castle grounds. The edge of Bria's cottage peeked through, where Rayhan had pressed me against the stone wall, and a blush struck my cheeks.

"Here." Maverick pulled open another door and stepped into a small bedroom. A petite fireplace glowed with warm embers, and heat seeped through my skin. A twin bed hugged the opposite wall, blocking the door from opening all the way.

"I'll get some water and rags." Maverick turned and disappeared.

Rayhan set me on the mattress and moved back, looking at me from a distance.

"Why the hell did you do that, girl?"

I knew the tone should make me angry. He couldn't have expected me to bypass the opportunity for freedom. Plus, I wasn't sure what he was talking about. The escape? Cutting myself during a hallucination? Angering a full-time mommy Suo? They were all dumb things to do.

"I don't know," I said. My voice sounded hollow, and I laughed again. I ran a finger across my eye and lip. The pain was gone, and the torn edges smoothed over. The magic was working.

Rayhan pressed his lips together and seemed to accept that he would not get a straight answer from me tonight.

"Let's get these things off you." His gentle fingers worked at the silver restraints, and they fell away in his palms. Immediately, an invisible weight lifted. Thick bands of damaged tissue layered around my wrists where the skin had half-healed before the metal cut fresh wounds. The magic wouldn't be able to erase the build-up of poorly mended flesh. These shackles would leave scars.

Rayhan bent and pressed his forehead against his palms. "I'm sorry," he said.

Slowly, I reached for one beaded lock and wrapped the trellis around my fingers. The vampire grew still under my touch. I followed the strand to his scalp and traced through the locks until his eyes closed. I let his hair fall and touched his high cheekbones. Stubble caught my fingertips, but it was rough and striking, paper against a match.

I hovered over his lips.

"What are you doing?" he asked, moving his mouth carefully.

I didn't know. I just knew the rich fluttering in my stomach burned too hot and too deep to be from a magic potion.

"Will you stay here tonight?" I asked. The thought of being alone, after Zhao, after seeing Penelope's body, felt like too much.

Rayhan shook his head, and my heart broke.

"Not like this, Natalie." He brushed a stray hair from my face. "It wouldn't be right."

I opened my mouth to protest, but Maverick jerked the door open and lugged a bucket of water near the fire. Gray towels and a light pink dress draped over her arms.

"Alright." She turned to me and rubbed her hands together like she was preparing to eat a delicious meal. "Let's get you cleaned up."

The two dipped rags into the bucket and wrung them out. Maverick helped me sit up and brushed the warm cloth over my dirty skin. I wanted to protest that I could do it myself, but my arms weighed more than solid lead.

"What possessed you to venture out in the state you were in anyway? You're lucky the Suo didn't just kill you. She must have been teaching her babies how to hunt," Maverick said.

I sighed. "My father is sick. I'm the only one who knows how to make his medicine."

"Why doesn't he take some of whatever potion we just gave you?" Maverick asked. "It seems to have done a fine job here."

I shook my head. "It's an autoimmune disease. We have tonic to bid it off, but not to cure him."

"Couldn't someone else make it?"

"They could try. My sister probably has, but it's very complicated. It took me years to learn."

"Hmm." Maverick sounded unimpressed. "Why didn't you do magic to fend off the Suo? Or heal yourself? Or kill Zhao before he took a bite out of you? I heard about that too."

I pressed my lips, but Rayhan froze. He turned those ocean eyes to me.

"That's a good question," he said, his tone cautious.

I considered lying, I didn't have the heart anymore. Any other witch in the same situation would have used magic to escape.

I wrapped my fingers together and drew a breath. "I can't." The words sank between us. "I can't do magic."

"That's not true." Rayhan sat back on his heels. "I've seen you do it. You used it on me!"

"I can't control it," I said. "When I was born, my power was very strong, and I couldn't control it. To keep me and our family safe, my mother locked my magic. When she died, the lock didn't go away."

"I've seen you do magic though," Rayhan repeated.

"I see a phantom." I gestured a generic ghostly shape. "It can force me to do magic."

"A phantom?" Rayhan's face pinched. "Like a hallucination?"

"Yeah." I shrugged. "Sort of."

"A hallucination forces you to do magic? So, in the woods when you read my mind?"

"The phantom."

"In my dad's room?"

"Phantom."

"When you escaped?"

"Well..." I pulled the silver knife from my shirt and pressed the metal into Rayhan's palm. "I actually used this to pull the bar from the window."

He turned the blade in his hand once, then slipped it into his clothes. He stood up. "So you can't help me find my father's killer?"

A raging sea rolled through his eyes.

I shook my head. "I'm sorr—"

He stepped through the door before I finished the words. It shut with a finality between us, the sound that would surely cement my return to the dungeon before sunrise. The sound that my father's coffin would make when I never returned home.

Tears fell in hot streaks, and I didn't hide them.

Maverick dropped her rag in the bucket with a splash. She looked between me and the door and pushed onto her heels.

"I'll talk to him." Her deep voice was soft, almost a whisper. "And I think I might have a way to help your father, but don't tell Rayhan I told you that. I'll come back for you soon."

Maverick pressed both hands against the sides of my face. She lifted my head and set her warm lips against my forehead. Then she left, and the door shut one more time.

I pulled on the new clothes, a thick, cotton shift dress and thigh-high wool socks, and stretched across the bed. The dying embers made the room a comfortable temperature, but I snuggled under the quilted blanket for an extra layer of protection. Rayhan may return to banish me to the dungeon, but I was going to soak up every second of comfort until then.

I closed my eyes and let the emotions churning in my chest settle over me. Guilt at leaving my people. Disappointment at my failed escape. Sadness that Father might not survive much longer. Doubt that I would ever see him alive again. The sinking feeling that the delicate string weaving between Rayhan and me had shattered into pieces.

CHAPTER SIXTEEN

A stack of dry wood sat in a wire basket near the fire, and I persuaded the faded embers back to life in a dancing haze of orange and red. The scent of freshly cut pine embraced the air. I didn't need a fire. It was a warm day, and the bedroom window faced the morning light, filling my room with blissful golden sunshine. Despite the tonic healing my body and the shackles no longer causing constant pain, I hurt. The flames soothed the ache in my bones and distracted me from my own thoughts.

The door smacked against the simple wooden footboard of the twin bed. Rayhan half-stepped into the room. His gaze skirted over my grip on the fire poker and the mattress I had made expecting a quick eviction.

I turned from him. I didn't want to see his anger at me, even if I deserved it.

"Come on, girl." Rayhan's throat sounded dry, cracked. "Let's go."

I pushed to my feet, and no arguments bubbled in my mind. He would march me straight to my old cell and then leave, and I wouldn't see him again. I wouldn't escape this place or save my father's life. I could only pray that Penelope was a better student than me and learned to make the tonic faster than I did.

The stones under my feet were softer than the iron knot in my chest. I deserved whatever Rayhan had planned for me. I had lied to him and failed him. I forced my chin up. I wouldn't go limp-hearted and ashamed. Everything I did was for someone else.

My people would hate me. Reef's pinched face burned through my mind. He may never forgive me for abandoning them. I may never forgive myself.

I padded behind Rayhan in the light pink dress and knee-high wool socks from his mother, tucked into the fur-lined black shoes Rayhan had given me my first day in the cellblock. I smoothed a hand through my dark tangles, but they didn't budge. We passed several people in the hall, all neatly pressed and bathed, but nobody turned my way. Probably because of Rayhan's towering presence rather than their lack of curiosity.

The vampire stepped from the staircase landing that led to the dungeon door. My heart froze. I may be trapped on this floor forever.

He spun right, descending another flight toward the ground floor.

I paused.

Rayhan stopped and turned around. "What, girl?" He pressed his lips into a thin line.

"Where are we going?" Maybe he'd determined I was more trouble to keep alive and he was leading me to the gallows outside.

"Come on." His tone softened. He lifted his hand, palm up, and reached out to me. His fingers twisted at the tips, inviting me to grab them. "I'll show you."

I bit my lip. I ached to take Rayhan's hand, to know that he wasn't mad or bitter at me, but I couldn't convince my arm to lift.

Rayhan dropped his palm, and his brows creased. The sea in his eyes twisted, and he stalked toward me. I backed up, but the edge of the stairwell halted my stride. Rayhan filled the space, and one hand on each side of my head locked me in place.

Anticipation, desire, and an undercurrent of fear spun in my gut, spreading warmth and nausea through me. The smell of sea salt and evergreen swirled between us, and I breathed it in like a dying man's last breath.

"What did I tell you in the woods that first day?"

"What?" I couldn't focus with his strong chest pressed against me. Every inhale put him closer to me.

Rayhan settled one finger under my chin and pushed my face up. His gaze poured over me, cold and fresh. "What did I tell you when we first met in the woods? Before the magic, before Kadence showed up. What did I say?"

The memories were crystal clear. Penelope's frightened expression, the thundering of my heart as I prayed he'd leave her alone.

"You said that you wouldn't hurt me," I answered.

His eyes turned from mine, brushed along the edge of my jaw, and settled on my lips. I parted them to draw a breath. Something dark and hungry burned through his gaze, lighting a fire in my core and scaring me at the same time.

"That's right, girl." His words were more of a growl. "Now, trust me."

He took half a step back, and my body cried at the sudden absence. Goosebumps trailed over my skin. Rayhan reached out his hand again.

I could turn from him, reject whatever trust our relationship had left. Maybe he'd let me stay in his little guest room or maybe I'd find myself back in the dungeon cell, but I'd never see him again. Or I could take his hand and find out if the fragile thread between us could ever carry any weight.

His grip was strong and solid and engulfed mine completely.

Rayhan's lips split into a savage grin, a hint of fang peeking through. My heart skipped a beat, remembering the pain of Zhao's teeth cutting through my skin, but then it settled. Rayhan wasn't Zhao. He would never hurt me.

He pulled me, and we descended the stairs together.

The winding staircase spit us out at the edges of a green field. Half a mile or so away sat a petite wooden stable. These weren't the cavalry horses bred for war and fighting. This would be the royal escort's personal herd.

"Aren't you worried that I know a way out of the castle now?" I settled into Rayhan's hurried rhythm, our feet tapping in unison.

He shrugged. "Doesn't seem to matter anymore, does it." The words weren't a question. I stared at the ground, my shoes, anything except his face.

The stableboy rushed to stand at our approach, knocking over the wooden bucket he'd perched on.

"S-sir," he stammered. "I've got the horses ready and packed the way you wanted. It's all in the bags, and I tied the easels on how you showed me."

Rayhan rested a hand on the kid's shoulder.. "Great job, boy. You can head home now. I'll get the horses settled when we return."

"Are you sure?" the stableboy asked, and a rosy glow softened his cheeks under Rayhan's praise.

"Yeah, kid. Get out of here before I change my mind." He shook the boy a little. The teen smothered a smile, then darted through the field and disappeared at the subtle edge of a hidden trail.

The two horses neighed at us and pulled against the rope securing them to the bar beside the stable. They each carried twin packs and one wooden easel. The delicate frames were tied outside of the leather bags, leaving space for a rider to slip their feet through.

Foresti hoofed the ground, his white-socked hooves drawing deep gouges in the dirt. He snorted at Rayhan and darted away from his reach, then paused to beckon the man again.

"You stupid creature," Rayhan growled. He held the worn lead in place and ran a hand across Foresti's ginger body. He lingered here and there, scratching a sensitive spot. The horse whined and complained but remained still when Rayhan's fingers brushed through his hair.

The second horse was a small chestnut mare. Her mane was long and clean, and the rich brown of her hide blended into white near her feet. She greeted me with warm eyes and buried her nose into my palm, searching for treats.

"I don't have anything." I showed her my empty hands, and she snorted and lowered her head to the grass to search for food.

"This is Juniper." Rayhan patted the mare's back as Foresti bickered in jealousy. "She's a good, dependable ride. This is Kadence's horse."

My hand froze against her velvet hide, and a tremor struck my fingers. "I don't want to ride Kadence's horse."

"That's too bad. She's the best for an inexperienced rider." Rayhan wrapped his arms around my waist and heaved me from the ground. A traitorous cry escaped my throat, and my feet buckled, looking for a place to stand. They found a solid ledge in the leather stirrup, and Rayhan flung my other foot across the saddle. He pressed the warm reins in my hands, and the animal did a happy sidestep under me. I rocked side to side, completely at her mercy.

"See? Riding Kadence's horse isn't that bad." Rayhan jumped into his saddle in a clean, easy motion and took an extra moment to settle into place.

My legs reached farther than felt physically possible. The horse's sides stretched with every breath, and she angled her head for a better look. My reflection lingered in her eyes.

Rayhan urged Foresti forward, and the two animals fell into step near each other. Juniper seemed content to trek behind the much larger steed.

Rugged forest extended around us. The sun was only a quarter through the sky, but it already stirred warm air over my skin. Branches bounced as birds and squirrels and smaller creatures scurried here and there through the green canopy. It certainly wasn't the dry desert landscape that juniper trees loved.

"Do junipers grow here?" I couldn't contain my curiosity.

"Huh?" Rayhan twisted in the saddle, and his blue eyes cut across the sweeping tree line. "Ah. No, they don't, but Kadence's mother tried to make them grow. It was always too wet, too much rain, and too cold in the winter. They died."

"But?"

Rayhan shrugged. "Queen Cameron had a stubborn heart. She was convinced she could make those trees grow. I remember running through the dying garden with Kadence, and the queen would be bickering with the staff gardeners, persuading them to try a new tactic." Rayhan shook his head, but a hint of a smile curled his lips.

"What happened to her?" I asked. Everyone knew the queen had died when Kadence was a child. I also knew the witches hadn't succeeded in her death, despite years of attempts.

"She died." Rayhan's face darkened, and I knew he wouldn't say anything more.

The silence stretched between us, but it soon melted away under the beautiful summer day. The horses talked to each other as we walked, and twice Rayhan jerked the reins hard to keep Foresti from snacking on an undesirable plant. I swore the horse turned to me with laughing eyes after the second time and sidestepped, making the redhead on his back sway and swear.

Almost an hour into the ride, Rayhan curved left and Juniper followed. The trees ended, and we popped into an open field.

The meadow stretched long and thin, covered in ankle-high grass and peppered with wildflowers. A small stream meandered through the middle, creating a pleasant background sound to accompany the pitter-patter of tiny creatures singing their songs. Something swirled through the space, something ethereal and special. If my mother was here, she'd say the ground was alive and this would be the best place to collect herbs. It sure felt that way. The earth almost rolled around us, full of joy and glee for our visit.

"Here's good." Rayhan pulled the reins, and Foresti trotted several more steps before stopping. Sputtering under his breath, Rayhan dropped from the saddle and began to unload the heavy bags.

The leather had warmed during our ride, and the sun-kissed material brushed pleasantly against my skin. I eyed Rayhan's quick, confident motions as he untied the latches. My hands were slower, less agile, but the cargo fell anyway.

"I'll get that." The vampire freed the wooden easel from the horse and settled it on the grass. He loosened the strap around Juniper's belly and pulled the brindle from her mouth. "We'll let the horses graze. We'll be here a while."

While Rayhan rummaged through the bags, I spun in a slow circle. The white tips and yellow centers of chamomile peeked between long strands of common reed. I could picture Penelope walking through the field, plucking a strand to suck the sugar sweetness from the end while we went. I had seen our mother do the same thing while I followed behind as we harvested for our tonics.

A swell of homesickness knotted my chest. My eyes burned with tears I refused to let fall. My mother would have loved it here, but she would have wanted to be home with my father and Penelope much more.

"Alright, it's all set up." Rayhan's voice drew me back. While I'd been lost in thought, he'd constructed two easels, each holding a blank white canvas. They faced the dancing river and half-risen sun. He shook a glass jar of paint and scooped a generous helping of a rich orange color onto a flat plate. The dish was already full of thick rainbow colors, a spectrum of vividness painted onto transparent glass.

"What's this?" I angled closer to the easels, and the heavy smell of pigments wafted over me, strong yet oddly pleasant.

Rayhan capped the jar and dug two brushes from a bag. He pressed a brush into my palm, folded my fingers over the top, and cradled my hand softly in his.

"You're the only one who can help me find my father's killer." His voice was softer than his grip. "I need your magic."

"I don't—"

"Hush, girl. Let me finish."

I closed my mouth, impatience tapping at me.

"You said you can't use your magic. Spellwork's supposed to die when the witch dies—at least that's what they teach us on the battlefield. Beat the witch's head in before they can cast a spell, that's training day number one." He grimaced at the harshness of his words. "Sorry about that, but it's true. If your mother's dead, her spell should be too. Maybe if we can help you to control your magic, you'll be able to use it. And I need you to use it."

I held up the brush. "What's painting got to do with it?"

Rayhan shrugged. "I've been on the battlefield my whole life. I don't go anywhere without a weapon." He gestured to the axe settled head-down on the ground near his easel. "But painting takes a different type of discipline and endurance. It's more than color on paper. You have to see the vision, see the heart underneath it. Then you have to make others see it too."

His eyes went far and glassy, and for a moment, the ocean was calm. Then, an undercurrent rippled and spread, and he came back to me. "Painting has freed me from more than one nightmare. It might not free your magic, but it doesn't hurt to try."

My messed-up magic would need much more than an art tutorial, but I pressed my lips shut. There was a sparkle in his eyes that said this meant something to him.

"Alright." I heard my own voice. "I'll give it a try."

Rayhan's grin spread ear to ear and forced a smile to my own face. His smile made him look years younger and like he'd shrunk to a normal size. If painting let me see that look again, I would paint the vampire a hundred pictures.

"This is your canvas, and I put out some paints already."

"So what do I do?"

He swept a massive hand toward the peaceful landscape in front of us. "You paint."

"I paint this?" The sprawling meadow suddenly looked intense and daunting. I would never be able to replicate the reaching grasses and dainty flowers.

"Yep." Rayhan stepped to his canvas, positioned behind my right shoulder. The thick scratching of his brush pressed confident strokes into the material.

I swirled the handle between my fingers and studied the terrain. Green. There was a lot of green. Hmm, not the deep color spattered on the glass plate. I peeked into the box of capped paints, but no other shades of green were visible. Dark green, then. I sank the bristles into the bubble of pigment, and it covered the utensil in a thick goop.

"Your mother died." Rayhan's words caught me off guard. I paused the brush above the canvas.

"She did."

"How long ago?" More soft strokes settled beside me, just out of view of my peripheral vision.

"Seven years ago." But it felt like yesterday. I still remembered the blood cooling on my hands. Heard the useless chanting as my numb lips moved over and over again, even when she was too far gone for the strongest magic to bring back.

I streaked the green across the canvas, and it resembled an angry smear of dying grass. My chest tightened, and a wisp of regret ran through me. I shouldn't have tried this.

"How'd she pass?"

The question settled over me like a cold, winter night. It was different than when Ella asked, by the cozy fireside in her room. Rayhan's own pain was raw and on display. He wasn't gouging for information.

"I don't want to talk about it," I said.

"Come on, girl. You saw the cup that poisoned my dad. Surely, you can spare me a few words about your mother."

I dipped the brush in a light blue hue. The green paint blended into the new pigment, creating a crazed sky the color of decay.

"She was the only witch with a healing affinity outside the city walls. The rest worked in battlefield infirmaries." My words moved slower than my brushstrokes. "She got called out to the neighboring village late one night. A woman was sick after having a baby, and only magic could heal her at that point." I could hear the panting horses and the man's begging as my mother buttoned her heavy coat over her shoulders and hurried out the door. Penelope had turned her little body closer to me, searching for Mother's missing heat.

"There was a raid." My voice shrunk.

"Vampires?" Rayhan asked.

"Yes," I said. The weight of war was familiar between us. It touched everyone and everything, leaving only death and destruction behind. "They thought she was a soldier because she could heal. They stabbed her and fled. She'd been training me, so the village brought her to our house. Except..." Her blood seeped through my clothes, too cold to be so fresh. Her mouth moved, trying to stretch into a smile even as darker fluid slipped between her lips. I chanted and strained against my trapped magic, but it didn't help. "My magic was bound. She hadn't taught me real healing yet, only theory and history. It was probably too late before she even got to me, but I'll never know."

Rayhan remained silent.

Anger twisted around the guilt consuming me. The buzzing insects that previously contributed to the ambience of the field turned to a ruthless timer—sand through an hourglass. Their frantic sounds urged me to paint faster, better, but I didn't have the skills. I beat the brush into the canvas. The fabric stretched, but I didn't grant it a reprieve. Pain that had been trapped inside for so long demanded an escape, and the brush became my only weapon. The fabric turned into a blend of color until it resembled something dark and angry, and certainly not the peaceful meadow and rolling river.

Failure churned in my gut. I couldn't save my mother. I'd abandoned Penelope alone in a forest. My father only had days left of his medication. It was all my fault. I didn't deserve the sunshine in my hair or the serene nature tunes. A loyal daughter would have asked to return to the cell she belonged in.

My fist tightened, and the brush snapped in my hand. Wood shards dug into my flesh, and I dropped the remains to the grass at my feet.

"Hey now." Rayhan's steps crunched, and his strong arms wrapped me in a hug. My eyes remained dry. I'd cried so many tears for my mother that only the flushing anger lingered in my soul. His strength pressed around me, and for a moment, I was in the eye of the hurricane instead of being beaten by the winds.

"You have as much fault for your mother's death as I do for my dad's murder." His muscular chest heaved against me. "I wasn't even home when he died. I was on the field with Kadence. He tried to tell me something was wrong, but I brushed it off. I should have listened. I should have been there."

I had a thousand comforting words on the tip of my tongue, but I swallowed them away. This level of grief, of true and complete internal blame, didn't listen to logic. It only obeyed the dark, twisting seed of doubt and destruction, and every day was spent pressing that seed to be a little bit smaller.

Rayhan's head turned. He went still in my arms. "What's that?"

I followed his gaze to my messy canvas and grimaced. "It's a painting."

"It's a curse."

"It's art."

"It needs to be burnt." An edge of laughter tightened his throat and pulled us both away from the cliff of regret. "I don't know how you made it look so bad. Are we seeing the same meadow?"

"Well, let me see yours."

I wrestled from his grip and peeked at his canvas. The early smears of light green grasses and a thick layer of sky blue streaked across the fabric. The river was just a suggestion, blocky and rough, nestled between the beginning edge of foliage. It wasn't the shape of the field that caught my eye. Underneath the natural hues, something alive and wild moved through the image. Rayhan had captured the mood and soul, this place's essence, into the soft colors.

I pointed to a woman's shape off to the left. "Hey, there's nobody else in this meadow."

His brows arched and a tilted smile unfolded. "There is from where I'm standing."

I leaned in to study the figure. Her hair was honey-toned and rolled in gentle coils down her back. Her waist pinched slightly and flared over large hips. A harsh dash of bright pink clothes settled around her.

The same blinding pink of my borrowed dress.

A hot blush covered my cheeks. "Oh" was the only word my mouth would form.

"Come here." Rayhan plucked his brush, not broken into a thousand shards, and wiped the paint off on a used rag. Settling in front of my painting, he fixed the tool in my palm and wrapped his hands around mine. He raised his arm, and my hand followed.

"You have to mix the paint." He dipped our brush into the mixture, grabbed a bit of forest green, and dropped it into the white blob. He spun my fingers, and they swirled the pigment into a rich, bright green. He ran the bristles across the plate until a heavy layer clung to the tips.

"Try small, thick strokes." He lifted my hand to the canvas and set the brush to the cloth. The ugly mess turned to new promise under his touch. The forest green hid beneath the fresh color.

"It doesn't look like the same meadow though," I said.

Rayhan shrugged, his big shoulders moving around me. "It's not always about painting what you see," he said. "It's about capturing how it feels."

Rayhan dipped the brush again, and we settled into a rhythm. He was so warm and solid, and his chest pressed against me with each breath. Sea salt and evergreen wrapped in the hurricane winds whipping over us. I breathed it in, gasping for air, until lightheadedness made me feel drunk on Rayhan's scent. His grip on my fingers turned softer, a caress instead of a grasp, and I knew we were both drowning in each other.

Underneath the whirlwind of our bodies, desire stoked a smoldering flame in my core.

I pulled out of his palm, dropped the brush, and grabbed his wrist. His empty hand froze above the canvas, and he stilled.

Taking both of his hands, I led his grip around my waist. His arms shook, from fear or anticipation. I turned to face him and blindly searched for the hem of his tunic in his breeches. The fabric tugged free. His skin against my palms stoked the fire inside me, and the rest of my body ached for him.

"What are you doing, woman?" His voice sounded raw.

I stood on my tiptoes and pressed my lips against his. He was soft and firm at the same time. He froze, eyes wide, and a groan slipped from his mouth and into me. His hand found the back of my head and he kissed me, hard and raging and demanding. His tongue brushed against me, asking for more. I parted my lips, and the taste of spice and cinnamon flowed into me.

Rough, calloused hands skimmed the tender place on my back, igniting a thousand tingles down my spine. My dress bunched at my waist, exposing my bare skin to the empty field, and I didn't care. Rayhan against me was everything right in the world.

I broke the kiss, thirsty for air, and reached for the buttons on Rayhan's shirt. My shaking fingers couldn't persuade them from the tiny holes. The vampire growled and pulled the garment over his head.

Rayhan's skin gleamed in the afternoon sun. His muscles stretched taut and sculpted. A hint of freckles grazed the tops of his shoulders, probably from training in the sunshine. His arms were particularly impressive, lined with thick indents that developed only after years of physical combat. His nose was long and flat, his cheeks wide and high, and laugh lines cut through his forehead. The expanse of the ocean roared in his blue eyes, and all that wild energy focused on me.

I was washed aglow in the light of his gaze.

I pulled the dress over my head, exposing the nude underwear and chest wrap underneath. They weren't pretty or special, but Rayhan's hungry stare rolled over me like a touch against my skin. He pressed one hand to his jaw, but no words escaped his gaping mouth.

His belt buckle was cold as I wrapped my fingers around the metal and tugged the leather from the clasp.

Two strong hands stilled mine. "Hold on." Rayhan's voice shook.

I pulled against the belt again, and a tremor caught the man's body.

"Natalie, stop for a minute."

I didn't want to stop. Fire twisted into a tornado through my soul, and it longed for chaos. It longed for Rayhan.

"Stop, girl, listen to me. I have something to tell you." His tone turned stern. I abandoned the clasp, disappointment painted across my face, but his eyes were shut.

"What?" The word broke through the longing in my heart, a fist through a canvas picture.

"We need to stop. It's not right." He grabbed my forearms, pressing them against my side.

My throat closed as my mind processed his words. The sharp stab of rejection buried into my chest and snuffed out the fire more completely than a bucket of water. The tears I couldn't find earlier filled my eyes, sudden and cold.

"Hey." Rayhan bent to look at my face, but I turned away. "What's this?"

He didn't want me. Embarrassment warmed my cheeks. Why would the vampire want to be with a witch, his sworn enemy? He'd be more comfortable killing me. The thought looped a thick knot in my throat.

"Stop whatever nonsense is going on in that brain of yours, girl." His eyes roamed my body once more, then he pressed them shut. "Of course I want you. You've got me wound tighter than weaver's yarn. But it wouldn't be right, to be with you now."

"What do you mean?" I pulled from his grasp, and he let me go with a pained expression. I plucked my dress from the ground and tugged it over my head. The cloth hugged me like a layer of body armor.

"I mean, you're a prisoner and I dragged you here with selfish intentions, but not *those* kinds of intentions." He scratched his naked back, pulling his stomach nice and tight, and I tried not to follow the movements. "It wouldn't be right for me to take advantage of you while you're technically my captive."

My heart dropped.

"That's all I'll ever be," I whispered. I knew our original deal was done. I had lied and cheated my way into the agreement, and it was never valid. It would be impossible for me to discover Manveer's killer before my father's tonic ran out.

"Well, I've been thinking about that, and if you'd listen to me, I've made a decision." He snatched my hand and pressed my palm to his chest. His heart beat a rhythm against me. "How much medicine does your father have left?"

"A week, probably."

"It's a three-day journey to your village, but we can do it in two if we ride fast. That gives you four more days."

"I don't understand."

"If you don't find my father's killer in four days, I'm taking you home anyway. I shouldn't have brought you here, and I need to make it right."

A shimmer of hope bubbled in my chest and expanded through me.

"You'd let me go home?" I couldn't hide the shred of disbelief from my tone.

Rayhan nodded. "I'd take you there myself."

I clutched at his hands, dragging them to my lips. I pressed kisses against his fingers, too lost in joy to remember his earlier statement. He groaned and closed his eyes, but I caught a flash of silver first.

"Look, girl, stop that." He untangled his grip from mine and took a step away. "Once you're home, maybe if you still want to see me again, we can figure something out. In secret."

"You'd come back? To visit?" I tried to picture the giant in my cabin, perched on the couch between Father and Penelope, and I smothered a laugh.

"If you'd want, and it'd have to be a secret. I don't need one of your people to try to kill me. Murdering your village would probably put a damper on the mood."

I laughed again, and a weight I'd buried in my gut started to lighten. My father would be okay. I would be home before his medicine ran out. I flung myself into Rayhan's arms, and the vampire nestled his head into my neck and took a deep breath.

"Alright." His words faded into my hair and tickled my skin. "Now, let's finish this painting before it summons the devil himself."

CHAPTER SEVENTEEN

The sun set long before we steered our horses onto the trail toward the castle. The ride back remained quiet, from exhaustion at the late hour and to avoid attracting Suos. Despite the reassurance Rayhan's axe brought, I didn't need any more Suo-related nightmares.

"Let's go through the city." Rayhan twisted Foresti's reins, and Juniper followed. "It's beautiful this time of night."

An edge of fear rubbed over me at the thought of waltzing through a town full of vampires. The fear conjured Zhao's face, red and pinched with anger, as he dug his teeth into me. Rayhan swayed easily on his horse, and the giant axe over his shoulder settled my nerves. There was something strong between us, the promise of a future.

We approached the city wall, and voices from the other side crested the cool night air. The sounds of clanking plates and pleasant chatter made me think we neared an eatery or tavern. My mouth watered at the scent of roasted meat and the bitter tang of baked root vegetables mingled behind it. Soft clip-clops of horse hooves stepped on cobblestone streets, followed by the crunch of wagon wheels. Torches lined the top of the wall in even intervals, casting light onto our path.

The main gate stretched higher than the rest of the structure. I hadn't been to the large city in Ededen, my own kingdom, very often. Occasionally, we had a rough harvest and I had to barter in the market for herbs and tonics, but the hustle and bustle of city life was foreign to me. Our walls were taller than these ones, which extended barely a head higher than me. The gate was made from crisscrossed iron bars similar to my cell doors, except these were pulled open and a pair of armored guards leaned against the doorway.

One man with dark skin and darker hair did a double take.

"Sir!" He snapped to attention. His partner's face twisted, then flashed with recognition and he straightened as well.

"At ease, men." Rayhan lifted his hand and led us through the iron gate.

The guards remained motionless until we passed, but I looked back and their gazes locked on our figures, mouths open. This was how rumors started. The rumor of Rayhan frolicking through the night with a mystery woman would spread like a disease through the troops.

I turned, words of concern in my mouth, but the city sprawled before us stole my breath.

The buildings were tall. Too tall. Impossibly tall. They stretched on both sides and almost pressed against the narrow street. These were several floors taller than any building in Ededen. Even more impressive than the height were the rainbow colors scrawled across the exteriors. The town could have been a tapestry, created only by the finest weaver, colored with fresh dye mixed by generations of life. A few buildings switched colors halfway up the structure, as though an artist had run out of paint and was forced to improvise.

Rayhan caught the look on my face, and a smug smile pulled his lips up.

The structures opened suddenly, and a brilliant little park greeted us. Several families were taking advantage of the cool night, and children screamed as they sprinted through the grass. Tiny bodies filled a rugged wooden climbing tower. Parents clustered in groups, passing mugs and nibbling off plates of food. An undertone of contentment shifted across the scene. The people here, although hundreds of years into the normality of war, hadn't stopped living. Thriving in hardship meant stealing joy in any way one could find it.

"Are you coming?" Rayhan asked. He'd trekked several feet in front of me.

"Oh yes." I hadn't realized I was pulling Juniper's reins, and the mare had paused at the edge of the park. I released the leather straps, and the horse shook her head, then trotted forward. I ran my fingers along her neck in a silent apology, and her ears flicked.

Turning to keep the park in view a moment longer, a shadowed figure half hidden inside the tree line caught my eye. It was a man, average height but bulky. He didn't watch the children or the families. Instead, he watched us as we slowly walked down the road. Something flashed under his face. His eyes turned to dark slits, and a set of reptilian scales peppered his skin. My heart jerked.

"Rayhan, who's that?"

He followed my pointing finger and squinted. "I don't see anything," he said.

I did a double take. The man was gone.

Rayhan eyed me up and down. "We need to get you some food. You're starting to hallucinate again."

My growling stomach didn't give me room to protest, but I knew the stranger had been real. An unsettled feeling churned in my gut.

The city ended, and we walked about half a mile along a cobblestone path before the main doors of the castle spread in front of us. We went around to the stables, and Rayhan unloaded the horses. He handed me a brush, and I combed Juniper's fine hair while she huffed contentedly. Rayhan led the animals to their stalls, and they turned to their piles of hay, already forgetting us.

The promise of food drove us up the castle steps and around the formal dining room toward Rayhan's suites. He didn't think it was wise for me to dine with the vampires, and I agreed.

We rounded the corner of the hall, and Maverick jumped from a red velvet chair, blocking Rayhan's path.

"There you are!" she said. "I've been looking for you for hours."

"I'm right here, Mom." Rayhan crossed his arms. "What do you want?"

"Me?" She pointed to her chest and rolled her eyes. "*I* don't want you. The council designated everyone who knows your name to go look for you."

Rayhan's red brows pinched. "What does the council want?"

"Kadence is due back tomorrow," Maverick said. "They need you to advise on preparations."

The blood rushed from my head at the king's name, and dizziness overwhelmed me. Even Rayhan's lips tightened at the mention of his best friend's return.

"Madeline is all hard-pressed about it too. She personally searched the dungeon, expecting to find you there visiting Natalie. She almost exploded when she learned Natalie was missing too." A smile slid up Maverick's face. "It was real funny, actually."

Rayhan sighed. "Fine. Let me drop Natalie off at my room, then I'll go to the council chamber."

"I can do it." Maverick must have heard her rushed words. Her next sentence was slower, careful. "I can take Natalie back."

Rayhan's expression flattened. "Why?"

"Do I need a reason? I like the girl. I can walk her to the end of the hall."

"What are you planning, Mother?"

"Planning?" Maverick beat her eyelids a little too hard. "Can't a mother just take her son's captive enemy safely to his room to lock her inside? Can't it just be because I love you?"

"No," he said.

Maverick narrowed her eyes. "Rayhan, the council has been looking for you for hours. Madeline is pissed. I've been in battle well before you were born, and I think I can manage getting this little witch to her room safe and sound. I can't say the same for you if Madeline finds you chatting in this hallway."

Rayhan let out a puff of air and looked at the ceiling as he took a deep breath. "Fine," he said. "But I don't like it."

"Wonderful!" Maverick snatched my palm and looped it through her arm. “We’ll see you in a bit. Although, apparently Kadence is right mad, so it’ll probably be a long meeting.”

“Mother.” Rayhan’s voice carried a growl. “Make sure you lock the door.”

“Of course, dear.” Maverick waved her other hand as we turned.

Her body stilled next to mine, and she dragged me to a halt. She tilted her ear toward the hall we’d just vacated. After a moment, Rayhan’s heavy footsteps pounded on the stone floors, then faded.

Maverick smiled. “Good. I didn’t think he’d actually leave you with me. Come on, we really do have to go to his room. I stashed some stuff there.”

“What are we doing?” I asked as Maverick dragged me toward Rayhan’s door. My much shorter legs struggled to match her stride.

“I told you I might have a way to heal your father.” She turned the key in the lock, and the door snapped open. “This is the perfect time to go look.”

Maverick disappeared into the dark room and returned with a satchel flung over one shoulder and a heavy bag on her left arm. Two wooden handles peeked through the top, but the tools were obscured inside.

I reached for the bag, but Maverick pulled it away from me. “Nonsense, dear, I’m a vampire. This is barely a feather. You can get the door though.”

It settled in the frame.

“Here’s the key too. Rayhan said to lock the door. He didn’t say anything about you being inside.” Maverick’s low chuckle vibrated through my arm where it rested against her. I twisted the metal key in the lock. “Now let’s go before anyone else shows up. Oh hell, we’re already too late.”

Silence spanned for several seconds, then dainty footsteps rounded the corner. Ella’s womanly shape strode through the hall, almost floating on the polished stones with her silk shoes. Her navy blue dress brushed the floor, and she had the spine of a book pressed open in one hand. Our shadows crossed over her path, and she froze.

Ella studied Maverick, and a look spread across her face as though she’d just tasted something sour.

"Maverick." Her glare tried to cut the other woman. "I hadn't heard you were back. What are you doing?"

Maverick squared her shoulders, barely noticing the weight she carried.

"Ella." False warmth ran through the word. "It's a pleasure to see you, as always. What brings you to this side of the castle? I thought the animals slept outside."

"Yes, and I thought the trash would be burned, but alas, here you are." Ella glanced at me, and her eyes widened like she hadn't noticed me before. "What are you doing with Natalie? Where's Rayhan?"

Ella raised her hand as though she'd reach for me, but Maverick jerked me back.

"I don't owe you any answers, Barton," Maverick snapped.

"It's Mrs. Whylde to you." Ella's face darkened.

"Manveer's dead. There is no Mrs. Whylde anymore."

Ella pressed her lips and examined the bags on Maverick's shoulders. She squinted, then widened her eyes in surprise.

"You're taking her to the catacombs." It wasn't a question, though she spoke it like one. "You can't. It's forbidden."

Maverick stepped around the woman, dragging me in her wake. Rayhan had stopped Nadeem from talking about the catacombs, so there was something he didn't want me to see. Although waltzing through a room of ancient dead bodies set a layer of dread over me, I suddenly wanted to go very badly.

"Look, Ella, we could do this all night, but I don't want to," Maverick said. We passed the woman, and she swiveled on her heels to keep us in sight but made no move to stop us. I'd seen the harsh line of a slim blade pressed against Maverick's side. I had no doubts Ella knew she was armed as well.

We rounded the corner, and Ella disappeared.

"That woman," Maverick said. "Manveer could have had the pick of the lot, but I don't know how he found that one."

"He wanted to marry you." Biting curiosity pulled the words from my mouth. Maverick didn't waver in her steps or ask how I knew that.

"Yes, he wished to get married." She shook her head, and her short, golden tendrils fluttered around. Some aromatic spice drifted toward me. "Could you imagine me as a wife? No, it was never my path. I'd rather make my own aisle of bodies on the battlefield than walk down a silk-lined one. And oh, I have made aisles. I have walked down grasses drenched in blood as headless bodies marked my steps."

An eerie light illuminated her face, and Maverick half-closed her eyes as though drunk. I had an urge to pull my hand from her arm, but I worried movement would remind her of my presence. My heart thundered in my ears, and I tried to steady it.

She blinked those round eyes and came back from her memories.

"Oh, I did it again. Sorry about that. The battle, it just calls to me sometimes." She awkwardly patted my arm. I could picture her with a young Rayhan, trying to comfort him but unable to find the right words. I could see his little eyes staring up at her as though she were his whole world, anyway.

We tumbled down the winding staircases until we reached the floor with Nadeem's old laboratory. Boxes stacked on the tables, overfilled with equipment, but the room was clean. A hollow feeling settled in my chest. I wanted to see Nadeem rolling through the lab and tending to rows of beakers full of mystery liquid. Instead, it was a gaping hole, dark and empty.

A sign pointed us toward the morgue, and Maverick led us that way. My feet tried to object, but I pushed them along. Even the chance that something down here may help my father was worth finding.

We passed the leather couches and went down the squished hallway at the back of the room. After several steps, a cutaway revealed a simple, gray, iron door. The other end stopped abruptly at a rock wall.

"Here we are." Maverick finally dropped my hand, and I wiped my palm on my dress.

I expected her to go to the metal door, but she ventured to the dead end and ran her hands along the ragged stones. These ones looked different from the rest of the castle walls. Darker and wider, they appeared old and waterlogged. A musty smell eased around them, the subtle scent of still liquid.

"I know it's one of these. Come here, help me find it." Maverick waved me over, and I dragged my feet to the wall.

The rocks were slightly damp, and the liquid left a slimy residue, oily and tinted green, on my skin. I crinkled my nose.

"What am I looking for?" Despite the unpleasant texture, the stones didn't look particularly interesting.

"There's a latch under one of these." Maverick's tongue poked between her teeth as she concentrated. Her fingers wrapped beneath the uneven surface of a stone, then disappeared into an invisible crevice. "Here it is!"

Something mechanical clicked between the rocks. Maverick groaned as she pushed the door open, and it swung into a darkened chamber.

"Here you go." She tossed a lantern into my hands, and I fumbled with the glass contraption. Oil splashed inside, but didn't spill. Maverick's light shimmered a soft glow across her impatient face as she waited for me to ignite mine.

I spun the knob on the lantern, and the flint rubbed against the starting paper. Sparks lit the oil, and a bright light twisted around us.

"After you." Maverick swept her hand into the depths of the catacombs.

My throat bobbed as I swallowed. The scent of stale water strengthened, and liquid dripped steadily in the background. A breeze that shouldn't exist this far underground drifted over me, cutting through the shift dress and chilling me to the core. I bit my lip and mentally grounded my feet so I wouldn't turn and run away.

If something in there could help my father, I had to look.

My mind didn't quite believe me.

I stepped through the doorway and lifted the lantern.

The narrow hallway continued. The stones were flat and thin, more bricklike than raw rock. My steps echoed, telling me a greater opening waited ahead. Each step I took toward the catacombs made me surer I wanted to turn around. My heart thundered, and my senses were on high alert. Every splash of water and whisper of cool breeze triggered a fresh shot of adrenaline.

The hallway launched us into an expanse of darkness. The lantern light surrounded me.

The room was round, and a wide column stretched straight through the middle. Offshoots of more hallways sprouted from the circle, each titled with a wooden sign in a language I didn't know. The floor was flat, unpolished marble, which made me think this space had once been a prestigious place. A ballroom perhaps, or a throne room.

The creepiest throne room ever.

Bones lined every surface. Empty skulls stared at me from all angles. They peered from the center column, lining the walls, even looking straight down from the ceiling. Some skulls were turned backward, their sockets forced to stare at a dark wall for eternity. Other bones, long and wide, filled the gaps between skulls. Smaller ones, like fingers and toes, were absent. The pieces were assembled so randomly, it would be impossible for whole bodies to remain together. They had been haphazardly tossed about until no space remained.

A presence swirled around the bones. A new scent arose, sweet and vanilla, and beckoned me closer. It felt warm and familiar, and I couldn't deny its call.

Magic.

Heavy magic twisted over me, rubbing along my skin. It wasn't magic the way I was used to it—the spark of life nestled in another witch's soul. This was fertile and wild and hungry.

I walked to the middle column, and one skull called to me. It faced backward, and the bone had that unhealthy look of aged paper, the kind that would crumble once touched.

My fingers lifted. I couldn't help myself. I had to know how it felt.

It was surprisingly soft and smooth. I caressed the remains and ran my fingertips along the tight ridge of the fused plates. Magic whispered through me, and some of it pushed into the skull under my palm. Tiny symbols etched into the bone suddenly illuminated with vibrant green light. The light strengthened, almost blinding, but I didn't cover my eyes.

The symbols looked familiar. I'd studied similar ones in my mother's spellbooks for years.

"It's a spell." I cupped my hands around the skull. "There's a spell engraved on this skull. It's a protection spell."

"Honey." Maverick's voice broke through the crystalline magic, and the green glow softened. "Look around."

I dragged my gaze from the object to study the cavern.

Every single bone illuminated green symbols. The dancing light filled the space, casting us into a soft, glowing cavern. The shapes shimmered and shined through their bone encasement, singing a melody just for me.

"What is this place?"

"Look." Maverick pulled a second skull from the wall. Something sharp sliced through my chest. The magic didn't like her plucking its spells.

She turned the head, and it took a minute to put the pieces together.

"It's a vampire skull," I said. Two pointy fangs frozen forever in the deceased's bones. More symbols etched into its surface. I scanned the walls and more skulls wore immortalized fangs, but many did not.

"Why are witches and vampires both buried here?" We didn't even bury our dead together on the battlefield. The vampires snatched bodies away before we could count casualties.

"We weren't always at war." Maverick settled the remains back into the wall, and the magic sang happily. "For hundreds of years, witches and vampires lived in peace in this castle. When one of us died, we immortalized their life with a new spell. This room is the largest spellbook ever made, locked away from where any witches will find it."

"We've only been at war for two hundred years." I tried to count the bones in the room, but there were too many. "The number of bodies here..."

"The war is new." Maverick's eyes sparkled with a long ago past. "Before then, there was peace and harmony."

"What happened?" I asked. "What led to us slaughtering each other?"

Maverick shrugged, but something locked her spine stick straight. "They say the witch queen went mad one day, just before her wedding to the vampire king. She killed him in their wedding bed, and the witches fled in the night." Maverick closed her eyes and swayed back and forth, listening to imaginary music. "Longing for revenge and answers, the vampires chased them. That was the first battle, and the worst. We lost half our people that day."

"We-were you alive then?" I couldn't wrap my mind around the numbers. If Maverick had been alive at the start of the war, she was well over two hundred years old. Her flushed skin was smooth and flawless. Her eyes glistened with a youthful glow. It was impossible.

She smiled and shrugged. "I've lived a long life. Sometimes it's hard to remember what's memory and what's a story you've heard one too many times." She looked around the room, but a weight blanketed her shoulders. Something in that past was heavy. "They want to get rid of this place, to bury these bones forever."

The thought of this knowledge disappearing hurt my heart.

"Why?"

"The water table has risen in the past few years. Apparently, it's a 'flood risk.'" She made air quotes around the words. "And it could 'collapse at any moment.' Since the rest of the castle is built on top of these, I guess there's some concern for its stability."

"There would be so much magic lost."

"They say that's a good thing. It would be dangerous for us if the witches ever found this place. Come on, I think the hallway we're looking for is over here. Just a warning, it gets spookier."

Maverick gestured to one offshoot from the circular room. The green glow spread through the little halls as well. I brought the lantern, although I didn't need it anymore.

I followed Maverick to the hall, and it immediately got spookier. Instead of the smooth, gray stones that lined the entrance to the main room, tombs covered this hall. Nestled between slabs of rock, panels of glass afforded a peek into skeletal remains, each bearing those enchanted spells. These bodies weren't random assortments of bones tucked into an artful display. They were carefully pieced together to form whole people.

One man lounged by himself, both arms raised above his head and his withered feet crossed, symbols and runes dancing from every bone. Even the tiny finger and toe bones were wound tightly with an invisible adhesive, or possibly magic. In another tomb, two faces peeked through the glass, the large skull of a grown adult and the daintier shape of a child. My chest tightened as I stared into the much too small eye sockets and mourned for a life lost early.

Relief covered me when we emerged from the hallway, and I didn't look back. I had a terrible feeling that the skulls may have turned to follow my path.

The next room was smaller than the circular entry and formed an almost perfect square. A second hallway branched deeper into the catacombs, and I hoped we wouldn't have to go that way. Bones and skulls lined the walls, but there was something more organized about them. These remains weren't placed for awe and decor. They were sorted by spellwork.

Maverick set her lantern down and grabbed one of the wooden handles from her bag. She tugged out a thick-headed pickaxe and handed it to me. My fingers curled around the sanded wood.

"Sometimes the bones have to be persuaded to come out," she said.

"What do you mean?" I creased my brows.

"These are all healing spells," she said. "If you see anything that might help your dad, you can chisel it from the wall to take with you."

The catacomb's magic twisted bitterly at Maverick's words. It was a collective expression from the years and years of spellwork stored here, but without a witch to wield it, it couldn't touch her.

"You think there's a spell here that can heal my dad?" I craned my neck to see the whole room. Thousands of bones glowed around me. It would require years to look over them all. "I can't understand the symbols."

"I thought witches studied stuff like this." Maverick ran her finger along the edge of one spell carved deep into a femur. "This cures bunions. Don't suppose that's your father's problem?"

I shook my head.

"Yeah, that seemed too simple." She turned to the next, a long, thin bone I didn't recognize. "This one helps with ailments of the gut. How's that sound?"

"No. He has an autoimmune disease. It inflames the rest of his organs and makes him weak."

Maverick pushed it back into place. "You can't read any of these?"

I gingerly pulled a bone from the wall. The smooth surface slipped through my fingers like dry paper. Symbols shimmered underneath, and the magic twirled over my hand.

"I recognize some." One curly rune represented cleansing or a new creation. It was likely some kind of disinfectant spell. It sat beside a boxy shape, with three dots spaced on top. I didn't know what it disinfected. "But not all of them."

"We can look through the bones, but it might have to come from your gut." Maverick settled her fist in the center of her chest. "It's going to have to be something you feel."

I placed the bone back into its spot and pulled another one out. I waited for my gut to tell me something, but it felt melancholy and perhaps a bit apprehensive about its calling. I had little faith in it anyway. It had yet to steer me in the right direction.

A thud banged from the circular room. I froze, my hand half-gripping the front of another skull, and strained to listen.

"What was that?"

"Huh?" Maverick turned from the bones in her hands and looked around. She shrugged. "I don't hear anything."

A new sound scurried across the floor. The soft chime of glass on stone followed by a simple, sudden spark of a match to paper.

The orb rolled to a stop by my feet. One of Nadeem's smoke bombs, but the match hadn't lit the accelerant yet. Clear liquid pooled at the bottom, not the black tar of an original bomb, but the kind that contained aerosol poison.

If the match ignited the poison, it would kill both of us.

I smashed my foot into the glass ball. The brittle orb broke, and thick shards shot through the soles of my slippers and into my skin. The sharp pain radiated up my nerves and drew tears from my eyes.

A shadow darted through the hallway, two blue-gold chains following her wake.

"Maverick!"

Both Maverick's and the attacker's heads swiveled toward me. The assassin altered her steps, and blue ropes swung my way.

Maverick jumped in front of me and blocked the coils with one arm. The ropes wrapped hungrily around her, and lightning burrowed into her skin, but the woman didn't flinch except for a locked jaw. She ran her other hand over the rope, and tendrils of lightning flicked to taste her.

"Interesting," she said. Maverick squinted at the assailant and jerked her arm back. The rope flung from the attacker's grip. The current died, and the weapon puddled on the damp ground.

The attacker whipped her second rope and studied Maverick's body through small slits in her mask.

"I think she's after you," Maverick said to me, and pulled a long, thin blade from the holster hidden at her waist. She twisted the weapon, and it turned to a steady, silver blur. I was glad she was on my side.

"Yeah," I said. "It's been happening."

"You will both die." The assassin's words came out rough and ragged. It wasn't her real voice, but was laced with a deep growl.

The woman attacked. She flung her rope whip at Maverick's face. Maverick raised her blade, and the weapons collided. Sparkes flew with an electric sizzle, momentarily flooding the cavern with blue light.

Maverick didn't give her opponent an opportunity to recover. She lunged, stepping in for a closer reach, and slashed across the woman's body. The attacker backstepped and sent a punch toward Maverick's face, which she dodged easily.

The two circled each other, then the blinding flash of the whip struck again, this time wrapping around Maverick's leg. The blue current flared stronger, and Maverick yelled sharply. She slashed at her opponent, and dark blood dripped from the knife. The attacker scurried away, one hand pressed to her chest.

"That's right." Maverick turned a bit slower as she favored a leg. "You might have that handy toy on your side, but I have decades more experience."

I couldn't see the attacker's face through her mask, but I thought her cheeks tightened in a smile.

The whip flashed again, too fast to track until it coiled around Maverick's blade. The woman drew her rope back, and the knife flung to the ground behind her. It skidded to a halt in the skeleton hallway.

Maverick swayed on her feet for a moment and blinked at the missing weapon. "Alright then." She turned to me, brows arched. "We should probably run."

Adrenaline pulsed through my mind, thinking through fight-or-flight options. It crashed against my magic, straining at the locked bars, but my mother's spell didn't budge.

I ran. The glass shards embedded deeper into my foot with every step. Hot blood slickened my toes, but the adrenaline didn't let me focus on the pain. I considered dropping the pickaxe to cut some weight, but without Maverick's blade, it was the only weapon we had.

We darted through a second hallway, with more skeletons smiling through glass panels. I swore their bony necks moved as I ran past.

The attacker's whip flicked, and blue-gold light flashed in front of me. Her rope smashed into a glass pane. The window shattered, and old, brittle bones fell on top of me. Chunks of dead skin and coils of dry hair dropped across my face. The scent of gauze and decay overwhelmed me.

I screamed. The sound filled the small space and echoed until my scream repeated a million times around us.

I flung the remains to the ground and tried to match Maverick's pace.

We split from the hallway into a new cavern. The whip flashed again. A blanket of skulls and shattered bones rained over our heads. My throat turned raw from screaming, but somehow my lungs found breath for another.

"Here!" Maverick grabbed my arm and jerked me to the right, just as the flash of the whip whirled past my ear. She dragged me into a shallow crevice cut into the wall, almost invisible from outside.

"This passage will lead to a larger room," Maverick said. I didn't ask how she knew. "But that room's a dead end. We have to hope she doesn't see us, or we'll fight her there."

I swallowed around the lump in my throat and the swell of bile that burned my chest. I remembered the paralyzing current of the lightning whip through my body. It made the glass in my foot feel like a lovely massage. I couldn't face it again.

We pressed through the passage. Rough stones cut at my arms, and I had to empty my lungs to squeeze through. Then it opened into a wider space, although it was generous to call it a room. The ceiling scraped the top of my head and forced Maverick to hunch down. More bones covered every surface.

A shadow flicked by the opening. We both held our breath.

It passed again and again.

She was looking for us.

I willed my pounding heart to settle. I drew silent, shallow breaths to fill my lungs. They screamed for more air, but I didn't dare. If she was a vampire, her hearing would far surpass my own.

The shadow disappeared, and the clean, green glow returned.

I finally took a deep breath.

The attacker's cloaked face appeared in the crack. I jumped and backpedaled until bones poked against my back.

The woman's head tilted. She examined the crevice and stuck one hand inside. An eerie, feminine chuckle escaped behind the black mask, and she turned. Her footsteps echoed away from us, unconcerned if we heard her anymore.

That couldn't be good.

"Is she going to wait for us to come out?" I asked. I hadn't considered that we'd be the ones trapped in here if she didn't pursue us.

Maverick's eyes became dark and broody. "I don't think so," she said.

A loud crash vibrated through the chamber. Something rattled under my feet. The catacomb's magic whispered a warning for me, but I couldn't understand it.

"What's she doing?" I asked.

Maverick shook her head.

Another crash. Bones above me banged together, and one skull fell from the ceiling. It spattered to the ground and landed upward, its gaping, empty eyes staring at me. A current of water billowed around the bone.

"Uh, Maverick." Panic tightened my throat, and I forced the words out. "Look!"

The water flowed faster, deeper. More liquid poured through the crevice. Another hard bang rattled our hiding spot.

"She's a madman!" Maverick said. "She's rupturing the water table. She's going to drown us. We've got to get out of here."

We both lunged for the narrow exit, and I slipped in first. I managed two steps, and the attacker appeared again.

I froze.

Her shadow disappeared, but she dragged something large and heavy behind her. She settled it over the entrance of the crevice with a groan. The green light of the adjoining room faded.

"She blocked the exit," I said. Water swelled around the blockage, squeezing through minuscule gaps.

We were going to drown.

"Let me try."

Maverick and I switched places. The cold water crested the tops of my shoes and flowed to my ankles. It settled the aching cuts. I might die, but at least my feet would feel better.

Maverick groaned, but the obstruction remained. "She reinforced it." Maverick's voice was flat. "We're trapped."

The sinking feeling in the bottom of my chest had less to do with the water creeping in my shoes and more with the realization that our air would not last very long.

"Where are we in relation to the castle? Is there another crevice we can go through?" I asked.

"We're right below the dungeons. And no. This way is a dead end."

"You're sure?"

Maverick slipped out of the gap. Her shoulders were squared, and a calm look settled across her face. She'd reached my same conclusions but was having a much more relaxed reaction.

"I'm sure. I've been exploring these tunnels well before you were alive."

Water churned up my knees, soaking the hem of my dress. My wool socks would keep my feet warm, but the cotton fabric would lower my body temperature quickly. It was a strange thought—that I might be cold when I drowned—but I couldn't stop the question from spinning through my mind. I should have asked for a wool dress to match the socks.

My pounding heart slowed. There was no reason to keep pumping adrenaline. My brain had analyzed the situation and determined the result, even as disbelief settled in the hollow space at the base of my chest.

Behind it all, something else pulled at me.

The water sloshed to my hips. Each inch it climbed introduced a new thought.

I would never see my father or Penelope again. Father would die quickly without his medicine, and Penelope would be alone in the world. I would never see Rayhan again. No. It was too much to bear. I didn't even remember the last words I'd spoken to him.

Cold crept up my waist. I gasped as water brushed the sensitive skin my on belly.

Maybe I would see my mother though. I hoped that would bring some comfort to my freezing limbs, but I knew it was an empty hope. Wherever my mother went, whatever afterlife she was given, I wouldn't be in the same place. My mistakes, the blood on my hands, were too great to let me in.

There. That same pull again. Like someone pinched me, not hard, but enough to be annoying. I rubbed my arms. The flowing water appeared clean and clear. Nothing floating in the depths could pinch me.

Pinch. Ouch. The skin on my left arm tingled.

"What's wrong?" Maverick asked.

"Nothing."

Pinch. To the left again. I arched my head, twisting to look above us. Skulls and bones shimmered their green light. Maverick looked calm and peaceful as her clothes swirled in the icy water.

Pinch.

I stepped left again, and heavy magic twisted around me. It brushed against my own trapped power and pulled at it. The box remained locked tight, but the tendrils recognized each other.

Wisps of my magic swept over the ancient bones and settled on one old, brittle skull, smiling down at me without a bottom jaw.

"You seem to have something else on your mind besides your impending death." Maverick tilted her head and followed my gaze.

"I think my gut is telling me something."

"Unless your gut has a way to drain this water or make a wall explode, it's a bit late."

The liquid gathered along the tops of my shoulders. The cold weighed my arms down as the muscles protested each motion. I stretched onto my tiptoes and wrapped my fingers through the empty eye sockets. The skull didn't budge.

"I don't think it wants to come down." Maverick waded to me. She grabbed the bone and pulled, but even her vampire strength could not persuade it from its tomb.

The panic leaked from my chest as the water crept along the bottom of my neck. The catacomb's magic wrapped around me and dragged me to a different place, a different time. *The brush of new silk on my skin from a dress I didn't own. The scent of wildflowers and fresh rain as I walked through a blooming garden. My hands on a dying man and an unfamiliar chant on my lips as I healed him. The feel of hot blood and a knife twisting through another man's chest.*

I had to have that skull.

I had almost forgotten the pickaxe in my numb fingers. The water pushed against me as I heaved the tool over my head. I dug the tip into the mortar above the skull. Pieces of stone broke apart, but the bone remained.

I hammered at it again. Water brushed my chin and slowed my swings. The axe ground into the rock, and the skull wavered.

A smile slipped on my lips, unbeckoned and unwelcome.

"You are terrifying." Maverick didn't look at the green, glowing skull or the rising water level with her chin. She focused on my face, and she flinched away from me.

She didn't know the half of it.

I heaved the axe into the mortar again and the skull fell from the ceiling. I caught it in one hand, dropping the pickaxe in exchange.

The fragile bone shimmered in my palms. I didn't recognize the words etched into the remains, but magic swirled hungrily around me.

This was the spell I was looking for. This could heal my father. I knew it.

The water pushed against my mouth, beating against my pressed lips. I had the spell, and it would die with me in the catacombs, lost and forgotten forever. Laughter bubbled in my chest. It was right and fitting. It was what I deserved.

A brush of warmth ran over my face. Maverick gasped.

A sliver of open air sat in the hollow where the skull used to be.

"It's a false ceiling!" Maverick said. "There's a room above it." She eyed my hands, which gripped the bone like the last match in a frozen wasteland. "Where's the pickaxe?"

"I dropped it."

Maverick rolled her eyes, drew a breath, and plunged into the depths.

The liquid crept into my nose. I angled my head up and pushed onto my tiptoes. In a moment, I would be treading water and then....

Then I would drown.

"Got it!" Maverick surfaced as the liquid ran over the top of my face. I sucked down one ragged breath, half full of water, and forced my eyes open despite the chill.

Maverick hammered away at the hole in the ceiling. The water resistance didn't seem to slow her down as she chipped at the remains and mortar above us. Bones split under her pickaxe and slowly sunk to the floor. Years of spells shattered in a desperate moment.

My lungs ached. The fluid I'd caught with my final breath threatened to make me cough, then it would be over. My heart pounded faster, using up the last of my oxygen. Bile burned the back of my throat.

I clutched the skull tighter to my chest.

Maverick dropped the axe. Her face appeared flat and calm, as though she didn't even need air. Maybe she didn't. Could vampires drown? I hadn't thought to ask.

A black hue covered the world. An element of peace wrapped over me, and it felt much warmer than the cold water. Maybe I could close my eyes and rest for a moment.

Strong hands locked around my ribs. Maverick launched me through the hole she'd plucked open. Warm air met my chilled skin, and my jaw chattered.

I gasped for breath, and my lungs rebelled against the fluid in my chest. I threw up, but it wasn't enough. My chest heaved with more convulsions.

Maverick slapped my back. "Take a breath in!"

I pulled oxygen into my stubborn body, and it settled the twisting in my stomach. I wiped the vomit from my lips with the back of my hand.

A pair of empty eye sockets gazed at me from the ground. I still had the skull. That was all that mattered.

Maverick took in our surroundings. "I know where we are." She tucked her hands under my arms and pulled me up. "This is the old passageway into the dungeons from the external floodways. I think you'll find it leads somewhere familiar."

I didn't care where the stupid passage led, as long as it was far away from the pit we'd almost drowned in.

"Is the whole castle going to collapse or flood?" I asked.

"I hope not," Maverick said. Her words did not comfort the unease in my chest.

The passage was composed of the same bricks as the hallway in the catacombs. I shivered, remembering the old, dead remains falling on me. Even as my mind tried to wrestle with the traumatic memories, I knew I'd do it all again.

I clutched the skull tighter.

"Here we are," Maverick said. The path ended at a brick wall.

"Let me guess, there's a latch here somewhere."

"Sure is," she said. I waited behind the vampire. I wasn't about to help her search for a latch in a mysterious stone door ever again.

She pressed on the hidden lever, and the door tumbled open. Warm, orange stones surrounded us. The musty scent of stale water and unwashed clothes flowed over me, somehow familiar and reassuring. A line of torches, evenly spaced opposite the iron bars, stretched along the hall.

My old cell block.

"Reef!"

I sprinted down the hall and skidded to a halt in front of Reef's prison. The man's face pinched, and his mouth rounded in shock.

"Natalie?" He asked as though he didn't quite believe it.

"Yes! Reef, I am so sorry." Guilt bit me from the inside. "I left you. I left all of you and I never came back to apologize."

A new coil of pain, one that had nothing to do with the glass shards in my feet or the icy clothes dripping a puddle on the dungeon floor, wound around me. I had abandoned Reef, Jolie, and the rest of my people. I was a traitor.

Reef walked to the door and put his fingers through the bars. I stumbled away from him until my back hit the wall.

"I'm so sorry." Tears flowed down my cheeks.

"Hey, come here. Stop that."

Reef held out his palm, and I clutched at his fingers.

"You're so cold." He rubbed my skin between his. "You're freezing. What have you been doing?"

"Almost drowning."

He chuckled, but his dark eyes turned concerned at my dripping clothes. He caught sight of the skull in my other hand and his brows rose.

"Look, Natalie, I don't blame you for what you did. None of us do." He gestured down the hall. "If any of us gets the opportunity to escape, we all expect them to take it. Maybe, hopefully, that escape can lead someone here to rescue the others. I'm only sorry you got caught."

I wiped the tears from my face. "I'm going to see if there's anything I can do to help you," I said.

"Give it a try, but don't put the guilt on yourself. It's not your fault we're in here. Besides, since you left, the food's gotten a whole lot better. I think they're trying to apologize for not telling us if you were alive or dead."

We both laughed, and the weight shifted inside me. It was still there, still heavy, but I could carry it.

A spark of light reflected from my old cell. I paused, watching the torch reflect from the golden letters of the book Bria had given me. I bit my lip. I didn't have a reason, but I slipped inside the space and snatched the item anyway. *Deathbringer*'s thin form felt much heavier than it should have. I returned to the hall, lugging my new burden.

Maverick pressed her fingertips to my arm. "We need to go," she said. "If we don't get some engineers down here, this floor might flood next."

"Please go do that," Reef said. "I have a vested interest in keeping this floor from flooding."

"Okay." I followed Maverick down the hall. "Thanks, Reef."

"And Natalie?" he yelled as we passed his gate. "I don't want to see you in here again."

I smiled and followed Maverick up the stairs.

CHAPTER EIGHTEEN

"Where the hell have you two been?" Rayhan's gaze raked over our dripping clothes, and anger burned across his face. "I thought you left her in my room hours ago?"

"We had a slight detour." Maverick's blonde hair sat flat on her head, and her soaked dress clung to her toned figure. Her shoulders were straight, one hand rested on her hip and the other swayed at her side. She could have been talking to a friend in the hallway and not being yelled at by a pissed off vampire after nearly drowning.

I had twisted my hair into a knot at my nape to stop the water from chilling my back, but it slipped down my neck, which was worse. My jaw chattered, and I'd already bit my tongue twice from its force. I settled the skull in my arms, locking it against my chest. Next to Maverick, I looked like a dejected child, and I didn't have enough energy to care.

"Look, son, I'd love to stick around and be verbally berated in the hall, but the catacombs are flooding and if I don't tell the engineers, we're going to drown about two hundred prisoners in the dungeons." Maverick put both hands up in a surrender sign. "Of course, that's your call. You technically outrank me, so if you want to flash execute all the prisoners, I have some great news for you."

Rayhan's jaw clenched. "The catacombs?"

Maverick grimaced. "Whoops. No. I meant, um, the kitchens."

"You know she wasn't supposed to see the catacombs, Mother."

"It doesn't matter anymore, does it? They're flooded now."

Rayhan pointed a stern finger at Maverick. Her spine straightened, an air of obedience on her face. She didn't care about the dynamic of son and mother. She was far more comfortable with soldier and superior.

"You go fix whatever's happening in the catacombs, and I'll forget I heard anything about that." Rayhan's usual warm, full voice turned deadly quiet. He flicked his pointing finger to me, and a splash of anger wound across my skin. It buried through me, warming my chilled body from the inside out, and nestled in a soft space in my core. I smothered a smile.

I liked him angry.

"You are going straight to my room, and I'm locking you there myself."

"Sorry to interrupt." Maverick poked her head around Rayhan's finger. He curled the digit into a shaking fist. "But she can't be alone. The assassin tried to attack her again."

Rayhan closed his eyes and pressed his lips together. His chest stretched in a deep breath.

"Okay." He exhaled. "The council meeting is almost over. You can sit in there, next to the fire, until it ends. Then we're going to have a long conversation about running away with strangers into an ancient tomb and getting attacked."

"That last one isn't my fault," Maverick said.

"Mother, don't you have something to do?"

"Oh, yes. I'll see you two later." She disappeared around the corner.

Rayhan's hard grip on the knob was the only indication of his lingering anger. He opened the door and gestured me inside.

The room stretched long and rectangular. A quaint fireplace sat against the right wall, half-hidden by chairs turned to face the center of the space. Most seats were occupied, but a few lonely ones skewed about. Black carpet lined the floor, except for a slab of stone nestled under the fireplace. An empty podium was at the front. There were no windows, despite sharing an exterior wall.

Everyone watched while I took a small step inside.

Rayhan nudged me. I stumbled forward and shuffled toward the lone chair nearest the fire. Madeline smiled at me, then she turned a harder glance to Rayhan.

"Let's finish this up," the vampire said.

The five others resumed a conversation that began before my interruption. I was too exhausted to wonder why Kadence's return merited an entire council meeting.

The chair's wooden bars dug into the tender flesh on my legs and back. I didn't care. The hard seat felt like heaven. The fire warmed me, and sharp tingles cascaded through my nerves. Stabbing pain cut at my feet. I peeled the shoes off, revealing a jagged mess of glass and skin and blood.

The skull smiled at me from my lap. A soft turn in my gut made me want to hold it tighter, but I needed two hands to work the glass. I set the bone on the thick carpet and adjusted the fabric so the remains would be cushioned and comfortable.

In case I had doubted my sanity before, this convinced me it was gone completely.

I drew my foot up and pulled the shards from my skin. Each shard that left my flesh settled another ache, and the fire soothed the chill from my body. My head drooped, and I jerked it up. Exhaustion made me heavy, but I couldn't sleep yet. Remembering the glow of the attacker's whip, the sharp crack of breaking glass, and my screams echoing through endless tunnels. I may never sleep again.

"I see Maverick took you to the catacombs," a soft voice said.

I jerked again, and the weariness faded.

Madeline sat in the chair beside me. She bent at the waist, and her long, black hair tumbled over one shoulder. Laugh lines filled her face, making me think she was in her early forties—except as a vampire, she was likely much older.

She pointed one slim finger to the skull staring at me but made no move to touch the bone. My fingers itched to pick it up, but I curled them. It was fine on the floor for a moment.

"Apparently, she wasn't supposed to do that," I said.

Madeline shrugged. “Maverick does a lot of things she’s not supposed to do. That doesn’t mean she shouldn’t do them though. We often find the things she’s not supposed to do are the very things she has to do.”

“That’s confusing.”

Madeline smiled. “Do you know what the spell says?” she asked. The green light had faded from the remains, but dark gray symbols were permanently etched across its forehead.

“No,” I admitted.

“I could look at it for you.” She didn’t move toward the skull. “As long as it’s not a spell to destroy vampires, I’d be happy to translate.”

“Why?” The word tumbled from my lips. “Since I’ve been here, nobody has held my heritage against me. But my people are locked in the dungeons. We are at war. Why are you so nice to me?”

“Would you rather be in the dungeons?” Madeline smiled and patted my hand. Her skin felt rough and dry, but I longed to grab her fingers and never let go. “Don’t answer that, I’m only jesting. It’s easy to believe that war is personal. I haven’t been on the battlefield in decades, but sometimes I still feel the weight of a hammer in my arms. I don’t miss it. I don’t miss killing strangers in cold blood. I don’t miss standing in the dark, wondering if my next breath will be my last.

“What we find, when we talk to someone, is that it’s harder to hate them. Generals teach recruits not to talk to the enemy. They’re stupid, evil, vile. They will spill lies with every breath. The truth is, if they speak to the enemy, the soldiers might realize they sound like them. And that makes it harder to kill them.”

Madeline smiled, but thick shadows clouded her eyes. The weight of more death than I could imagine. “I quite like you. Would you rather I translate your spell or go find my hammer for good times’ sake?”

I couldn’t stop the smile from spilling across my face. Her bright gaze stilled away some of the trauma from the night and centered me.

“I’d appreciate it if you translated the spell,” I said.

“That’s what I thought.”

I scooped the skull from the carpet and placed it in Madeline’s grip. Her knuckles were thick and swollen, and I recognized the inflammation as chronic arthritis. Autoimmune, meaning her vampire power couldn't heal it. Her hands were still and steady, though, as she cradled the remains.

"It's a healing spell." She traced the ancient runes. "Very strong, but very dark. Do you need me to write it down?"

"No, I'll remember it." My mother made me do memory drills as part of my training. It's vital to memorize symptoms, pain, spells, and tonics within moments of hearing them. Forgetting a single, slight symptom could end a patient's life.

"It says the spell must be completed by a witch with strong magic. It may drain the life from a weaker spellcaster."

If I could free my magic, that wouldn't be a problem.

"The instructions are very simple. The witch must sacrifice the one they love the most while chanting '*tuuma lux memum.*' It recommends doing the spell outside, but as a mere suggestion." Madeline handed the skull back to me. "Probably to make cleaning up the mess easier."

A faint buzz ran through my mind, but every thought froze. "What does *tumma lux memum* mean?"

"It's the ancient language." She settled her hands in her lap. "It means 'The one that is my heart.'"

"The witch has to sacrifice the one they love most?" My words sounded far away, like I was still drowning in the cave and someone was screaming at me, but I couldn't hear them through the thick water as my life left my body. Maybe I *was* still drowning. Surely this was hell.

"Yes, it's a dark spell. I wouldn't recommend completing it, to be honest. Who could you possibly heal that you'd value more than the one you love?" Madeline shook her head. "Witches are a confusing lot."

"Does it say what it cures?" I asked. Maybe it couldn't help my father anyway. Maybe the thick, dark slime in my chest was unnecessary.

"Anything," Madeline said. "It says it can heal any ailment, permanently."

My throat locked. It became harder to breathe than when Maverick had dragged me from the water.

"Are you okay?" Madeline patted my hand.

"I'm okay," I said, or at least I thought I did. My mind was far away.

Healing my father would require sacrificing someone I loved. That was impossible. Faces rolled through my thoughts. Penelope's wide, youthful gaze. My father's face, thin and stretched, but always smiling.

Rayhan.

No. I didn't *love* the vampire. Wisps of desire, at most. His death wouldn't fulfill the spell.

From across the room, Rayhan must have felt my burning gaze on his back. He caught my eye, and his lips curled into a brilliant smile. A secret danced over his face, something sweet and delicious and just for me.

He turned away.

I didn't love him *yet*.

A new memory folded over me. It was blurry and rough at the edges. One borrowed from when I picked up the skull for the first time. It had shared the remnants of the spell that was carved into its bones. The memory of blood on my skin, my blade cutting through flesh, and pain so sharp the wound could have been my own.

The owner of this skull had sacrificed her greatest love to heal someone else. And when she died, they engraved the spell into her head.

My stomach was long empty, or the nausea would have brought up my dinner again.

"Are you ready to go?" Rayhan startled me.

I jumped from the chair and ignored my complaining feet. "I'm ready." I forced a smile.

Rayhan held out his arm, and I grabbed it. I studied his face and imagined plunging a knife through his heart. I thought about the heat as my magic healed my father with Rayhan's stolen life.

I chased the thoughts away. It didn't matter. I didn't love the vampire.

"Wait," I said. Picturing Rayhan's blood covering my hands reminded me of a different question for Madeline. "What can you tell me about the children's book *Deathbringer*?"

She rolled her eyes. "It's nonsense," she said. "Written to keep children familiar with death. They see it at too young an age, unfortunately."

"But why would so much emphasis be placed on the king's blood?" I asked. "She needed it to make the poison, but couldn't any blood do?"

"If you tell Kadence I've repeated this story, I will deny it." Madeline waved her finger at Rayhan. He made an X over his heart. "Before the war began, the witches and vampires lived in this castle together." She paused for a moment. "I see the look on your face, but no, I wasn't alive then. Anyway, the witches and vampires married and had children. The royal line was particularly known for intermingling. It helped maintain the peace, but it meant every witch in the lineage had vampire blood and every vampire had witch blood."

"What would that do?"

Madeline shrugged. "It doesn't seem to do anything. At least, Kadence seems like a perfectly normal vampire, and so did his parents. The myths say there's magic in the royal blood. If it's given freely, it lends the person immense power and can save them from death. If stolen, it turns to vile poison. The myth inspired the story, but it's not true. Kadence has taken many hits in battle, and his blood hasn't killed anyone."

"What if someone drank the blood?" I ignored Rayhan's tug on my arm. "Would it be poison then?"

Madeline wrinkled her nose. "Vampires don't drink vampire blood," she said. "It's particularly nasty. Akin to wastewater, I'd say."

"Come on, girl." Rayhan flicked his gaze down my still damp clothes. "You need to change and sleep."

I couldn't argue with him.

"Myths say the blood has to be purified though." Madeline raised her voice as Rayhan pulled me from the room. "It can't be straight from the vein."

Rayhan shut the door, and Madeline's words disappeared.

I'd plucked the glass from the slipper, but I didn't trust the fur not to hide any more shards. My bare feet dragged along the floor, as if my body was protesting standing for so long. I leaned a little more on the vampire and pretended not to see his smile.

We trekked up the stairs, and the decorated walls blurred as we passed. Rayhan twisted the key in the lock with a soft murmur about why his mother would even bother locking the door at all, and we stepped inside his room.

Flickering candles set a golden glow through the space, and a castle staff member had made the bed. The scent of a sea breeze through fresh cut trees brushed across me. The cracked balcony door let in cool summer air that chased away the heat of the day.

"Here, I've got some dry clothes you can borrow." Rayhan turned the lock and rummaged through a carved trunk near the footboard. The wooden eyes of a great beast stared at me from the lid while the man pushed aside stacks of folded linen.

"Here." He thrust a plain, white tunic into my arms. It looked big enough to drown me in fabric. "You can change out here and I'll start a fire in your room."

He slipped through the partially open door into the guest space.

I could see the edge of Rayhan's red hair and the scoop of his shoulders while he bent over the fireplace to stack the wood, but the sudden expanse of his room felt too big, too lonely. Panic crept up the back of my throat. I swallowed it, but the coiling in my stomach refused to settle. I couldn't quite convince myself that I wasn't alone. Rayhan was mere steps away.

I set the skull on top of the wooden trunk, replacing the hollow-eyed creature with the half-smiling head. I threw my clothes into a dripping pile near the door. Rayhan's shirt felt soft and warm. A line of little buttons climbed up the middle of the garment, and I rolled the sleeve several times before my hands were free. The garment hit above my knees and was much too wide.

Rayhan still wasn't back. The edge of fear roared through me again. My heartbeat quickened, and a bead of sweat dotted my forehead despite the cool night.

I almost died today. The attacker had been close to killing Maverick and me with her strange blue ropes. Then she'd tried to drown us. The memory of cold water climbed up my neck. I scratched at my skin, but nothing was there. Just me and the memories.

I forced my shaking legs toward the bedroom. My body didn't want to cooperate. Adrenaline crashed through my veins, looking for the threat. The danger was over, but my mind refused to believe it.

An amber spark erupted in the fireplace, and Rayhan set a larger log across the rack. The fire reflected in his eyes and the rolling sea and wildfire danced together. He sat back on his heels and breathed into the flames, which stretched higher and higher, hungry arms seeking more. Rayhan complied, stacking more logs, and the fire licked them greedily.

He turned and jumped.

"Natalie. I didn't hear you." His voice held the edge of a growl. His gaze roamed across me, taking in the places where his shirt didn't quite cover, burning me with something much hotter than flames. "What are you doing?"

I don't know.

"Waiting," I said. "Waiting for you to finish the fire."

Rayhan's throat bobbed with a thick swallow. "Well," he said, "it's finished."

He stepped around me through the doorway, but I didn't move. His body pushed against mine, warm and strong and safe. It eased the memories of drowning, feeling my nose burn with water and my stomach turning at the expectation of death. When he was this close to me, his muscles against my chest, he left no room for fear.

His breath paused, and a flash of silver burrowed in his eyes. He closed them and turned away, attempting to squeeze through the narrow passage.

"Wait." I caught his arm, and a current rippled between us.

"What?" Rayhan whispered.

"Don't leave me."

The quiver in his body stilled, and the warm man that had been against me moments ago cooled to ice.

"Don't do this, girl. I already told you how I feel."

"You're worried that you'd be taking advantage of me."

"Yes."

I pulled his arm, and his back pressed against the doorway. He sucked in his gut, putting as much space between our bodies as he could—a mere finger's length.

"What if I told you that you weren't?" I ran my fingers over the edge of his jaw, burrowed under his neat red beard. His skin felt soft along the scruff of rough hairs.

"Natalie." He put his hand on top of mine and pressed my palm harder to his face. His nostrils flared. "I can't risk hurting you."

He dropped his touch, and a blanket of fear wrapped around me. He was going to leave me alone in this little room. He'd be right next door defending the only entrance, but it wasn't enough. I needed his skin, his scent, to keep the panic at bay.

"Please, don't." Hot tears poked my eyes. *I need you to stay.* "I want you to stay."

He turned to me, his mouth open, but I didn't dare let the words escape. He had a thousand excuses on the tip of his tongue, ready to push me away because of fear, because of honor, but I didn't care. I pushed to my tiptoes and pressed my lips hard against his.

Something uncurled amid the panic and fear, something instinctual and long forgotten. It blossomed inside my chest, sending sparks through my fingertips and down to my toes. A whirlpool of need and want mixed into a desire so violent and demanding.

I wanted to give it everything, and it wanted Rayhan.

I pressed against him and wrapped my hand around his head. I pulled him down, running my tongue across his lips. He growled low in his throat but kissed me back. He tasted sweet and spicy and everything in between. The whirlpool twisted harder, threatening to capture us both.

Rayhan's arm circled my waist and ground me into him. His hardness pressed into my stomach, and I rubbed against him. His hips buckled, searching for more. I had plenty more to give him.

I broke the kiss and drew a gasping breath. His silver eyes darkened with anger, and twin fangs peeked through parted lips.

A naughty smile caught my mouth. I pulled from his embrace and dashed to the bed. Catch me if you can.

It was a short chase.

I'd barely managed two steps, and he locked a rabid grip around my waist. He pulled me against his chest, and his hands wound under the long shirt, caressing my thighs and massaging my ass. My sore muscles yielded under his palms as tingles cascaded down my skin.

We reached the bed, and Rayhan draped me over the edge on my stomach. The fabric bunched at my lower back and pulled tight across my breasts. His gaze rolled over me, a spring rain after a long drought. He covered his mouth with a hand, and his silver eyes were wide.

I ground my ass into him. This wasn't a one-way show. He groaned, grabbed my hips, and pressed against me.

The whirlpool twisted and turned faster with every motion he made. I was going to drown again, this time in passion and desire, and I was okay with that. I would accept death at those terms.

I flipped in his grip and grappled with the buttons on his tunic. The material parted and fell to the floor. His breeches were fastened with a single button, and they joined the rest.

I pulled at my borrowed clothes. Rayhan stilled my hands.

"No," he said. "Leave that on."

I circled my arms around his neck, and his hands flittered beneath the fabric, brushing sensitive nerves under my breasts. He rubbed my nipples with his thumbs until the buds peaked and ached for more. I groaned and leaned my head back. The rough scratch of Rayhan's beard across my skin twisted with his gentle touches until I rocked in a wild sea and my body longed for relief.

I stepped away. "Get on the bed," I said.

"What?"

"Lay down."

He scampered up and propped himself on the pillows. The dash of my nude undergarments had to go. I pulled on the fabric, and they topped off the piles of clothes on the floor.

Rayhan spread before me like a sunset across a glorious ocean. His body was wide and hard and carried crevices of sculpted muscle. His abs cut into a neat triangle, and there was a natural curve to his thighs that came from agility training. The twisting edge of desire burrowed through me, turning my center warm and ready.

I took Rayhan into my mouth, and the vampire pressed both palms to his eyes. A quiver ran through him, and he arched his hips, inviting me for more. I delivered. I ran my tongue over him, sucking lightly. Each groan that slipped from his lips encouraged me to take a little more. I pulled him deeper, and he shifted under me.

"Come here." His hands caught my arms, and I let him escape my mouth. His silver eyes were wild and hungry. "I need you. I need all of you."

He settled me across his hips, and I adjusted. I groaned as he slipped into me, stretching and filling me. I rocked against him, and he leaned his head back.

"You'll be the death of me, girl."

I grabbed his hands and drew them under the white shirt. He massaged my breasts and teased my aching nipples. That whirlpool in my core roared and turned, and I sank into it with open arms.

I moved against Rayhan, taking him deeper with every thrust. There were no words now. We each found a pulsing rhythm and tried to keep our heads above water. The ache and need in my chest built into a violent storm, lightning flashing through me until I thought it would consume me completely.

The whirlpool paused for a moment, then pleasure and thunder rolled through my body. My climax tightened me against Rayhan, and his head tipped back. He gave a final thrust, jerking my hips harder onto him and sending another wave of release through me. His grip softened, and his hands fell to the side.

I collapsed across his chest, and he wrapped his arms around me.

For a moment, nothing remained except our breath and our matching heartbeats.

Rayhan's fingers drifted through my hair, pulling me from my half-asleep state. He smoothed away the locks until my face was clear.

"I told you not to do that, girl," he said, but there was no anger in his eyes. He traced my lips.

"Actually, you never said that." I fumbled with the words. My mind twisted, drunk with afterglow and exhaustion.

"Come here."

Rayhan pulled me to his side and nestled one great arm around me. He tugged up a soft blanket and settled his head into my hair. The fire crackled from the open door of the guest room, and Rayhan's breathing became soft and steady.

The ancient skull, which I swore I had turned to face away, watched me with its gaping eyes. It knew. It knew the truth that I had tried to deny myself.

I loved Rayhan. Maybe it was just the beginning, but the whimsical tendrils crisscrossing through my chest were more than lust, more than one night could fulfill. I craved a future where his arms would be around me always.

You'll be the death of me, girl, Rayhan had said. The words floated through my head. They may be true.

Because if I wanted to heal my father, I would have to kill Rayhan.

CHAPTER NINETEEN

A loud bang pulled me from the warm cocoon of Rayhan's arms. Light spilled around the open door, and someone stepped into the room. I caught a hint of a splintered doorframe. Wood twisted away from the stone wall, and the metal bolt in the lock protruded into empty air.

The stranger hesitated. Rayhan sat up, snatching the blanket, and a draft flicked my exposed skin.

The intruder grabbed my arm and pulled me from the bed. My hands and knees smacked the ground, and the rough stones scraped away the tender flesh on my palms. Panic slipped through my chest as I expected the blue coil of a lightning rope to wrap around my neck, but it was the sharp edge of a sword that nestled there instead.

"What the hell, Kadence?" Anger simmered in Rayhan's words. "You broke my damn door! It's the middle of the night!"

"It's true then." The king's voice sounded calm and poised, a drop of ice from the tip of an iceberg. "You have been seeing her."

"This is about Natalie? You could have asked me before destroying my room."

"Why have you gone against my specific wishes to keep enemy prisoners where they belong—in the dungeons?"

"She's helping me solve my father's murder." Rayhan shuffled around the foot of the bed. He pressed his lips, and anger highlighted his face.

"Looks like she's helping with more than that," Kadence bit. "The coroner determined your father died of natural causes."

"You've always known my thoughts about that," Rayhan said.

Kadence fit the flat edge of the blade under my chin and forced my head up. His dark eyes shot daggers into me, cutting through the panic and fear and igniting my anger. My trapped magic flared in my soul, longing to slice him.

"Is that what she's doing?" The king spoke to me, and the blackness in his eyes bled to a rich, molten silver. "She's helping you? Do you know what happened during my return trip home?"

"No," Rayhan said.

"We were attacked. Ambushed in the pass."

"By who?"

"Who else, Rayhan! The witches!"

"How many?"

"We didn't see them. It was a covert team."

"Did they take the supplies?"

Kadence paused. "No."

"How many vampires dead?"

"None."

Rayhan's shoulders sagged. "Then what's the problem here?"

"They made it to my tent and drew my blood before we drove them away." Kadence pressed the tip of his sword into my neck. My body locked, the air froze in my chest. A single breath and I would risk cutting my own throat. "That's all these creatures are, Rayhan. Mindless, bloodthirsty, and best left dead. Then, I get home and my catacombs are destroyed, my top tier general is dead, and you've been caravanning around the castle with this witch."

"Kadence, put down the sword." Rayhan's voice had turned deadly, but I didn't dare move my eyes from the king.

"Or what, *friend*? Would you take up arms for this enemy?"

The sound of Rayhan's axe scraped across the floor. "Yes, Kadence. I will."

Kadence glanced at Rayhan. I used his distraction to scurry away from the edge of his sword and lunged toward the open door. He snatched a handful of my hair and dragged me back. Sharp pain along my scalp drew an uninvited cry from my lips. I hit the wall beside the wooden headboard.

Kadence dropped my hair and circled his palm around my throat. He dragged me up until the tips of my toes barely touched the floor. My air was gone, my throat turned narrow and dry. I wheezed a slight breath, and Kadence tightened his grip, stealing even that from me.

"Let her go," Rayhan said.

"She deserves to die."

I dug my fingernails into Kadence's hand, but the vampire didn't flinch. My mind screamed that I needed oxygen. The memory of water burning my chest made my rapid heartbeat pound faster. Blood struggled to pump under the king's grip, and my vision blurred.

A silver axe swung at Kadence. He hesitated, watching Rayhan's weapon streak toward him. He dropped me and stepped to the side.

I collapsed to the floor and drew a ragged, painful breath.

Kadence swiped at Rayhan with his sword, and the giant jumped back. Rayhan lugged the great axe over his head, his hands blending into a blur of silver, and aimed at the king. Kadence was already gone, halfway across the space with his weapon aiming at Rayhan's side.

I couldn't follow their impossible speed. I caught them in snippets as they danced around the room, never quite catching each other.

"Stop this." Sparks flew as Kadence's blade rubbed against Rayhan's axe. The king pulled away.

"I will if you'd listen to me."

"There's nothing to hear."

Rayhan raised his arms for another swing, and Kadence struck at his exposed stomach. The sword streaked along Rayhan's skin, and a trickle of blood escaped before the wound sealed. The giant's lips curled into a harsh smile.

Rayhan lunged, his axe leading the way, and Kadence spun to the left. Rayhan was already there. Kadence dashed right, but an iron weapon blocked his escape. The vampire bared his pointed teeth, but Rayhan unleased a ruthless assault. One dodge at a time, he corralled the king into the back corner until the man had nowhere to go. Kadence lifted his sword, but his shoulders tensed with resolve. He knew this battle was over.

Kadence's eyes darkened again. He glanced over Rayhan's shoulder and caught my gaze. The fire of hatred burned hot across his face, but it wasn't for me. A long-ingrained loathing, built on years and years of war and death, looked at me from a madman's eyes.

The king's sword crashed to the floor. "You care for her," he said. "You would kill me for her."

Rayhan lowered his axe, sweat shining on his brow. "I do. I would."

"You think she can solve your father's murder?"

"I know she can."

Kadence nodded. Slowly, he stretched one hand toward his friend. Rayhan stilled, but he let Kadence grab his shoulder.

"For you, I will spare her life. But I can't have a witch running rampant through my castle. Once your father's murderer is discovered, she's going straight back in the dungeons. That's the best I can do, Rayhan. You know this."

Rayhan pressed his lips and gave a stern nod. "Thank you, Kadence."

"Don't thank me. This just gives me an incentive to find Manveer's killer myself—and make sure she returns where she belongs."

The king picked up his weapon and slid it into a leather sheath draped over his black slacks. His face remained carefully blank as he strode toward the door, but something wild and feral peeked underneath. His frame caught in the ruined doorway, and flickering lanterns danced like hellfire around him.

"Wait." The words burned my throat. Kadence froze, trapped by a grip stronger than my voice. Trapped by his loathing for my kind. "You said the attackers spilled your blood."

"I won't talk to you," the king hissed.

"What did they do with it?"

He turned and his brows rose. “What do you know?”

“Did they keep it?” I staggered to my feet. I refused to kneel for the man any longer. I stretched my shoulders until my back groaned and raised my chin to meet the king’s eyes. “Did they cut you and steal your blood?”

Silence. One hand caressed the top of his hilt as though he considered pulling the weapon again.

“They did,” he said finally. The king spun on his heels and disappeared into the hall.

I sagged onto the bed, draping my arms across the mattress for support. Coils burned around my throat where Kadence’s fingers had pressed into my skin.

Rayhan’s hand brushed along my back, and the soft tingles felt good through my aching body. I leaned into him, and his breath rolled against my neck. His heartbeat settled mine, and his breathing reassured me we were both okay.

“You think the person who killed my father attacked Kadence on the road?”

I nodded. My throat was too raw to speak.

“That means they have more poison.” Rayhan slumped over the bed, the defeated line of his posture speaking volumes. “Who knows what they’re going to do with it.”

Rayhan’s soft body screamed at me to join him on the bed. We’d been interrupted from our first night together, but it felt wrong to go back to him now. His breathing softened and his face relaxed as sleep settled through him. I never understood how men could fall asleep so fast, but his chest rose and fell in a steady rhythm.

He had been willing to kill Kadence, his best friend and king, for me. A knot twisted deep inside my heart. I had skirted around the words, the feelings, but this was love. He would kill for me because he loved me.

My burning throat had nothing to do with Kadence’s assault. Tears caught in my eyes. My mother had died. My father was crippled and sick. I’d abandoned Penelope in the woods and could only hope she made it home safely. Everyone I loved was dead or hurt.

Would I condemn Rayhan to a similar fate?

CHAPTER TWENTY

"Mom says you can't be alone, but I don't trust leaving you with her." Rayhan settled his axe into the leather sheath on his back, and it peered at me from around his shoulder. "Kadence would be pissed if I took you to the council meeting."

The king had called an emergency meeting to discuss the unexpected attack on his way home. I was sure my name would come up as well, and I didn't want to be there for that.

"So Ella is going to babysit you."

My heart sank. "I think it's safe if I stay in here," I said. "We can barricade the door."

We both turned to the smashed door. One hinge had succumbed to gravity during the night, and it swung around, threatening to collapse at any moment.

Rayhan arched his eyebrow at me.

"I can scream really loud if anyone comes in," I tried again.

"You're going to stay with Ella, girl. She's never been a warrior, but she'll surprise you if it comes to a fight."

I opened my mouth to protest, but a voice cut me off.

"Natalie! Dear, I've missed you." Ella stepped around the sagging door and into Rayhan's room. She wore an emerald green dress that was barely visible under a stack of other dresses in her arms. Her hair was pinned into a complicated bun on top of her head that resembled either a crown or a pastry, depending on the angle. She scattered the gowns across the bed as a second silhouette lingered in the hall.

"Wilson." Rayhan's voice came out flat.

"Oh, uh...hi, Rayhan." Wilson held his hand out, and Rayhan shook it with a tense expression.

"Ella didn't say you would be here. Shouldn't you be in the library?"

"Ha ha, that's funny." Wilson bounced on the balls of his feet, looking everywhere except at his stepbrother. I tried to avoid staring at him, but that rich scent of flowers floated around me, and I peeked from the corner of my eye. Despite his ordinary form and skinny nose, I couldn't look away. "I don't have any projects to work on today, actually. We've finished the last one for a while."

Rayhan hesitated at the door. He looked back, and I forced my hands to my sides instead of wrapping them around myself.

"I'll return soon," he said. I didn't know if it was a promise or a prayer, but he left.

"I thought we'd start with a change of clothes." Ella ran her hand across the rich fabrics. She squinted at my thick cotton shirt, and I sucked in my gut. "Then maybe a walk in the garden together. It's such a lovely summer morning. A bit dry perhaps, but it is that season."

"I was hoping to go to the blood bank." My words were rushed. Ella's face pinched in surprise.

"Heavens, dear, you shouldn't be anywhere near that place."

Wilson's eyes sparkled with an eager light. His iris glimmered, and I took half a step closer before I'd realized it. I ground my feet into the floor. Something was strange about that man.

"Why would you want to go there?" His voice wasn't deep or high, it landed somewhere in the middle, ordinary. "Are you interested in making a donation?"

I pretended not to see his tongue dart across his lips in anticipation. "No, I borrowed a book from Bria, and I'd like to return it." Not quite a lie.

Wilson's face fell. He walked past me and slipped into the chair near the footboard, suddenly less invested. That wild scent rolled over me again. Memories trekked from my mind, words we'd shared in the library. The unnatural attraction that drew me toward him.

"Are you wearing..." What had they been called? "Pheromones?"

Wilson's face split into a smile. "Yes!" He leaned forward and rested his elbows on his knees. "How can you tell? Are you having a reaction to them? Mother, get the notebook, we need to record observations."

"I didn't bring the notebook, dear." Ella's tone was hard, but Wilson didn't notice.

"Um." I refused to admit a physical attraction to this strange man. "You smell good."

"Ah, yes! I knew this batch turned out better than the last one. Remember the last one, Mother? Everyone walked on the other side of the hall to avoid me. It couldn't have been that bad."

"It was pretty bad, dear," Ella said.

"Do you always test your research on yourself?" I asked.

Wilson's face fell, and he sent a worried glance to his mother. A careful mask covered Ella's expression.

"Yes, we do," Wilson said, still watching Ella. "Ever since—"

"Since Nadeem barred us from the laboratory." Ella's tone chilled my blood. "But that's neither here nor there. It's unwise to speak ill of the dead."

Wilson nodded. "We used to be allowed in the lab part-time, after Nadeem's work was finished. Then the old man accused us of stealing his stuff. He said his smoke explosions were missing." Wilson rolled his eyes. "What use would we have for an incomplete experiment with a fifty-percent failure rate? We didn't take his junk, but he kicked us out anyway. Now we have to test things on ourselves. It can be a little annoying, because after a while we build a tolerance to certain substances. That's why I couldn't smell the pheromones. They all smell the same to me."

Wilson opened his mouth to say more, but Ella interrupted.

"I'm not sure Rayhan would want you to go to the blood bank," Ella said.

Her mask slipped for a moment, and annoyance flashed across her face. I bit my tongue and plastered on a smile.

"Rayhan never has to know," I said. "Besides, I would love to walk around the castle in one of these beautiful dresses. It's such a far walk from here, everyone would get a chance to admire your handiwork in my appearance."

A brilliant light twinkled in Ella's eyes.

"It is quite a ways." She looked over the garments hungrily. "I'll have to fix your hair too, of course. And cosmetics. It's a shame there isn't time to draw a bath."

I nodded and hurried to her side. "Which dress should I try on first?"

It took several outfit changes and a fist-curling length of time before Ella stepped away from her craft and looked me over. She'd settled me into a long, rose-colored gown that pinched at my waist and turned to swirls of floral lace near the bottom. My dark hair was wound into curly ringlets and pinned into a braided bun at the back of my head. The black slippers had been ruined when I crushed the poison ball, so Ella had found a simple pair of cream flats that were significantly less comfortable.

"Do a twirl for me, dear."

I twirled in place, and the hem of the dress wrapped around me. I bit my lip, both to keep my face neutral for Ella and to avoid admitting to myself that the twirl was sort of fun.

"Are you ready yet?" Wilson asked. He looked up from a thick book in his lap and did a double take. That shimmer of interest I'd doused earlier returned in force. "Woah. You, uh, look great."

I offered him a small smile but remained silent.

"Yes, Wilson, we're ready now." Ella pulled her cosmetic bags shut and gave me one more lingering gaze. "Are you quite sure you want to go to the blood bank? Perhaps Bria can meet you for the book later."

Rayhan would be back later, and I had some private questions for Manveer's ex-best friend.

"I'm sure," I said.

Ella led the way out of the room, and I trotted behind her. Wilson brought up the rear, his gaze painting an unwelcome line down my body.

Now that I knew the attraction was fabricated, the lingering looks and open staring made my skin crawl.

A few women stopped and chatted with Ella. They stole veiled glances at me, and I smiled with my back straight. I had bribed Ella with the ability to show me off, so I stood as an obedient dress form at her side.

After far too much small talk, we finally reached the blood bank. The same blonde attendant sat at the wooden desk, and the white curtain billowed behind her. She looked us over, and that pristine smile slipped.

"I'm here for Bria," I said.

"She's not taking visitors today," the woman said in a clipped tone.

In the past two days, I'd been attacked by an assassin, almost drowned, been assaulted by the vampire king, and been threatened with being thrown into the dungeons again. I was done being nice.

"I'm pretty sure she is."

I went around the woman, but she moved in front of me. We faced each other, barely a foot apart, the scent of fresh linen and spice settled between us.

"You're not allowed back there," she said.

I leaned in, and she tilted away from the unexpected proximity. I stepped forward, and she staggered back, fear suddenly lining those perfect features, until she brushed against the white waterfall curtain and tangled into its wrappings.

I set a firm grip on her shoulders and drew her close to me. Her hitched breath spread across my face as I settled my cheek against her soft skin. Years of fear trapped her in place. Vampires and humans in this kingdom were taught that witches were vile and evil, and I used those lessons to my advantage.

"I have a thousand-year-old skull under my bed." I sucked in her scent, and she shivered against me. "I have enough magic to open a cavern and sink you into the depths of hell. Unless you want to be the next body I stash today, I suggest you let me by."

Her jaw locked, and for a moment I thought I'd have to defend my words with my fist, but the quivering woman stepped aside. She didn't turn her head as I pulled the white sheet away.

I glanced at Ella and Wilson. Their mouths gaped, and they made no moves toward me.

"I'll be right back." I headed down the hall.

The blood bank had been mostly empty last time, but it was full today. Moans and slurping sounds escaped closed doors, and some suspicious banging that suggested a different activity altogether. Through one sliver, I glimpsed a woman clinging to a man's body and her face buried in his neck.

Bria's door was locked. I rapped my knuckles on the wood.

Silence.

"I know you're in there," I called.

Muffled footsteps and the door opened a crack. A bloodshot eye glanced at me, then scanned over my shoulder.

"What do you want?" Bria's previously calm voice sounded hitched.

I pushed on the door, but it didn't budge. "I want to return your book." I held up the well-read copy of *Deathbringer.*

"You can keep it." She leaned against the door, but I propped my foot in the gap.

"I know about the poison made from the king's blood," I said. "I know about the plot trying to kill him."

Bria paled. She looked over my head again, then pulled the door open enough for me to slip through.

"Okay. Come in."

The office was a mess. Books scattered the floor, spines bent and pages torn. Sheets of words stared at me, begging for help, but there was no salvation for them now. A large trunk sat in the center of the room, half-filled with papers and personal goods.

Bria walked past me to the sprawling desk and pulled handfuls of stuff from the surface. Her perfect hair was a mess atop her head, and her clothes were creased and wrinkled. Her fingers shook as she emptied the drawers, throwing some books into the cluster on the floor and tossing some into the trunk.

"You can put the book on the desk. Or the floor. It doesn't matter," she said.

"Are you leaving?" I asked.

"Yes. I should have been gone hours ago, but King Kadence had some questions about Manveer. I shouldn't have talked to him. They'll know now for sure."

"They?" I asked. "Know what?"

Bria smashed the lid on the chest and pushed the iron buckles down. "They." She waved her groomed hand. "The murderers."

"You knew Manveer was murdered?"

Her tasseled head bobbed. "Of course. Once he showed me the letter, I knew he was in too deep. Then he died a week later."

"You said Manveer never showed up for your meeting."

"I lied." Bria spun on her black heels, and spit flew from her bared teeth. "Manveer came here that night. He brought a note. It was written in ancient script, and I couldn't read it, but I'd seen it before."

My heart clenched. "Where?"

She pressed her lips and held her hand out. I set the book in her palm. She flipped through the pages and turned the book back to me.

She brewed a poison from the King's blood and hosted a feast for the whole kingdom.

The words sat on a blank page. There were no illustrations, no plethora of mysterious equations.

"I don't understand." I looked at Bria.

"Neither did I," she whispered. "But Manveer did. Nadeem was his best friend. He was in the lab all the time. When Manveer met with me, he brought a page filled with some sort of formula. He said he'd found it in his chamber and didn't know what it was. The only symbol I recognized was the ancient script for blood, specifically royal blood. That's when Manveer saw this book on my shelf and realized it was the formula to brew Lexliv, the only poison that can kill vampires."

"I thought the formula to Lexliv was lost." I recalled Nadeem's words from our first visit.

Bria shook her head. "I think the witches have a traitor in their castle.

Someone rediscovered the formula, then passed it to a vampire. Somehow, it ended up in Manveer's room. He became obsessed with King Kadence's safety."

"That's why he had the map to Kadence's room." I remembered the folded paper I'd taken from Manveer's locker. "He was strengthening defenses."

"Yes. He asked me to help, and I told him no. The king didn't need a ragtag team of spies protecting him. He has the entire Royal Guard. Cynthia could defend him by herself. But Manveer was persistent. He knew someone would try to attack the king and use his blood for something terrible."

"So they killed Manveer to get him out of the way of the king?"

"No." Bria shook her head. "I don't think that's it at all. Manveer must have figured it out. They killed him, and when you passed Nadeem that note in the library, they killed him too." She pointed a finger at her chest. "Now I'm next."

"Did Manveer figure out how the poison worked? How Lexliv kills vampires?"

Bria sank into the black leather chair and ran a hand down her face. "Do you know why vampires drink blood?"

I creased my brow. "They can't produce enough of their own. Their healing, immunities, immortality burn through blood faster than they can make it."

"Yes, that's all true, but there's something more." Bria cupped her hands in front of her chest like a little bowl. "When witches do a strong spell, it may require chanting or a circle. Those elements strengthen the power inside the witch. But blood and death have a power of their own. Something similar happens when a vampire takes blood. We get essential nutrients and iron that our bodies produce in limited amounts, but we also gain power, an essence of the donor. The power expires quickly because we're not magical beings and we can't retain magic, but it gives us a boost, so to speak.

"Manveer discovered that Kadence's blood has a specific protein other vampires don't have. It's genetic, his parents had the same thing. This protein collects and stores power from his blood meals. It's not spellwork, exactly, but it's likely derived from years of interbreeding between the vampire and witch royal lines. There's certainly a magical element involved. If Kadence gives his blood, it heals. If someone steals his blood, it kills."

"It kills anyone?"

"Anyone who drinks enough of it," Bria nodded. "When the blood is brewed in a specific way, that protein is isolated and concentrated. That's Lexliv. That's the poison that can kill vampires. Don't you see why I have to leave? Kadence's attack is public knowledge. The murderer has his blood, and it's gotten out that Manveer met with me before he died. I'm an obvious target." She looked at me with a new expression.

"Thank you. That was very helpful." I stood. "I'll let you go now."

Bria trailed me to the door. "Listen." She leaned in. "The note wouldn't have ended up in Manveer's room if the killer wasn't close to him. I don't know if Rayhan could kill his father, but they were truly best friends. It doesn't get much closer than that. Be careful."

Rayhan idolized his father. He could never hurt the man.

She opened the door and peered down the hall. "Do you have someone to escort you?"

"Ella and Wilson are waiting."

Bria snorted. "Ella would be keeping an eye on you."

I creased my brow. "What do you mean?"

"She hates witches." Bria's voice was casual, as though a jolt of surprise wasn't cutting through my chest. "You didn't know? She blames them for her first husband's death. He was King Kadence's uncle, Firat, second in line to the throne. He and Madeline co-ruled until King Kadence became of age. Firat died in battle, and Ella found a vendetta against the witches. She was one of Nadeem's top assistants for a long time."

"Ella?" I tried to picture the woman in a lab, but the images wouldn't form. "Are you sure?"

Bria's eyes darted impatiently down the hall again. "Yes, yes, I'm sure. She only stopped working in the lab after she married Manveer. She may not look it, but she's smart as a whip beneath those silk dresses."

I stepped through the door, and Bria visibly relaxed. There was one more question on my lips, one that refused to let my feet take another step.

"Bria, what happened to Sion?" I studied the ground, avoiding meeting Bria's gaze. I didn't need to see guilt or regret in her eyes.

"Sion," she said softly, in a tone that was brittle and worn. "So stupid, really. It was my fault, but he died protecting me. He gave me a second chance at life."

A melancholy silence stretched as we both remembered those we'd loved and lost.

"Thank you," I said. The door shut and locked behind me.

Ella waited at the edge of the white curtain, her green dress twisting around her like a python. Her hands clasped, and a smile set across her lips. I tried to see her in Nadeem's basement laboratory, illuminated by flickering burners, but it was easier to imagine Rayhan in a pink dress.

She reached for me as I approached and tucked my palm into her elbow. "Did Bria decide she didn't want the book?"

I realized *Deathbringer* was still in my hand.

"No," I said. "She told me to keep it."

"She's quite an interesting woman. Her poor husband. They never figured out what happened to Sion."

I kept my mouth shut.

Our footsteps fell into a walking rhythm, and Wilson's intoxicating scent wrapped around me. I let Ella guide me as my mind replayed Bria's conversation. We reached the council room door, but I hadn't found any revelations.

Ella stroked my hand while we waited for the council meeting to end. Her fingers were gentle and soft, bearing no remnants of years working with harsh chemicals.

The door snapped open. Rayhan barreled out. His face was red and sweaty, palms clenched tight. Kadence stalked behind him, spine straight but expression equally livid.

Rayhan spun to his king and pointed a finger at the man's chest. "How can you call me your friend after this? You have betrayed me twofold now."

"Rayhan, I know you're upset, but there's nobody else who could have done this." Kadence swung his arm into the room, gesturing to someone invisible from my place in the hall. "All the evidence points to her."

"What evidence?" Rayhan's words turned to daggers, but the king didn't flinch.

"She admitted to stealing magic tonics from dead witches—maybe she would steal poison too. She doesn't have an alibi for the night when I was attacked. And we found this when we searched her room." Kadence jabbed a square of paper into Rayhan's chest. The giant's fingers trembled so badly, I worried he would split the page in two. He pressed the wrinkles flat, and the ancient symbols peered out. It was the page we'd discovered in Manveer's suite that had gone missing from Nadeem's body.

"It's a formula to make poison that can kill vampires," Kadence said. "The witches call it Lexliv."

"You can read this?" Rayhan brushed his fingers over the page.

"I had it translated. They didn't know every symbol, but they knew enough."

Rayhan's shoulders sagged. His red face turned blush, then pale. The fight fled his form.

"Rayhan, I'm sorry." Kadence dropped a heavy hand on Rayhan's shoulder. "I know it's unfortunate, but I hope there's some relief. You know who murdered your father. You can have your revenge."

Rayhan leaned against the wall and closed his eyes. The page slipped from his grip to settle on the floor, and Kadence snatched it.

The king looked back into the council room. "Take her to the dungeons now, level four. Let her stand in the water from my catacombs that she destroyed."

My throat tightened, and I angled to peek through the doorway. It couldn't be...

Two guards stepped through, and Maverick walked between them, her chin held high, despite both hands being bound with a thick chain behind her back. She moved in step, as though about to direct a dangerous battlefield tactic march to the dungeons.

She paused when she passed the king, and the guards jerked her forward.

"You know I didn't do this, Kadence. Why do you insist on torturing my son, your best friend?" Her voice was tight, but clear.

"I have no choice, Maverick. You had the only evidence."

"Someone else put that page in my room."

"There's no proof of that. Take her."

The guards passed us, and Maverick winked at me with a sly smile.

Rayhan was immobile with his eyes shut. Kadence reached for him but drew the touch back. The king's lips pressed tight, and another emotion flashed across his face. It was gone when he turned to me.

"Since Manveer's murder is solved, you're going back to the dungeons. Guards."

More guards moved at Kadence's command. Ella's hand on mine tightened as though she might draw me away, but her feet didn't move. I forced myself to hold still. If Maverick could go to the dungeon with poise, I could too.

"No," Rayhan said.

"We had an agreement."

"I know." Rayhan pushed from the wall, and his first step was staggered. He recovered, standing tall and rolling his shoulders. "I will take her. She's my responsibility."

Kadence looked between us. "A guard will escort you."

Rayhan shrugged. "Fine."

"I'm not preventing you from seeing her." There was an edge to the king's voice. He could feel his friendship sinking away like quicksand, and something inside of him wanted to fight for it. "But enemies can't roam free in the castle."

"Kadence, I understand." Rayhan smiled, and he offered his hand to the king. Kadence stared at it for a moment, then clasped Rayhan's palm. "We're good."

Kadence nodded, but he didn't see the pain and savage rage painted across Rayhan's face when he turned to me. Rayhan held out his palm. I plucked my fingers from Ella's arm, and his skin was warm and familiar.

We abandoned the group in the hallway. Rayhan's stride was brisk and focused. The guard fell into a quiet step beside us. We reached the dungeon door, and the inner soldier stood up. We strolled past him. Our accompanying guard lingered on the landing.

My stomach coiled as we neared my old cell door. I didn't want to be trapped here. Surely the window had been repaired. They couldn't risk another escapee. Sweat beaded on my palms, caught between Rayhan's hand and mine.

Scuffling followed us from Reef's cell, but I didn't turn to look at the man. We reached the iron doors of my prison, and Rayhan froze. The echoes of shifting prisoners and our ragged breath trickled through the stone space.

"I'm sorry," Rayhan said.

"I understand," I said, but I knew the cell was more than a trap. It was a death sentence for my father. Kadence would never let Rayhan take me home, and Rayhan needed to clear his mother's name. I couldn't help him with that. He knew my magic was locked away and useless. He required real aid, not the remnants of a failed witch.

"Listen." Rayhan turned me to face him and clasped both my hands between his. "I'll return later tonight. I promise."

I nodded. He would be back tonight. I believed that with my whole heart. But eventually, he would realize this was a dead-end relationship. Losing my family would be crippling. He would find Manveer's actual murderer, and our relationship would have less priority. The visits would grow short and far between, then dry up like an old riverbed.

That's assuming the assassin didn't kill me first.

Rayhan swung the gate open. It banged against the wall with a ring of finality.

I stepped through the gate.

"Wait." Rayhan pulled me back, hard against his chest. He was solid and smelled like a fresh sea breeze through a rich pine forest. I dragged the scent deep into myself, trying to lock away its memory.

Rayhan's hand slipped against my palm, but it was something cold that planted itself between my fingers. I curled a fist around the item and clutched Rayhan in a tight hug.

He pulled me to arm's length and studied my face. "Tonight," he said.

"Tonight," I nodded.

The cell looked the same as when I left it. The iron bar in the window had been returned to place. The trickle of water flowed into little puddles on the floor. Even the black blanket Rayhan gave me was crumpled in a pile on the low bench against the far wall. The hot summer sun set an uncomfortably warm temperature and painted the walls in a rich, golden glow.

The door settled into the latch, and Rayhan disappeared down the hall.

"I was hoping you wouldn't be back here," Reef said once the footsteps had faded and the upstairs door slammed shut.

I uncurled my fist, and the shiny silver of a small knife glinted under the sunlight.

My lips curled into an unwilling smile, and my rolling stomach settled.

"I don't think I'll be here very long," I said.

CHAPTER TWENTY-ONE

This time, when my feet hit the ground under the cell window, they were strong and steady. No fever stole my logic, no hallucinations played mind games. It was just me and the sliver of moonlight peeking over the tree-lined horizon.

Horses snorted a moment before Rayhan rounded the corner, mounted on Foresti. Rayhan's red hair bounced around his head with each step, and his trim beard emphasized his bold jaw. He sat proudly in the saddle, a half-grin plastered on his face. He resembled a savage king more than a rogue vampire attempting a jailbreak. A nondescript brown mare trailed behind.

"What are you doing?" I asked when Rayhan approached.

"It's time to go home, girl. Kadence will make our lives miserable if you stay here."

"He'll make your life miserable if you take me home." A knot caught in my throat. "He might kill you if he finds out."

Rayhan shrugged. "He won't find out."

He glanced at the window where the single bar was missing. When he turned back to me, a smile was painted across his face.

"Don't worry about me. Come on."

I ground my feet into the grass. “What about your mother? We both know she didn’t murder your father.”

Rayhan rolled his eyes. “Hell, if he’d died from a sword through the heart, Mom might have done it. I’m going to work to set her free, but your safety is my priority. She’ll get a trial before her execution, so I’ll have a few weeks to set it straight.”

“Execution?” The word weighed in my mouth.

“That’s the punishment for murder, and Kadence is a swift judge,” Rayhan said. “But she’d be pissed if I let you rot in a cell mourning your father when I could prevent his death. Speaking of that, Mom said you’d need this.”

Rayhan opened the leather saddlebag, swaying near his feet. The spelled skull from the catacombs smiled, empty and hollow, from the depths of the pouch. I pressed my lips. Unless I was willing to kill Rayhan or Penelope, it was useless to me.

“You need to get home to save your dad. One more time, woman, come on.”

I clambered up the saddle, and the scent of hay and mud wafted around me. Rayhan tugged his horse forward, and my mare trotted behind.

“We’re going to have to ride at a hard pace for a while. I want to put distance between us and the castle before morning.”

I hadn’t ridden horses much, and the thought of desperately clinging to a galloping beast made my skin itch. But a layer of excitement settled beneath the nerves. I was going home. I could picture Penelope’s face pinched with joy, her tiny arms around my waist. My father would laugh and smile and exhaust himself stammering to give me a hug. The house would smell like firewood and fresh herbs and flicker with the gentle glow of candlelight. Worry also lingered. My father had been taking half-doses of his medication. He would be weak.

We rode over the manicured lawn of the castle grounds as the moon painted a dim path of the trail in front of us. As we skirted the edge of the property, waiting for a break in the trees to run the horses, a shimmering shadow caught my eye.

My phantom, dark and twisting, watched as we passed. Its ghostly head swiveled to keep us in sight. The promise of chaos stretched in its gaze, and dread shot through my chest.

I turned back, clutching the reins as Rayhan urged us into a fast gallop. The castle's glowing torches faded into the depths of night.

"Are you sure it's safe to stop and sleep?" I dug my sharpened stick into the hot coals of the fire. The flames simmered against the moist wood, hissing its displeasure at my offering. "Maybe we should ride straight through."

Rayhan cupped water into his hands from the small spring bubbling beside our campsite. He splashed the clear liquid on his face and shook his head. Crystal droplets scattered across me.

"Hey, stop that." I couldn't halt my smile.

Rayhan flicked his fingers, splashing more water on me. "You let me do the worrying." He dried his palms on his dark breeches and flopped onto a pile of blankets and pelts, which were more nest than bed. "We've ridden for almost two days. The horses need a break, and so do you."

I bit my lip, but he wasn't wrong. We'd ridden through the night and the entire next day, only stopping to relieve ourselves and let the animals drink. Painful knots wound up my legs, and my feet cramped when I pointed them. A strange vibration pricked at my toes and fingertips, even though we weren't riding anymore.

We'd made good time, Rayhan assured me, but we were miles away from my family's cottage. Kadence knew we were missing by now, and Rayhan wasn't any closer to clearing his mother's name.

"Why don't you rest a bit? I'll stay up and keep watch."

"You need sleep too," I said.

Rayhan waved. "Not as much as you. Besides, I'm used to pulling all-night shifts. Can't trust other soldiers to be as motivated to protect my life as I am."

I settled into a second wad of blankets beside the fire. Bright and vivid coals danced a molten rainbow just for me. Rayhan fished through his bag and urged out a small canvas and a handful of brushes. He propped up the canvas with one hand, and his brush scratched across the tight fabric with the other. The sound lulled me into a hypnotic state as the first tendrils of sleep pulled at my mind.

The phantom appeared, hovering beyond the stream, staring at me with blank eyes. Adrenaline jerked me upright, and a soft blanket fell from my shoulders. My heart sped up, a metronome in my ears.

"You okay?" Rayhan's brush paused.

The ghostly imprint didn't move. It watched and waited.

"Yeah." A hard brick blocked my throat, but I forced it aside. The panic faded, leaving me on edge and vulnerable. I craved Rayhan's touch. "What are you painting?"

"You're supposed to be asleep," his gravel voice said, but eagerness bled through his words. He was happy I was awake.

"Lemme see."

I clamored out of my bed and kneeled onto the furs beside him. Rayhan scooted over and drew an arm around me until I nestled into his side.

"Here." He held up the canvas, and the soft, fiery glow livened the paint.

The painting was partially finished. It bore the silhouette of a woman against a window with a rainbow sunset through the glass. The pigment pressed into thick strokes, each one a slightly different color. The subject faced away from the observer, clutching a hand in a grip of dark drapes. The sun shimmered and glowed, more colorful and livelier than she, but only half as intriguing.

"Who is she?" I resisted the urge to touch the wet paint.

"I don't know." Rayhan eyed the canvas critically. "She's been appearing in my drawings, but I can't quite capture her. It's like she's a ghost."

His words unsettled me. I tilted my head and angled the image toward the fire. There was something familiar about the woman. Her grip on the drapes was firm but desperate. There was a stiffness to her stance as she studied the landscape. I could almost picture her face, although I had never seen it. She was ethereal, eerie.

I didn't look at the phantom hovering across the river, even as its presence drew chills down my spine.

Rayhan tightened his arm around my shoulders. The heat between us chased the chill. The press of his body from my shoulder to my knees warded away the unease. The gossamer of need bubbled in my core, urged by his proximity and the ticking sands of time. Once I was home, Rayhan would return to the castle. This could be our last night together, for a very long time.

"I'll help you find her," I whispered. I crawled between Rayhan's legs and settled against his chest. His heart beat in my ear, and a soft breath rustled my hair. I wanted to freeze time, to stay here forever.

I slipped the paintbrush from his fingers and set it on a flat rock near the blankets. The canvas went beside it. I pulled Rayhan's arms around me, running them across my breasts. My nipples hardened, and I held back a groan just from the simple contact.

"What are you doing? This isn't painting." Rayhan's hardness against my stomach as I climbed higher countered his complaint.

"Sometimes painting is about capturing what you feel," I whispered.

A chuckle shook us as he remembered the words from our time in the meadow. I cupped his face and studied the bent bow of his lips. I drew in the scent of sea salt and evergreen. Rayhan remained motionless beneath me, watching every movement with half-closed eyes.

I pressed my mouth to his, and tingles streaked to the center of my body. He tasted fresh and new and like everything I'd ever craved. The warmth in my core revived, and clawing flames sprouted from the coals.

He pulled from the kiss and groaned, hot breath through my hair. I twisted in his arms, and his blue eyes raged with a stormy sea. Forgotten were our parents' murders, the wrongs that family and war had done to us. It was only me and Rayhan and the wild heat between us.

He plucked the buttons on the back of my dress as I pulled his tunic open. The expanse of his chest, solid lines of muscle running toward his hips, called to me. My fingers itched to trace every crease until I knew his body better than my own.

The garment peeled from my shoulders, exposing my bare skin to the summer air. Rayhan's hands replaced the fabric, exploring me as I explored him.

I stroked his jaw where the soft flesh met the hard line at his beard, and a fist wound tight in my gut. This could be the last night we spent together. Panic swelled as an icy spring, and my breath cut short.

"What if..." I couldn't force the words out.

"What?" Rayhan kissed the side of my neck and trailed to my breasts. He pinched at my nipples until my mind spun and my spine arched toward him for more.

"What?" he repeated.

Thoughts escaped the waves of pleasure. I snatched his hand, forcing him to stop stealing my focus.

"What if Kadence doesn't let you visit?" The creeping fear returned. "What if I never see you again?"

Rayhan turned red. He grabbed the sides of my face and locked me in place. I searched his gaze, suddenly serious and cold.

"Nothing will ever keep me from you." His voice was rough, husky, and sharp. "Kadence will have to turn from the witches and rage war against me if he plans to keep us apart. I will paint our wedding aisle with the bodies of his soldiers."

There was no room for argument in his words, and I bit my tongue. Rayhan believed what he said, but he underestimated Kadence's hatred of my people. I'd seen the longing for death and revenge on the king's face. Rayhan may very well find himself against an army to ever see me again.

I needed to make tonight count. I needed to feel him as a part of me.

His fingers traced the edge of my neck and slipped into my hair. He slipped them through the long strands, letting the tendrils fall against my skin. Each brush was a new wave across our private ocean, one that would soon roll over us both.

I pulled his hands away and drew the dress over my head. A silver glint in Rayhan's eyes froze me in place. He ran his fingers over his mouth, and his hungry gaze took in my naked body. His look burned my skin, down my neck, across my breasts, and lower and lower. He painted a line of desire through me, a wildfire only he could extinguish.

"Come here," he demanded. One strong hand circled my waist and pulled me on top of him. He ground against me, only the tightened fabric of his breeches between us, and a moan slipped from my lips. He wrapped his mouth around mine, catching the sounds.

"I want you," I groaned into him. He moved away.

"Say it again."

"I want all of you." I nipped his bottom lip, and he grabbed the back of my head. He rolled us over, and we traded places so that he was above me. His remaining clothes disappeared, and the full length of him rubbed against me.

Lightning flashed through Rayhan's eyes, and thunder rocked us. One hand balanced his weight and the other explored my body, sending trails of desire across my skin. He took a nipple in his mouth and teased it with his tongue. I arched into him, the pleasure making me beg for more. Rayhan complied, playing with his mouth until the pressure at my core reached a fever pitch.

I raised my hips until he pressed inside, and I moaned as he filled me. The tightness of my core clenched around him, and his hands teased at my breasts. I clutched his back and rocked against him. His ocean eyes turned molten silver, and he hovered over me with a new hunger.

Unbeckoned, memories of Zhao's lips against my neck and his fangs in my flesh brought the pleasure to a halt. My heartbeat filled my ears, and I pushed both palms against Rayhan's chest.

"Wait, wait."

He paused, but the tilt of his head had turned predatory. The vampire was here.

"I don't want you to bite me," I said.

"It's a bit late for that, girl."

"Don't, please. I can't take that pain again."

Rayhan's gaze softened, the sea storm finding a temporary respite. He stroked a strand of hair from my face.

"It won't be like that, Natalie," he said softly. "I'd never hurt you."

The memory wound around me, smothering the joyful moment. I squeezed my eyes shut, trying to dim the flashbacks.

"Hey." Rayhan brushed my eyelids, and I forced them open. "Don't you think you can trust me by now?"

I recognized the irony in his words. It was impossible for us to be more intimate, and he had to ask me to trust him again.

"Look, I'm all in." His voice was deep, husky. "If I take you home and you want nothing to do with me, that's fine, but there won't be another woman. I've waited my whole life for you, I just didn't know it. Every battle I've fought, every victory, pales compared to what I feel right now. I would never hurt you, Natalie. Let me prove it."

I bit my lip and wound my fingers through the tight locks of his hair.

"You're it for me too," I said. "I'm not who I used to be."

Tears trailed down my neck. Grief for the life I'd lost, the love I'd found, and the fragility of it all. I tilted my head back, and Rayhan leaned toward me.

I expected the sharp cut of fangs, but he pressed a soft kiss against my flesh. He rocked his hips, rekindling the spark that had faded. Waves of pleasure spun through me, spreading the smell of sea salt and spice around us, until the forest and the fur and the fangs receded and it was only Rayhan and I.

His lips parted against my neck, and a sharp pain cut into my skin. It disappeared in an instant, drawn away by Rayhan deep inside me and some twisting sensation that could only be magic.

Rayhan groaned and rocked harder and faster. I ground against him and arched my head, trying to give him more space. He took me greedily, demanding more and more, and I gave him everything I had. The arching sea swelled between us, threatening to capsize us into the waves. The joy and love grew and grew, until I wasn't sure I could take any more. The pleasure crested, then my body released in a hard orgasm.

I clenched against Rayhan, and his back tightened under my fingertips. I pressed them harder, grounding myself with his flesh. He drew away from my neck. Warm gasps of his breath flooded against my cheek. He collapsed and rolled to the empty spot on the bed beside me.

Our ragged breathing broke the still night.

One arm slipped beneath my head, and Rayhan turned my tired, content body against him. He pulled up the edge of a soft blanket and tucked it around my naked backside. His hair brushed me, and I soaked in every feeling.

"Maybe we'll both sleep." His tilted voice exposed how close he was to doing just that. "Let the horses keep watch."

Laughter slipped through my throat. It wasn't long before the vampire's body turned soft beside me and his arm grew heavy with slumber.

I wanted to stay here forever. I wanted to ignore the slipping avalanche as time pressed closer against me, threatening to suffocate everyone I loved. I hadn't lied to Rayhan. I had never spoken truer words before. There was no one else for me. He would be the only one, even if I never saw him again.

CHAPTER TWENTY-TWO

"Are we there yet?"

My legs dragged. They didn't want to take another step, but sheer determination pushed me forward. We hadn't stopped since our rest in the forest last night. My stomach growled. We'd finished the dried meat in the saddlebags hours ago. I foraged as we walked, but a few bites of mushrooms weren't filling either.

"You grew up in these woods." Rayhan led the horses behind us. After so many days of riding, the thought of climbing back on the beasts made me grimace. "You tell me if we're there yet."

The terrain changed through the journey. The widespread grasses turned to rocky mountains, then to a new forest. This one was wet and marshy. The animals kept a wide berth, suggesting they knew the dangers of people in these parts. Some of the land looked familiar. The twist of a rotten log we'd passed hours ago. The shape of the river's mouth to our right. But the darkness stole away the fine details. I wasn't quite sure where we were.

"I think—" A sharp scent pricked my nose. Smoke, too strong to be from a simple firepit. "Do you smell that?"

Rayhan nodded. A shadow cast across his face. "I should scout ahead."

He pulled the horses and offered me the reins. “I don’t like the way this feels.”

I reached for the straps.

A scream cut through the night. It pierced my ears and sent a pulse of recognition through my mind. Memories of that sound flooded back. The death of a thief on the road. The look of horror in my sister’s eyes.

Penelope.

There was no choice. I had to go to her.

I sprinted toward the sound. Adrenaline coursed through me, driven deeper with each pump of my heart. The way became clear. My feet knew where to go.

“Natalie!” Rayhan yelled and cursed, but his words were meaningless. My thoughts narrowed to the direction of the scream and the thick, billowing cloud of smoke that fluttered into the sky.

Penelope screamed again. I ran faster.

The flat ground turned into a steep hillside. My lungs burned as I climbed, but there wasn’t time to catch my breath. The dampness slowed my steps. My foot slipped, and I stumbled.

Panic tightened my throat. I might not make it up this hill.

A strong grip circled my forearm. Rayhan pulled me to my feet.

“Let’s go, girl.” He dragged me up the slope. “You’re wasting time.”

His strength aided my tired body up the slope. We peeked over the crest and peered down on the quaint village that had been my home for twenty-two years. I remembered the wooden slates of our cottage, could almost smell the sweet yeast of fresh bread and hear crinkling as Father turned the pages of his book.

Amber flames sprouted from our cottage. Golden-red claws scratched at the sky, and a twisting tornado of embers spilled into the air.

My heart stopped. My fingertips numbed, and my eyes tried to convince my mind that it was another hallucination. Please, please let this be dehydration, disease, or psychosis. Anything but real life.

The front door snapped open, impossibly small from my distance, and a little figure tumbled through the opening, dragging a much larger person in their wake.

Penelope and Father.

This couldn't be happening. It wasn't real.

I ran down the hill. I didn't need Rayhan's help as determination and desperation pushed me forward. Even at my full speed, the vampire sprinted ahead.

Crackles and pops echoed as we neared, and the first tendrils of heat brushed across my skin. Smoke, dark and thick, churned through the night air and choked me while I ran.

"Penelope!" My scream was raw and primal. "Penelope!"

My sister's eyes widened when she saw me. Her mouth turned round, and she started screaming, but I couldn't make out her words. My father's limp and lifeless body flopped in her arms.

Rayhan stopped in front of Penelope, several yards ahead of me. He took Father from Penelope's grasp and flung him over one shoulder. He grabbed Penelope's arm in his other hand and dragged them from the flaming doorway.

Rayhan set Father in the cool mud beside the riverbank. The vampire staggered back and ran his hand over his jaw. He tried to flatten his face, but emotion flashed behind his eyes.

I fell to Father's side as Penelope pulled her sweater off and plunged it into the river. She settled the wet garment across Father's motionless body and rubbed the coolness into his soot-covered skin.

"Natalie!" Penelope's golden hair had escaped its bands and twisted near her delicate face. "What are you doing here? Isn't this the vampire who took you?"

I yearned to wrap my arms around her and pull her close, but wild flames danced through the windows of the first story. I could see them teasing the bottom edge of the staircase.

"Yes, his name is Rayhan. Listen, are Mother's books still in there? Father's recipe?" I asked.

"Everything's in there, Nat. Everything but us."

"Good." I nodded as I tracked the blaze. "Stay with Dad. I'll be right back."

"Whatever you're thinking, girl..." Rayhan's tone had a dangerous edge. "...don't do it."

I ran for the house.

Rayhan swore, and his thunderous footsteps pounded the ground as he followed. I had a head start, and his pursuit was too late. Adrenaline blanketed a layer of false calm through me. My heartbeat turned slow and steady, and my lungs expanded with deep breaths.

Clear purpose painted my mind. My mother had poured her life's work into her books. They were the only copies of Father's medication. Without them...

I couldn't think about it.

A wave of heat wove over me when I crossed the threshold. My body tried to fight the hot air, but I forced a ragged breath down and held it. Smoke seeped through the doorway and blinded me. I crouched low and crept through the house.

Two doors rose to the left-hand side. One was Penelope's tiny room that used to be a closet, but we'd shoved a little bed into the corner. The other was my father's room, but only twirling flames swarmed the space now. The staircase pressed against the side of the cottage, raw pine leading to the attic that was once Mother's infirmary and was now my room.

"Natalie!" Rayhan stepped into the inferno. Sweat fell from his skin. "Get out of here right now!"

"Not without my mother's spellbooks."

I dashed away from the vampire. Heat ate at me as one rogue flame licked a line of blisters on my arm. I bit my cheek against the pain. If I let it slow me down, I would burn alive.

I sprinted for the stairs, and the wood groaned under my feet. Rayhan cursed again. His steps stalked mine.

"This is stupid, woman." His anger was as hot as the fire. "You're going to get killed."

"If I don't save these books, my father will die." My ankles rammed against the hard edge of the first stair. "I don't have a choice."

"There's always a choice, Natalie."

The brush of his hand slipped against the back of my dress, but I was out of his reach. The steps squeaked as I clambered up them.

"Damn it."

Rayhan stepped up the stairs, and a sharp creak snapped through the house. The wooden board collapsed under his weight. A swell of flames escaped the void and consumed the steps I'd just climbed.

I swallowed. If I'd been any slower, I'd be dead.

The fire blocked Rayhan's path. He stared at me through its twisting, devilish arms, and his eyes reflected its hungry claws. He knew he couldn't reach me.

"Be careful," he said. "And be quick. I'll take care of your dad."

Rayhan turned and left, but there was tension in his shoulders.

Quick, I could do.

I jumped up the final step. It was too hot up here. The thick air burned when I forced in shallow breaths, and the world twisted as I staggered toward my bed. A stack of books peeked under the quilted blanket across the mattress. They were hardbound, with wide spines that my mother glued together years ago. Her handwriting, in wide painted letters, greeted me as I fell to my knees beside them.

An inferno raged beneath me, eating the foundations of the house. The floor would collapse me into a hellhole at any moment. I pushed the thoughts away. *Be quick,* Rayhan had said. Lingering was not quick.

My mother's books were large and heavy. I drew the first stack out from under the bed. Sweat dripped down my forehead and flooded my eyes with stinging salt water. The colorful covers blended together.

Had I grabbed the one with Father's medication? I couldn't make out the titles.

Be quick. Time was running out.

My blistered arm stung as I gathered the tomes. The stairs were gone completely. I couldn't go down that way.

That left the window.

I dropped the books to the floor. The hardwood groaned and rocked. My heartbeat thundered, and more sweat dripped with each pulsing rhythm. I pushed the glass panes open. The fire was too close and too hot for the night to offer any relief.

I heaved the first book out the window, and it fell onto the grass. Something in my chest whispered that this was wrong. My mother's books deserved respect. But it was worth sacrificing a few pages to rescue my father's recipe. I tossed the pile to the lawn and turned around for another stack.

Two steps toward my bed and the house rolled beneath my feet. The floor shifted and, for a moment, froze completely. Then, like the changing of an ocean tide, the foundation buckled, and my bed fell into a flaming, red-orange crevice.

I backpedaled, slinking away from the edge of the pit. The floor wobbled under me as the excessive heat warped the wood.

The rest of my mother's books were gone. The quilt she'd made me as a child, lost in a single moment. Every memory we'd built in this house, the house that I'd been born in and that she'd died in, turned to ash before my eyes.

My tears evaporated instantly in the hellish temperature.

"Natalie!" Rayhan screamed from outside. "You have to jump!"

My senses came back. My mother's books were gone forever, and I was about to be too.

I peeked my head out the window and gauged the distance. Twenty feet or so. It was going to hurt.

The floorboard shifted as they bowed away from the wall. Tendrils of flames buzzed around my ankles, burning another layer of blisters into my flesh.

The wooden boards gave up and slipped beneath me.

Now or never.

I jumped through the window. There was no technique, no time to plan my landing. I leaped through space, and gravity welcomed me with hard, solid ground. I reached my hands out to catch my fall, and my right wrist buckled. Shards of pain exploded down my elbow, hot and sharp like molten glass.

Someone screamed, and the raw ache in my throat said it was me.

"Natalie! Nat!" Penelope gripped under my arms and dragged me from the smoldering fire, Rayhan at her heels. The house cried once more, and the roof gave way. Embers and sparks erupted around us.

"Let me see it." Penelope pulled my injured wrist from my chest before I could protest. The throbbing settled numbly, a defense the brain developed when it couldn't handle the pain. "Oh, that's not good."

My wrist bent at an impossible angle and twisted harshly to one side. A bruise blossomed beneath the skin as the joint swelled. Broken or shattered, it was hard to say. Either way, it would need a healer or a miracle.

Rayhan stood behind my sister, his lips pressed tight.

"I'm okay," I whispered. The effort to speak through my burned lungs made me pant. New sweat soaked down my back, and it wasn't from the heat this time. "Check the books. Did I get the right book?"

Penelope left my side. The world spun and everything hurt. The cool grass countered my throbbing skin. I cradled my wrist against my chest, too afraid to look at it again.

Penelope returned. An expression of horror etched into her face. She shook her head.

My throat squeezed. "I didn't get it?" I whispered. "I didn't get the one with Father's medicine."

"I'm sorry, Nat." Penelope's blue eyes sparkled, and she cried for both of us.

Rayhan turned his back to me and strode into the darkness behind our ruined home.

"Help me get to Father."

I stretched my better arm, wrapped in blistered skin, toward Penelope. She helped me to my feet, and the ground tilted for a moment. The muddy riverbank masked my slowed pace. Everything hurt, but not as much as my heart as I drew near to my father.

His clothes were black and charred, and blisters swelled across his cheeks. His chest rose and fell in a shallow rhythm. A slight gasp escaped his lips between exhales.

"The fire started in his room," Penelope said. "We had to run through the flames to get out."

I pushed my fingers into his neck. It took a moment to find his pulse with my left hand, and when I did, it beat irregularly. I leaned my ear to his chest. His breathing was erratic and abnormal.

"How long has it been since he's had his medicine?" I asked.

"We went to a half-dose when you were taken," Penelope said. "He takes it every other day. I tried to make more, but it wasn't right."

"He hasn't had any since yesterday?" I asked. Penelope nodded.

I bit my lip.

"What's wrong with him?" Penelope's voice was soft. She already knew.

"His body is too weak from his illness. His lungs couldn't handle the smoke inhalation." The adrenaline faded, replaced by something sharper and more focused. Something familiar with death. "He's dying."

Penelope gasped. "No!"

Rayhan's steps crunched across the grass as ash floated like a melancholy snow around us. He kneeled beside me. His gaze brushed over my father's figure, and resignation filled the ocean waves of his eyes. He recognized death too.

"Maybe this could help." Rayhan thrust his arms forward, and the empty sockets of the ancient skull stared out of his palms. A glimmering green shine ran through the engraved spell, but it could have been an illusion from the pain. "You and my mom risked your lives for this thing. She must have thought it may help your father."

A knot tightened in my throat. I recoiled from the bone.

"This won't help me." I pictured plunging a knife into Rayhan's chest. "It can't help anyone."

Rayhan shrugged and set the bone on the grass. "It might be worth trying." He pushed to his feet and rested his hands on his hips. "I know if I had a chance to save my dad, I would have tried anything."

I shut my eyes. I could exchange Rayhan for my father's life. I could give Penelope her father back, healthier than he'd ever been. But it would cost me everything.

"How'd the fire start?" Rayhan's voice drew me from my thoughts. His sharp gaze surveyed the flaming remains of our home.

"We were reading before bed and something broke through the window of Father's room." Penelope rested her hand on Father's chest. Her fingers rose and fell with each breath. "Some kind of round, glass ball."

My heart jumped.

"It would take some advanced pyrotechnics to light a house this quickly. There must have been accelerant poured outside before an ignition event started inside." Rayhan continued to talk, but the world faded from my mind. My attention gravitated on a single word.

"What did you say?" I asked.

Rayhan snapped to me, his lips paused midsentence. "It burned white hot?"

"No, before that."

"Pyrotechnics?"

"Yes." The word fell slowly from my mouth. "That one."

The glass balls containing smoke bombs, aerial poison, and now fire ignitors. The knowledge of making technical weapons. The stack of books in a pristine bedroom and one blaring the title *Pyrotechnics*. Someone close to Manveer with a motive to injure Kadence.

"I know who killed your father," I said as the thoughts rolled through my mind. "It was Ella. She poisoned your father's tea and had Hayleigh deliver it." I had a sinking suspicion that wasn't the last deadly duty she'd assigned her daughter. The memories of blue-gold chains burned my arms.

Rayhan creased his brows. "That's impossible," he said. "You said Hayleigh also drank the tea. Ella wouldn't have let Hayleigh drink poison. She loves her children more than anything."

I already had this conversation, when I'd asked Wilson about the pheromones.

"She's immune," I said. "Wilson said he experiments with pheromones on himself, and he can't even recognize them anymore. Hayleigh must have been exposed to the poison enough times that it stopped affecting her. Maybe they tested diluted amounts or something. She had immunity, but your father didn't."

Emotions flashed across Rayhan's face. "Ella had the knowledge from working in Nadeem's lab for years." Anger slipped through his tone, hot and rough. "She studied the ancient language and would know about Lexliv. Ella always thought her children belonged on the throne. Maybe she was willing to kill to put them there."

"Natalie!" Penelope screamed and pointed toward the dark depths of the forest. I squinted as my heartbeat pounded in my throat, but nothing moved between the still trees.

A flash of blue reflected from the damp ground. It was gone as quick as it came.

I jerked to my feet, and the world swayed. We'd figured it out too late. Ella and Hayleigh were already here.

"You people can't do anything right. You can't even die right." Ella's voice hissed from the quiet woods.

A shadow moved between the trees. The figure stepped closer, and the outline of a woman sharpened. Ella and Hayleigh followed her. She wore a tight black outfit with ropes in both hands. My mind flashed back to the night I was attacked in my cell. I could see her now. Hayleigh's face smiled out of my nightmares.

Rayhan's gaze darkened at his stepmother.

"You killed my dad?" There was an undercurrent of danger in his tone. "Why?"

"Why?" Ella's mocking voice rose an octave. "Your father couldn't keep his mouth shut. He confronted me, said he had suspicions about my loyalties toward the king." Her lip curled. "I don't have any, of course, but Manveer would do anything for duty and honor. So I made sure he died for them."

"Do you miss your daddy?" Hayleigh snapped the whip at her side. "Don't worry, you'll be with him soon."

The weapon glowed bright blue with the lightning current. Hayleigh lunged at Rayhan and snapped the rope at him. The vampire jumped back, narrowly avoiding the cracking weapon, and patted his body. His hands came up with a long blade.

Hayleigh charged, and the whip bit into Rayhan's leg. He shouted and jerked away. Smoke leaked from the new wound. He studied the woman, and her death reflected in his eyes.

Hayleigh and Rayhan danced in front of the smoking remains of our home. Rayhan dashed under Hayleigh's chains and sliced a bloody trail across her chest. She hissed, and the whip cracked at Rayhan's feet. He dodged, barely.

The two drew apart, chests heaving and sweat running down their faces.

"Why would you kill my dad?" Rayhan asked.

Hayleigh flicked the tendril, and he ducked easily. "He was in our way," Hayleigh growled. "He would have stopped us."

"From what?"

"They planned to kill Kadence," I said. "She wanted the throne."

"The throne." Hayleigh spat on the ground. "Wilson can have the throne. I'm after something much, much more."

"What then?" Rayhan stepped closer, pushing Hayleigh back.

"Godhood," she said, and a wild shimmer flashed in her eyes.

Rayhan's brow creased, and he glanced at me. I shrugged. I didn't know what that meant either.

"Well, good luck with that." Rayhan lunged at the woman, and the two reengaged.

"He's pretty good, huh?"

The warm tone settled an ache in my heart. Childhood memories flooded from the depths of my mind. My father, soft-spoken but smart and funny.

Penelope's head swiveled to the voice only a second before me. Father's hazel eyes were open, and he watched the fighting duo as they navigated around the yard. A smile set across his lips, and his gaze turned to Penelope and me.

"Father!" Penelope clutched his hand to her chest. I touched his forehead, disbelief boiling through my soul.

Father focused on me. His narrow eyes pinched a bit, then shone with a layer of fresh tears. His face, so familiar and comforting, broke into a smile. A rattle sounded from his lungs with every inhale, and a blue tint spread across his lips as his body fought for oxygen. The price of consciousness was steep.

"Natalie." His voice was weak but steady.

"Shh, Father, it's okay."

He wrapped his shaking hand around mine and drew it to his face. "I thought I'd never see you again." He smiled against my palm. "This is a final blessing from your mother. Or perhaps I'm already dead."

He coughed at the end of his words, and a sprinkle of bright blood speckled his lips.

"No, Father, you're not dead. I'm back. They let me go."

He shook his head. "I know that tone. It's the same tone you gave your mother as a child. I'm sure you gave them hell until they were forced to let you go."

"They actually begged me to take her back," Penelope said through tears. "I tried to tell them no."

"Hey!"

Dad's laugh was soft and flat. He drew another rattling breath. "Who is this vampire?" he asked. "Your phantom hasn't killed him yet."

"He's...different," I said carefully. Confessing my love of a vampire may have been enough to kill Father in his weakened state.

"So you care about him." Father struggled for his next word. He tracked Hayleigh and Rayhan's battle. "Tell me about him. Tell me about our mortal enemy you've decided to care for."

"He's a vampire," I said.

Dad laughed. "No kidding."

"He carries a huge axe." I couldn't help but smile. "And he likes to paint. I wish you could see his paintings. He has a way of bringing the most stagnant landscapes to life."

"Listen to you." Father's grip slacked in mine, and the air caught in my throat. "You sound like your mother. Babbling on and on about a man who could never deserve you."

He swallowed, and I saw a flash of blood in his mouth. His hold suddenly tightened until his knuckles turned white.

"Listen." He staggered for breath, and the blue beneath his skin deepened. "You girls and your mother were the best things I've ever had. I've lived a good, long life. I got to see the beautiful women you've become. Looking at you two, I see miracles on this planet. You can let me go." His words faded. "I'll be okay."

"No, Father!" Penelope couldn't scream around her tears.

His eyes fluttered closed, but his chest rose and fell in quick, shallow paces. He was still alive, but not for long. I settled his hand on his stomach and patted his thin skin softly.

Rayhan's shout drew me back to the fight. He reached an arm over one shoulder, and his fingers came away red with blood. He turned, and I saw a small knife hilt protruding from his back.

Ella stood on the other side of the clearing. She must have circled the house, and she held a second throwing blade in her hand.

"I don't like getting stabbed." Rayhan plucked the weapon from his skin. The wound closed, leaving a bloodstained hole in his tunic as a reminder.

The blue whip wrapped around his ankle, and the current locked his leg. Rayhan's jaw clenched, and he slashed at the edge of the whip with his knife, knocking the coils loose. He retreated, an eye on each enemy, trying to hide a limp.

"Well?" He took a new stance, one foot slightly in front of the other and the blade out. "What're you waiting for?"

The women charged.

Ella's second shot went wide, and she ran forward with a sword in her hand. Rayhan dodged her strike, and Hayleigh met him with her blade.

He slashed across Hayleigh's stomach, and her intestines tumbled out in a heap of pink and gray. For a witch, it was a killing wound. For a vampire, it was an inconvenience. The skin tried to repair itself, but the mass of organs remained in the way. Hayleigh's expression scrunched in pain, and she missed her next strike. She tumbled forward, one hand trying to press her guts back inside.

Ella ran for her daughter, but Rayhan blocked her path. He hammered a fist into her face, and Ella's eyes rolled back. She dropped and scurried backward with her palm pressed against her nose.

Rayhan didn't let Hayleigh suffer for long.

He stepped behind her, grabbed a handful of her blonde hair, and forced her head up. He stabbed his knife through her neck, and the pointed blade exited through her throat.

"I'll be taking this." Rayhan jerked the weapon to the side, slicing halfway through Hayleigh's neck. Blood trailed down her chest and splattered onto the exposed organs she still juggled in her hands. Her eyes widened as her mouth went slack. She sagged, supported by Rayhan's grip in her hair. He ran the blade through her throat, and Hayleigh's head separated from her body.

Rayhan tossed the head to Ella's feet. "I believe this is yours." His grimace revealed tight, pointed fangs.

Ella screamed. She grabbed the blue whip that had fallen from Hayleigh's grasp. She flicked the coils, and it wrapped around Rayhan's wrist. The currents pulsed through him and locked his muscles. He fought against the pain, grunting with the effort, but his reach was too slow. Ella found her daughter's second whip and primed the charge.

No!

I swayed on my feet. The world tipped and turned, but I staggered toward Rayhan.

Penelope grabbed my hand. "Stop! You can't help him!"

I shook her off. If Rayhan fell, Penelope would be next. I couldn't let that happen. I couldn't lose Father and her at once. I wouldn't survive.

"Stay with Dad," I whispered. "Protect him."

My feet protested. Burned blisters popped and warm fluid leaked down my flesh. My vision turned black at the edges. I was so weak. There was no plan once I reached Rayhan, except to make sure I died before he did.

Ella flicked the second whip. Rayhan jerked away, but the coil wound around his neck. She flashed the blue lightning, and his body convulsed. Ella screamed as Rayhan's eyes rolled in his head.

The memory of my mother's death suddenly painted over my mind.

She was feverish and limp in my arms. Her lips arched into a hesitant smile as her heartbeat slowed. She tried to talk, to tell me it wasn't my fault, that she was going to a better place, but her lungs didn't have any more air. Her eyes rolled back in her head, and my tears covered her cheeks as I wished I could freeze time. I would have given anything for a few more minutes with her.

I would give even more to save Rayhan.

"No!" I screamed. I wanted to run, but I struggled to walk.

The blood fled Rayhan's face, and he turned paper-white. A trail of spit leaked from the corner of his lips.

"No." I reached for him. I was too far, and too late, but I reached anyway.

A black shape appeared in front of me. I jerked my fingers back. The phantom stepped into my grasp, my hand sunk through the creature, and magic pulled from my soul.

CHAPTER TWENTY-THREE

The recoil from the magic the phantom stole bounced me backward into the thick, cold mud. My injured wrist smashed into the ground, and the pain rocked through me. My mind spun. Twinkling stars covered my vision. I would never reach Rayhan. I pinched my eyes and waited for Ella's victory.

Silence.

I blinked as the sharpness cleared to a dull throb. I rolled over. Several yards away, Ella and Rayhan were frozen, the blue-gold whip still tight around his throat.

I staggered to my feet. They didn't move. I forced myself the rest of the way forward, and neither of them glanced at me. Even their chests remained immobile. I waved my hand in front of Rayhan's face. Nothing.

"They can't move. You froze time." A soft, feminine voice said from behind. I jumped, and a blanket of familiarity settled over me, thick and warm. I knew that voice.

"Mother?" I spun around. I didn't dare hope it was really her. We'd buried her body in the local cemetery. The funeral had filled the entire field with grateful patients, paying their last respects. But I had to look. I had to know.

The phantom stood with the smoldering house behind its darkened frame. It was a demonic image, similar to the mess I'd created when Rayhan tried to teach me to paint. As I watched, the ghostly shape twisted and turned. Its waist pinched, and the barrel chest rounded into a feminine outline. Its fingers slimmed, and a wisp of a haunted dress clothed the figure. Her face shifted until the swirling depths became recognizable.

My mother, a gray-black shell of her former self, smiled at me.

"Mother?" I asked again.

"Who else would it be?"

A stabbing ache chewed through my chest. I swallowed a sob, but an ugly sound escaped.

"It can't be you," I whispered. "You died."

"It is me, Nat." Her voice brushed over me like a warm bath on a winter's night. I longed to feel her arms around me, but I didn't dare take one step closer. The phantom had haunted me for years. This was just a new trick.

"It's not." The loss felt fresh, a scab torn from a wound. My mother had died. I would lose Penelope, my father, and Rayhan tonight. Death, when it came for me, would be welcomed. "This is another lie. Unfreeze everyone and let this night finally end."

"I can't, Natalie."

My knees gave out from emotional turmoil and physical exhaustion, and I sank into the mud. Water seeped through the delicate layers of my dress, but I barely felt it. I barely felt anything at all.

"Of course you can't." Despair colored my words. "You can't do anything I want you to. You killed the thief who tried to rob us, but you couldn't heal Father. You invaded Rayhan's memories but couldn't find Manveer's murderer. You're useless."

The phantom stepped toward me. My mother's face that it wore remained impassive. Instinct urged me to my feet to scramble back, but I didn't move. I was ready to defeat this demon once and for all.

She stopped five paces back. "Are you done complaining now?" She tilted her head and arched her brows.

"What?"

"I asked, Natalie, if you're done complaining now." She bent her wrist, as though looking at a timepiece. "If not, I can pencil you in more time."

I heard those same words a thousand times before, usually after whining about healing lessons or mixing a complicated potion just right. It couldn't be...

"Mother?"

"Did you forget my face after all these years?" she asked.

I jumped from the riverbank. The throbbing in my wrist and my protesting joints didn't stop me from running to her. I stepped to the phantom, and she watched me with an amused expression.

I halted at the last minute. She was so close, she looked so real. I wanted to smell her scent of dried herbs and fresh paper, but there was only smoke. I lifted one hand to her cheek and brushed her skin. My fingers fell through empty air.

She grimaced. "Sorry, Nat. I'm not really here."

I let my hand fall to my side and wished, more than anything, that she was here.

"What are you?" I looked behind me to Penelope's still form. "Why are you doing this?"

"I'm not doing this, Nat. Dead witches can't do magic. I taught you that."

I fought the urge to roll my eyes, and a smile found my lips. I wanted Mother here to trigger a hundred eye rolls.

"Can you at least answer the first question?"

"I am me. I'm the piece of me you couldn't leave behind."

I shook my head. "I don't get it."

"A witch's spell fades when the witch dies. It's why the vamps bash our heads in, right? Witches can't do spells if they don't have a head."

"That's not funny, Mother." The word felt foreign on my tongue.

"Of course it is. You sound like your father when you say that. I raised my girls with a sense of humor." The dark chuckle looked wrong on her smoky lips. "When I died, the bonds were lifted from your magic. You were free."

"No, my magic has always been trapped. I could feel the bonds, Mom. I could feel the remnant of your spell."

"I know, but it wasn't because of me. It was because you wouldn't let me go."

My brows pinched, and I shook my head again. "I tried to get rid of them a hundred times. I wanted to use my magic. I could feel the spell was still there."

"It was only there because you wanted it to be."

"But the phantom." I gestured to her eternal form. "This controlled my magic."

"I never did anything." She reached for a strand of my hair, but her ghostly fingers had no substance. "This creature is the physical manifestation of my magic that you've kept trapped inside yourself. You called to me whenever you used your powers, and I was always there. I can't leave you, Nat. I never will."

"I've been binding my own magic?" I asked. Emotions twisted through me. Pain at killing the thief, at failing to heal my mother. Regret at the times when my magic could have helped someone. I looked at my own hands, speckled with blisters, burns, and mud. "I've killed people."

"Yes, thank goodness." My mother sighed. "Once that crook grabbed Penelope's arm, I've never been happier to see someone die."

"I thought he was going to kill us."

"He was! You knew that as soon as you saw the knife. You did the right thing, Nat. You always do."

"I did this too?" I gestured to the immobile people around us.

"You willed your magic to stop time. You're very powerful."

My tongue stuck to the roof of my mouth. "I don't know how to use it."

"You have a lot to learn, and I believe in you." She turned and her hands lifted again, then fell to her side. I ached to touch her skin, to feel her one more time. "But you're going to have to let me go."

Fear blasted through me. "I can't," I said. "I just found you." Tears bled over my cheeks. "I need you."

"I'm gone, Nat. This part of me, the speck of magic you've been clinging to, it's not alive. It's holding you back."

"I can't lose you," I said. "It's my fault you died in the first place."

"Oh, you sweet child. It's not your fault I got caught in a vampire raid. Did you take up a broadsword and run it through my chest?"

"No, but—"

"There is no 'but.' You didn't do it. Let it go."

"You don't understand!" Years of frustration and fear wound together and ignited inside me. My throat ached from screaming and crying, and my body was on the edge of collapse. "I can't do it! I can't control my magic and I can't save people and I can't lose you!"

My mother's eyes sparkled with unshed tears. She turned from me and walked toward Father and Penelope. I wiped my cheeks and followed her.

"I miss him. I miss you all," she said, and a hollow space lingered in her voice. "I only ever wanted to heal him, to give him the best life."

"He had the best life. He loved you."

"He had the best life because you girls were in it."

Another eye roll smothered. "Thanks, Mother."

"And this is the vampire." She turned to look at Rayhan, trapped in Ella's whips.

"It is."

"He saw me a few times. Snippets here and there, through you. He's very insightful. He has an artist's vision."

I recalled the hauntingly familiar image Rayhan had captured in his last painting. He'd seen the shadow form of my mother's magic better than I had.

"The spell will work, you know," Mother said. Her gaze had turned to the abandoned skull in the grass. "You can heal your father."

"I would have to kill Rayhan."

She nodded. "But would he have to stay dead?"

"That's how death works."

"Is it? I'm still here."

"You're only magic," I said.

She kneeled in the short foliage strands beside Father. "You're very strong, Nat. You couldn't heal me, but maybe fate is giving you a second chance."

Her phantom hands hovered over Father's blank face.

"Time can't stay frozen forever." Mother's voice turned soft. "Not even you are that powerful. It will start again whether or not you want it to. If you let me go, if you unlock the full potential of your powers, then you will have your magic when time begins again. You'd be undefeatable. You could save everyone."

A hot jab of anger stabbed into me.

"I don't know how to let you go." My jaw ached as I clenched it.

She rose to her feet, and her wispy dress fluttered, despite the absence of a breeze. Her black hair, which had been blonde in her life, twirled and twisted around her shadowed face. She smiled at me, and it felt like sunshine on my skin.

"Natalie, I'm always with you." She held out her hands, palms up, and I hovered mine above her. I could almost feel the heat from her body.

"Close your eyes," she said. "Remember our lessons. Ground yourself in your senses."

I didn't want to miss a single moment of seeing her face, but years of lessons had ingrained a strict obedience. I pressed my lids closed and drew a deep breath until my rib cage expanded and my shoulders straightened.

"What do you smell?" Mother asked.

The fresh river water, layered with aquatic life, iron and minerals.

"What do you hear?"

Our frozen landscape remained hushed, but I could imagine the soft snort of the horses at the riverbank. The pops and crackles of the fire at my back.

"What do you taste? Feel?"

Rayhan's flavor in my mouth, sweet and salty and so, so intoxicating. His fingers along my skin. The flames of desire in my core.

"Your mind is free, Nat. Now search for your magic, release the remnants of the binds that fear makes you cling to."

I reached for my magic, and it greeted me, wrapped in the same thick chains that always bound it. I could feel my mother's power caught in the tendrils, swirling through the spell. Mentally, I clutched at the cords and heaved.

They didn't budge.

"It's not working," I ground out. The calmness from centering myself faded away.

"Relax." Mother's voice held a singsong rhythm. "Try again."

I pressed my lips until my teeth pushed against the tender flesh. My wrist ached. My blistered skin was oozing. My knees wobbled from exhaustion. I wasn't sure I had anything left to give, but I closed my eyes again.

In my mind, I wrapped both hands around the chains and dug my feet into the ground. I strained against my mother's power, pulling until sweat covered my spine and my breath turned ragged. The bonds groaned and shook, but Mother's spell remained secure.

I let the chains go, and they snapped back into place, firm and thick, locking my magic away forever.

The anger was long gone. I would never unleash my magic. I didn't know how to let go of my mother's spell, how to let go of my mother. Rayhan would die at Ella's hands. Penelope, and my father, and then, me.

A shade of darkness eclipsed my eyes—not real darkness, but an imagined covering of hopelessness and depression.

A deep hue of forest green.

Below the dread and grief, a shard of memory pulled at me. A white canvas, covered in strokes of angry dark green, a landscape of bitterness. The memory overwhelmed me, enveloping the senses that grounded me, thrusting me back into that place.

The thick meadow grasses tickled the unmarred skin on my feet. The morning sun brushed streaks of gold across Rayhan's fingers as he rescued the paintbrush from my destructive fingers. His rich scent washed around me, and I drew it in, thirsty for more.

"It's about how it feels." Rayhan's breath trailed against the side of my neck.

My faulty memory twisted his words. I turned to see his face, which I hadn't done that day in the meadow. His sharp nose was straight and narrow, and his eyes, which I'd expected to be glued to the canvas while he guided my hand over the fabric, stared down at me. Something wild and expansive twirled through the depths of his irises, promising forever and delivering much, much more.

How did I ever imagine it was the ocean trapped in his gaze? The rolling turquoise and blue orbs were an impossible expanse. There was no beginning or end. The universe stretched through them, and my reflection stared back.

“It’s like this, girl,” he whispered. He cradled my hand in his massive palm and reached out. The canvas faded away, the sunlight fled, and the prison where my magic dwelled extended in front of us. “Slow and precise.”

Together, we reached for the first chain. It was cold and solid. My grip tightened to clench the coil, but Rayhan pressed my palm against it until my fingers uncurled. He drew our hands down the metal, and the chain chimed a happy note.

We found the end of the tendril, where the magical clasps anchored to my psyche. We brushed across the grounded stake. The chain burst from its hold and fell away.

A sliver of fresh magic turned in my chest.

“See?” Rayhan’s voice held the heat of excitement. “You’re the one making it difficult.”

I nodded, too afraid that speaking would break the mirage.

Together, we painted away the chains around my magic. Each one that broke released a swell of power through me. The magic poured into my soul. More than I ever thought possible unleashed, and it threatened to drown me. It felt like a piece of myself, of my physical body, had been missing and was suddenly reattaching. My breaths came easier. My feet felt lighter.

We reached the last chain. It held down the final swell of my power, and the magic cried for freedom.

Rayhan halted behind me. He reached for the last bond, but our hands froze as though hitting an invisible wall.

“Sorry, Natalie.” The warmth of his body faded as he stepped away. “Looks like you have to do this one on your own.”

“No, I can’t.” I turned around, aching for Rayhan’s touch again, but he was gone. The meadow memory fled. It was just me, and the last chain binding my magic.

I reached for the restraint, but a cold twist of fear caught my hand. It froze, inches from the remaining clasp.

Maybe unleashing my magic wouldn't change anything. Even with my powers, Rayhan could still die. We could all die, and it would be my fault. There would be no excuse, no final reason for my failure. I couldn't blame the bindings or the phantom. Their deaths would be all my fault.

But doing nothing would be my fault too. I had to try.

I reached for the final binding, and the anchor slipped under my fingertips.

I fell.

The magic swept my feet away and poured into my soul. It filled and expanded my chest, stole the air in my lungs, and demanded more. It sank through my stomach and ran down my fingers and toes, but there still wasn't enough room. The magic chewed through me, an odd mix of pain and, finally, wholeness. The excess power leaked into a cocoon of wild-caught magic.

The magic wrapped around my wrist, a tendril of wind across my skin. It fluttered through me, unhappy at our injury.

I could heal it.

The thought barely crossed my mind, and a bud of warmth erupted through my flesh. The distorted bone bent back, a rush of endorphins smothering any pain. Purple bruises faded.

The magic didn't stop. I jerked at the power, but it brushed me aside as easily as a gnat buzzing near its head. It ran down my body, healed the blisters and burns in a heartbeat, and pushed out, stretching from me. It was hungry for more.

A rock of fear sunk into my gut. I didn't have any control. The magic was too wild, too dangerous.

I tried to pull it back, but it was like lifting a boat onto a dry dock with my bare hands. Sweat broke across my forehead with the effort, and my shaking knees finally collapsed. I didn't feel the ground meet my legs. The strain of fighting my magic stole all my concentration.

"Mother!" I screamed. My throat turned raw, and the words burned. "Help me!"

There was no reply. She was gone. I'd shed the last of her magic, and the phantom disappeared with it. I was alone, and my crazed magic was bloodthirsty.

The power flung around me, a broken compass searching for north. It rolled and curled in anger, looking for someone to hurt, someone to kill, and it wasn't picky. Healing me had been like flicking water into an inferno. It only urged the power on.

The magic stretched until it brushed against Penelope. It ran along her skin and sang a joyful song only I heard. It touched Ella's frozen whip, and the pain and anger roared back, turning my vision red.

The magic longed to be used. The only way to calm its rage was to spend it. I searched the scene for an outlet, anything that would dispose of the hot, bitter power.

Shining under the silver moon, dusted with hues of orange from our smoldering house, sat the ancient skull from the catacombs. My magic licked the bone and purred in contentment.

Maintaining control of my power made my head swim, but between the strained thoughts and physical exhaustion, the pieces clicked.

I knew what I had to do.

I forced myself to my feet. The mud sucked at my steps, and cold water seeped into my dress. I ignored the chill and the fatigue. I focused on Rayhan's face.

The magic coiled over Ella, the way her whip had wrapped around Rayhan's throat. It longed to kill her now, before time unfroze, before she had a chance to even see Death coming. I drew it back. My magic was too angry and unpredictable. It was too strong. Ella would die, but so would the rest of my family.

I closed my eyes. Strings of power stretched through the night. They crisscrossed each other and wrapped through the border of the clearing. Time settled around us, caught in the wisps of my power. I reached my hand out and could almost feel the soft tendrils.

I drew my magic away from the waves of time. It fought me, clinging like a stubborn child. I was merciless. I wrestled the power back into my soul.

Time snapped into place.

Rayhan's blue face gasped at me beneath Ella's whip. I strode toward them. Rayhan's fist held his blade. I pushed my fingers beneath his and persuaded the knife from his locked muscles. The weapon was heavy and unfamiliar in my hand.

"Come to say goodbye, dear?" Ella hissed through clenched teeth. My magic flailed, a whirling tornado. My control stretched too thin to provide her a response.

I sliced the blade through her whip, and the coils fell away. She yelled, but I only saw Rayhan's swaying form. I set one hand on his shoulder to steady him, and he clutched my forearms.

"Thank you." The blue tint on his lips faded. His gaze shifted behind me. "Now let's finish this."

Yes. Once and for all.

I grabbed the front of his shirt and pulled him toward me. Confusion creased his brows, and his mouth parted, but I didn't wait for his words.

"*Tuuma lux memum,*" I said.

Bending down to match his kneeling height, I pressed my lips against his. He froze, then yielded. His head tilted, and he kissed me back. I took in his smell, his taste, the feeling of his heartbeat so close to mine.

I plunged the knife between his ribs.

Rayhan pulled away, his mouth open and gasping in disbelief. He leaned from me and studied the blade in his chest.

"*Tuuma lux memum,*" I said again, and twisted the weapon as hard as I could, until his ribs trapped the blade.

Rayhan sucked in a breath, but red blood poured from his mouth instead. He jerked and fell to his back. One hand reached out, and the face I loved most in the world judged me with hatred—and beneath that, sorrow.

He closed his eyes, and his chest stilled.

"You did it." Ella sounded far away. "You killed him."

A foreign magic rose from Rayhan's body. Unlike the violent arms of my power, this was light and delicate. It spun around me, silent and invisible, but as real as a twisting wind.

I held my hand toward this strange power, and it reached for me with eagerness. It brushed over me, familiar and warm and intoxicating.

Rayhan's life force—not a soul exactly, but the magic that every living being possesses. It was separate from the soul, but intertwined as they lived together. In death, this magic would escape immediately, as there was no more body or life to sustain it. But the spell I had chanted captured the power and bound it to me. It was mine now, to do with as I wished.

My magic was hungry. It stretched toward the death magic and wanted to consume it all. The red over my vision painted a picture of me devouring Rayhan's life force, of the rush of power I would get.

There was a reason human sacrifice was illegal in spellwork. Once a witch caught a taste of the power of death, they always longed for more.

My magic ached to enact revenge in blood, but Rayhan's death magic wrapped me in a blanket of calm. It slipped over my hand, wound up my arm, and settled around me in a firm embrace. I breathed it in, and under the smell of river water and mud was Rayhan.

"I have to let you go," I told the magic. It didn't understand me, but it responded to the tone of my voice.

I stepped toward my father, whose chest barely rose under his burned clothes. His own life force was thin and weak. I dropped to my knees and put both hands on his head. Carefully, fighting my own reluctance, I pushed Rayhan's power into my father's body. It was slow and hesitant, like squeezing honey through a vial.

Finally, my father absorbed the last of Rayhan's magic. He shuddered once, then went still.

"Natalie." Penelope's wild eyes gazed across Rayhan's body and our father between us. "What did you do?"

I wasn't sure. Father gave no indication that the spell had worked, but gasps slipped between his bloodstained lips.

"I healed him." At least, I think I did. I hoped I did.

"But you killed the vampire." Penelope's voice turned small, and tears swelled across her eyes. "You killed the man you cared for."

My magic raged at the pain in her face. It tore at me, pulled against the thin constraints that barely restrained it. I jerked against its murderous desires, but it was too strong. Years of neglect and my lack of training made me too weak to control the magic. I yearned to pour it into Ella, but we were too close. Everyone else would be caught in the crossfire.

I held my hands out and looked at my palms, as though that's where the power congregated.

"You want out?" I whispered, and the power swirled in anticipation. "Then get out."

I poured the magic into Rayhan's body. The vampire's limbs jerked, and an eerie orange glow stretched across his skin. He lifted inches from the ground and convulsed. My power, overfull from years of unuse, eagerly filled his lifeless form, replacing the life force I'd stolen. My magic couldn't heal my father, but it might bring Rayhan back from the dead.

A flash of movement. From the corner of my eye, Ella approached. I tried to turn, to switch my focus, but the magic refused to halt its process. Ella held one arm over her eyes as though protecting them against a strong wind. She struggled with each step, then her movements halted. She reached out, and her palms flattened against an invisible wall. My magic made sure she couldn't reach us.

Ella's mouth opened in a silent scream. She pulled a dagger from her dress and flung the weapon through the air.

My magic was a black hole. It expected her move and greedily sucked the blade up. It evaporated into a thousand glittering shards before it neared us.

The power roared.

I tried to pull the power back, but it was too strong. My control was gone. It snapped to Ella and gnawed on her skin. She screamed, a long, piercing noise like an animal pleading for its life. The magic had no mercy. Her flesh dissolved into red powder, painting the ground a rusty shade. The metallic scent of blood billowed around us. Her bones fell apart and turned to ash before they hit the grass. Where Ella had been was just mist and memory.

The magic continued to pour from me, and I couldn't stop it. It dumped into Rayhan and filled him with the entirety of my power. As it drained, my body reminded me I was tired and achy. My limbs grew heavy. I sagged forward onto my hands and knees.

Maybe my mother was wrong. Maybe reviving Rayhan would drain all my power and we'd both be dead.

The red over my vision faded. Hues of blue and green pushed and pulled like ocean currents, rinsing the pain and fear. My steady heartbeat turned to a dancing drum, balancing in rhythm with the washing waters. As the magic flowed, I welcomed the quiet and the calm. Maybe this was death, or maybe it was freedom.

The current stopped. The ocean disappeared. I was on my stomach in the mud, struggling to persuade oxygen into my lungs.

"Natalie!" Penelope ran to my side, her golden curls knotted with sweat and soot. She brushed her hands across my body with a healer's precision. "Are you hurt?"

I tried to shake my head, but I was too tired. I sagged to the ground. My eyes drifted closed. It was over. I could rest now.

A glass bulb fell from the sky and settled between me and Penelope.

I stared at the round container. My mind recognized it but couldn't quite place the pieces together.

A flame danced in the bottom of the bulb, and a clear liquid ignited.

An aerosol poison.

"Hold your breath!" I yelled at Penelope. She turned to me, her mouth slightly open, then she leaned forward and coughed. "Go away! Get out of here!"

Penelope scrambled to her feet and staggered. She headed for the river and threw up in the grass.

My father and Rayhan were trapped. As the smoke spread, my father began shaking. His throat tried to cough as the poison air filled his lungs. There wasn't much time until it would be too late to save him, and I wouldn't be able to use the skull's spell and bring Rayhan back from the dead again.

My limbs screamed as I scrambled up. My body weighed a million pounds and was anchored to the bottom of the sea. The fire and the effort of using my magic had drained me. I staggered to my feet, and my ankles rolled as though trying to stand during an earthquake.

I grabbed the orb, and the smoke leaked toward my face. I held my breath, but the poison burned my eyes. Its slight weight was too much for my weak grasp, and my arms threatened to drop the glass bulb. I didn't have the energy to throw it far enough where the mist wouldn't reach us.

I forced my feet to take a step. They listened, slow and reluctant, but they moved. I took one step and another. My vision blurred, either from the poison or the tears that trailed down my cheeks. I paused for a moment to look back, and I had traveled enough for the poison to stop reaching my father. I just needed to set the bulb down and walk away.

My legs collapsed. I fell face first into the grass, and the bulb rolled from my hand. It settled inches from me, and the smoke billowed over my face. My lungs burned. I couldn't hold my breath much longer.

An edge of calmness blanketed over me. The poison smoke would kill me. That's okay. My sister was alive. Rayhan was alive. My father might be healed.

It was a good time to die.

I let the air from my chest and drew in the bitter scent of the poisoned air. I couldn't even feel its effects through my overworked body. Darkness curled at the edge of my vision, and I welcomed it. I needed the rest.

Footsteps echoed through the dimness. A hand reached down and plucked the bulb from the ground.

"How about I get this out of the way?" It sounded like Maverick, but I couldn't see her face. There was a splashing sound from the river, and warm hands flipped me to my back. She patted my cheek. "You'll be okay. I'll go check on the others. Looks like Rayhan's made quite the mess. What else is new, huh?"

She stepped away, and Rayhan's surprised voice chimed behind me. He must have woken up. I did it. I brought him back from the dead. I waited for the relief, but exhaustion was too strong.

"Mom! What are you doing here?"

"Prison break, I suppose." Maverick's voice faded as she walked farther from me. “Also, I found this in the woods.” There was a thumping noise, and a man shouted.

“Wilson,” Rayhan said. I wanted to look, but my body refused.

“Please, please, I didn’t do anything.” Wilson’s words trembled. “I wasn’t involved in this. My mom, Hayleigh, they’re both crazy.”

“Then why’d you throw the poison smoke bomb at those nice folk over there?” Maverick asked. There was a sharp crack, and I suspected she had slapped Wilson. “Yeah, I saw you throw it. Oh, look. Now he’s running away.”

“Mom.”

“What?”

“Go stop him!”

“Oh fine. But then we have some things to discuss. Primarily, what you’re going to tell Kadence to keep me out of the dungeons.”

Grass crunched as her steps grew farther away.

A face appeared through the fog. Rayhan kneeled beside me. “You killed me.” There was a growl in his voice.

I tried to say, “I’m sorry,” but only a hiss escaped.

He kept talking, but my hearing faded. The poison cleared from my head with each deep breath. I gave into the exhaustion I’d been fighting. The grass felt nice and cool, a good place for a nap.

“What’s going on?” I thought I heard my father’s voice from somewhere in the land of consciousness, which I was no longer a part of. “Who are all you people?”

EPILOGUE

"Now remember, just a slice." Madeline nestled on the picnic blanket she'd spread under a shady tree. The golden leaves announced the early days of fall. It was a still day, no breeze to distract me.

I squinted at the watermelon perched on the wooden table twenty yards in front of me. I drew a deep breath, and my mother's words came to me.

What do you smell, hear, taste, feel?

The sweet scent of freshly tapped sap. The crunch of people stepping over dried leaves. The yeasty dough of dessert drifting from the kitchens. The warmth of golden sunshine across my hair.

I let my air out, and coils of magic wrapped around my body.

"Only this much magic." Madeline pinched her fingers until they almost touched.

I focused on the watermelon. It sat there, menacingly.

One coil of my power slipped out, excited and eager to be used. I drew it back. It was hesitant, but obeyed. Good start. I let the magic creep out, a sliver, and pushed it toward the melon.

The fruit vibrated.

I ground my teeth.

A little....bit...more...power...

The watermelon and the table exploded. A cloud of dirt and wood showered around us. I jerked my arm over my eyes as debris splattered against me. Madeline screeched, and watermelon parts rained over her blanket.

I clenched my fists. I couldn't get this right.

Madeline jumped up and clapped her hands. My mouth dropped in surprise.

"Good job, that was much better!" the older woman squealed.

"What do you mean?" I gestured toward the crater in the ground, then at her dirty, wet clothes. "You have melon in your hair."

"Well, yes." She pulled at the chunks. "But look, the crater is half as large as it was last time. Your magic can be controlled, you just have to learn and practice."

I studied the carnage. The watermelon and table were long gone, but Madeline was right. It was a smaller divot this time.

I sighed. "Should I try again?"

"Yes, of course, but let's do it later. I have to take a bath now."

We both laughed, and it felt good.

"Hey!" Rayhan's voice drifted over the field. I couldn't help but smile as the giant lumbered toward us. His red hair resembled a rugged mane around his face, and his eyes smiled as soon as they saw me. A spark erupted in my core. I wished we were alone in our room.

The sun illuminated the new armor across his chest. I squinted at the breastplate, critiquing the line of symbols along the bottom edge. My power hummed, happy that he wore the armor. I'd been infusing it with spells and magic for the past few weeks. As he neared, I thought of a couple more I needed to add.

"I've been looking for you." He wrapped his arms around my waist. Madeline smiled and turned away, offering the illusion of privacy.

"Is something wrong with my father? Penelope?"

"What?" Rayhan's brow pinched. "No, they're fine. Last I saw, they were in the dining hall, bugging the contractor about when he'll be done with the plans for their new cottage. That poor man can't hide from them."

A smile curved my lips. Soon they'd be back in our village, in a new fire-resistant house, and not lingering among the vampires. Penelope was far too interested in our ancient enemies.

"Kadence wants to see you."

A cold dagger buried in my chest.

"Why?" I asked, and I couldn't quite hide the fear in my voice.

Rayhan rubbed my arms. It had been tough for him to balance me and his best friend. Kadence and I hadn't spoken since he'd almost killed me in Rayhan's room and then banished me to the dungeons. I would rather keep it that way.

"He said it's important." Rayhan shrugged. "If you don't want to see him, I'll let him know."

"No," I said. The vampires were constructing new prisoner of war camps, complete with cells with real beds and an outside recreation area. Partially because Rayhan couldn't stand my brethren being locked in the cold cells, and partially because the lower level of the castle was slowly flooding. The catacombs and their years of history were truly lost. If Kadence had a question about the camps, I needed to know. "I'll go."

Rayhan's hand was warm and comforting in mine. He guided us up the stairs and through the castle. We went past Manveer's suite, patched up from the explosion, and a shiver of cool air blew over me. I caught an outline of a humanoid shape, but when I turned my head, there was only an empty hall.

Kadence's door stood open, and Rayhan led us inside. I expected the room to be a dark cave, where a demon would live, but it was light and airy. The walls were naked stone, but almost completely covered in bright, vivid paintings. I recognized most as Rayhan's work, among some more abstract pieces. An unlit fireplace sat opposite a simple wooden bedframe.

The vampire king lounged in the open balcony doorway. He turned to us and tried to smile, but the look was hard and foreign on his face.

Anger bubbled hot in my chest, but I pushed it away. He was still the king, and my father and sister were finding refuge in his castle.

"Can we sit?" Kadence gestured to the semicircle of chairs that looked like they'd been dragged into the room for this meeting.

Rayhan took the first chair, and I followed his lead. The plush velvet cushion didn't distract me from the king across from us. A low wooden table spanned the middle, and a black box perched on it.

"The war is over," Kadence said. "Scouts reported that the witch king and queen disappeared with ten thousand soldiers. We march tomorrow to siege the castle."

Dread sat heavy in my gut.

"Why are you telling me this?" I forced the words around my unwilling tongue. "Aren't I one of those enemies?"

"Yes. No." The king dropped his head into his hands, and for a moment, his hard shell cracked. Through the sliver, I saw something I hadn't before. A person. A boy. Alone with a crown, navigating this dark world. "I don't know. Defeating the witches is all I've wanted, but Rayhan..." His voice trailed. He drew a deeper breath. "Rayhan has shown me another option."

My curiosity piqued.

"Rayhan thinks a peaceful surrender would be more beneficial." Kadence lifted his head and studied me. His eyes burned, and a predator looked out. "We would gain laborers and supplies."

"And not have to slaughter thousands of innocents," Rayhan said. The tilt in his voice made it sound like an old argument.

"Yes, that too." Kadence nodded.

"Who's heading the kingdom?" I asked.

"The princess."

"Princess Salvatore?"

Kadence nodded again.

"You'd let her live?"

He shrugged. "If she agrees to a surrender, then yes."

I bit my lip. Princess Sal had worked hard to gain the trust of her people, but she had skeptics in Ededen. She would have an uphill battle, but she'd do anything for her people, for us.

“Why do you need me?” I asked. I didn’t have power for negotiations, and I wasn’t worth a ransom.

Kadence and Rayhan looked at each other. Kadence opened the black box on the table and turned it to face me.

Inside the thick cushion sat a plain silver bracelet.

“The only way I can control the witches is to control the princess’s magic,” Kadence said. “Rayhan thought you might be able to enchant this bracelet to bind her magic, the way your mother once bound your own.”

I remembered the years of pain as I struggled to use my trapped magic. How it felt having a piece of my soul locked away, as though part of myself were missing.

“Why would I ever place that curse on someone else?” I asked.

“I’m tired of this war.” Kadence’s mask disappeared. Pain echoed in deep lines on his face. It wasn’t a king across from me. It was a hardened warrior who didn’t want to survive one more battle. “It will end, Natalie. You can decide how.”

I thought of my father and Penelope, who were promised the opportunity for a new home. I thought of other witches holding family members close as they prepared to die in war. I thought of our kingdom, our princess, who was tired of picking up bodies from the battlefield.

I turned to Rayhan and wrapped my hand around his. If this war ended, we would have a future together. All the witches and vampires would have a future.

“I’ll need a lot of practice first,” I said, watching the universe dance in Rayhan’s eyes. “But I’ll do it.”

Thank you for reading! Did you enjoy? Please add your review because nothing helps an author more and encourages readers to take a chance on a book than a review.

Don’t miss from A.N. Payton available at anpayton.com

SNEAK PEEK OF CLAIMED BY DARKNESS

NORA

Every day when I wake up, my first thought is how badly I want to die. My eyes flutter open and burn from the rays of sunlight pouring in through my lacey, sheer curtains, and I want to drift back off to sleep and never have to open my eyes again. The lake outside my window sends its waves rising and falling, crashing onto the shore in tumultuous chaos, mirroring the feelings I carry inside of me. I squint my eyes as I stand and peer out the window, the Mackinac bridge taunting me in the distance, like a ghost from my past life that will stand and haunt me forever. Every morning is the same.

I can't tell my therapist any of this. He'll send me back to the psych ward, a place where misery reigns and dreams go to die. I'm not like them, the people who dissociate from reality and can no longer decipher between reality and imagination. I know someday I might heal from my trauma, from the loss of the two greatest people I've ever known, and that someday I will move on. I know, and yet it changes nothing.

Life feels so meaningless.

As I pull on my cutest sundress and quickly smear make-up across my eyelids and lips, my limbs feel heavy and worn down. I have nothing left to give, but I must keep up the façade. Smile. Laugh. Tell them I'm alright. If the past year has taught me anything, it's that people see what they want to see. Grabbing my keys off the counter, I glance at the clock above the stove, the ticking sound ringing through the air and reminding me that time is still moving. Most days I forget.

I rush through town, savoring the quiet calm of the place now that tourists have left the island to avoid the isolation that comes when winter hits and the lake freezes over. They crave the peacefulness that comes from a town that prohibits cars and allows travel only by horse-drawn carriage, like some fairytale world where time moves slower and things are simpler. Yet, the thought of not being able to leave, of being stuck here with no way out terrifies them. I guess some fairytales aren't meant to last forever. I wouldn't want to live anywhere else.

The ferry ride takes twenty minutes, and I barely remember going from point A to point B. There are many times I struggle to remember what I've done or where I've been. Every day passes in a blur of faded colors and muted sounds. Jumping off the ferry and onto the dock in Mackinac City, I push my shoulders back and remind myself to appear normal as I stride toward Dr. Cooper's office.

Smile.

Laugh.

Everything is just fine.

As I sit in the dimly lit waiting room, the walls covered in sickly green wallpaper, I pick at the skin on the edge of my nails, impatiently waiting to be called back.

"Come on in, Nora." Dr. Cooper's bright smile radiates positivity as he holds the door open wide and watches me pass through. "How are you today?" We both sit down.

"Hi, Dr. Cooper! I'm doing good, thanks. How are you?" My voice is too high and too bright and too much like anyone but me.

"Good, good." Bradley shifts in his seat in front of me, crossing one leg over the other, and looks down his nose at me through his thick, black-rimmed glasses. "Tell me, Nora. How have you been, *really*?" His voice is silky and velvety, a sound that seems to caress deep into my mind and soul.

Dr. Cooper's voice is like a dark velvet dipped in honey, deep and comforting and sweet. It has always reminded me of my boyfriends voice in a way, and I'm pretty sure Ere's voice alone is enough to heal anyone in all the right places. His smile is small, but it's there. He truly wants the best for me, and I know it, but I can't trust him. I can't trust anyone around me anymore. I glance behind him at the cherry oak wood shelf lined with books from floor to ceiling and briefly picture him sitting at home with his favorite book and a glass of wine by the fireplace. It seems like a very Bradley thing to do after a long day of talking the crazy out of people like me. The thick curtains block out the sunlight, giving his office a cozy, relaxing atmosphere. If I try hard enough, I could maybe let my fucked-up thoughts and feelings seep out and leave them in the dark here in this place with him. But trying is hard. It's so tiring and I'm tired of being tired.

I give him my best *'I swear I'm not suicidal anymore* smile,' tucking my red locks behind my ears and fluttering my eyelashes up at him, attempting to convey innocence and a happy demeanor. I shrug my shoulders, my hands clasped in my lap, and my body relaxed and still. I will not let the truth show. I've practiced this so much now that it has gotten easy, fooling everyone into believing I'm fine. I will not cry. I will not let my hands shake or my mind spiral in front of him. I. Am. Healed. They will not lock me up again.

I take a deep breath before speaking, hoping to let the calm demeanor shine bright in the tone of my voice as well.

"Truly, I feel great," I giggle, shrugging my shoulders. "I've had a rough year. Like... really rough, I know. But I've learned a lot about myself and about life and the world around me. I know now how to handle challenging situations when they come my way. I'm so thankful for you. Thankful to be alive." I let my smile reach my eyes, and this time it is real. I appreciate everything Bradley has done to help me. He doesn't need to know that it was all for nothing.

He leans forward, placing his arms on his legs, and letting his hands hang freely. His facial hair is neat but scruffy, and his brown locks are messy yet stylish, making him look much younger than the forty-five-year-old man he is.

He sighs quietly and smiles in a way that immediately makes me feel awful for all the lies I've fed him these past few months. "Great. Hearing that makes me so happy."

He believes me. Every lie and every half-truth and every forced, fake-ass smile. I started coming in with my hair curled and golden eye shadow to brighten up my blue eyes, and the prettiest, brightest sundresses I could find, to fool him into seeing me as someone I'm not, and it fucking worked. How did it work so easily?

As I breathe in deep, the scent of leather and deception burns its way into my lungs and beats through my heart.

"I'm happy, too. For the first time in a long time, I am. I'm moving on. This is what my parents would want for me, and I know that now." I don't blink or move, keeping my eyes locked on his to show no signs that I'm attempting to deceive him.

"I'm so proud of you, Nor. You should be proud, too. Your mind tried to break you, you fought hard, and you won. You're a warrior." His leather chair creaks as he stands and makes his way over to his desk. "I'm writing you a one-month prescription for the medications I have you on. Increasing the dosage is no longer necessary with how well you're doing now." He leans on the edge of his desk, crossing his arms over his broad chest, smiling as if he feels so accomplished for healing me. For saving my life.

I'm an asshole. That's all there is to it. I'm a liar and a fraud and if God is looking down at me right now, he is surely shaking his head in disgust and disappointment. I don't care, though. I just want to be free.

I smooth the wrinkles out of my dress as I stand, tossing my curls over my shoulders and smiling over at him. "Does this mean our visits are over? Now that I'm... better?"

His smile vanishes, and he places his hands in front of him, palms facing toward me in a gesture to slow down. He shakes his head. "That's not what I'm saying. Not yet, at least. Let's see how you do with monthly visits instead of weekly. How does that sound?"

Horrible. Like a waste of time.

"Sounds great!" I beam, knowing it's what I should say and do. "I'll see you in a month, then?"

"See you in a month. Of course, if you need me at any time before then, please don't hesitate to call, okay?" He straightens up and walks to the door, then opens it and turns toward me. "Your prescriptions will be ready for pickup on your way home. Don't...forget it." He says sternly, probably remembering back to all the times I 'forgot' to pick them up after our visits before.

It doesn't matter. They'll end up down the drain where the rest of them have gone to die.

"I won't forget. Thank you, Dr. Cooper. For everything, really. I don't care what people say about you, you're not such a bad guy." I smile playfully and his deep, carefree laugh follows me out the door even as he shuts it behind me.

On my first day seeing him I told him the truth about what I'd heard from the others at the mental health facility. They'd all agreed he was an emotionless, abrasive jerk. I've never seen that side of him. He's not a bad guy at all, he is just slightly bad at reading people and picking up on emotions. Or maybe I'm just a really good actor. Too good, even. Standing in the waiting room, the receptionist scribbles my next appointment date on a business card, then slides it across the counter.

"September ninth at 10 o'clock, sweetie. See you then." Her smile doesn't meet her eyes. It's barely even a smile at all.

Her hazel eyes hold a sadness within them that she isn't very good at hiding. She isn't rude or unkind or bitter, she's just sad. Probably from a life full of pain and loss and heartbreak that never healed like she hoped it would. Looking at her feels like a glimpse into my future. She is me and I am her, and we both deserve much better.

The smile I give her is no longer the fake or forced one I show to Bradley, my sister Olivia, or my best friend Katie, and it's still far from the semi genuine one I save for my boyfriend Ere. I give her the real one. The one that's barely a smile at all, just like hers. As I walk out of the office and the sunlight hits my eyes, I block it with a hand and head toward the diner. It's almost dinner time and Liv will be waiting for me already. She'll be thrilled to hear the news that I'm healed.

Shattered glass and a high-pitched scream from behind the rough, beaten-up counter of Lake City Diner has me raising my eyebrows and smiling at the young waitress who giggles with the busboy passing by her. "That's the third one this week. Jenny is going to kill you." She rolls up the white towel she uses to wipe the counter with and playfully slaps his back with it. He pushes the squeaky swinging doors open and winks at her as he disappears into the kitchen.

They're probably only a few years younger than me, but somehow, they seem much younger and more alive. I'm twenty-three but Olivia and Katie tell me all the time that I might as well be ninety. They see an introvert who would rather read than go out. What they don't get is that my real hobbies the past year have been trying to fight off nightmares about monsters and simply making it through the day. Surviving is my main hobby. That's hard enough most of the time.

"Liv!" I squeal as my sister enters the diner, strutting toward me in her black dress and heels.

The old, faded paintings hanging on the walls, and the dated chandeliers hanging above our heads are not bright enough to distract from Olivia's entrance. She always looks stunning, and today is no different.

"Hey sis!" Her high-pitched sing-song voice echoes in my ear as she wraps her arms around me and squeezes tightly. "I've missed you so much." Pulling back and looking down at me, her blue eyes sparkle like sapphires as the sunlight dances across them.

She releases me and slides into the leather booth, her wavy dark hair bouncing as she takes a seat in front of me. The bright white smile she wears almost seems plastered to her face, like it couldn't possibly be real, but it is. She's always smiling, and I love that about her. She reaches across the table to take my hand in hers, and her bronze skin against mine makes my own look almost translucent. She resembles our dad, and everyone always called me my mom's little twin, my freckled cheeks and red hair reminding them of her. God, she was so beautiful.

"How did your appointment with Bradley go?" She smirks, raising her eyebrows up and down at the mention of his name.

She is obsessed with him. She saw him once and hasn't been able to shut up about him since. She thinks he has a thing for me, but I've never noticed or cared. I think she's just so eager for me to find happiness or to fall in love that she imagines it wherever we go. Also, there were whispers in town this past year of him having a relationship with a girl about my age, and Olivia always says I need an older man in my life to help level me out. It should be enough that I have a boyfriend at all, and technically, he is older. Only by a few years, but still, Ere helped me through my struggles these past five months. If it weren't for him, I'm not sure where I would be right now, or if I would be at all.

My sister doesn't agree with his choice in letting me sink into grief and darkness when I choose to. She believes I need someone who forces me into the light, to help guide me through my dark days. I never told her that I met him during my time at the local psychiatric hospital and that he understands the struggle with darkness as well as I do. She'd freak. She'd worry. She would convince herself he's even more of a bad influence on me, but Ere gives me exactly what I need. There's no need to pretend to be anything with him, I can just be. I consider myself lucky to have found someone as accepting and understanding as him.

"Dr. Cooper, you mean?" I correct her with a roll of my eyes and a smile. "He thinks I'm doing great. He said he's proud of the progress he's seeing in me and moved my sessions to once a month."

She nods once before taking a sip of the water the waitress places in front of her, and then we order our usual burgers and fries. It never changes, no matter how many times we've been here. I guess that makes us boring, but why change a good thing?

"I'm proud of you, too." Her eyes gloss over and I know she's about to cry before the first tear even falls.

"Liv. Don't. Don't you dare," I tell her, knowing that every time one of us cries the other one isn't far behind.

"I'm sorry." She dabs the tears away with a napkin. "I just... at one point I didn't know if I would ever get my sister back. I was so scared of losing you."

"Damn it, Olivia." My eyes sting as tears well up and warm my cheeks as they fall, and we both let out a laugh. "I'm sorry. That the past year has been a mess. That you've dealt with so much alone. That I couldn't be there for you like I should have been." I pick up my napkin and blot my tears away. "I've been such a shitty sister, haven't I?" I shake my head and look up at the ceiling, not wanting to face her and the truth.

My sister visited me every day for months while I was in the psych ward, whispering about a missing necklace holding secrets and monsters who are coming for me next. She was scared shitless, I could see it in her eyes even though I wasn't myself then. All she could do was tell me over and over that she believed me, but that I was safe for now and shouldn't worry. We haven't talked about those things since I got out, but I often wonder if a part of her did believe me. She has always had a strange obsession with supernatural occurrences, and there was nothing natural about the way our parents died. She has to wonder if maybe I was right. If maybe I did see things she didn't. I'm too afraid to bring it up again. I don't want the semblance of a normal life I have now to be ripped away.

I don't know how she has stayed so damn strong when she's the one who lost the most. A mom, a dad, and a sister. All gone in the blink of an eye. But I'm here. She has been the strong, supportive big sister for long enough. I hate that I've made things harder for her than it needed to be. My heart hurts knowing she needed me and I couldn't be there to comfort her. Guilt eats at me still, even though at the time I was too broken to care. I was too lost then to know how much it'd torture me later on for not pulling myself together for her. All I can do is be here for her now that I can be.

"No, Nor, not at all." She reaches across the table and squeezes my hand. "Please don't think that even for a second." Her voice is calm and reassuring.

She will never just let me take the blame for things. She makes excuses and pretends there's hope for me even when there isn't, and sometimes I hate her for it. Other times, I want to prove her right and turn my life around, only I don't know how to anymore. I've tried everything.

I stare out the window and watch as cars and people pass by, wondering if they've ever felt even remotely the way I do right now. Lost and defeated. Alone yet not alone at all. Olivia never seems to feel this way. She always finds a way to see the light even when there is none to be found. I envy her for that.

"I'm going to do better, Liv. I promise. I'll be a better sister and friend. I'll do all the crazy things you and Katie beg me to do, no matter how badly I want to say no."

She rolls her eyes but smiles over at me as if hearing this makes her happier than I could ever imagine.

"I want to be better. I will be." I sit up straighter with my head held high, for a second believing I can will it into existence.

"You are better. So much better than you were before. Just promise me something, okay?" She leans forward, watching me carefully.

I nod my head, my eyes crinkling slightly, not knowing what she's about to ask of me and fearing I won't be able to keep the promise.

"Promise me that if you find yourself spiraling again. If you find yourself losing control or having thoughts of hurting yourself, promise you'll tell me. Don't keep it inside this time until... until it's too late." She swallows thickly, and I know why it's so hard for her to talk about what happened just six months ago.

Finding your sister pulseless on the floor surrounded by empty bottles of prescription pills probably isn't something you get over easily, if at all. A pang of guilt shudders through me at the thought of her there, panicked and alone. I'd never make the mistake of letting her be the one to find me if someday I chose to try again. She deserves better.

I take a deep breath in and out, just as Dr. Cooper taught me to do when I'm feeling overwhelmed. "I promise," I whisper, giving her a half smile that should give my lie away.

It doesn't, because she believes me, or at least she pretends to. She gets up to go to the bathroom, and when she does, I fumble with her key chain to find the card attached to it that leads in and out of the Mackinac Bridge. Our dad had special access because he worked for the city, and he used to take us to the top all the time. His card still works, surprisingly, I know because she still uses it at times. We used to go up there together until I became a suicidal mess who couldn't be trusted anywhere, let alone on a bridge three hundred and fifty feet above a large body of water. Olivia will be pissed that I stole his access card, but I haven't been there since our parents died, and haven't been to the top in years. I just want to enjoy the view of the city alone. There's a peacefulness up there away from the noise and lights that I've never been able to find anywhere else. Up there, all my scattered, broken thoughts slowly disappear.

After dinner and hugging my sister goodbye, I make my way down the street toward the bridge. I've been so afraid to face reality, to face my fear once and for all, but I will not let fear rule my life. I want to try for her, for Olivia. She deserves a sister who can always be there. A sister who she never again has to find lifeless on the floor. As badly as I want to take the ferry home, to just forget about healing and give up hope again, tonight hope calls to me. So just for tonight...

I will try.

Don't miss more from A.N. Payton available at anpayton.com

And now, discover CLAIMED BY DARKNESS, by City Owl Author, S.R. Hartley

Sometimes, to destroy evil, you have to embrace it...

The night Nora's parents were murdered, something ancient and malevolent stirred beneath the waves—and it never let go. No one else felt it. But Nora did... she still does.

The darkness whispers her name, curls through her thoughts, tempts her with release. On the edge of the Mackinac Bridge, Nora is ready to surrender. But fate has other plans.

A flash of burning green eyes. Wings of midnight. And everything changes.

Saved by Kairos, a powerful celestial, who claims she's his *fated mate*, Nora is thrust into a hidden world of otherworldly beings and ancient prophecy. Her past—wiped away. Her future—bound to a war that began long before she was born.

A century ago, the demon queen Nyx stole everything from Nora. Now she wants her soul. But Nora won't go down without a fight.

To save the world—*and the ones she loves*—Nora must unlock the terrible truth of who she is. Even if it means binding herself to a dark king who promises love... and carries deadly secrets.

As Heaven and Hell collide, Nora must choose between the mate who holds her heart and the darkness that calls her name.

Because the God of Shadows is coming. And he won't stop until she belongs to him.

Claimed by Darkness is a fantasy romance filled with fated mates, celestial warriors, forbidden magic, and a heroine torn between light and shadow.

Please sign up for the City Owl Press newsletter for chances to win special subscriber-only contests and giveaways as well as receiving information on upcoming releases and special excerpts.

All reviews are **welcome** and **appreciated**. Please consider leaving one on your favorite social media and book buying sites.

Escape Your World. Get Lost in Ours! City Owl Press at www.cityowlpress.com.

ACKNOWLEDGMENTS

As always, I'd like to acknowledge my family – particularly my children, Eve and Eli. Without them, this series would be finished by now. Thank you for making me slow down and appreciate the little things in life.

Thank you so much to my editor, Danielle DeVor, who put so much time and work (and patience) into this book. I'm grateful for City Owl Press and the opportunity to continue this series. Sal and Kadence, Belle and Alex, and now Natalie and Rayhan would also like to say thank you – without your support, they wouldn't have their lives memorialized in ink.

And of course, the biggest thank you to all my readers. I hope these books can take you to a new world, at least for a little while. I hope you'll all stick around for the journey to the next one.

About the Author

A.N. PAYTON is a fantasy romance author who is also navigating the tides of motherhood. She has a degree in biology and is passionate about the intersection of fantasy and science. When not writing or chasing a toddler, she can be found working on one of her many side projects, playing video games with her husband, or sleeping.

www.anpayton.com

x.com/anpayton2

instagram.com/anpayton.author

ABOUT THE PUBLISHER

City Owl Press is a cutting edge indie publishing company, bringing the world of romance and speculative fiction to discerning readers.

Escape Your World. Get Lost in Ours!

www.cityowlpress.com

facebook.com/CityOwlPress
x.com/cityowlpress
instagram.com/cityowlbooks
pinterest.com/cityowlpress
tiktok.com/@cityowlpress

www.ingramcontent.com/pod-product-compliance
Lightning Source LLC
Jackson TN
JSHW082339010526
101785JS00004B/4
9781648985560